A
PERRY
MASON
OMNIBUS

A
PERRY MASON
OMNIBUS

Erle Stanley Gardner

*

The Case of the Singing Skirt

The Case of the Blonde Bonanza

The Case of the Horrified Heirs

*

William Morrow and Company
New York

THE CASE
OF THE
SINGING
SKIRT

FOREWORD

Gertrude Stein once sagely wrote "A rose is a rose is a rose."

To date no one has ever contradicted this statement.

In the field of legal medicine, however, when someone remarks "A coroner is a coroner is a coroner," there is an immediate chorus of discord.

Actually there are coroners and coroners and it is a far cry from the politically adept mortician in the small community who elects to run for the office of coroner and public administrator to my friend, Dr. Nicholas J. Chetta, the coroner of the Parish of Orleans, who has done such a splendid job of making New Orleans a bright spot in the field of legal medicine.

All of which goes to prove that no matter what title a man may be given, the sort of job he does depends upon his vision, his determination and his capabilities.

7

Dr. Chetta realizes that the ultimate function of the autopsy is to protect the living. The cause of death in any obscure case may be of the greatest importance not only to surviving relatives but to society.

In New Orleans, due to the fact that Coroner Chetta is ex-officio city physician, he has been able to bring about reforms that have helped legitimate law enforcement and have checked abuses in the field.

For instance, Dr. Chetta has placed a resident doctor on duty at the central police lock-up to examine all persons arrested, establish drunkenness or sobriety when persons are arrested and to supervise the welfare of the jail inmates.

Under Dr. Chetta, the parish has modernized and revitalized the coroner's office. Duly accredited pathologists now perform autopsies, and necessary pathological techniques are used in order to bring the coroner's office up to date as an aid to law-enforcement agencies in determining causes of death.

A photography department has been installed which is equipped for both color and black-and-white slides as well as prints. Autopsy findings are expedited through adequate inquiry by a special investigator.

A coroner's commission composed of doctors, lawyers and medical-school representatives serves in an advisory capacity.

Those who have had experience with law enforcement know the importance of determining with speed and accuracy the real cause of death, and it is my hope that my many millions of readers will come to understand something of the importance of legal medicine.

It has a day-to-day impact upon their lives, their safety
and the safety of their loved ones.

And so it gives me pleasure to dedicate this book to

My friend,

NICHOLAS M. CHETTA, M.D.

Coroner and ex-officio physician
of the Parish of Orleans

ERLE STANLEY GARDNER

CHAPTER ONE

GEORGE ANCLITAS looked at Ellen Robb with the shrewd appraisal of a cattle buyer inspecting a shipment of beef. "Black stockings," he said.

Ellen nodded.

"Long black stockings, way up," George said, making a gesture which included the hips.

"Leotards," Slim Marcus added parenthetically.

"I don't care what you call 'em," George said. "I want the black shiny ones that are tight and go way, way up."

"That's the stuff," Slim said. "Leotards."

"And the skirt," George went on, eying Ellen appraisingly, "about halfway down to the knees with a little bit of a white apron. You know, that thing about the size of a pocket handkerchief with a lot of lace on it that you tie on."

"Tonight's the night?" Slim asked.

"Tonight we take him," George said.

"All of it?"

"Why stop halfway?"

"Now, he likes you," George went on to Ellen. "He can't take his eyes off you when you're in your working clothes. Every time after you finish a number, grab

11

the tray and come on in. Always walk on the side of the table where he can see you and keep his attention distracted, except when I give you the signal."

"Now, don't forget that signal," Slim said. "George takes his right hand and rubs it along his head, sort of smoothing back his hair."

George raised a well-manicured hand to black, wavy hair and illustrated the signal.

"Now, when you get that signal," Slim explained, "you come right over to the table, but come up behind him. Now, get this. If he's only got two pair or three of a kind, you say, 'You want a cigarette, Mr. Ellis?' Remember, whenever you say 'you,' that means three of a kind or less. Now, if you stand back and say impersonally, 'Cigars, cigarettes,' that means a full house, and if you say 'Cigars or cigarettes' twice, that means the full house is higher than jacks. If you just say it once, it means it's below jacks—three tens and a pair of something, or three nines and a pair of something."

"And," George went on, "if he's got better than a full house, if he's got a straight flush or four of a kind, you reverse the order and say—"

Ellen Robb spoke for the first time. "No," she said.

Both men looked up at her incredulously.

"I'm not going to do it, George. I'll sing and I'll show my legs but I'm not going to help you cheat Helman Ellis or anyone else."

"The hell you aren't!" George said. "Don't forget this is a job you've got here, sister. I'm running this joint. You do like I tell you. What's the matter? You falling for that guy?" Then after a moment he added, less roughly, "It's only if I give you the signal, Ellen. I don't

think we'll have to do it. I think we've got this sucker
staked out cold. But he likes you. He likes to look you
over. That's one of the reasons he hangs around. We've
been fattening him up, letting him lose a little, then
letting him win a little, then letting him lose some
more. We know just about how he plays. But there'll
be a couple of other fellows in the game tonight and
that may make it a little more difficult to size up his
play."

"I'm not going to do it," Ellen Robb repeated.

"Well, I'll be damned!" Slim said.

George pushed back his chair and got to his feet, his
features dark with rage. Then he took a deep breath and
smiled. "All right, girlie," he said, "go get dressed. If
you don't want to, you don't have to. Just go ahead with
your singing. Just forget all the signals. We'll play it
straight across the table, right on the up and up, won't
we, Slim?"

Slim seemed bewildered by this abrupt change of
manner. "Well," he said . . . "yes, I guess so . . .
sure, if that's the way you want it, George. We can
take him."

"Sure, we can," George said. "Forget it, Ellen. Go get
your things on. Remember, black stockings."

Ellen Robb glided from the room. Slim Marcus
watched her hips until the green curtains had settled
into place behind her retreating figure.

"Nice scenery," George said. "But it's strictly for customers. Sucker bait."

"What the hell's the idea?" Slim asked. "I thought
you were going to give her the works, tell her to follow
orders or else."

Anclitas shook his head. "It would have been the or else," he said. "That dame has a mind of her own."

"So what?" Marcus asked. "Who's running the place?"

"We are," George said, "but we tie the can to her, take five grand from Ellis tonight and then she'd go to Ellis' wife and tell *her* the game was rigged. You know what'll happen then."

"Keep talking," Slim said.

"The minute she refused to ride along," George Anclitas explained, "she was done as far as I'm concerned. But there's no reason to be rude about it. When I get rid of 'em I get rid of 'em *right*."

"What you going to do?" Slim asked.

"Frame her," George said, his face darkening. "Frame her for stealing and kick her the hell out. Tell her if she ever shows her face in these parts again, she'll be thrown in the can. I'll give her enough money for a bus ticket to Arizona and tell her if she isn't out of the state within twenty-four hours, I'll prosecute.

"She knows too much now. We have to discredit her. Remember that other broad we framed? She's still in."

"Think we can take him without signals?" Slim asked.

"Sure we can take him," George said. "We've done it before, haven't we?"

Slim nodded.

"Well, then, quit worryin'."

"I ain't worryin'. I just want to be sure."

"In our game, that's worryin'," George said.

CHAPTER TWO

DELLA STREET, Perry Mason's confidential secretary, stood in the doorway between the lawyer's private office and the passage leading to the reception room. An amused smile tilted the corners of her mouth.

At length, Mason, sensing her immobility, looked up from the volume he was studying.

"You have always said," Della Street observed archly, "that you didn't like cases involving figures."

"And that's right," Mason observed emphatically. "I want cases involving drama, cases where there's a chance to study human emotions. I don't want to stand up at a blackboard in front of a jury and add and subtract, multiply and divide."

"We now have a case waiting in the outer office," Della Street said, "involving a figure, rather a fancy figure I might add."

Mason shook his head. "We're booked solid, Della. You know I don't like routine. I . . . ." Something in her manner caused a delayed reaction in Mason's mind. "*What* did you say the case involved?"

"A fancy figure."

Mason pushed the book back. "Now, by any chance,

young woman," he said sternly, "is this an animate figure?"

"Very animate," Della Street said.

Mason grinned. "You mean it undulates?"

"Well," she said thoughtfully, "it sways."

"Smoothly?"

"Seductively."

"The age?"

"Twenty-four, twenty-five, twenty-six."

"And the figure?"

"Superb."

"The name?"

"Ellen Robb, formerly a photographic model. Now a singer in a night club, doubling as a vendor of cigars and cigarettes."

"Show her in," Mason said.

"It will be some show," Della Street warned. "She's garbed."

"Most women are," Mason said and then added, "when they visit offices."

"This," Della Street said, "will be different."

Mason placed the fingers of his left hand on his right wrist, consulted his wrist watch. "Pulse a hundred and twenty-eight," he said. "Respiration rapid and shallow. How much more suspense, Della? Now that you've aroused my interest to this extent, what are we waiting for?"

"What was the pulse?" she asked.

"A hundred and twenty-eight."

"In exactly five seconds," Della Street said, "take it again, and if it hasn't reached a hundred and eighty, you can cut my salary."

She vanished momentarily, to return with Ellen Robb.

Mason glanced quizzically at the determined young woman, who was wearing a long, plaid coat.

"Miss Robb, Mr. Mason," Della Street said, and then to Ellen, "If you'll slip off your coat so Mr. Mason can see what you showed me, he will . . ."

Ellen Robb opened the coat. Della Street's hands at the collar of the coat pulled it back and slipped it off the girl's shoulders.

Ellen Robb stood gracefully and without the least self-consciousness. She was clad in a tight-fitting sweater, a skirt which terminated some six inches above the knees, and black leotards. A small diamond-shaped apron, about the size of a pocket handkerchief, adorned with a border of delicate lace, was tied around her waist.

Despite himself, Mason's eyes widened.

"Miss Robb," Della Street explained, "won a bathing-beauty contest which included a trip to Hollywood, a screen test and a certain amount of resulting publicity."

"The screen test?" Mason asked.

Ellen Robb smiled and said, "It was part of the publicity. I never heard anything from it again. I sometimes doubt if there was film in the camera."

"The trip to California?"

"That was real," she said. "I had to wait to travel when the plane had some extra seats. However, it was nice," and then she added, "while it lasted."

"When did it quit lasting?"

"About six months ago."

"And you've been doing?"

"Various things."

"The last," Della Street said, "was being employed as a cigarette girl and novelty singer at a place in Rowena."

"Rowena," Mason said frowning, "that's the small town where—"

"Where gambling which doesn't conflict with the state law is authorized by city ordinance," Della Street said. "The place is just big enough to get incorporated. It pays its municipal expenses from the gambling and nicking the unwary tourist who goes through the eighteen blocks of restricted speed limit faster than the law allows."

"The police force," Ellen Robb said with a smile, "consists of one man. When he's at the east end of town, he makes it a rule to issue at least one citation on his westbound trip. People who are going east are immune if they go tearing on through. On the other hand, when the city's police force is at the west end of town, people going east had better crawl along at a snail's pace or they'll have a citation."

"I take it the officer is exceedingly impartial," Mason said.

"Completely impartial. He only gets one driver on every eastbound trip, one driver on every westbound trip. In an eighteen-block restricted district there's not room for a much better average than that."

"I see you have a sense of humor," Mason said, "and now that Della has arranged the dramatic presentation of the principal figure in the case, why not sit down and tell me what's bothering you?"

Ellen Robb walked easily across the office, settled herself in the big leather chair, crossed her long legs and smiled at Perry Mason. "After all," she said, "I'm accustomed to being on display. I've had people looking me over so much I feel I could take a bath in a goldfish bowl at the corner of Seventh and Broadway without the least trace of self-consciousness—but that doesn't prevent me from being good and mad, Mr. Mason."

"And what are you good and mad about?" the lawyer asked.

She said, "Five months ago I got a job with George Anclitas. He's running a place in Rowena, a little night club with a room in back where there are legalized games."

"And your employment terminated when?"

"Last night, and very abruptly."

"What happened?"

"George and his right-hand man and crony, Slim Marcus, were—"

"Slim?" Mason asked.

"His name is Wilton Winslow Marcus, but everyone calls him Slim."

"Go ahead," Mason said, noticing that Della Street was making notes of the names.

"They wanted me to do some crooked work. They wanted me to look at the hands of a sucker and signal what he was holding."

"And you did?"

"I did not."

"So what happened?"

"I should have known better," she said. "George is

dangerous. He has a terrific temper and he was furious.
Then all of a sudden he took a long breath and smiled
that oily, suave smile of his, and told me it was all right,
that he'd handle the game without my help."

"And he did?"

"I don't know. I didn't last long enough to find out."

"What happened—to you, I mean?" Mason asked.

"George told me the cashier had become ill and had
to leave. I was to take over the cash register and let some
of my singing numbers go. Well, there was a hundred-
and-twenty-dollar shortage."

"While you were in charge?"

"Yes."

"A real shortage or—"

"A real shortage. The cash simply didn't balance."

"What happened to it?"

"Frankly, I don't know, Mr. Mason. I think George
did a little sleight of hand on me when he inventoried
the cash with me at the time I took over. George is very
swift and very clever with his hands. He can deal from
the bottom of the deck or deal seconds, and it's almost
impossible to catch him at it. I think that when he
counted the cash in the cash register with me at the time
I took over, he used his sleight of hand. All I know is
that when I came to balance up, there was a shortage of
a hundred and twenty dollars."

"Who found it?"

"I found it."

"And what did you do?"

"I communicated immediately with him. I told him
about it; that is, I told one of the waitresses to tell him.
He was in this game."

"And what happened?"

"He fired me. I had about a hundred dollars coming in back wages. He handed me forty dollars and told me that was enough to get out of town on and if I wasn't across the state line within twenty-four hours, he'd have a warrant issued for me. He called me a thief and everything else in the—"

"Anyone present?" Mason asked.

"Quite a few people in the place could hear him," she said. "He wasn't particularly quiet about it."

"Know any of their names?"

"A couple. Sadie Bradford was there."

"Who is she?"

"One of the girls who does all-around work. Sometimes she acts as attendant in the powder room, sometimes she's a hat-check girl, sometimes she works in the motel office."

"There's a motel?" Mason asked.

"Yes. George and Slim own two whole city blocks. They have a motel with a swimming pool, a trout pool, a night club and bar, and a sort of casino.

"Some of the construction is modern, some of it is rambling old-fashioned buildings. The night club, for instance, started out as an old barn. George modernized it, put on an addition, kept the barnlike atmosphere and called the place 'The Big Barn.' "

"This Sadie Bradford," Mason said, "heard him call you a thief?"

"Yes."

"Would she be a witness?"

"I don't know. Her bread and butter might be at stake."

"What happened after he called you a thief and told you to get out of the state?" Mason asked.

"I wanted to go to my locker to get my street clothes, and he told me whatever was in the locker might be evidence, that he thought I had money secreted there. He handed me my coat and told me to get started."

"A rather spectacular way of discharging help," Mason said.

"He did it," she said, "for a purpose."

"To get even with you?"

"That was only part of it. They'd been playing poker for the last few weeks with this man, Helly Ellis—his first name is Helman—Helly is his nickname."

"And I take it this Helman Ellis was the man they wanted you to signal about."

"That's right. Last night they were ready to really take him to the cleaners and, of course, George was afraid that if I told what he had asked me to do, it might make trouble—so he chose this method of getting me discredited, firing me under a cloud, giving me just enough money to get out of town. He said he'd have my things packed up, put in a suitcase and sent to me at the Greyhound Bus Depot at Phoenix, Arizona. They'd be there in my name. I could call for them there."

"And when he cleans out your locker?" Mason asked.

She met his eyes steadily. "You don't know George," she said. "I do. When he cleans out my locker, he'll have some witnesses with him and they'll find a wad of bills."

"This was the first time you'd ever been in charge of the cash register?"

"No, I'd had charge before."

"Were there other shortages?"

"I think there were," she said, "but not in the cash register. I had heard George complaining that some nights the receipts dropped way down although business was good. He intimated that someone had been knocking down—only ringing up a part of the sales. He threatened to get private detectives on the job and said everybody was going to have to take a lie-detector test."

"I take it he hasn't won any popularity contests with the help," Mason said.

"Not recently," Ellen Robb said dryly.

"And somebody has been knocking down on him?" Mason asked.

"He seems to think so, and I would assume he probably is right."

"Could that person or those persons have tampered with your cash register?"

She shook her head. "Most of the knocking down that is done," she said, "is done at the bar. People who buy drinks at the bar pay cash, and if the bar is very busy and the bartender takes in four or five payments at once, he can ring up varying amounts in the cash register and there is no one to check on him. For instance, let us suppose one man has a cocktail which is seventy-five cents or a dollar. Another man has a drink which is sixty cents. Another person has bought drinks for three or four, and his bill is two dollars and eighty-five cents.

"By timing things just right a good bartender can be preoccupied at just the right moment so that every glass gets empty at about the same time. That makes for a rush of business and a lot of payments being made all at once.

"So then the bartender picks up all the money, goes over to the cash register and starts ringing up sales of varying amounts.

"If the bartender is good at mental arithmetic, he can add up the figures in his mind and ring up an amount that is exactly two dollars short of the real amount. Then he gives each customer his exact change. Various amounts have been leaping into sight on the cash register, staying there for just a moment only to be superseded by another amount. Nobody can tell for certain what check is being rung up. If the bartender sees someone paying attention to the cash register, he is scrupulously accurate in ringing up the amounts, but if people are talking and not paying too much attention, he'll knock down a couple of dollars and no one is any the wiser. He'll do that perhaps ten to twenty times in an evening."

"Were you doing any of this work at the bar?"

"Not last night. I was handling the main cash register. I had the only key to it while I was on duty—at least, it was supposed to be the only key. I would sit there on the stool, and people would come to me with their checks, or the waitresses would come to check out the amounts due at their tables. I'd take in the money and give out the change."

"Was there any reason why you couldn't have knocked down if you had wanted to?" Mason asked.

"There's more of a check on the main cash register. The waitresses issue dinner checks and keep a carbon copy which has to be filed when they go off shift. Theoretically the cash register should show a total income equal to the exact total amount of checks issued by the waitresses. But there are lots of ways of beating that game."

"How?" Mason asked.

"Walks, for one."

"Walks?" Mason asked.

"A customer pays his bill directly at the cash register," she said. "The amount of the bill is two dollars and eighty-five cents. He gives you a twenty-dollar bill. You pretend to be very much interested in the addition on the check, then apparently something goes wrong with the key on the cash register. You concentrate on that. Eventually you ring up two dollars and eighty-five cents; still without apparently paying too much attention to him, you hand him fifteen cents, then give him two one-dollar bills, then hand him a five, then look back at the cash register for a minute. Nine times out of ten the man will pocket the change and walk away. If he starts to pocket the change and then stops suddenly, or if he still waits there, you take out two additional fives and give it to him with a smile, then start looking back at the cash register again."

"You seem to know all the tricks," Mason said thoughtfully.

"I've heard *some* of them," she said.

"And you sing?"

"Yes."

"Let's hear," Mason said.

She tilted back her head, sang a few bars of a popular song, then stopped and said, "My throat's always a little thick in the morning—I love to sing—I like melody, always have, but singing in rooms filled with stale tobacco smoke is hard on the throat."

Mason nodded, studied the young woman's face.

"You've had ups and downs?" he asked.

"Mostly downs," she said, "but I'm in there fighting. I think I'll go back to modeling. I can get by doing that —only there's no future in it."

"How does George Anclitas stand in Rowena?" Mason asked.

"It depends on whom you ask. He owns the justice of the peace and he has something on Miles Overton, the chief of police. As far as official circles are concerned, George stands ace high. Some of the citizens don't like him but they all kowtow to him. He's powerful."

"I think," Mason said, "we're going to interrupt a somewhat busy day to call on George Anclitas. You don't happen to know his telephone number, do you?"

"Rowena 6-9481."

Mason nodded to Della Street. "Get George on the phone, Della. Let's see what he has to say."

A few moments later Della Street, who had been busy at the dial of the telephone, nodded to Perry Mason.

Mason picked up the receiver. "George Anclitas?" he asked.

"Sure," the voice at the other end of the line said. "Who are you? What do you want?"

"I'm Perry Mason. I'm a lawyer."

"All right. What does a lawyer want with George?"

"I want to talk with you."

"What about?"

"About an employee."

"Who?"

"Ellen Robb, a singer."

"That tramp. What about her?"

"I'm coming out to see you," Mason said. "It will take me about half an hour to get there. Miss Robb will be with me. I want all of her personal possessions, I want all of the money that she has coming to her, and I'll talk with you about the rest of it."

"All right," George said. "Now I'll tell you something. You bring Ellen Robb out here, and she gets arrested quick. If she wants to spend the next sixty days in the clink, this is the place for her. Tell her I've got the reception committee all ready."

"Very well," Mason said, "and since you're planning a reception committee, you might go to the bank and draw out ten thousand dollars."

"Ten thousand dollars! What are you talking about?"

"I am about to file suit on her behalf for defamation of character, for slanderous remarks and false accusation. If you have ten thousand dollars available in cash, I might advise Miss Robb to make a cash settlement rather than go to court."

"What the hell you talking about?" Anclitas shouted into the telephone.

"About the business I have with you," Mason said, and hung up.

The lawyer looked across the desk at Ellen Robb's startled eyes. "Want to put on your coat and go?" he asked.

She took a deep breath. "No one has ever talked to George Anclitas like that. I want very much to put on my coat and go."

Mason nodded to Della Street. "Bring a notebook, Della."

CHAPTER THREE

THE BIG BARN in Rowena was a two-story frame building, the front of which had been made to resemble the entrance to a barn. Double barn doors were half open. A recessed partition in the back of the doors, which was not over two feet deep but to which the ends of bales of straw had been fastened, created the impression of a huge barn crammed with baled hay.

A motel was operated in connection with the other activities, and a sign at the road blazoned TROUT FISHING POOL. RODS, REELS RENTED. FISH BAIT SOLD. NO LICENSE NECESSARY.

Perry Mason parked his car, assisted Della Street and Ellen Robb to the curb, then walked across to open the door to the night club.

After the bright sunlight of the sidewalks, the interior seemed to be encased in thick gloom. Figures moved around in the shadows.

A man's voice said, "I'm Miles Overton, the chief of police of Rowena. What are you folks doing here?"

Ellen Robb gave a little gasp.

"Where's George Anclitas?" Mason asked.

"Here I am."

George Anclitas pushed his way belligerently forward, his deep-set eyes glittering with hostility at Perry Mason.

Mason's eyes rapidly adjusted themselves to the dim light.

"I'm Perry Mason. I'm an attorney," he said. "I'm representing Ellen Robb. You threw her out of here last night without giving her a chance to get her things. The first thing we want is to get to her locker and get her belongings."

"All right, all right," George said. "You want to go to the locker. The chief of police is here. He'll search the locker."

"Not without a warrant he won't."

"That's what you think," the chief said. "When she opens that door I take a look. George Anclitas owns this place. He's given me permission to search any part of it I want."

"The locker is the property of my client," Mason said.

"She got a deed to it?" George asked.

"It was designated as a place where she could store her things," Mason said.

"While she was working here. She isn't working here any more. I want to take a look in there. I want to see what's in there. I'll bet you I'll find some of the money that's been missing from the cash register."

"You mean," Mason said, "that she would have taken the money from the cash register last night, then gone to her locker, unlocked the locker, opened the door, put the money in there, then closed and locked the door again?"

"Where else would she have put it?" George asked.

Mason regarded his client with twinkling eyes. "There," he said, "you have a point."

"You're damned right I got a point," George said.

"And you don't have a key to the locker?" Mason asked.

"Why should I have a key?"

"I thought perhaps you might have a master key that would open all of the lockers."

"Well, think again."

"You can't get in this locker?"

"Of course not. I gave her the key. She's got it in her purse, that little purse she keeps down in the front of her sweater. I saw her put it there."

"And you have been unable to open her locker?" Mason asked.

"Of course. Sure, that's right. How *could* I get in? She's got the key."

"Then," Mason said, "how did you expect to get her things out and send them by bus to Phoenix, Arizona?"

George hesitated only a moment, then said, "I was going to get a locksmith."

The police chief said, "Don't talk with him, George. He's just trying to get admissions from you."

"First," Mason said, "I'm going to get my client's things. I'm warning you that any attempt to search her things without a warrant will be considered an illegal invasion of my client's rights. I'm also demanding an apology from Mr. Anclitas because of remarks he has made suggesting that my client is less than honest. Such an apology will not be accepted as compensation by my client, but we are suggesting that it be made in order to mitigate damages."

George started to say something, but the chief of police said, "Take it easy, George. Where's Jebley?"

"That's what I want to know," Anclitas said angrily. "I told my attorney to be here. This tramp is going to show up with an attorney, I'm going to have an attorney. I—"

The door opened. For a moment the light from the sidewalk poured in, silhouetting a thick neck, a pair of football player's shoulders and a shock of curly hair. Then the door closed and the silhouette resolved itself into a man of around thirty-seven with dark-rimmed spectacles, a toothy grin and hard, appraising eyes.

"This," George Anclitas announced, "is Jebley Alton, the city attorney here at Rowena. The city attorney job isn't full time. He takes private clients. I'm one."

George turned to the attorney. "Jeb," he said, "this man is Mason. He says he's a lawyer and—"

Anclitas was interrupted by Alton's exclamation. "*Perry* Mason!" he exclaimed.

Mason nodded.

Alton's hand shot forward. "Well, my gosh," he said, "am I glad to meet you! I've seen you around the Hall of Justice a couple of times and I've followed some of your cases."

Alton's fingers closed around Mason's hand.

"All right, never mind the brotherly love stuff," George said. "This guy Mason is representing this woman who's trying to blackmail me and—"

"Easy, George, easy," Alton warned. "Take it easy, will you?"

"What do you mean, take it easy? I'm telling you."

Alton said, "This is Perry Mason, one of the most famous criminal lawyers in the country."

"So what?" Anclitas said. "He's representing a broad who's trying to blackmail me. She claims I accused her of being dishonest."

"Oh, George wouldn't have done that," Alton said, smiling at Mason. And then turning to Della Street, bowing, and swinging around to face Ellen Robb, "Well, well," he said, "it's the cigar and cigarette girl."

"That's the one," George said.

"What's the one?"

"The one who's making the trouble. Ellen Robb, here."

The chief of police said, "There's been a program of pilfering going on in the place. George has run up against a whole series of shortages. He's asked me to make an investigation."

Alton's eyes swept over the chief of police with skeptical appraisal. "The law of searches and seizures is rather technical, Chief," Alton said easily. "Several decisions of the Supreme Court in California and the Supreme Court of the United States haven't simplified matters any. I'll take charge here."

Mason turned to Ellen Robb. "Do you have a key to your locker?"

She nodded.

"Get it," Mason said.

Her hand moved into the front of her sweater, came out with a small coin purse. She opened it, took out a key.

"Let's go," Mason said.

Ellen Robb led the way. Mason and Della Street came next, then the chief of police. George Anclitas, striding forward, was checked by Jebley Alton who, laying a restraining hand on his client's arm, drew him back to one side and engaged in rapid-fire, low-voiced conversation.

Ellen led the way into a room marked *Employees,* through a curtained doorway which had the word *Female* painted over the top, and paused before a locker.

"Open it," Mason said.

She fitted a key and opened the locker. In it there was a cheap suitcase, a pair of shoes, a suit and a raincoat.

"These all yours?" Mason asked.

She nodded.

"Do you want to put those things in that suitcase?"

"They came in that way. They can go out that way," she said.

"You have some other things?"

"Yes."

"Where?"

"There's a motel unit assigned to us girls. We sleep there. It's a sort of dormitory. Sadie Bradford, another girl and I share the unit. He wouldn't let me get my things out of it last night. I was virtually thrown out."

"Better start packing," Mason said.

She pulled out the suitcase and flung back the lid.

"I think Miss Robb would like some privacy while she changes her clothes," Mason said. "My secretary, Miss Street, will wait with her and—"

Mason broke off at the startled exclamation from Ellen Robb.

"What is it?" he asked.

She instinctively started to close the lid of the suitcase, then checked herself.

"Let's take a look," Mason said.

"I'll take a look," the chief of police said, pushing forward.

"What is it, Ellen?"

Ellen Robb reopened the lid, then pulled forward the elastic which held closed one of the compartments in the lining of the suitcase. A wad of currency had been thrust hurriedly into this compartment.

"I'll take that into my custody," the chief of police said.

Mason moved so that he interposed a shoulder between the officer and the suitcase. "We'll count it," he said.

Ellen Robb glanced at him in questioning panic, then with trembling fingers counted the money. "Five hundred and sixty-eight dollars," she said.

"Good," Mason told her. "We'll give George credit for that on the amount of back wages due and our claims against him for defamation of character."

George, who had quietly entered the room with Alton at his side, started to say something, but just then the curtained doorway was flung back with such violence cloth was almost ripped from the guide rings on the overhead pole. A woman's voice said angrily, "Defamation of character, indeed! *That's* a laugh—pot calling the kettle black, I'd say!"

Her eyes blazed hatred at Ellen, then she turned back to George.

"But I didn't come here to see that husband stealer, I

came to see you. Just what do you think you're doing to my husband?"

"Why Mrs. Ellis!" George said, stepping forward and smiling cordially. "This is—that is—we aren't really open for business yet. I had some people come in and— Come on with me and I'll buy a drink."

She ignored the man's proffered hand, said furiously, "You've been trimming my husband in a crooked game here and I am tired of it. He tells me you took him for six thousand dollars last night. We don't have that kind of money to lose, and I'm not going to let you make a sucker out of my husband. I want the money back."

"You want it back!" George said incredulously.

"That's right, you heard me. I want it back."

George said soothingly, "Your husband was in a little private game last night, Mrs. Ellis. I don't know how he came out. I believe that perhaps he *did* lose a little, but I haven't tried to figure up just how much. I can assure you that the game was on the up and up. I was in it myself. If we gambled with people at night, let them take a chance on winning the place, and then, if they weren't lucky, gave them back the money they had lost the next morning, it wouldn't be very long before I'd be selling apples on the street corner."

He laughed at the idea, his mouth making the laughter, his eyes anxiously watching her, appraising her mood.

"As far as I'm concerned, that's exactly where you belong," Mrs. Ellis said. "I want our money back. That's money my husband earned, and I have other uses for it than giving it to you. I'm *not* going to let you cheap crooks rob us of that money and get away with it."

The chief of police said, "I hope I don't have to take you into custody for disturbing the peace, Mrs. Ellis. If you continue to make abusive statements of that sort in public, I'll have to take action."

"You!" she snapped at him. "You fatheaded nincompoop! You're just a shill for these gambling houses. George Anclitas has you right in his hip pocket. You don't dare to hiccup unless he gives you permission. Don't tell *me* what I can do and what I can't do!"

"You're using loud and profane language in a public place," the chief said.

"I haven't moved into profanity yet," she told him, "but I'm getting ready to, and when I do, I'm going to have some very biting adjectives and a few nouns that may startle you . . . you—"

"Just a minute," Mason interposed. "Perhaps *I* can be of some help here."

"And who are you?" Mrs. Ellis demanded, turning to regard Perry Mason belligerently. "You . . . I've seen your pictures . . . why, you're Perry Mason!"

Mason bowed, said, "I think it might be better to control your temper, Mrs. Ellis. Apparently you aren't going to get anywhere making a personal demand, and I think perhaps a written demand made in a more formal manner through an attorney would do you more good."

"What are you talking about, through an attorney?" George said scornfully. "You know as well as I do that when a guy loses money gambling he can't get it back."

"Can't he?" Mason asked.

George laughed sardonically. "You're damned right

he can't. Even if the game was crooked, he can't. He was engaging in an illegal activity and—"

"Careful," Jebley Alton interposed. "Let us put it this way, George. There are certain contracts that are against public policy as far as the law is concerned. It's against the policy of the law to raise those activities to the dignity of legitimate business enterprises. Therefore, the courts are not open to persons who have participated in those activities."

"Never mind all that double talk," George said. "Let's give it to her straight from the shoulder. Tell her she can't get a dime back."

"That's right, Mrs. Ellis," Alton said with his toothy smile. "You can readily understand how things are in that regard. A man can't sit in on a game at night, trying to win money, and then come back the next day and say that the activity was illegal and that he wants the money back that he's lost. If he could do that, he'd keep all of his winnings and then whenever he'd lost he'd recoup his losses. Now, George is in a legitimate business and—"

"And they've rigged up a deal on my husband," she said. "They had already got him for something over four thousand dollars. I was willing to let that ride. He promised me that he wouldn't do any more gambling, but they started in easy last night and lured him into the game. Then they started to take him. He thought his luck was bound to turn and stayed with it and—"

"And there you are," Alton said, shrugging his shoulders. "He was trying to win. If he *had* won, he'd have pocketed his winnings and both of you would have been very satisfied this morning. But he didn't win, so—"

"So I want my money back," she said. "The game was crooked."

"You can prove that?" George asked ominously.

"I don't need to prove it," she said. "*You* know it was crooked. Everybody here knows it was crooked. You aren't running this place on the square. Don't be silly."

"Those are words that would lay you wide open to a claim for damages," George said. "I suggest you be more careful, Mrs. Ellis."

"All right," she said, raising her voice. "All I know is that my husband has lost something like ten thousand dollars here within the last few weeks and I'm not going to stand by and see him robbed. Now, are you going to give him his money back or—"

"Definitely, absolutely, positively not!" George Anclitas interrupted firmly. "Your husband doesn't get back a nickel, and in view of what you've just said and the scene you've created here, he doesn't even get back inside this place. I'm leaving orders with the doorman not to admit him. If you'd come to me like a lady and told me that you didn't want your husband gambling here, he couldn't have got in last night. But you never said a word about it. He came and went just like any other man and he gambled. He's a good poker player. He knows what he's doing but he just happened to have a run of bad luck last night. That's all there was to it.

"However, now you've said you don't want him gambling here, that's good enough for me. We won't ever let him sit in another game."

Jepley Alton said, "I think that's fair enough, Mrs.

Ellis. If you didn't want your husband gambling, I'm quite certain that George wouldn't have wanted him sitting in on the games. I don't think you ever said a word to George about not wanting Helly to gamble. After all, he's been trying his best to win. You don't have any legal recourse and—"

She whirled to Perry Mason. "Will *you* take my case against this crooked outfit?"

Mason smiled and shook his head. "That's not in my line," he said, "and I'm pretty well tied up with cases right at the moment. However, I suggest you do get an attorney."

"What are you trying to tell her?" Jebley Alton asked scornfully. "You know that an attorney wouldn't do her any good. A man can't recover money he's lost in gambling. That's one of the most elemental features of the law."

"That's right, Jeb," George said. "Make this guy put up or shut up. It's easy for him to say a lawyer can get the money back, but he don't dare to back up his words. Now, go ahead and pin him down if he thinks he's so damned smart. Personally, I'd like to hear how some smart lawyer can get gambling losses refunded."

"Do you have a pen and notebook handy?" Mason asked Mrs. Ellis.

She looked puzzled for a moment, then said, "Yes, there's one in my purse."

"Take this down," Mason said. "You can tell your attorney about it, and you, Mr. Alton, might like to look up some law on the subject."

"I've looked it up," Alton said. "What kind of a run-around are you trying to give us? Ellis can't sit in a game trying to win and then come back and recover the money he lost."

Mason said, "Mrs. Ellis, if you'll just take down this citation to give to your attorney when you call on him, it may make a little difference.

"You see, Mrs. Ellis, there's a peculiar situation in the law of California. Ordinarily, gambling debts cannot be recovered, and since the gambling activity is against public policy, the courts leave the parties in the same status where they find them.

"However, as your attorney will tell you, in California where we have community property—that is, property which is acquired *after* marriage as the result of the joint efforts of the husband and wife—the husband has the care and management of the community property. In business transactions it is presumed that his judgment is binding upon the wife. But he does not have authority to give away the property of the community or to squander it without a consideration.

"So in a case where your husband lost community property gambling, *you* may well be able to recover it."

"What are you telling her?" Alton asked angrily.

"I'm telling her," Mason said, "to make a note of a most interesting case, the case of Novo versus Hotel Del Rio, decided May 4, 1956, and reported in 141 C.A. 2nd at page 304. It's in 295 Pac. 2nd 576. In that case it was held that a husband has no right to gamble with the community property. His action is not binding on the wife. She can follow the community funds and recover them from the gambler who won them."

"What the hell are you talking about?" Jebley Alton

said. "A decision like that . . . why, that would put gambling out of business."

"I suggest you look up the decision," Mason said. "It's an interesting law point. It may well put certain types of gambling out of business."

"What were those figures again?" Mrs. Ellis asked.

"141 C.A. 2nd 304," Mason said, "295 Pac. 2nd 576. Ask your lawyer to look up the decision."

Mason turned to George Anclitas. "I'll be in touch with your attorney about Miss Robb's claim for damages on defamation of character and on being discharged without cause, on being thrown out with only the sheerest of garments to cover her body.

"And as far as you're concerned, Mrs. Ellis, I would suggest that you get an attorney, preferably someone who is not living in Rowena and dependent on the local political machine for any favors."

Mrs. Ellis said with feeling, "If that's the law, if wives can get back what their husbands lose in these joints, there's going to be a cleanup in Rowena. I know a dozen women who are fighting mad over the way this thing's been run and the way their bank accounts melt away only to reappear in the hands of these men who run dives of this sort."

"It's a thought," Mason said. "The situation has very great possibilities, and that decision of the court may have far-reaching repercussions. Perhaps your attorney would like to appear before one of the local women's clubs and give a talk on California law and the management of community property."

Mrs. Ellis said, "I'm tremendously indebted to you, Mr. Mason."

"Not at all," Mason said.

"This guy's nuts," George Anclitas said to Mrs. Ellis. "I don't know what his idea is in filling you up with this stuff but I know what the law is. I've been in the gambling business for a long time and . . ."

His voice trailed away into silence as he got a look at Jebley Alton's face.

"What the hell, Jeb!" he said. "You don't think there's anything to that cock-and-bull theory, do you? I know what the law is in regard to gambling."

Jebley Alton said thoughtfully, "Apparently this case was decided in regard to community property. It *may* be there's a quirk in the law that—I'll go up to the office and look up the decision."

"You do that," Mason said, smiling. "It is a very interesting case."

George turned to Mrs. Ellis. "Now, you look here, Mrs. Ellis," he said, "you and I aren't going to get at loggerheads with each other. My attorney's going to look up that decision. There's no need for *you* to go getting a lawyer and *you* don't need to bring anyone in to make any talk before any women's club. That stuff is for the birds."

Mrs. Ellis laughed throatily. "What a wonderful coincidence," she said. "It happens that I'm in charge of the entertainment program for the next three months at the Rowena Women's Club. We have a regular monthly meeting about ten days from now, and I was wracking my brains, trying to think of some really entertaining program that would be of universal interest.

"This is a program that will bring everyone out.

There must be dozens of women here who will want to learn about the law of community property as it relates to gambling."

"And now," Mason said, bowing to George Anclitas and his openmouthed attorney, "I think we'll go out to the car, Della, and let our client finish dressing. She can pack her things and leave here at her convenience."

Mason turned to Ellen Robb. "I'm quite satisfied you won't have any more trouble, Miss Robb."

"What about this money?" she asked, pointing to the money in the suitcase.

"Remember the amount," Mason said. "Give George credit for that as payment on account. Go to a hotel, get a room, and let me know where you are."

"They'll arrest me the minute you leave here," she said.

"I don't think so," Mason replied, smiling. "I think they'll treat you with every consideration."

Mason turned so that the others could not see him and gently closed his right eye. "As it happens, Miss Robb, I am primarily interested in the better administration of justice and don't care particularly about fees. I hate to see people pushed around just because they don't have political influence. In case you want to make some settlement with George Anclitas on your own, it's quite all right with me. Just make any kind of a deal you think is fair and don't worry about my fee. There will be no charges.

"If, on the other hand, the slightest indignity is offered you or any threats are made, don't fail to call me at my office."

Jebley Alton said, "I don't know what you mean by a settlement. As far as Ellen Robb is concerned, she's getting out pretty easy if she keeps that money and—"

"You get the hell back up to your office," George Anclitas interrupted, "and look up that damned decision. If that thing says what Mason says it says, there are certain things we've got to do—fast."

"It is," Mason said, "a decision which presents an interesting problem to you people who are making a living out of gambling."

Mason extended his arm to Della Street and together they left The Big Barn.

Mason held the car door open for Della, then walked around and got in behind the wheel.

The lawyer was chuckling as they drove out of Rowena.

"Chief," Della Street said in an awed tone, "does that case of Novo versus Hotel Del Rio lay down the law that you said it did?"

Mason smiled. "Look it up when you get back to the office, Della. The doctrine laid down may be limited in future cases, but in that case the court said very plainly that transfer by a husband of community funds in payment of a gambling debt was within the meaning of the law a transfer without the consent of the wife and without the receipt of any valuable consideration by the husband. It's quite a decision.

"I can imagine that when some attorney delivers a talk on the law of community property to the housewives of Rowena and reads this decision, the meeting will be very, very well attended."

"And you deliberately walked off and left Ellen Robb

there so that George could make a settlement with her?"

"I thought perhaps under the circumstances he *might* have a change of heart. You know, Della, I wouldn't be too surprised if he didn't also reach some sort of an understanding with Mrs. Ellis.

"I think on the whole it's been a rather unprofitable morning for George Anclitas."

"Well," Della Street sighed, "you can't say he's the only one. We've lost half a day from the office, given some attorney a whole lot of fees on a silver platter, making him the fair-haired boy child for the women of Rowena. We've thrown any fee in the Robb case out of the window, in addition to gasoline and mileage on the car."

"I know," Mason said, "but think of the enjoyable morning, the sunshine, the fresh air, the scenery."

"Particularly the scenery," Della Street said sweetly.

"Yes, indeed, the scenery," Mason agreed. "And somehow, Della, I have an idea we'll receive a phone call from Ellen Robb shortly after we get back to our office."

"Wanting to know about what to settle for?"

"Something like that," Mason said.

"What should she settle for?"

"About anything she can get," Mason said. "I think George Anclitas has learned his lesson. I think Ellen Robb has been fairly well compensated for whatever inconvenience was caused her by being thrown out clad in nothing much but a sweater and stockings."

"She doesn't mind that," Della Street said. "She's accustomed to appearing in public with nothing much on. She likes it."

"Tut, tut," Mason said, "don't sell our client short."

"If it had been a man," Della Street asked, "would you have done as much in the interests of justice?"

Mason thought for a moment, then met her eyes. "Hell no," he admitted.

"Leotards," Della said somewhat wistfully, "are hardly suited for office wear, but they certainly can do things for a girl."

"They certainly can," Mason agreed.

CHAPTER FOUR

PERRY MASON latchkeyed the door of his private office.

Della Street, who had been sorting the mail, looked up with a smile.

"Well, Della," the lawyer said, "I wonder what adventures the day holds."

"Let us hope that it's nothing that will take your mind from the brief in the Rawson case or the stack of mail that I've marked urgent and have been calling to your attention for the last two days."

Mason settled himself in his swivel chair and sighed. "I presume one can't go through life just skimming the cream off existence," he said. "Sooner or later one has to get down to chores, routine drudgery. But I really did enjoy yesterday, Della. It was in the nature of an adventure.

"Now I'm somewhat in the position of the housewife who has given a very successful party, has ushered the guests out with cordial good nights and walks out into the kitchen to find a sink full of dirty dishes."

Mason sighed and picked up the folder Della Street had marked urgent. He opened it, hurriedly read through the letter that was on top, tossed it over to Della

and said, "Write him that it will be impossible for me
to be in San Francisco and take part in the case, Della."

Della Street raised her eyebrows slightly.

"I know," Mason said. "He makes a nice offer, but I
don't want to try a case with him. He has the reputation
of being a little too zealous on behalf of his clients, particularly in connection with producing witnesses who
swear to alibis. What's the next one, Della?"

Della Street's telephone buzzed discreetly.

Della picked up the instrument, said, "Yes, Gertie,"
then looked at Mason and smiled. "A little more cream
to be skimmed," she said. "Our friend, Ellen Robb, the
singing skirt with the long legs, is in the reception room.
She wants to know if it would be possible to see you. She
says she'll wait the entire morning if you can give her
just a few minutes. Gertie says she seems rather upset."

"Of course I'll see her," Mason said.

"Tell her to wait just a few minutes," Della Street
told the receptionist, "and Mr. Mason will try to see
her."

Mason pushed the file of urgent correspondence back.

"I thought we might have time for the other two letters that are on top. They're both urgent," Della Street
said. And then added, "Miss Robb is probably conventionally dressed this time."

Mason grinned. "So the cream won't be as thick."

"Something like that," Della Street said. "Let us say
that the scenic dividends may not be as great."

"You don't like her, do you, Della?"

"She has her points," Della Street said. "I should say
her curves."

"And you don't approve?"

"There's something about her, Chief," Della Street said, "and frankly I don't know what it is."

"Something phony?"

"You have the feeling that she's . . . oh, I don't know. The girl's an exhibitionist. She's been capitalizing on a pair of wonderful legs and a beautiful figure. She uses them. Her singing voice is pleasing but it doesn't have much range. Her figure is her best bet."

"Pushing herself forward?" Mason asked.

"Oscillating is the word," Della Street said. "Of course, a woman with a figure like that, who is working in a place of that type is pretty apt to have been around, and . . . well, it would be interesting to know just what there is in her background, how she happened to be making her living that way."

"You mean she's probably done about everything?" Mason asked.

"Except teach Sunday school," Della Street said dryly.

"And you're warning me," Mason said, "not to become so fascinated by a pair of beautiful legs that I lose my perspective."

"Not only legs," Della Street said. "I have a feeling that she deliberately puts herself on exhibition in order to get what she wants."

"But this time," Mason said, "she will be conventionally garbed."

"She may be conventionally garbed," Della Street said, "but I'm willing to bet she's wearing something that's cut rather low in front and that, during the course of the conversation, she finds occasion to bend over your desk for some reason or other."

"It's a thought," Mason said. "Cough when she does it, will you?"

"Why?"

"So I can keep my perspective," Mason said, grinning. "Let's get her in, Della, and then we can get back to the routine of the urgent mail."

Della Street nodded, walked out to the outer office and a moment later came back with Ellen Robb.

Ellen Robb was wearing a skirt which was tight around the hips, with a band of pleats around the bottom which flared out as she swung around, displaying her knees. Her silk blouse revealed shapely curves. She wore a heavy pin at the closing of the low V-cut neckline.

"Oh, Mr. Mason," she said impulsively, "I feel like a heel coming in and taking up your time this way, but I desperately need your advice."

"About a settlement with George?" Mason asked.

She made a little gesture with her shoulders. "George is a lamb," she said. "He was as nice as I've ever seen him. He thanked me, Mr. Mason. He positively thanked me."

"For what?" Mason asked, indicating a chair.

Ellen Robb sat down and almost immediately crossed her knees. "Thanked me," she said, "for showing him what a heel he was. He told me that he was too accustomed to having his own way, that he was ruthless with other people and that it was a trait he was trying to overcome. He begged me not to leave him but to stay on, and he raised my wages twenty-five dollars."

"A week?" Mason asked.

"A week," she said.

"And you agreed to stay?"

"For the time being."

"So you're all straightened up with George?"

She nodded.

"Then what did you want to see me about?"

"The Ellis situation."

"What about it?"

"I'm afraid you started something with Mrs. Ellis."

"That was the general objective I had in mind," Mason said.

"Well, it goes a lot deeper than just a legal point, Mr. Mason. There's friction between Mr. Ellis and his wife. He thinks it would make him look like a piker for her to try and get back the money that he lost."

Mason said somewhat impatiently, "I tried to help you, Miss Robb, because I felt you had been wronged, but I can't adopt the troubles of the whole neighborhood."

Ellen Robb inched forward in the chair until she was sitting on the edge. She leaned forward to put her hands on the arm of Mason's chair. *"Please,* Mr. Mason," she said, "I didn't mean it *that* way."

Della Street coughed.

Mason looked at Ellen Robb, then glanced at Della Street. "Go ahead, Miss Robb," he said.

She said, "I'm so anxious that you understand, Mr. Mason, that I . . . I'm just coming to you because . . . well, because you do understand."

She sighed and straightened up once more in the chair, glanced down at her knees, pulled the hem of the dress lightly with her thumb and forefinger and said, "Helly has gone overboard."

"Helly?" Mason asked.

"Helman Ellis, the husband."

"Oh, yes. And what's he done?"

She said, "Look, Mr. Mason, I'm under no illusions about myself. I'm on display. I'm sucker bait. I have a good figure and I know it, and I'm supposed to let other people know it. That's part of the job."

"And Helly, as you call him, has noticed it?" Mason asked.

"I'll say he's noticed it! He noticed it right from the start. Last night he—Mr. Mason, he asked me last night if I'd run away with him. He wanted to throw up the whole business and start all over again."

"What did you tell him?"

"I told him no."

"Well?" Mason asked, somewhat impatiently.

"All right," she said, "I'll get to the point. Nadine Ellis went to an attorney, a Mr. Gowrie. Do you know him?"

"Darwin Gowrie?" Mason asked.

"Darwin C. Gowrie," she said.

"I've heard of him," Mason said. "Quite a divorce lawyer, I believe."

"That's right. Mr. Gowrie called early this morning. He wanted to talk with me. He said he was Nadine's attorney—I thought, of course, it was about the legal point you had raised about the gambling, but I couldn't imagine why he wanted to talk with me. I thought he would want to talk with George."

"But you saw him?"

"I saw him," she said, "and it seems what he really wanted was to question me about Helly."

"Getting evidence for a divorce?"

"I don't know. He asked me all about my relationship with Helly, how long I'd known him, how many times he had been at the club, whether he noticed me and . . . well, whether he'd ever made passes at me."

"Had he?" Mason asked.

"Of course," she said.

"And you told this to Gowrie?"

"No."

"You lied?"

"I lied."

"Convincingly?" Mason asked.

"I hope so," she said. "Isn't a woman supposed to . . . well, isn't there supposed to be sort of a code of ethics about—?"

"Professional confidences?" Mason asked.

"Something like that."

"I wouldn't know," Mason said. "Why do you come to me?"

"Because I want your advice."

"On what point?"

"I want to go to Mrs. Ellis and tell her."

"Tell her what?"

"Tell her she is wrong about Helman and me and shouldn't make a fool of herself. She has a very fine husband. She'd better hang on to him. I've seen too many instances of women divorcing a man over some little thing and then regretting their action."

"Making passes is a little thing?" Mason asked.

"Of course. They all do—that is, nearly all—and I wouldn't give a snap of my finger for those who don't. Most of them don't really mean a thing by it. It's just the normal biological reaction of the male animal."

"You intend to explain that to Mrs. Ellis?"

"Not that so much as . . . well . . . the facts of marriage."

"What," Mason asked, "are the facts of marriage?"

"A man asks a woman to marry him because he enjoys her companionship. As long as he enjoys her companionship he's going to stay home with her. When he begins to wander around, it's because something has happened to take the keen edge off that enjoyment."

"Doesn't that happen with time?" Mason asked.

"It can," she said. "But the point is that when it does, the natural thing for the woman to do is to start reproaching the man, throwing it up to him that he's neglecting her, that he's getting tired of her now that she's given him the best years of her life, and all of that."

"You seem to know a lot about it," Mason said.

"I've been through it," she said.

"And played your cards wrong?" Mason asked.

"Just as wrong as I could have played them," she said. "I lost a mighty good man. If I'd only had sense enough to make it a pleasure for him to come home, he'd have stayed home. Instead of that, I made the home a hell on earth for him and pushed him right into the arms of a cheap little tramp who took him to the cleaners."

"But then he came back?" Mason asked.

She shook her head.

"Why not?"

"Let's not go into that," she said.

"All right," Mason told her. "What do you want to know?"

"Whether you think, under the circumstances, I

should go to Mrs. Ellis and tell her exactly . . . well, put my cards on the table. I don't want her husband. I wouldn't have him on a bet. He's . . . well, he just doesn't appeal to me, that's all."

"But you appeal to him?"

"Apparently," she said. And then added, "And to about ninety per cent of the other customers. Otherwise I wouldn't have lasted for the five months I've been there.

"I'm sorry for Helly. I've given him some sisterly advice. I'd like to talk to her. I—"

The phone rang.

Della Street answered it, then cupped her hand over the mouthpiece and said, "It's for you personally, Mr. Mason."

Mason raised his eyebrows.

"Want to take it in the law library?"

"I'll take it here," Mason said. "Who is it?"

"An attorney," Della Street said.

Mason, suddenly warned by something in her manner, hesitated. "It is . . . ?"

She nodded.

Mason said, "Oh, well, I may as well take it here anyway. Let's find out what it is he wants."

Mason picked up his own phone, and Della Street threw a switch which connected both phones.

"Hello," Mason said.

"Perry Mason?" a man's voice asked.

"That's right."

"I'm Darwin C. Gowrie, Mr. Mason."

"Oh, yes, Mr. Gowrie."

"I'm calling you on behalf of Mrs. Helman Ellis—

that is, it's in relation to a matter you discussed with Mrs. Ellis yesterday."

"What can I do for you?" Mason asked.

"That's a most interesting case you gave Mrs. Ellis yesterday," Gowrie said. "I feel rather guilty going before a women's club and stealing your thunder. Wouldn't you like to appear with me and take the credit for having ferreted out this decision?"

"Not me," Mason said. "If that's all that's worrying you, you have a complete clearance and a free hand. Go ahead and tell them about it. You don't need to mention my name."

"I've looked up the case," Gowrie said. "It's certainly a very interesting and yet a very logical application of the law. But do you realize what it's going to mean if this case is publicized? It's going to put the gamblers out of business. They just can't afford to buck a situation like that."

Mason said, "I spread it on a little thick for the benefit of George Anclitas. Actually, it's an appellate decision. The State Supreme Court or the United States Supreme Court may not go that far."

"I understand," Gowrie said, "but right now that decision is on the law books in California. The gamblers are going to have quite a time over that. What do you suppose would be the effect if some married man went to Las Vegas and got in a really big game where he lost perhaps eighty or a hundred or a hundred and fifty thousand dollars of community property?"

Mason said rather impatiently, "I don't know. You can cross that bridge when you come to it. As a matter of fact, Gowrie, I have a file of a lot of unusual decisions, feeling that the time may come when I can use them. But I don't go out of my way looking for an opportunity to use them.

"Take, for instance, the case of a person shooting another person, inflicting a mortal wound, but before the wound actually proves fatal, while the victim is lying there mortally wounded, another person comes along and fires a second shot into the victim, and the victim dies as the result of that second shot—who's guilty of the murder?"

Gowrie thought for a minute, then said, "Both of them."

"That's wrong," Mason said. "There are quite a few well-reasoned decisions that hold to the contrary. There's a case in Arkansas—the case of Dempsey versus State, where one man stabbed a victim in the heart. Another man inflicted a fatal blow on the head. The last one was held to be guilty of the homicide."

"What!" Gowrie exclaimed incredulously.

"That's right," Mason said. "In fact, in California we have an early case holding somewhat the same thing."

Gowrie became very much excited. "Look, Mason, I don't want to poach on your private preserves—but now that you've given me the clue, I could pick up the citations at the law library. Would you mind giving me the citations, if you have them?"

Mason nodded to Della Street, said, "Just a minute, Gowrie."

Della Street opened a small card file, ran through the cards, picked out a card, handed it to Mason.

"Here are the citations," Mason said, "that I have on my card. Dempsey versus State, 83 Ark. 81; 102 S. W.

704; People versus Ah Fat, 48 Cal. 61; Duque versus State, 56 Tex. Cr. 214; 119 S. W. 687."

"Well, I'll be damned," Gowrie said. "You mean if I should shoot you and just as you were dying somebody else fired a shot that was instantly fatal, I wouldn't be guilty of any crime?"

"I didn't go so far as to say that," Mason said. "What I said was that you couldn't be convicted of murder—unless, of course, two people were acting together in accordance with a common plan, as the result of a conspiracy, or in the commission of a felony. In that event you would both be guilty of first-degree murder. But I think the law is quite plain that where a person has received a fatal injury but is not yet dead, and another entirely independent agency inflicts a wound which is immediately fatal, the second person is the one who is guilty of the homicide. However, I just mentioned that as an illustration. I have a whole drawer full of unusual decisions, and this gambling decision just happened to be one of them. You go ahead and use it any way you want to.

"Now, while we're on the subject, Gowrie, your client, Nadine Ellis, feels that Ellen Robb has been breaking up her home and—"

"Not at all, not at all," Gowrie interrupted. "I'm afraid Miss Robb had the wrong impression. I will admit that I was questioning her, trying to find out something about Helman Ellis and I'll also be perfectly frank to state that I don't know just what Mrs. Ellis is going to do about it. There's no question but that Ellis has been hanging around The Big Barn because he was interested in Ellen Robb. That's why they kept the girl there. They have her appear in clothes which show off her figure, and she has a figure that's worth showing off.

"Helman Ellis became completely fascinated. I'm not blaming the girl. I don't think she was guilty of any wrongdoing at all, but naturally, as Mrs. Ellis' attorney, I *would* like to know a little of what was going on. You might tell your client, Mr. Mason, that I think she was a little less than frank with me. I don't blame her under the circumstances, but if she'd co-operate with Mrs. Ellis, I think she'd find Mrs. Ellis very broad-minded and very understanding."

"Actually," Mason said, "my client was thinking of doing just that. She was thinking of going direct to Mrs. Ellis and having a heart-to-heart chat with her."

"I think that would be a wonderful thing," Gowrie said.

"No objections as Mrs. Ellis' attorney?"

"None whatever."

"All right," Mason said. "You go ahead and put on your talk to the women's club. I think I'll tell my client to go talk with Mrs. Ellis."

Mason hung up the phone, turned to Ellen Robb. "Look, Miss Robb," he said, "why don't you just go see Mrs. Ellis and tell her something of what you've told me? Don't talk too much about her husband as an individual, but talk about the problem of marriage in general. I take it you've given the subject quite a bit of thought."

"I have," she said. "I've given it thought during a lot of sleepless nights, and, believe me, that's when you really cover all the angles of a problem. Right now Mrs. Ellis may feel rather vindictive, but, believe me, it's a lot better to make sacrifices and save a marriage than to go rushing into something where you win a little alimony and then have years of loneliness to think things over."

"All right," Mason said, "you go see Mrs. Ellis and I'll get to work."

She seemed rather hurt at his brusque manner of dismissal. "I have money now, Mr. Mason. I want to pay you for your services."

Mason hesitated a moment.

"Fifty dollars," Della Street said.

Ellen Robb opened her purse, took out two twenties and a ten.

"Right this way," Della Street said. "If you'll step out to *my* office I'll give you a receipt."

"I take it you can spare that money," Mason said. "You made some sort of a settlement?"

"I received a present, Mr. Mason. It wasn't a settlement. It was for the purpose of paying my expenses in the matter and—"

"Did you sign anything?" Mason asked.

She shook her head. "George said my word is good enough for him."

Mason nodded.

"Right this way," Della Street interposed. "I'll get your receipt."

When Della had returned to the office, Mason picked up the file of urgent correspondence. "Don't you think fifty dollars was a little steep?" he asked.

"It should have been two hundred and fifty," Della Street said. "Do you realize you made a trip out of the office, killed half a day, and then she had the temerity to come back and see you? You mark my words, Chief, that girl is one who could become a pest. She's got her eye on you."

"On me?" Mason asked.

"On *you!* You don't react the way she's accustomed to having men react. You noticed the way she bent over when she leaned over to put her hands on the arm of your chair?"

"I noticed," Mason admitted.

"You were supposed to," Della Street said. "That's why she did it. I'll tell you something else. She's a pretty good shorthand stenographer. While you were talking with Gowrie over the telephone, she was taking notes."

"What!" Mason exclaimed incredulously.

"That's right."

"You're sure it was shorthand?" Mason asked.

"It was shorthand," Della Street said. "I couldn't see the point of her pencil but I could see the way her shoulder moved, and I would say she was a very clever shorthand stenographer, and she was taking down your entire conversation with Gowrie."

"Well, isn't *that* interesting," Mason said, his eyes narrowing. "And do you suppose that Mr. Gowrie called quite by accident, that the fact he made his call while Ellen Robb was in the office was pure coincidence?"

"Not pure coincidence," Della Street said flatly.

CHAPTER FIVE

PERRY MASON latchkeyed the door of his private office to find Paul Drake, head of the Drake Detective Agency, visiting with Della Street over a cup of coffee from the office percolator.

"Hi, Perry," Drake said. "Della was telling me about your Rowena case."

"Quite a case," Mason said.

"Well, I'll be on my way and let you get to work. I just dropped in to make a report on that Finsley case. I gave it to Della. There's nothing you need to take any action on at the moment."

"Don't run away, Paul," Mason said. "We haven't had a visit for quite a while. I don't have anything pressing this morning."

"On the contrary," Della Street said firmly. "This is the morning you *are* going to dictate replies to the letters in that file of urgent mail. On your way, Paul."

"I've been ordered out," Paul Drake said, grinning.

He started for the door, paused midway and said to Perry Mason, "You're all cleaned up with that bunch down in Rowena?"

"Uh-huh."

"It's rather a mess down there," Drake said. "The joints actually control the town. It's a prosperous little community as far as outside money pouring in is concerned, but this fellow Anclitas you tangled with is quite a guy."

"How come?"

"I don't know too much about him," Drake said, "except that he's supposed to be bad medicine. He fights dirty. He has the city attorney and the chief of police in his pocket. I don't know whether you remember reading about it, but about a year ago there was a case in the papers."

"Involving him?"

"That's right. He filed charges against a girl who had been working there, claimed that she had been stealing money from the cash register and that she had stolen a gun. They found the gun in her possession, and she claimed the whole thing was a frame-up. There was an investigation. I guess the kid had been smoking marijuana. Quite a lot of those people connected with music go for that type of junk. The police found some marijuana in her apartment along with this stolen gun. Then George's friend, the chief of police down there, took the girl's fingerprints and from them dug up an FBI record which showed a prior conviction for marijuana."

"What happened?" Mason asked, interested.

"I think the girl went up, as I remember it, but she was making some wild accusations, claiming that George and his partner had framed her. Just keep an eye on those boys, Perry, and remember they've got the town all sewed up. If you have any trouble with George Anclitas, don't leave your car parked in front of a fireplug

in Rowena or you'll be in jail for six months. And if
they can get you where there are no witnesses, they'll
charge you with resisting an officer and show bruises
on *your* face to prove the charge."

"A nice cozy little setup," Mason said.

"It is for a fact," Drake told him. "Well, I'll be on my
way, Perry. I'm keeping on the job on that Finsley case.
I expect to hear something definite by tomorrow. You
get back to your dictation."

"Thank you, Paul," Della Street said sweetly.

"I like to make him work," Drake said and left the
office.

Perry Mason sighed, said, "One cup of coffee and one
cigarette, Della."

"All right," she said, "only answer those two top letters while you're sipping the coffee and smoking the
cigarette."

"Slave driver!" he charged.

Della Street adjusted her shorthand notebook on her
knee. "I'm the slave," she said. "What do you want to
tell that fellow?"

Della Street's phone rang while she was in the midst
of taking Mason's dictation on the letter.

Della said, "Hello," listened, then cupped her hand
over the mouthpiece and said to Perry Mason, "Your
girl friend."

Mason raised his eyebrows.

"Ellen Robb," Della Street said.

"All right," Mason said, "we've wasted enough time
with her, Della. She can't keep dropping in on us this
way without an appointment. Tell Gertie to explain to
her I'm busy, that I see clients only by appointment and

. . . well, you'd better go out and tell her yourself. I don't want to be too obvious with the brush-off. I'm afraid this is getting to be one of those things."

"*I'll* send her on her way," Della Street said.

She pushed back her chair, walked quickly out of the office, and Mason, waiting to resume his dictation, studied the letter to which he had been replying. After some thirty seconds he began to frown impatiently. He put the letter down, took a cigarette from the silver case on the office desk and was just lighting it when Della Street returned to the office.

"Perhaps I've been uncharitable," she said.

"What is it?" Mason said.

"This time," Della Street said, "she has a story and a black eye."

"How come the black eye?"

"George."

Mason's face darkened. "I'm afraid," he said, "George needs something in the way of a lesson."

"I thought you might feel that way."

"How's she dressed?" Mason asked.

"Same outfit she had on yesterday," Della Street said, "and she'll probably lean over and put her hands on the arm of your chair. But . . . well, Chief, you have to feel sorry for her. She's been batted around, and, after all, that figure of hers is her showcase. And someone has planted a gun in her baggage."

"A gun?" Mason asked.

Della Street nodded.

"So," Mason said, smiling, "I take it you didn't send her on her way."

Della Street shook her head. "I told her that I thought

perhaps you'd be able to see her, that you were very busy this morning and that you usually only saw people by appointment but that you *might* be able to see her. She's quite upset."

"Let's take a look," Mason said. "Bring her in. This gun business—I don't understand that. Tell her to come in. But I warn you, Della, I'm going to put her through a wringer this time."

"The poor kid is pretty much upset," Della said.

"You've changed your tune quite rapidly," Mason observed.

"I have," she admitted. "If there's anything that riles me it's the idea of these big burly men who demonstrate their manhood by hitting a good-looking girl in the eye. I hope you take this man George and put him through the hoops. After all, Miss Robb didn't sign anything, and there really wasn't any settlement within the legal meaning of the term. I think sticking George for about five thousand dollars would teach him a mighty good lesson."

"Let's get her in," Mason said. "I'm interested in the gun."

Della Street returned to the outer office and ushered Ellen Robb into Mason's presence.

Ellen Robb tried a lopsided grin. "Isn't it a beaut?" she said, fingering her swollen eye.

"All right," Mason said, "let's cut out the window dressing and get down to brass tacks. What happened?"

"I don't know. George was in a terrible mood last night. Every time I said anything he'd snap me up, and finally I couldn't take it any more and I told him I didn't have to. Then he really gave me a bawling out."

"What sort of a bawling out?" Mason asked.

"I think a lawyer would refer to it as loud, vulgar and obscene language."

"And then what?"

"Then he said something I just wouldn't take, and I slapped his face and . . . well, I have a shiner to show for it."

"No one interfered with your packing up?"

"No one interfered with my packing up. I got out and took a taxi to another motel. This morning when I was going through my things, I looked in my bag and . . . well, there was a gun in it."

"What sort of a gun?"

Ellen Robb opened her purse. "This," she said. "And I'm quite certain it's one of the guns he keeps there for protection. He has three or four of them by the various cash registers. This looks exactly like one of those guns. So, what do I do?"

Mason took the gun, motioned to Della Street to take her notebook. "A .38-caliber Smith & Wesson revolver with the number stamped in the metal, C 48809," he dictated.

He pushed the catch which released the cylinder, swung out the cylinder, said, "One empty cartridge case in the cylinder."

Mason put the gun down on his desk, then after a few seconds picked it up and dropped it in his right coat pocket.

"Let's assume someone put this revolver in your bag," Mason said. "When was it done—before your altercation with George Anclitas or afterwards?"

"Before. The minute he hit me I went right to my

locker and started getting my things out, then I went to my room in the motel and packed my bag."

"Could he have gone to your room while you were getting your personal things out of your locker?"

"I suppose he could have, but somehow I don't think he did. I don't know. I have an idea . . . it's hard to tell, Mr. Mason, but I have a definite feeling that George had decided he was going to pick a fight with me over something and get rid of me. I think the whole thing had been carefully planned and was all cut and dried."

"Did you go and see Mrs. Ellis?"

"I tried to, but I never got to see her."

"What do you mean, you tried?"

"They have a yacht. I rang up the house and tried to talk with her. I found she and her husband were going on a cruise and she was supposed to be aboard the yacht, getting it ready for the cruise. I went down to the yacht, but she wasn't on board."

"Did you go out to the yacht?"

"Yes. I got a skiff, rowed out and went around the yacht calling her name. Then I went aboard. There wasn't anyone there. I thought it over and felt that since they were going cruising together they had probably patched things up and it would be best for me to say nothing."

"This was before your altercation with George?"

"Oh, yes, quite a bit before. The fight didn't start until nearly eleven o'clock, but I felt he was just looking for an excuse to pop me one from the minute I started to work."

"What time did you go on duty?"

"Eight o'clock."

Mason said, "Look here, Miss Robb, you have had stenographic training, haven't you?"

She seemed surprised. "Yes. How did you know?"

"You were taking down my conversation yesterday when I was talking on the phone."

She flushed, seemed embarrassed, then said, "Well, yes. I— You were talking about me and . . . well, you were talking with Mrs. Ellis' lawyer, and I just wanted notes on what you said."

Mason said, "You told me that you'd been married?"

She nodded.

"Want to talk about it?" Mason asked.

"No."

"And you've been around?"

"I've been around. I'm twenty-four years old and thought I was smart. I won a beauty contest. I thought I was going to be a Hollywood actress. I had a darned good husband and I guess I just took him too much for granted. When he started getting restless and playing around, I played the jealous wife to perfection. I nagged him and made his home life a hell. I drove him right into her arms. I told you that before."

"And then?" Mason asked.

"Then," she said, "I just didn't seem to care. I went out and tried to get away from everything and everybody I knew. I found that *good* stenographic jobs were rather difficult to get. I got a job as hat-check girl in The Green Swan. We only got to keep a very small percentage of our tips there, and George had his eye on me. He found out I liked to sing and he offered me a good job with a salary and a chance to keep all my tips— Look, Mr. Mason, your time is valuable. If I tried to tell you about all of my career, you'd have to charge me more than I could afford to pay."

"Have you ever had any trouble with the law?"

"Never."

Mason turned to Della Street, said, "If you'll excuse us, Miss Robb, I have to make a rather confidential phone call at this time." Mason walked around his desk, opened the door to the law library and nodded to Della Street.

She joined him and Mason pulled the door shut.

"Well?" Della asked.

"I don't like it," Mason said. "I have a feeling that I've been suckered into a trap."

"By Ellen Robb?" she asked.

"By George Anclitas," Mason said, "and I don't like it."

"What do you think happened?"

"George resented me when I first appeared on the scene Monday morning. He realized, however, that I had him in a position where he was hooked, and struggling or resentment wouldn't do him any good, so he capitalized on my weakness."

"Your weakness?" Della Street asked.

"Exactly," Mason said. "I should have been a hard-boiled lawyer. I should have made a settlement on behalf of my client, charged her thirty-three and a third per cent of it and had proper releases signed. In place of that, I left it to her to make her own terms with George so she wouldn't have to pay me any fee, and I walked out.

"That's where George saw a heaven-sent opportunity. He started playing up to Miss Robb. He ate a little crow

and told her he was sorry. He got her to stay on. All the
time he was planning to jockey her into a position where
she'd be in trouble, and if I tried to help her I'd be in
trouble."

"The gun?" she asked.

"I think in due time he's going to charge her with
stealing the gun. He may even plant some dope in her
baggage."

"When do you think George will spring this trap of
his?" Della asked.

"When I have filed an action on behalf of Ellen
Robb."

"You intend to do that?"

"Sure I intend to do that. I have to, to protect her interests and to save my own face. The point is, Della, that
I started something that is destined to raise the devil
with the gambling interests. They aren't going to like
that. They're going to try to smear me in some way, and
Ellen Robb is their point of contact.

"You can see from the way she tells her story that they
laid plans very carefully and then George punched her
in the eye."

"She slapped his face," Della pointed out.

"He egged her on," Mason said.

The lawyer was thoughtful for a few minutes, then
he said, "Della, we've got quite a collection of guns in
the safe, guns that have been surrendered by clients from
time to time. Do you suppose we have a Smith & Wesson
in there—one of the police models with a two-and-a-
half-inch barrel?"

"Yes, I'm certain we do."

"Get the gun and bring it in here," Mason said.

Della Street went to the safe and after some two minutes returned with the gun.

The lawyer extracted one of the cartridges, pried the bullet out, shook out the powder, put the empty cartridge shell back in the revolver and, going over to the coat closet, exploded the percussion cap with the hammer. He replaced the other cartridges, put the revolver in his left coat pocket and returned to the office.

"I'm sorry we had to keep you waiting, Miss Robb," he said.

"It's all right."

"Is Ellen Robb your true name or a professional name?"

"Let's put it this way, Mr. Mason, Ellen Robb is as near my real name as you or anyone else will ever know. The man I was once married to has become a big businessman now. I wouldn't drag his name into . . . into the sort of work I'm doing."

"Where were you intending to go?" Mason asked, absently lighting a cigarette.

"I want to take a bus to Arizona. I have an offer of a job at Phoenix. A girl that I know has the photographic concession in a night club, and there's an opening for a girl to sell cigars, cigarettes and double as a hat-check girl. But what do I do about the gun?"

Mason reached in his left pocket, took out the gun he had placed there, weighed it in his hand as though debating what was to be done with the weapon. "I don't like to have you turn it in to the police," he said. "It seems to me that . . . well, I don't know . . . after all, we don't want to borrow trouble."

The lawyer pushed the gun toward her and said, "Perhaps you'd better keep it, Ellen. Remember that you showed it to us and told us about it."

"Shall I keep it in my purse?"

"Heavens no. You don't have a permit," Mason said. "Put it back in your bag where you found it."

"And what shall I do with it?"

"Keep it for evidence," Mason told her. "You have no idea how it got in your bag?"

"No idea whatever."

"Well, you've done everything you can. I'm going to file suit against Anclitas. Where are you staying?"

"Unit 19, the Surf and Sea Motel at Costa Mesa."

"Go back to your motel. I want to know where you are at all times. If you leave there, let me know."

"If you're going to file a suit, you'll want some more money," she said. "This is—"

Mason shook his head. "No more money. Not unless something else turns up. We're all fixed. Save your money until I ask for it.

"Go back to the motel and wait. By the way, what about Helman Ellis? Was he there when you and George were having this altercation?"

"No."

"You said you had heard he and his wife were going on a cruise. Do you know if they actually went?"

"I don't know. Helly was in The Big Barn last night before the altercation with George. He said his wife had marooned him aboard the yacht. They'd had a fight."

"Keep in touch with me," Mason said. "I want to know right where I can reach you."

She impulsively gave him her hand. "Thank you, Mr. Mason," she said. "I'll never forget this."

"I probably won't myself," Mason said.

Della Street ushered her to the door, shook hands with her, returned to the office.

"Did you switch guns?" she asked.

"I switched guns," Mason said.

"And she has no idea?"

"I hope not," Mason said. "I hope I wasn't crude—Just where did that gun I gave her come from, Della? What about it?"

"According to our records," Della Street said, "that gun is a .38 Smith & Wesson Special with the number 133347. You may remember that when George Spencer Ranger came to us and wanted you to represent him, you asked him if he carried a gun. He said he always carried one, that he didn't have a permit because he didn't need one, that he'd been appointed a deputy sheriff in Arizona. You told him that he'd better leave the gun with us. This is the gun that he gave us."

"All right," Mason said. "Give this other gun to Paul Drake. Tell him to first trace the registration, then take it to Maurice Halstead, the ballistics expert who does his work. Tell Halstead to fire some test bullets through it and save the bullets. Then bring the gun back here. You can lock it in the safe.

"Then, when George Anclitas swears to a complaint charging Ellen Robb with stealing one of his guns, gets a search warrant and finds a gun in her baggage, he'll naturally assume his little scheme is working perfectly."

"Then you'll jerk the rug out from under him?" Della asked.

"Then I'll jerk the rug."

"But what about this gun that was planted in Ellen Robb's baggage?"

Mason grinned. "If Paul Drake's investigation shows that it's George Anclitas' gun, it will be right back in George Anclitas' place of business and no one can ever prove it had been missing."

"Is that legal?"

Mason said, "I know of no law which keeps one from returning lost property to the owner."

CHAPTER SIX

WHEN DELLA STREET had returned from Paul Drake's
office, after leaving the gun with him, Mason said, "Let's
get Gowrie on the phone, Della. I want to see how *he's*
feeling this morning."

Della Street put through the call, nodded to Perry
Mason.

Mason picked up the telephone, said, "Hello, Gowrie.
Perry Mason speaking."

"Oh, yes, Mr. Mason. How are you today?"

"Pretty good. My secretary and I want to sit in on your
talk to the women's club at Rowena, Gowrie. We may
have some trouble getting in, but if you would invite us
as your guests we probably wouldn't have any trouble."

Gowrie hesitated a moment.

"You there?" Mason asked.

"I'm here," Gowrie said. "I was just trying to marshal
my thoughts."

"What about your thoughts?" Mason said. "Why do
they need marshaling?"

"I am not going to make the talk at Rowena."

"You're not?"

"No."

"Why not?"

"Well, for one thing, Mrs. Ellis hasn't completed the arrangements that she had agreed on."

"What do you mean?"

"I was to receive a fee from the women's club for the talk, and there was to be a retainer in connection with her case."

"She hasn't paid anything?"

"Not a cent. And I can't reach her. I can't find her. Apparently she went yachting. Under the circumstances, I rang up the president of the Rowena Women's Club and told her that the talk would have to be postponed."

"Like that, eh?" Mason asked.

"Like that," Gowrie said. "You know how it is yourself, Counselor. A lawyer can't go around giving his services away."

"All right," Mason said. "Let me know when you hear from Mrs. Ellis, will you?"

Mason hung up the phone. "Did you listen in on that, Della?"

She nodded.

"Well," Mason said, "I guess there's nothing much to be done at the present time."

"Except that mail file," she said. "We still haven't got at those important letters."

Mason sighed, picked up the mail file and spent the rest of the day in dictation.

In the late afternoon Paul Drake's code knock sounded on the door.

Della Street got up to let him in.

Paul Drake stretched himself out on the big overstuffed chair in the lawyer's office and said, "What the hell have you been doing, Perry, juggling guns again?"

"Why the again?" Mason asked.

Drake said, "I don't know, but any time you get in a case and a gun figures in it, you certainly seem to play three-card monte with the prosecution and the police."

"Anything wrong with that?" Mason asked.

"Not if you get away with it," Drake said.

"And what brings up all those remarks?" Mason asked.

"That gun you wanted me to trace—a .38 Smith & Wesson number C 48809."

"What about it?"

"It's one of four guns that were purchased, all on the same date, by W. W. Marcus, full name Wilton Winslow Marcus. He's supposed to be some sort of a silent partner of George Anclitas in a restaurant deal in Rowena. The restaurant is mostly a front for gambling."

"Permit?" Mason asked.

"Apparently no permit. They own the chief of police at Rowena. He appointed them some sort of special officers. Apparently both Anclitas and Marcus are specials. That gives them an opportunity to carry firearms without any written permit other than their authorization as special officers."

"And this gun is one of the four that were purchased?"

Drake nodded.

"All right. What else?" Mason asked.

"I had a ballistics expert fire test bullets from it and then replace the cartridges that were in the gun just as they were when you handed them to me."

"And the test bullets have all been marked for identification?"

Drake nodded.

"Okay," Mason said. "Where's the gun?"

Drake took the gun from his pocket and handed it to Mason. "You be careful you don't get into trouble with that," Drake said.

"What sort of trouble, Paul?"

"Darned if I know, but . . . you evidently have the idea the gun has been used in committing some sort of a crime."

"What gives you *that* idea?"

"Otherwise, why would you want test bullets fired from it?"

"Perhaps," Mason said, "I merely wanted to date the gun."

"What do you mean by that, Perry?"

Mason opened the drawer of his desk, took out a piece of steel that was bent at the end into a small, sharp point, said, "This is a tool for etching steel, Paul."

Mason inserted the tool in the barrel of the gun, drew it along the length of the barrel, then inserted it once more and again drew the tool along the length of the gun barrel.

"What's the idea?" Drake asked.

Mason said, "If we fire a bullet through that gun now, there will be striations that are in addition to and different from those of the test bullets that have previously been fired through it. Is that right?"

"If you want to be sure, better make a couple of more marks," Drake said.

Mason repeated the process of scratching the barrel. "How's that?"

"That should do it very nicely," Drake said.

Mason opened the drawer of his desk and dropped the gun down in the drawer.

Drake regarded him thoughtfully. "You know, there's a law about tampering with evidence."

"Evidence of what?" Mason asked.

"I don't know," Drake said.

Mason grinned. "We're not supposed to be clairvoyant, Paul. If you adopt that attitude, you could never change anything in connection with any object. You couldn't even tear up a piece of paper and throw it away. You couldn't wash a dirty dish. You'd be altering or destroying evidence. Any object doesn't become evidence until you know or have reason to believe that it has become identified with a crime in some manner."

"And you have no reason to believe that this gun is connected with a crime?"

"Very definitely not," Mason said. "I am simply protecting a client."

"And that will protect the client?" Drake asked.

"It may help," Mason said. "I'm sitting in a game where I don't know what cards have been played and moreover I don't know what are trumps. But we've been dealt a hand. It may not be a very good hand. It probably was dealt to us from a cold deck with the idea that it was the lowest hand in the deck. I've got to play that hand so it becomes a winning hand."

"Without knowing trumps and without knowing what cards have already been played?"

"That's right."

"That's a job you can have," Drake said. "I'm glad I'm not a lawyer. Anything else before I go home, Perry?"

"Not right now."

Drake got to his feet, moved lazily toward the door, paused at the entrance door to look back at Mason. "This deal in Rowena could be bad business," he said. "There's a lot of money involved."

"That's right," Mason said.

Drake hesitated a moment longer, then shrugged his shoulders, opened the door and walked out.

Della Street looked at Mason and raised her eyebrows in silent inquiry.

"Now then," Mason said, "we know this gun is the property of George Anclitas. I want to get it back to his place of business. We have to—"

The lawyer was interrupted by the ringing of the telephone.

"That's Gertie," Mason said. "See what it is, Della."

Della Street picked up the telephone, said, "Yes, Gertie," then said, "Just a minute." She looked at Mason. "Mr. Helman Ellis is in the outer office and says it is very important that he get in touch with you at the earliest possible moment. He realizes it's after office hours but he wants to know if you can see him immediately."

Mason hesitated a moment, appraising the situation, then said, "I'll see him immediately, Della. Go out and bring him in."

Della Street said, "I'll be right out, Gertie," and hung up the phone.

"Go through the usual routine," Mason instructed her. "Get his name, address, telephone number where he can be reached, and then bring him in."

Della nodded, then walked out through the doorway to the reception room.

A few minutes later she returned and said, "Mr. Mason, Mr. Ellis."

Mason got up to shake hands.

Ellis was a tall individual in his late twenties. He had high cheekbones, a somewhat Slavic cast of features, a long, thin mouth, steady blue eyes. He was big-boned and wrapped powerful fingers around Mason's hand as the two men shook hands.

"Sit down," Mason said. "Is there anything I can do for you?"

"I don't know," Ellis said. "It depends on how you're tied up."

"I am representing Ellen Robb."

"That's why I'm here," Ellis said.

"What is your trouble?"

"My wife."

"I don't take divorce cases," Mason said. "I try to specialize pretty much in trial work. A good deal of my practice is criminal cases. Domestic relations, contracts and all that just don't appeal to me."

"My wife," Ellis said simply, "is going to kill your client."

Mason raised his eyebrows.

"There is no real cause for jealousy," Ellis said, "but my wife has in my opinion become temporarily insane."

Mason said, "Let's get certain facts straight. You have been playing a lot of poker at The Big Barn and you've lost rather heavily?"

"That's right."

"Your wife didn't take kindly to the idea?"

"Wives don't take kindly to the idea of husbands sitting in poker games and losing money."

"And Ellen Robb was rather conspicuous around The Big Barn?"

"They made her conspicuous," Ellis said.

"And you became interested in her?"

Ellis took a deep breath and said, "Mr. Mason, I love her."

"And yet you say your wife has no reason to be jealous?"

"I'll put it this way, Mr. Mason. I hadn't—I have been keeping it to myself."

"You mean you think you've been keeping it to yourself," Mason said.

"What do you mean by that?"

"A wife can smell a situation of that sort a mile away," Mason said. "If you're in love with Ellen Robb, you can rest assured that your wife knew there was something more to your excursions to The Big Barn than a desire to sit in a poker game."

"She doesn't know how I really feel," Ellis said, "because it was only recently I faced the situation myself and realized I had fallen in love."

"She knew it before you did," Mason said, "otherwise, why should she have become so jealous?"

"She's always been jealous. She's jealous of any woman that I look at twice."

"Have you looked at many women twice?"

"Not much more than that."

"All right. Tell me what happened."

"Well, I knew that Nadine, my wife, was building up to terrific emotional tension. I'd lost some money playing poker but I could afford to lose money playing poker. Then she made a scene. You know all about that—that was one thing I couldn't afford, to be branded as a welsher.

"Mr. Mason, if Nadine had filed suit against George Anclitas on account of money that I lost playing poker, I would be branded from coast to coast as a piker, a welsher."

"Suppose the game was crooked?"

"That, of course, is different. If anyone could *prove* the game was crooked, the situation would be different."

"All right. What happened?" Mason asked. "Let's get down to brass tacks."

"I learned that my wife had made a scene down at The Big Barn. I learned that you had given her some legal authorities which would enable her to try to recover the money I had lost. I learned that she had gone to an attorney and retained him to file suit. So I told Nadine that we simply had to talk things out. We decided to go on a cruise on my yacht. We would be uninterrupted that way. We could sail out beyond the harbor and try to get the whole thing settled. We'd done that once or twice before during periods of crisis in our married life, and things had worked out all right."

"How long have you been married?" Mason asked.

"Seven years."

"All right, go on. What happened?"

"We left the house," Ellis said, "to go to the yacht. We told the neighbors that we would probably be out all night or perhaps two nights. We planned to sleep on the yacht. We planned to have dinner on the yacht. We stopped to buy some provisions.

"It seems that almost immediately after we left the house, Ellen showed up. She wanted to talk to my wife.

The neighbor told her we were down on the yacht so Ellen went down there, rented a skiff and rowed out to where the yacht was moored. She rowed all around it and called out several times. Then she tied up the skiff and went aboard. When she didn't find anyone there, she took the skiff and rowed back to the place where she had rented the skiff.

"Now, that was the last straw that touched everything off. While Ellen was on the yacht, she apparently had dropped a handkerchief that had her name embroidered in the corner. We got aboard the yacht and went down to the cabin and . . . well, my wife found Ellen's handkerchief.

"That really started things going. My wife was frantic. She wouldn't listen to anything I had to say.

"Of course, at the time I had no way of knowing how Ellen's handkerchief got aboard the yacht. I thought somebody had planted it. I tried to tell my wife that it was simply a scheme by which someone was trying to discredit me, and perhaps it was something the gamblers had done to get her mind off the idea of recovering some of the money I had lost gambling."

"What happened?"

"Nadine was crazy. Mr. Mason, she just went temporarily insane. She took the gun—"

"What gun?" Mason asked.

"A revolver that we keep aboard the yacht for protection when we're at sea or when we're sleeping aboard the yacht while its moored in the harbor."

"You don't carry a gun?"

"No. We kept a gun there on the yacht. That was the only place I thought we ever might need one. I understand that sometimes there have been holdups on some of the yachts that were moored in the harbor—vicious young thugs who get aboard a yacht and commit all sorts of atrocities—tie up the men, submit the women to indignities, take money and all of that."

"What sort of a gun?" Mason asked.

"A revolver."

"Do you know the make?"

"Smith & Wesson."

"Where did you get it?"

"It was a present."

"Who gave it to you?"

"George."

"George Anclitas?"

"Yes."

"Do you know the number that was on the gun?"

"Heavens no!"

"How did George happen to give you the gun?"

"Well, George and I have been rather friendly over a period of several weeks. I like to play cards and . . . well, we played with varying results. Sometimes I'd win, sometimes George would win, and we became friendly. I happened to see this gun when George and his partner were discussing firearms. They had made some sort of a bet about it. George explained that he kept several guns around the place so that in case of a holdup there would be more than one person who could get his hands on a gun. I told him I was thinking of getting a gun for the yacht because I'd read about a situation where a group of three thugs had boarded a yacht and tied the owner up and . . . well, he pressed the gun on me, told me to take it."

"Where is that gun now?"

"I told you. Nadine has it."

"All right, she took the gun," Mason said. "What happened after she took the gun?"

"She told me if I wanted to have a rendezvous aboard the yacht with my paramour, she wasn't going to stand for it. She told me that she was going to invoke the unwritten law and kill Ellen. It was a terrible scene. I have never seen her like that before. She was utterly insane."

"What did she do?"

"Got in the skiff and rowed away and left me marooned on the yacht."

"Didn't you object to that?"

"Of course I objected to it. If I could have got close enough, Mr. Mason, I'd have knocked her down and taken the gun away, but she was too smart for that. She made me keep my distance and she kept me covered. I believe she would have killed me. In fact, the idea in her mind at that time was to kill me aboard the yacht, then kill Ellen and then kill herself."

"But why leave you marooned aboard the yacht?"

"She was afraid I would try to warn Ellen."

"Go on," Mason said. "What happened?"

"That's about all I know. She rowed away in the skiff. I was marooned aboard the yacht until nearly nine-thirty. Then I was able to attract the attention of a party of yachtsmen and got taken ashore."

"Couldn't you have started the engine on the yacht and gone into the pier?"

"No chance," Ellis said. "She took the keys to the starting switch with her. I had had a burglarproof lock put on there so that when the keys are out it's impossible to start the motor. I suppose an electrician could have short-circuited the wires back of the locking mechanism but I didn't know how to do it and I'm not too certain it could have been done. I had the sort of lock installed that would keep people from stealing the yacht and taking it for a joy ride.

"It's not a particularly large yacht, Mr. Mason; only forty-two feet, but it's very expensive and perfectly appointed. I have spent a lot of money trying to make it very comfortable."

"All right," Mason said, "you got ashore about nine-thirty. Then what?"

"So then I tried to find my wife and I couldn't find her. I went to talk with Ellen but I didn't want to alarm her. I just told her to be careful, that my wife was on the warpath. So then I went out looking for Nadine.

"Then this morning my wife showed up very briefly at the house. She made further threats. She said Ellen Robb had been meeting me secretly aboard the yacht, that she was going to prove that fact by having finger-print experts develop her latent fingerprints.

"She also said she felt Ellen was waiting for me on the yacht right then and that if she was, she was going to kill her."

"What did you do then?"

"Nothing. Ellen had never met me aboard the yacht. I knew Nadine was barking up the wrong tree, so I let her go. . . . But I want you to know that my wife is in a murderous rage so you can take steps to protect Ellen."

"Did you know that Ellen Robb and George Anclitas had had an altercation?"

"What about the altercation?"

"He fired her, and gave her a black eye to boot," Mason said.

"What!" Ellis exclaimed, half rising from the chair.

"Gave her a black eye," Mason said.

Ellis said, "I'll kill him for that. That . . . that boorish, arrogant, crooked . . ."

Ellis quit talking, compressed his lips in a thin, straight line.

Mason said, "On behalf of Miss Robb I'm filing suit against George Anclitas and several John Does, who I think are partners in the business, for six thousand dollars exemplary damages and fifteen hundred dollars actual damages for pain and suffering."

Ellis said, "Mr. Mason, I am beginning to be satisfied that game was crooked. I think that . . . I think that Ellen could tell you something about that. I want to get even with George Anclitas. If he struck Ellen, I'm going to give him the beating of his life. I'll—"

"And how will that look when your wife files suit for divorce and names Ellen Robb as correspondent?" Mason asked.

Ellis' face showed dismay.

"There are some things you have to take into consideration," Mason said dryly.

"Look," Ellis said, "I'll do anything I can in this matter, Mason. I'll—I'd like to pay your fees for prosecuting that case against George."

"And how would *that* look in the divorce action?" Mason asked.

Ellis hesitated, then said, "All right. I have lost

around ten thousand dollars there in The Big Barn. I'm now satisfied the game was crooked. If you want to act as my attorney to recover that money, I'll pay you fifty per cent of the recovery and give you all the expense money you need to prosecute. You can hire detectives or do anything else you need to do."

"I may be disqualified on that action," Mason said. "I already advised your wife—gratuitously, of course —that she could probably recover the community funds that had been lost gambling, regardless of whether the game was straight or crooked."

"Mr. Mason, don't you understand what that would do to my reputation? I'd be the laughingstock of—"

"I don't think so," Mason interrupted. "I think if a few women would take action of this sort, it would give the big gamblers something to think about, particularly the ones where the games are crooked."

"On the contrary," Ellis said with some feeling. "It would have exactly the opposite effect, Mr. Mason. The ones who were running square games couldn't afford to stay in business. If they were faced with the prospect of having to give up their winnings when some woman filed suit claiming it was community property that the husband had lost, the ones who were running a straight game would find that the percentage was too much against them and they'd go out of business. On the other hand, the crooked gamblers would stay in business. Or I'll put it this way. The gamblers who stayed in business would be crooked."

"You have a point there," Mason said. "I don't know, of course, what's going to happen when the doctrine laid down in this decision is tested in the Supreme Court of this state or the Supreme Court of the United States. This, however, is at present a new angle on the law of community property. It's an interesting legal development, and I'm going to watch and see what happens."

"Well, I'll say one thing," Ellis said. "You certainly threw a monkey wrench into the City of Rowena. George would do almost anything to keep that information from being made public. I guess you know that my wife intended to have a meeting and retained an attorney by the name of Gowrie to address the meeting, and George promptly bought him off."

Mason raised his eyebrows. "Bought him off?"

"Sure he did. Oh, nothing crude. He didn't go to Gowrie and offer him money not to appear at the meeting, but Gowrie now has some new clients who brought him some rather important business and I think conveyed the idea to him that they would be very unhappy if he addressed a meeting of the Women's Club of Rowena on the subject of gambling."

"He told me," Mason said, "that he couldn't get hold of your wife."

"Sure, he was trying to reach her but he was trying to reach her to tell her that he'd have to postpone the meeting and that he didn't think he'd be available. I think he also was going to tell her that after thinking the matter over and looking up the law on the subject, he had decided that the point probably wasn't well taken."

"How do you know all this?"

"He talked with me on the telephone. He was feeling his way," Ellis said.

"All right," Mason told him. "I'll think over the information you've given me. If you get in touch with your wife, let me know at once."

"Tell me, Mason, is Ellen in a safe place? That's what I want to know. Can you guarantee protection?"

"I can't guarantee protection to anyone," Mason said.

"How about the police?"

"They can't either," Mason said. "If the police tried to put guards around every woman who is threatened with death at the hands of a jealous spouse, they wouldn't have enough officers left to direct traffic."

"But she's in actual danger."

"That may be," Mason said. "She is, however, fairly well concealed. I'm going to keep her under cover for the time being and I appreciate the information you've given me.

"However, these things happen. You pick up the paper almost any day and you'll find where some jealous ex-husband went to the apartment of his divorced wife, made a scene, killed her and killed himself. Or where a woman threatened to leave her husband, and he told her that if he couldn't have her, no one else was going to and pulled out a gun and killed her, then gave himself up to the authorities. These crimes of emotion account for the majority of our murders, but for every person who is actually killed under circumstances of that sort, there are a thousand who are threatened. The police simply can't cope with any situation of that sort."

"You sound cold-blooded about it," Ellis said heatedly. "Ellen Robb is a beautiful woman, a sweet, good young woman. Oh, I know she's been around, but essentially she's a mighty fine, sweet young woman and

. . . well, you simply can't sit back and let my wife go all out on the warpath this way."

"Where do you think your wife is now?"

"I think she's in Arizona. The story was that Ellen was to get a job at one of the night clubs in Phoenix. She had some connections there, and I suppose that's where Nadine went. If Ellen is here, I certainly hope Nadine is in Arizona—I'm hoping she'll cool down by the time she gets back."

"Well, we'll see what we can do," Mason said. "I'll try and protect my client to the best of my ability, but you understand we can't furnish absolute protection in a situation of that sort; even the police can't."

Ellis said, "Look here, Mr. Mason, if the police can't protect her, we can hire a private bodyguard for her. I want to pay for it, no matter what it costs. Armed guards who can watch her day and night."

"And how will *that* look in the divorce suit?" Mason asked.

Ellis thought over the lawyer's remark. "I guess I'm licked," he said, getting to his feet. "However, Mr. Mason, I'm telling you there's a real danger to your client and to me."

Mason merely nodded.

Ellis seemed reluctant to leave the office, but Mason arose, signifying the interview was terminated.

As soon as Ellis left the office, Mason nodded to Della Street. "Get Paul Drake, if he hasn't already gone home, Della. Have him come down here right away."

Less than a minute later, Drake was in Mason's office.

Mason said, "Ellen Robb is staying at the Surf and Sea Motel in Costa Mesa. She's registered under her real name. She may or may not be in some danger. Apparently an irate wife is on the warpath and is looking for her with a gun."

"Bodyguard?" Drake asked.

"Bodyguards," Mason said, "the 's' sound signifies the plural, two or more, and without her knowing anything about it. I want you to keep an eye on the place. Have men on duty down there where they can watch the door of Ellen Robb's motel apartment. If any woman asks for Ellen or if any woman shows up, have your men get on the job. If the woman is about twenty-seven, red-haired, streamlined, perhaps a little on the thinnish side, I want your man to stop her, no matter on what pretext, and if her name should be Nadine Ellis—Mrs. Helman Ellis—I want your men to take some action."

"How much action?"

"It depends on the circumstances," Mason said. "Divert her attention and . . . well, in any event, stick right with her. If this woman sees Ellen Robb, I want at least one of your men there. I want him to make certain there isn't any opportunity for Mrs. Ellis to pull a gun and go bang, bang."

"I get it," Drake said. "We do a lot of that stuff. I've got some pretty good men. However, it runs into money. How long do you want them kept on the job?"

"As long as there's any possibility of trouble," Mason said.

"How long will that be?"

"Until we locate Mrs. Ellis and find out more about the situation."

"Okay," Drake said. "Will do."

After Drake had left, Mason turned to Della Street. "Now," he said, "we have the question of the gun."

"How do you mean?"

"We start out with four guns that George Anclitas had," Mason said. "He gave one away. That leaves three. Now, one of them shows up in the personal effects of Ellen Robb. Presumably, George is going to claim that gun was stolen from him. That leaves George with two guns."

"What are you getting at?" Della Street asked.

"Simply trying to keep the guns straight," Mason said, grinning. "Usually when I get in a case the district attorney accuses me of introducing additional guns and juggling them around and—"

"And that's exactly what you've done in this case," Della Street said.

"I have, for a fact. Won't it be nice when George Anclitas 'discovers' that one of his guns has been stolen and accuses Ellen Robb of having committed the theft? He'll get a search warrant for her baggage. Then the officers will discover the gun, and then George will swear to a complaint. The matter will be brought into court and when they start introducing the gun in evidence, I'll ask that the number of the gun be read into evidence. Then we'll check the records to get the numbers of George's gun and then it will turn out that the gun that was found in Ellen's baggage wasn't the gun that was 'stolen' from George Anclitas."

"And then?" Della asked, smiling.

Mason grinned gleefully. "Then," he said, "We'll have another suit for damages against George Anclitas.

Perhaps after a while, Della, we'll teach him not to pick on women and black their eyes."

"But," Della Street asked, "suppose someone finds you're holding George's gun up here?"

"Why, the very idea!" Mason exclaimed. "I wouldn't *think* of holding George's gun up here. I told you we were going to return it to the owner as soon as we knew who the owner was."

"You'll just hand it to him?" she asked, her eyes twinkling.

"I said we'd *return* it," Mason answered, grinning.

"Do you have a plan?" she asked.

Mason said, "Downstairs at the soda fountain they use ice in the drinks that is round, about an inch diameter with a hole in the center and—"

"Go ahead," Della Street said, as Mason broke off and started to chuckle.

"I think," Mason said, "they make that ice around the outside of a pipe. They have some process by which they fill a larger pipe with water, freeze it, then get the ice out in lengths and cut it into pieces to put in the drinks.

"Suppose you run down, Della, talk with whoever is in charge and find out if you can get a piece of ice about . . . oh, say twelve inches long."

Della Street regarded him quizzically for a moment, then smiled and said, "On my way, Counselor. I take it we're about to freeze the evidence."

"On the contrary," Mason said. "We're going to melt a hard heart. Also, Della, pick up a shoe box and fill it half full of dry ice."

Della Street nodded, left the office.

Mason was once more pacing the floor when Della Street returned with a shoe box under her arm.

"Get it?" Mason asked.

She nodded.

She reached in the shoe box which contained dry ice and pulled out a twelve-inch cylinder of ice.

"All right," Mason said. "We'll try it for strength."

The lawyer took the gun which Ellen Robb had brought with her, ran the tube of ice through the trigger guard, then moved up two chairs and suspended the revolver between the two chairs, the cylinder of ice resting on the back of each one.

"Perfect!" he said, quickly removed the tube of ice and put it back in the box containing the dry ice.

"Now what?" Della Street asked.

"Now," Mason said, "we go down to Rowena. I stop on the block back of The Big Barn, where there's an entrance to the motel. You get out, walk through the motel, around the swimming pool and into The Big Barn by the back entrance. You go to the women's powder room—"

"Carrying this shoe box?" Della Street asked.

Mason shook his head. "You'll be carrying a purse by that time. The purse will be filled with dry ice, this tube of ice and the gun. We'll also stuff the hollow of ice with dry ice. You go into the women's powder room and look for a place to plant the gun, either high up by suspending the gun from two corners of a partition, or preferably, if you can find a washbowl that has open plumbing underneath it, and I think you can, you can suspend the two ends of the ice tube from the two shut-off valves which you'll find underneath; one on the hot water, one on the cold water pipes."

"And then?" she asked.

"Then after a period of time, depending on temperature, the ice tube melts enough so the gun drops down to the floor. The ice will melt into a pool of water, and someone will find the gun on the floor."

"And they'll connect it with us?" Della Street asked.

"If you do it right," Mason said, "and go in from the back entrance this early in the evening, no one is going to see you. I don't like to ask it of you, Della, but I am an attorney of record now with interests adverse to George Anclitas, and it's not ethical for me to talk with him except in the presence of his attorney. If I should go there, he'll want to talk with me. And I want the gun found in the women's powder room."

"Why there?" she asked.

"Because there's an attendant there," Mason said, "and because it's right near the back door which leads to the motel. You can pop in there, wait until some other woman comes in, plant the ice tube, give the attendant a quarter and leave the place. You can rejoin me in the car. We'll have stuffed the hole in this ice with dry ice, which will keep it from melting for some little time. When the gun falls to the floor, either the attendant will see it, or some woman who is in the place will see it within a few minutes after it has fallen. If we're lucky, the attendant will swear the gun couldn't possibly have been there over four or five minutes."

"And we'll be long gone?" Della Street asked.

"We'll be long gone," Mason said.

"How much of a crime am I committing?"

"I've told you," Mason said, "we're returning lost property. That's highly commendable."

"How about suppressing evidence?"

"Evidence of what?"

"Of theft."

"I didn't steal anything," Mason said.

"How about Ellen Robb?"

"She's a client."

"She's a client," Della Street said thoughtfully, "but don't go overboard on that girl. She knows which side of the bread has the butter and she doesn't intend to have anyone give her bread that isn't buttered."

Mason grinned. "Meaning, perhaps, that she might butter up people?"

"Particularly her lawyer," Della Street said. "I wish you'd play this one close to your chest, Chief."

Mason nodded. "That's why I want to get that gun back where it belongs."

"What will George Anclitas think when the gun is reported as having been found in the women's powder room?"

"That, of course, depends," Mason said, "on what he's planning to do."

"You think George Anclitas intends to file charges of theft against Ellen?"

Mason's forehead puckered into a frown. "I wish I knew the answer to that, Della," he said. "I certainly thought that was what he had in mind when he planted the gun in Ellen's suitcase, but why is he holding his fire? He's waiting for something. What is it?"

"Perhaps waiting to find out where she is," Della Street said.

"I doubt it—and there's one thing that bothers me."

"What?"

"Suppose he's playing a much deeper game than that?"

"What could it be?"

"I don't know," Mason said, "but I want to get that gun back into his possession. I want it planted in the women's powder room. The attendant there will find it. In all probability she's frightened to death of a gun. She'll cause something of a commotion and . . . well, George will know he's got his gun back."

"Of course he'll suspect you," Mason said. "And he'll also conclude that he waited too long before lowering the boom on Ellen Robb, that she found the gun in her suitcase and managed to return it. George will naturally be furious."

"When do we go?" Della Street asked.

Mason said, "You go down to the shop that sells handbags, on the corner, and get a leather handbag in which you can stuff the dry ice, the gun and the tube of ice. Then we're on our way."

CHAPTER SEVEN

PERRY MASON eased the car to a stop.

"Everything okay, Della?"

Della Street put her hand on the catch of the door. "Everything okay."

"Now, look," Mason said, "there's just a chance something may go wrong at either end of the line. If anything goes wrong with you, if anybody catches you, you send for me. I'll come in and we'll face it. I'll state that you were acting under my instructions, that I was returning a gun that had been planted in my client's baggage. We'll take it from there.

"Now, get that straight, Della. I don't want you to try this on your own. If anything goes wrong, you just step back out of the picture and I step in and take the responsibility. Understand?"

She hesitated a moment, then nodded.

"Now, those are instructions," Mason said. *"Don't* try to take the responsibility if you get into a jam. Now, here's the other situation. Something may go wrong out here. Someone may spot me.

"I'm going to drive around the block, into the alley and turn my lights on. If you see my lights on, everything is clear. You come on out and get in the car. . . . You can see those lights from the end of the swimming pool there.

"If, however, anything goes wrong, I won't have my lights on. If you come to the end of the swimming pool and see that my lights are off, don't come anywhere near the car. Understand?"

"For how long?" she asked.

"Until you see the car in the alley with the lights on. Then come across and join me."

"And if it's a long time, say over half an hour?"

"Under those circumstances," Mason said, "get back the best way you can. Take a bus or hitchhike."

"Okay," she said, "I'm on my way."

She opened the car door, slid out to the sidewalk, crossed the sidewalk and walked past the entrance to the motel around back of the swimming pool.

Mason circled the block to the left, came to the alley, drove down the alley until he was in a position where he could see the end of the swimming pool, then shut off his motor and waited, with his lights on.

So intent was the lawyer on watching the swimming pool that he failed to keep an eye on the rearview mirror and did not see the car which pulled up behind him.

Two men got out and walked up to where Mason was sitting.

Miles Overton, the chief of police, said, "This is the lawyer I was telling you about."

Mason snapped to quick attention, turned and said casually, "Hello, Chief."

"Want you to meet a friend of mine," the chief said. "This is Ralston Fenwick, Mr. Mason."

A heavy-set, bullnecked individual with smiling lips and cold green eyes extended a pudgy hand on which a scintillating diamond made sparks of fire. "How are you, Mr. Mason? Mighty glad to know you."

"What are you doing here?" the chief asked.

"Parking," Mason said wearily, switching off the lights on his car. "Looking over the lay of the land. I want to make a diagram of the premises."

"How come?" the chief asked.

"My client is suing George Anclitas for seventy-five hundred dollars. Or hadn't you heard?"

"I'd heard," the chief said noncommittally.

Fenwick pushed the chief of police slightly to one side, eased an elbow over against Mason's car, smiled at the lawyer. "I'm just sort of getting oriented here, Mr. Mason. I wanted to see the lay of the land myself. Then I was going to come and have a talk with you."

"Yes?"

"That's right."

"What's your interest in me?" Mason asked.

"Well," Fenwick said, "I'm in public relations. I represent an association. George Anclitas is a member of that association."

"What's the association?" Mason asked.

Fenwick grinned. "It wouldn't mean a thing to you if I told you. It has a high-sounding name, but there's no reason for you and me to beat around the bush, Mason. The association is composed of men who are in the gambling business."

"I see," Mason said.

"You have some peculiar ideas about the law," Fenwick went on, "but because of your position, Mr. Mason, and the fact that you are a pretty shrewd lawyer, those ideas of yours could do us a lot of damage."

"They're not ideas of mine," Mason said. "They're ideas of the courts of the State of California."

"So I understand," Fenwick said.

Mason saw Della Street walk quickly to the end of the swimming pool, look across at the car, then as she was aware that the lights were not on and that two men were talking to Perry Mason, she moved around the end of the swimming pool and out of sight.

Fenwick said, "You know, this association is pretty powerful, Mr. Mason. That is, we have a lot of mighty nice people who are members, and it isn't just in this county. In fact, it isn't just in this state, although my territory is all within the state—places in Nevada, for instance, have—"

"I take it," Mason said, "you also look after the legislative interest of gambling establishments."

"Among other things," Fenwick said. "You know, Mason, a lot of people like to knock gambling; but, after all, there's nothing wrong with it. Gambling is an outlet for the emotions. All people gamble. It's universal. You can't stop it. Prisoners in penitentiaries gamble, every fraternal organization has its little gambling setup. Even the society women with their bridge clubs gamble.

"I'll tell you something else, Mason. Gambling makes good business. It puts money in circulation. It encourages sociability, and it's darned good business for a community. Now, you take right here in Rowena. You'd be surprised how much money comes into this city from gambling. People come in from all over this part of the country to do a little card playing—and they leave money here."

"I take it," Mason said, "the gamblers don't quite break even."

Fenwick threw back his head and laughed. "You're a card, Mr. Mason, you really are! Of course that's the whole principle of organized gambling, Mr. Mason. The customer doesn't break even. Hell's bells, he doesn't want to. If he wanted to break even, he'd stay home. He wouldn't go out to a gambling place at all.

"That's the real philosophy back of gambling. Sometimes the customer makes a profit. The gambler always makes a profit. Everybody knows that. The gambler isn't doing business for nothing. Some people lose and some people win. More people lose than win, but the people that win, win heavy. They sit in a game with fifty dollars and they leave it with five hundred or fifteen hundred. That's the lure. That's what keeps the wheels running.

"On the other hand, a gambler knows that while somebody may win fifteen hundred dollars in a game in the course of a week, the majority of people who sit in the game are going to contribute. That's where he makes his living, and, believe me, Mr. Mason, gambling is a good thing for a community."

"It's a matter of opinion," Mason said.

"Now, you look at this place here at Rowena," Fenwick went on. "It's well policed, orderly, quiet and law abiding. You don't have any holdups here. You don't have any problems with gangsters. The place just runs along smoothly, and people like George Anclitas are heavy taxpayers—I mean really heavy taxpayers."

"You mean gambling is a good thing for the community," Mason said, "for the citizens who make up the community?"

"That's right. Now you're getting the idea."

"Then there's no reason why we shouldn't tell the married women that the husband has the management of community property but he can't gamble it away. If a gambler wins the wife's share of community property, he can't keep it."

The smile faded from Fenwick's face. "Now *that's* a horse of another color, Mason. You're getting things all mixed up. I didn't say that, and we don't feel that way.

"In the first place, I think that when you make a careful study of the law you'll find you're mistaken, and frankly I'd like to have you make a careful study of the law. That's going to take some time, Mr. Mason. You're a lawyer, and we don't want you to do it for nothing. My association needs some representation here, and we'd like to retain you to sort of keep us advised on the law.

"One of the first things we'd like to have you do would be to take a year or so and really study up on the decisions relating to gambling and games of chance. We'd put you under a retainer of, say, fifteen thousand a year."

Mason grinned. "What do you want *me* for, Fenwick? You've already hired Gowrie."

Fenwick's eyes widened. "How did you know?" he asked.

Mason grinned.

"Well," Fenwick said, "after all, Mason, we're both of us grown up. Think this proposition over, will you?"

Mason shook his head. "I'm busy with trial work," he said. "I don't have many interests outside of that."

"Well, you sure knew some law that threw a monkey wrench in the machinery of *our* organization," Fenwick said. "Boy, they got me on the telephone and told me to get down here so fast it'd make your head swim. I was on a vacation down at Acapulco and had a very pleasant, understanding little companion along with me. Wham! Boy, did I get a telephone call! Get on the plane, get up to Rowena, talk with George Anclitas, talk with Perry Mason, talk with Darwin Gowrie, talk with Mrs. Helman Ellis!"

"You evidently made good time," Mason said.

"I made good time. I can get along without sleep when I have to and still keep going."

Fenwick hesitated for a moment, then met Mason's eyes. "Well, why not?" he asked. "Sure, I've seen Gowrie."

"And what about Mrs. Ellis?"

"I'm looking for her," Fenwick said. "That's why I'm still hanging around here. We can't find her. She is in some kind of a ruckus with her husband. She was away for a while. Her husband thinks she was in Arizona. But she came back early this morning, then got in the family yacht and sailed off somewhere."

"Where?" Mason asked.

"I wish I knew. I'm figuring Ensenada on a guess. I've got men covering Ensenada and Catalina. The minute her boat shows up, I'll take a plane and go talk to her. I was going to ring you up at your office and make an appointment. Finding you here has saved me a lot of trouble."

"I understood Mrs. Ellis was looking around in Arizona," Mason said.

"That's where she was. She didn't stay long. The party she was looking for wasn't where she expected to find her. She got a hot tip from some place and came back here, all worked up. She thought she'd been deliberately sent on a wild-goose chase."

"Who tipped her off?" Mason asked.

"I don't know. I heard about it, that's all, just the sort of gossip a man can pick up."

Mason stretched and yawned.

"Look here," Fenwick said, "I'm not an attorney, Mr. Mason, and I'm not in a position to question your judgment about the law, but if—now, I'm just saying *if*—that decision you mentioned is out of line with the law generally or if there's been a rehearing, or if the case hasn't been decided by the State Supreme Court and this represents just an outstanding departure from the ordinary doctrine of law, I know you'd want to be the first to find out about it.

"Now, I'll tell you that we've got a battery of high-priced lawyers looking into this thing and we'll know the answer within a day or two. If, of course, your ideas about the law are wrong, you'd want to be the first one to correct the erroneous impression you gave Mrs. Ellis.

"Now, as I told you, we're willing to pay for research. We don't want you to start looking this point up for nothing. In fact, I'm authorized to give you fifteen thousand dollars just to start looking it up."

There was silence for a moment.

"In cash," Fenwick said.

"I heard you the first time," Mason said. "Right at the moment I'm busy. I won't be able to do any research work."

Fenwick extended his pudgy hand. "Well, you know where I stand, Mason. Think it over—but if you're too busy to research the point, my associates here in Rowena certainly wouldn't want to do anything that would interrupt your schedule."

"In other words," Mason said, "if I'm so damned busy, why don't I stay in my office and mind my own business."

"Something like that." Fenwick grinned, gripping Mason's hand.

The chief of police touched two fingers of his right hand to the brim of his cap, turned back toward the police car. Fenwick walked back and joined him. The car purred into motion, glided past Mason's automobile and turned to the left down the block.

Mason turned on his lights.

Della Street came out to stand by the edge of the swimming pool.

Mason started his car, drove out of the alley, across the street and swung in close to the curb.

Della Street, moving rapidly, walked across to the car, jerked the door open and jumped in.

"Everything okay?" he asked.

"Everything okay," she said. "There was one other woman in the place. When she had the attendant occupied, I went to work. There was a washbowl with open plumbing, and I got the tube of ice suspended from the two shut-off valves just as you suggested. The gun's out of sight unless someone should happen to get down on the floor and look up."

"Okay," Mason said, "we'll be on our way."

"I see that you had company."

"The chief of police and a lobbyist for the gambling interests," Mason said.

"What do the gambling interests want?"

"To retain me," Mason said. "They think I'm working too hard. They'd like to pay our expenses to Acapulco and have us keep out of circulation for a while."

"And you told them?" Della Street asked.

"That I was busy," Mason said.

"And so, now?" she asked.

"Now," Mason said, "we get out of Rowena—fast."

CHAPTER EIGHT

THURSDAY AFTERNOON, while Della Street was out of the office on an errand, the unlisted telephone in Mason's office buzzed its signal.

Mason, knowing that Paul Drake was the only outsider in possession of the unlisted number, dropped the book he was reading, picked up the telephone, said, "Hello. What is it?"

Paul Drake's voice, clipped with urgency, came over the phone. "Perry, have you heard from your client in that Rowena case?"

"Ellen Robb?"

"Yes."

"I haven't heard from her all day, Paul. Why?"

"Better get her," Drake said.

"What's happened?"

"I don't know for sure. I can give you some of it."

"Shoot."

"Mrs. Ellis boarded her yacht and took off for destinations unknown."

"I know," Mason said. "I talked with the lobbyist for the gambling interests, and he had an all-points bulletin

111

out for the yacht. He thought it was due in Ensenada or in Catalina."

"Well, here's the thing," Drake said. "Sometime late this morning a submarine that was quite a ways out beyond Catalina Island noticed a boat in proscribed waters. It was drifting aimlessly. The submarine hailed the boat, got no answer and went aboard. The boarding officer found the cabin was locked, found the tanks were out of gas, that no one seemed to be aboard. He forced the cabin door and right away knew something had happened."

"Such as what?"

"Murder."

"Go on," Mason said.

"The body inside had been there for a while. It was the body of Mrs. Ellis. She had evidently tried to protect herself. There were evidences of a struggle. The gun that she had evidently tried to use was lying by her hand. One shot had been fired from it. The gun was cocked, ready for a second shot, which Mrs. Ellis never got a chance to fire. There were two bullet wounds in the body, apparently both of them chest wounds. Either one would have been fatal within a matter of minutes. There had been a massive hemorrhage, and the inside of the cabin was a mess.

"Now then, there's something that links Ellen Robb to the case. I don't know what it is, but I understand police are looking for her. They have out an all-points bulletin and they're really making a search."

"Anything else?" Mason asked.

"That's all."

"Okay," Mason said. "I'll get busy. Where are you now?"

"At the office."

"Stay there," Mason said. "Hold a couple of good men in readiness. Now, you have bodyguards watching Ellen Robb's motel?"

"That's right."

"You've had a recent report from them?"

"Within an hour. She's at the motel."

"Any visitors?"

"Apparently she's been pure as the driven snow, if you mean has she been entertaining Helman Ellis in the motel."

"That's what I meant primarily," Mason said. "Anything else?"

"Nothing else."

Mason said, "I'm going down there, Paul, and you'd better pull your men off the job. When the police show up, if they find private detectives on guard, they'll start asking questions. We may not want to answer those questions."

"Okay," Drake said. "I'll get busy."

Mason called the receptionist on the intercom, said, "When Della comes in tell her to wait for a call from me, Gertie. I'm going out on an emergency. Cancel any appointments for the next hour and a half."

He picked up his brief case, grabbed his hat, left the office and drove to the Surf and Sea Motel at Costa Mesa. He tapped on the door of Unit 19.

"Who is it?" Ellen Robb's voice asked.

"Mason," the lawyer said.

"Oh," she said. Then, after a moment, "I'm not even decent, Mr. Mason."

"Get decent," Mason said. "This is important."

"How important?" she asked, sudden alarm in her voice.

"Important enough to get me down here," Mason said.

Ellen Robb turned the key in the lock. "Come on in," she said.

Mason entered.

"Don't mind me," Ellen Robb said. "I can stand it if you can. Did you bring the papers for me to sign?"

"I brought the papers," Mason said. "I want you to do two things."

"What?"

"Sign this complaint and get some clothes on."

"Which first?"

"The complaint."

She seated herself on the stool at the dressing table, took the papers that Mason handed her, said, "Is it all right for me to sign?"

"It is," Mason said. "You're suing George and Marcus for seven thousand, five hundred dollars. Sign now, then dress, and after you dress read the complaint carefully."

She signed, then pushed back the stool.

"Want to talk to me while I dress?"

Mason hesitated a moment, then said, "It's better you don't know what this is all about," he said. "Just get dressed. Now, remember, if anything happens before we leave here, I simply came here to have you sign these papers."

She regarded him with a puzzled expression as she carefully smoothed stockings up on her long legs, pulled a dress over her head.

"You're a deep one," she said.

Mason said, "Ellen, I want to know one thing. I want you to tell me the truth."

"What is it?"

"Were you cutting corners with Helman Ellis?"

"Why?"

"George Anclitas says you were. His partner, Slim Marcus, says you were."

"Slim!" she blazed. "He's a great one. That guy was making passes at me from the moment I came on the job, pulling the kind of stuff on me that the way to get ahead was to co-operate with the people who could help me and—"

"Never mind that," Mason said. "I'm talking about Ellis."

"Ellis," she said, "I think was . . . well, fascinated."

"How about you?" Mason asked. "Did you give him a tumble?"

"I strung him along a little bit. I was supposed to. I—"

Knuckles sounded on the door.

She looked at Mason in surprise, then called, "Who is it?"

"Police," Lt. Tragg's voice said. "Will you open up, please? We want to ask you some questions."

"This is it," Mason said.

She hurriedly buttoned her blouse.

Mason walked to the door, opened it and said, "Why, how are you, Lieutenant?"

"You!" Tragg said.

"Whom did you expect?"

Tragg took a deep breath. "I *should* have expected you. Where's Ellen Robb?"

"I'm Ellen Robb. What's the trouble?"

Ellen Robb stepped forward.

Tragg sized her up. "You know Helman Ellis of Rowena?" he asked.

"Yes. Why?"

"His wife, Nadine?"

"Yes."

"Any trouble with Nadine?"

"Now, wait a minute," Mason said. "Before you start throwing a lot of questions at my client, let's find out what it's all about."

"That's a good one," Tragg said. "No idea what it's all about, eh? What are *you* doing *here* if you don't know what it's all about?"

Mason said, "I am suing George Anclitas and his partners for claims which Miss Robb has against George for giving her a black eye, for kicking her out of her room and into the cruel, cold world when she was garbed only in her professional working attire, consisting of little more than a pair of tights and a look of extreme innocence.

"In case you want all of the details, I have just had the papers prepared in my office and I came here to get Miss Robb to sign them."

"We'll look around," Tragg said.

"Got a warrant?"

"That's right. Here it is."

"What are you looking for?" Mason asked.

"A murder weapon, in case you didn't know."

"Who's dead?" Mason asked.

Tragg smiled and shook his head.

"Now, you look here," Ellen Robb said, "you can't pin—"

"Shut up, Ellen," Mason said. "I'll do *all* the talking."

"That's what you think," Tragg told him. "You're leaving."

"Not until you've finished with the search," Mason said.

"Look around," Tragg told a plain-clothes man who was with him.

Tragg seated himself on the bed, looked from Mason to Ellen Robb. "It certainly is lucky finding you here. Let's take a look at those papers you say she just signed."

Mason opened his brief case, took out the signed copies, said, "Here you are, Lieutenant."

Lt. Tragg carefully inspected the signature of Ellen Robb. "It *looks* as though she had just signed it," he said. "Perhaps she did. I—"

"Lieutenant," the plain-clothes man said.

Tragg turned.

"This way," the plain-clothes man said.

Tragg stood, peering down at the revolver that had been uncovered in the suitcase.

"Well, well, well! What's this?" he asked.

"I don't know," Ellen Robb said. "It's a revolver that I found in my baggage when I left George Anclitas' place—you know, The Big Barn in Rowena."

"And when was that?"

"I left Tuesday night."

"And you noticed this in your things this morning?"

"Yes."

"And what did you do about it?"

"Let's not answer any questions about that gun right now," Mason said. "Let's wait until we know why Lieutenant Tragg is interested in the gun."

"I'm interested in it," Tragg said, "because it's a .38-caliber Smith & Wesson revolver, and I want to know about it."

"My client found it in her baggage," Mason said. "She told me about it as soon as she discovered it. I advised her to leave it there."

"She didn't know anything at all about it, about where it came from or anything about it? It isn't her gun?"

"That's right. She just found it there. Someone evidently put that gun in her suitcase."

"How nice," Lt. Tragg said sarcastically. "How perfectly nice that Ellen Robb has an attorney representing her. What a happy coincidence that you were here."

"What's so important about the gun?" Mason asked.

"We'll tell you about that a little later," Tragg said.

"Well, let me give you a little advice," Mason told him. "Just so you don't stick your neck out too far, Tragg, don't make any statements about that gun until you know what you're talking about."

"What do you mean?"

"I think you'll find that gun has absolutely no significance whatever."

"What do you mean, no significance whatever?"

"Just what I said. I can't elaborate. I'm giving you a personal, friendly tip, Lieutenant."

"Thanks," Tragg said. "I could hardly hold down my

job if it wasn't for your personal, friendly tips, Perry."

"This one may be a little more significant than you
think at the moment."

"Why? What do you know?"

"Not very much as yet," Mason said. "But there is a
chance I may know more than my client."

"Should you hold out on her that way?" Tragg asked
sarcastically.

"It may be for the best interests of all concerned,"
Mason said.

Tragg said, "Miss Robb, would you mind letting me
take your fingerprints so I can make a comparison with
certain photographs?"

Ellen Robb looked questioningly at Perry Mason.

"Let him take your fingerprints," Mason said.

Tragg opened the bag he was carrying, took out a por-
table fingerprint outfit, took Ellen Robb's fingerprints,
then studied them carefully with a magnifying glass.

He looked up at Ellen Robb, said, "You knew that
Helman Ellis had a yacht that he called *Cap's Eyes*?"
She nodded.

"You've been aboard that yacht?"

"Yes."

"When was the last time?"

"Early Tuesday evening."

"What time?"

"I don't know. About . . . oh, I'd say along about
dusk."

"What were you doing aboard?"

"Looking for Mrs. Ellis."

"Did you find her?"

"No one was aboard. I heard that she and her husband were going on a cruise. I wanted to catch her before they left."

"Why were you so anxious to see her?"

"I wanted to talk with her."

"What about?"

"About various things. About . . . well, frankly, because I wanted to discuss her husband with her."

"Why should you be discussing her husband with her?"

"I think she had become jealous of me."

"Why?"

"I worked at The Big Barn, and her husband, Helman, spent some time there."

"And you talked with him?"

"At The Barn?"

"Yes."

"Of course I talked with him. That was part of my job, to keep the customers feeling good."

"And Mrs. Ellis resented that?"

"Frankly, I don't know. I heard she was jealous and I wanted to see her."

"Why?"

"I wanted to tell her there was absolutely no ground for any jealousy whatever."

"So you went aboard the yacht?"

"Yes."

"And you had this gun with you?"

"No."

"No?"

"No. Definitely not. That was before the gun was put in my bag."

"How do you know?"

"Well, I . . . well, I'll say this. That was before I discovered the gun in my bag."

"That's better. You don't know when it was put there?"

"Not definitely, no."

"And you left The Big Barn that night?"

"Later on, yes."

"And you didn't see Mrs. Ellis on the yacht?"

"No."

"Did you see Mr. Ellis that night?"

"I saw him later, shortly before the trouble with George Anclitas."

"Did you tell him you were looking for his wife?"

"He told me his wife had been looking for me, and I told him that there was absolutely no reason for her to be jealous, at least as far as I was concerned."

"And what did Helman tell you?"

"He said his wife got these unreasoning spells of jealousy, and when she did, that you couldn't reason with her or anything. He said that he had been planning on going on a cruise with her but that she'd taken the skiff and gone ashore and left him marooned on the boat."

"And when was that?"

"That was Tuesday night."

"Did you also talk with him last night?"

"Now, just a minute," Mason said. "I think this questioning has gone far enough, Lieutenant."

"Okay," Lt. Tragg said rather cheerfully. "I just want to ask Miss Robb one question. Did you at any time ever enter the cabin of Ellis' yacht, the *Cap's Eyes*?"

"At any time?"

"At any time."

"No."

"You knew the yacht?"

"Yes."

"You'd been aboard it?"

"Well . . . yes, I went aboard once with Helman, when he was showing me around."

"Did you go in the cabin then?"

"I . . . I may have."

"When was that?"

"Oh, some time ago."

"How long ago?"

"Two weeks ago."

"Did you kill Nadine Ellis while you were on that yacht?"

"Did I kill Nadine Ellis? *What* are you talking about?"

"I'm talking about murder," Tragg said. "Did you see her Wednesday and kill her?"

"Good heavens no! I didn't— Why? Is she— You mean she's been—?"

Mason said, "Now, I'm going to give you some instructions, Ellen. Don't answer any more questions. You have given Lieutenant Tragg a very fair, straight and direct statement. There is no reason for Lieutenant Tragg to browbeat you, bully you, cross-examine you or try to give you a third-degree. If, however, Lieutenant Tragg wants you to accompany him, do so. But don't make *any* statement under *any* circumstances. Don't say one more word about this case or about your relations with George Anclitas, about the suit that I'm going to file or about anything, unless I am present and instruct you to make a statement."

"All right, Mason," Tragg said. "You've spoken your piece. You can leave now. There was a chance we might have been able to get an explanation which would have prevented a lot of notoriety for Miss Robb. But in view of your instructions to her, she's going to have to come to Headquarters."

"That's fine," Mason said. "She'll go to Headquarters — How long are you going to hold her there?"

"Probably until we can have some test bullets fired from this gun," Tragg said, "and have the test bullets compared by the ballistics department with the fatal bullets which killed Mrs. Ellis."

"Go right ahead," Mason said. "Accompany him, Miss Robb. Make no statement to newspaper reporters. Don't talk to anyone. Simply clam up and keep quiet. You've made your statement. Now then, when Lieutenant Tragg tells you that you can leave, get in touch with me at once."

"You mean if," Tragg said, "not when."

Mason grinned. "Once more, Lieutenant, you have failed to understand me. I mean when. I said when and I meant when."

CHAPTER NINE

MASON, pacing the floor of his office, made comments from time to time to an attentive Della Street.

Della, knowing that the lawyer was simply thinking out loud, used her knowledge of his character to facilitate the thought processes. At times she would nod her head, at times listen with rapt attention, and at times interpose some shrewd question.

Mason, pacing back and forth, said, "That probably explains why they didn't make any commotion about the gun."

"Who?" Della Street asked.

"George Anclitas," Mason said. "He was framing a crime on Ellen Robb, all right, but it wasn't anything simple like the crime of stealing a gun."

"Then he must have known a murder had been committed?"

"Yes."

"How would he have known that?"

"There's only one way," Mason said. "He must have killed her. He must have killed her with that gun and then planted that gun in Ellen Robb's suitcase."

"Then Mrs. Ellis was killed before the gun ever came into Ellen's possession?"

"That has to be it," Mason said, and resumed pacing the floor.

After a moment Della Street ventured an inquiry. "Where does that leave us?" she asked.

Mason stopped abruptly in his pacing, snapped his fingers and said, "Damn!"

Della Street raised her eyebrows.

"I hadn't thought of it from that angle," Mason said. "I've been too busy trying to unscramble what must have happened in connection with the murder so I could protect my client's interests."

"You're thinking of it from that angle now?" Della Street asked.

"I'm thinking of it from that angle now," Mason said, "and I don't like what I'm thinking."

"Why?"

"As long as the gun was simply an article of stolen property, we had every right in the world to restore it to its rightful owner and we could do that by returning it to his place of business, but if that gun becomes a valuable piece of evidence . . ."

Mason broke off and resumed pacing the floor, his eyes level-lidded with concentration.

"Isn't it our duty to report any evidence to the police?" Della Street asked.

Mason nodded, then said tersely, "It's also our duty to protect our client."

"But if the evidence came into her possession *after* the crime had been committed . . ."

"Suppose they don't believe that, Della?"

"Then, of course . . ." It was Della Street's turn to break off in the middle of a sentence and start thinking.

"Exactly," Mason said. "It puts us in the devil of a predicament."

"Can I take the sole responsibility?" Della Street asked. "After all, I was the one who took the gun back."

"You were acting under my orders," Mason said. "Don't be silly. I was taking the responsibility, and if there's any responsibility I take it all—*all*, you understand?"

"The facts," she said, "speak for themselves. I took the gun back."

Mason said, "I take the responsibility. Now, just remember that. Don't try to get yourself involved in this thing out of a sense of loyalty. Hang it! The trouble is I don't know . . . suppose she *isn't* telling the truth?"

"Who?"

"Our client," Mason said.

"She could be lying?" Della asked.

"Of course she could be lying," Mason said. "And she's just the type who would lie. She's a young woman who has sharpened her wits against the seamy side of life. She knows her way around and she's doubtless learned that everyone must look out for himself. That's the code of the society in which she's been living."

Della Street said, "Then she would have stolen the gun from The Big Barn, gone aboard the yacht, only instead of not finding anybody aboard, she had a session with Nadine Ellis and killed her. Then she came here and handed you the gun, telling you her story about having found it in her baggage."

"That's right," Mason said.

"And at that very time Mrs. Ellis must have been lying dead on the yacht."

"In that case," Mason asked, "how did the yacht get out there beyond Catalina Island?"

Della Street gave his question thoughtful consideration. "The yacht was safely moored in the harbor after you switched guns?"

Mason grinned. "It must have been," he said, "and that fact is going to give Hamilton Burger, the district attorney, and Lieutenant Arthur Tragg of Homicide, a terrific jolt. That fact, Della, puts our client in the clear and puts us in the clear."

"Just how will the D.A.'s office get jolted?" Della Street asked.

"Finding a gun in Ellen Robb's possession, thinking that it's the murder weapon, getting everything all built up, turning the fatal bullets over to the ballistic department and then finding that they didn't come from that gun at all."

"In that event, what gun did they come from?" Della Street asked.

Mason stroked the angle of his jaw with the tips of his fingers. "I wish I knew the answer to that," he said. "It doesn't seem possible that the bullets could have come from the gun that we returned to The Big Barn . . . but if they did . . . *if* they did, we're in one hell of a predicament, Della."

"What would we have to do?"

"I'm darned if I know," Mason said. "If I keep quiet I'm perhaps compounding a felony, perhaps making myself an accessory after the fact—to use a legal expression—in a murder case."

"And if you go to the police and tell them the story?"

"If I go to the police and tell them the story," Mason said, "they won't believe me. They'll think I am simply trying to work some elaborate scheme to trap the police and throw the prosecution off the track. And in any event I'd still be in a jam, this time for betraying the interests of a client."

"Are you honor bound to keep all the facts in connection with her case confidential?"

"Probably not," Mason said. "Strictly speaking, a privileged communication is rather limited. A lawyer is technically only entitled to protect the confidences of his client within a very limited field. The confidences are those that are given to the attorney in order to enable him to represent the interests of his client.

"That's the narrow, technical rule. Practically, by both usage and custom, the rule has been expanded. I know as far as *I'm* concerned, I'd rather have my hand cut off than betray the interests of a client. If I'm representing a client, I want the representation to be honest, loyal and efficient. I make it a point to believe everything my client tells me and to act accordingly in order to protect the best interests of that client."

"Yet you recognize there's a possibility the client may lie?"

"I recognize the possibility the client may lie," Mason said.

"Well," Della Street said, "as I see it, there's nothing to be done until the police get a report from the ballistics department on those bullets."

"That's right," Mason said. "*After* they find out that the bullets that killed Mrs. Ellis didn't come from that gun, then the question is, did they come from the gun we took from Ellen Robb? If they didn't, we're in the clear. If they did, then we're right slap-bang behind the eight ball."

"We can find out?" Della Street asked.

"We can find out," Mason said, "because fortunately I had Paul Drake get a ballistics expert to fire test bullets from the gun. We have those test bullets. Paul Drake can get photographs of the fatal bullets, and we can compare the striations. That's not the best way of making a comparison, but it will do under the circumstances. We can reach a pretty fair opinion. In other words, if the test bullets don't match the fatal bullets, we can tell. If they do, we can't be *absolutely* certain. But if we get enough lines of striation in the photograph, we'll know that there's a very good possibility the fatal bullets were fired from that gun."

"And then?" Della Street asked.

"Then we'll cross that bridge," Mason said. "We should be hearing from Paul any—"

Drake's code knock sounded on the door. Mason nodded to Della Street, who opened the door and let Paul Drake in.

Mason, standing in the middle of the office floor where he had paused mid-stride when Drake knocked on the door, nodded to the detective, said, "What's new, Paul?"

"I hate to bring bad news," Drake said, "but if the ballistics check shows that Nadine Ellis was killed by a bullet from the gun that the police took from Ellen Robb's motel room, she doesn't stand the faintest whisper of a chance."

"And if the bullets don't check?" Mason asked.

"They've probably got a case against her," Drake said, "but it won't be dead open-and-shut."

"I don't see what evidence they have," Mason said, frowning.

"Well, naturally they're not telling," Drake said. "From what I can pick up in the way of scuttle butt around Headquarters, they seem to feel they have an air-tight case—and, of course, once the ballistics experts show Nadine Ellis was killed by a bullet from that gun the police took from Ellen's motel, they have a case that neither you nor any other lawyer can win. That ballistics evidence will make it a copper-riveted cinch."

"All right, Paul," Mason said. "I've got some confidential information for you. The gun won't check. Now, start working on the case from that angle and see what your investigation shows up."

"You mean the bullets weren't fired from that gun?"

"They weren't fired from that gun."

"How sure are you, Perry?"

"Positive."

"That's going to make a difference," Drake said. "But, look, Perry, you *can't* be positive. You never know when a client is lying to you and when she's telling the truth. Particularly a girl like Ellen Robb. She can be convincing as a liar. She's a past master at pulling the wool over your eyes."

Mason said, "Nobody's pulling the wool over my eyes, Paul. The bullets won't check."

"Well, that's something," Drake said. "There's one thing certain. If they don't check, that will hit the district attorney an awful wallop right between the eyes."

"He's going to be hit a wallop, then."

Drake was thoughtful. "There's only *one* way you could be certain, Perry."

"How's that, Paul?"

"That gun you gave me to take to Maurice Halstead, Perry."

"What about it?" the lawyer asked.

Drake was thoughtfully silent.

"Well?" Mason prompted.

"Look, Perry," the detective said, "if you pulled one of those gun-switching acts of yours, and if that gun I gave Halstead should prove to be the murder weapon . . . well, I'm bailing out, that's all. I can't go that far."

"No one's asked you to, Paul."

"I'd have to tell what I know."

"When?"

"As soon as I knew it made any difference in the case."

"We'll let it stand that way," Mason said.

"I'm not going to sleep tonight, Perry," Drake said.

"Take a pill."

"That won't help. Good Lord, Perry, do you know what you're doing?"

"It's not what I'm doing that worries me," Mason said. "It's what I have done."

"So what do I do now, Perry?"

"Wait until you're certain," Mason said.

"Maurice Halstead will also be doing some thinking as soon as he's seen the papers," Drake pointed out.

"Let him think, Paul," Mason said.

The phone rang.

Della Street picked up the telephone, said, "Yes," then to Paul, "It's for you, Paul."

"That'll be a report on what ballistics found out," Drake said. "I told my office to call me here if they got that report but not to bother me otherwise."

Drake picked up the telephone, said, "Hello . . . uh-huh. . . . They're sure? No chance of a mistake . . . well, *that's* interesting. . . . Okay, I'll be back in the office in a few minutes. 'Bye now."

Drake hung up the telephone, cocked a quizzical eyebrow at Mason, and said, "Why were you so damned sure those bullets weren't going to match, Perry?"

The lawyer grinned. "Call me clairvoyant or psychic, Paul."

"Well," Drake said, "you'd better throw away your crystal ball and try tea leaves. The fatal bullets that killed Nadine Ellis were fired from the gun that Ellen Robb had in her possession when the police arrested her."

CHAPTER TEN

DONOVAN FRASER, a relatively new and somewhat eager-beaver deputy district attorney, arose to address the Court.

"If the Court please, we expect to show that the defendant in this case, Ellen Robb, was attempting to break up the home of the decedent, Nadine Ellis, that quite understandably friction developed between the two women, that the defendant surreptitiously and with malice aforethought entered the yacht belonging to Mr. and Mrs. Ellis, knowing that Mrs. Ellis was aboard, that she fired two shots into the body of Mrs. Ellis and then, having assured herself that her enemy was dead, she pointed the yacht out to sea, started the motors and trusted that the natural risks incident to marine navigation in a small boat of this sort would result in the loss of the boat and its grisly occupant.

"We expect to show that a gun found in the possession of the defendant, Ellen Robb, inflicted the fatal wounds upon Nadine Ellis and we shall ask that the defendant be bound over to the Superior Court for trial."

Judge Staunton Keyser looked down at the young

man thoughtfully, said, "You don't need to make an opening argument to the Court in a preliminary hearing, Mr. Deputy District Attorney. As I understand it, this is simply a question of showing that a cime has been committed and that there is probable cause to believe the defendant committed that crime."

"I understand, Your Honor," Fraser said, "but in view of the well-known tactics of defense counsel, who always tries to put on a case at the time of the preliminary examination, I felt that the Court should be advised of what we are trying to do."

"You go right ahead," Judge Keyser said, "and never mind the tactics of opposing counsel. Just put on your proof. Call your first witness."

Fraser called the captain of a Coast Guard cutter to the stand.

"Are you familiar with a yacht called *Cap's Eyes*?"

"I am."

"Are you familiar with the documents of registration in the Coast Guard records as to ownership of that yacht?"

"Yes, sir."

"Who owns that yacht?"

"Helman Ellis."

"Did you have occasion to see that yacht on Thursday, the eleventh day of this month?"

"I did. Yes, sir."

"Will you explain the circumstances."

"We were notified by the Navy that the yacht was drifting helplessly with a murdered woman aboard. I called the FBI and the coroner's office. I was instructed to take Dr. Andover Calvert out to the yacht, together with a representative of the sheriff's office and an agent of the FBI. We had to wait a short time until these men arrived. Then we flew to Catalina, picked up a deep-sea patrol boat there and proceeded at high speed to where the yacht was located. At that time we made an inspection of the yacht. Do you want me to tell you what we found?"

"In general terms, yes."

"The fuel tank of the yacht was quite dry. The yacht was drifting in an area which is devoted to naval maneuvers and where small craft are forbidden to venture. The body of a woman was lying in the cabin. We took photographs of the body."

"Do you have those photographs?"

"I do."

"We'd like to have them introduced in evidence."

"No objection," Mason said.

"Very well," Judge Keyser ruled, "they may go into evidence as People's Exhibit— How many are there, Counselor?"

"Seven."

"All right, People's Exhibits A-1, A-2, A-3, A-4, A-5, A-6 and A-7. Proceed."

"What did you do?"

"After completing inspection of the yacht we fastened a tow cable and brought the yacht into port."

"Cross-examine," Fraser said.

Mason arose and approached the witness. "How long have you been with the Coast Guard, Captain?"

"Some twenty years."

"You are quite familiar with the waters around Southern California?"

"I am, yes."

"The waters where the yacht was found?"

"I am not familiar with those waters except in a general way. Most of our work is done a lot closer to the shore line."

"I understand. But you know generally the waters, and quite particularly you are familiar with the waters between the coast line and the place where the yacht was found?"

"Yes, sir."

"That yacht was some distance on the other side of Catalina Island?"

"Yes, sir."

"Now, then," Mason said, "what are the chances that the yacht with no one aboard except the dead woman could have started out from Los Angeles yacht harbor or the Deep Sea Cruising Yacht Club near Long Beach with the steering mechanism locked in position so that it would have gone in a straight line and have sailed out to the place where it was found without mishap—and without attracting attention because of failure to follow regulations or display running lights—assuming, Captain, that there was no one aboard the yacht other than the body of the decedent?"

"Ordinarily I would have said the chances would be pretty slim," the captain admitted, "but here we are confronted with an established fact. Regardless of the percentage of chances, the yacht did do that very thing."

"Now, just a moment, Your Honor," Fraser said. "I don't see the purpose of this examination. I don't see what counsel expects to accomplish by it."

"It's legitimate cross-examination," Judge Keyser

said. "Anyway, the question has been answered. Let
the answer stand."

"What was the cruising radius of the yacht? With a
full tank of gasoline, how far would it have gone?"

"We don't know the tank was full," Fraser objected.

"This is simply cross-examination," Judge Keyser
said. "He can ask anything he wants to about the yacht.
The Court, frankly, is interested in this. It's rather a
significant phase of the case. At least, it seems so to the
Court."

"The cruising radius would have varied depending
upon wind, tide and weather conditions, but if the
tanks had all been full, the cruising radius would have
been . . . well, somewhat beyond the point where we
found the yacht."

"You're assuming, then, that the tanks were not full
when the yacht was started on its journey. Is that
right?"

"Yes."

"There was some sort of a steering mechanism on
the yacht which would hold it to its course?"

"That is right. There are several variations of mechanical devices which hold a yacht on course. Some of
them are quite elaborate, working with compass directions so that a yacht can be set on a compass course and
will hold that course. Some of them are simply devices
to hold the yacht steady after the course has been manually selected."

"Assuming that you were on that yacht at Long
Beach, that you wanted to point it in the direction
where it was located by the Navy and picked up by you,
would it have been possible for you to have set that

steering gear so that the yacht would have been pointed in that direction and gone on until the fuel tanks became dry?"

"I think it *could* have been done, because I know it *was* done."

"If the yacht had started from its regular mooring, wouldn't it have had to sail right through Catalina Island to arrive at the place where it was found?"

"Not necessarily."

"What do you mean by that?"

"I think it might have been difficult, although not impossible, for the yacht to have been sailing blind through all the ocean traffic without being noticed. It *could* have cleared the westerly end of the island, then, after the fuel was exhausted, drifted to the portion of the ocean where it was found."

"You think the yacht did that?"

"I feel certain it must have."

"Then you feel the murderer was not aboard after the yacht left its mooring?"

"Not unless he was an exceptional swimmer."

Judge Keyser frowned at the titter of the audience.

"What are the chances that the yacht could have made the trip without collision, without having wind and tidal currents get it off course so that it would have run into trouble?"

"That depends on what you mean by trouble. Once the course had been set so as to miss Catalina Island, there was very little to stop it."

"Except the normal small-boat traffic on the water?"

"Yes."

"That is a considerable factor?"

"That depends. It depends on *when* the yacht was started, it depends on conditions."

"There were no running lights on the yacht?"

"You mean that were lit?"

"Yes."

"No, the lights were not lit."

"Indicating that the yacht had made its journey during daylight hours?"

"Either that or it had violated the regulations in regard to navigation."

"And if the yacht had been detected violating those regulations, something would have been done about it?"

"Yes."

"Now, this yacht was found in a restricted area?"

"Yes."

"It is customary for the Navy to use radar in that area for the purpose of detecting small boats which may have entered the area?"

"I believe so, yes."

"Therefore, if the person who started that yacht on its way had wanted the yacht to vanish, to sail on into oblivion, that person would hardly have selected that particular area?"

"Not if the individual was familiar with the restricted areas."

"And this was a restricted area?"

"Yes, sir."

"And if the person had wanted the yacht to sail on into oblivion, the fuel tanks could have been filled, and the yacht would then have gone a very considerable distance beyond the point where it was picked up, before running out of fuel?"

"Yes, sir, depending of course on whether the murderer had to accept the condition of the fuel tanks as he found them. He or she may not have dared to attempt to refuel with the body aboard—or if the murder was committed at night, there would have been little opportunity to have replenished the fuel."

"Thank you," Mason said. "That's all."

Donovan Fraser said, "Call Dr. Andover Calvert."

"I'll stipulate Dr. Calvert's qualifications, subject to the right of cross-examination," Mason said cheerfully. "Just go right ahead and ask him your technical questions."

Fraser regarded Mason with some surprise but very quickly took advantage of the opportunity. "Very well," he said. "You'll stipulate that Dr. Calvert is an examining physician connected with the office of the coroner, an autopsy surgeon, a duly qualified physician and an expert in all fields of forensic medicine?"

"Subject to the right of cross-examination," Mason said. "I'll stipulate to his general qualifications, subject to cross-examination."

"Very well. Be sworn, Dr. Calvert," Fraser instructed.

Dr. Calvert held up his right hand, was sworn, and took the witness stand.

"You boarded the yacht, the *Cap's Eyes* on Thursday, the eleventh?"

"I did."

"That was then on the high seas?"

"Yes, sir."

"What did you find?"

"The cabin door, which had been locked by a spring lock on the inside, had been forced open by some party before we arrived. I understand this was done by Navy personnel who had boarded the boat before the Coast Guard was notified."

"Go on," Fraser said. "What did you find in the cabin?"

"In the cabin we found the body of a woman about twenty-eight years of age. The first stages of decomposition had set in, and I estimated the woman had been dead for somewhere between twenty-four and forty-eight hours. The woman was lying on her back on the floor of the cabin. There was an open handbag near her hand, and a cocked double-action Smith and Wesson revolver was lying near her right hand. One bullet had been discharged from this revolver and then the weapon had been cocked, apparently preparatory to firing a second shot."

"Did you find the one bullet which had been discharged?"

"We found a bullet embedded in the woodwork of the cabin near the door. I believe that it was checked out by ballistics and shown to have been fired from the weapon which was lying there on the floor of the yacht near the hand of the woman."

"You subsequently performed an autopsy on the body of this woman?"

"I did, yes, sir."

"And what did you find?"

"I found that she had been killed by gunfire. Two

bullets had entered the chest cavity, slightly above and to one side of the heart. The two bullet holes were less than an inch and a half apart, and the courses of the bullets were, generally speaking, parallel."

"Had the bullets gone through the body or were they still embedded in the body?"

"One of them had been deflected and had embedded itself in bone. The other had just penetrated far enough to go through the body. It was found in the clothing of the decedent."

"These bullets were, in your opinion, the cause of death?"

"Yes."

"Cross-examine," Fraser said to Perry Mason.

Mason arose and walked toward the witness. His manner was casual and his voice was calmly conversational. "Two bullets, Doctor?"

"Yes."

"Which one inflicted the fatal wound, Doctor?"

"They both inflicted fatal wounds."

"Which one was the cause of death?"

"Either could have been the cause of death."

"Pardon me, Doctor. I'm not asking you about *could have,* I'm asking you about which *did* cause death."

"Both of them inflicted fatal wounds."

"Would you say both bullets caused death?"

"Yes."

"Would you say that a person could die twice?"

"That isn't what I mean."

"What *do* you mean?"

"I mean that either bullet might have caused death and either bullet could have caused death."

"How far apart were the bullets?"

"Around an inch and a half at the point of entrance."

"And which one was fired first?"

"I have no way of knowing."

"Were the bullets instantly fatal?"

"That depends on what you mean by instantly."

"Well, what do you mean by it?"

"When I say instantly I mean instantaneously."

"Did either of these wounds inflict an instantaneously fatal wound?"

"Both of the bullets instantaneously inflicted a mortal wound."

"How long after the first wound before the victim died?"

"That I don't know. It couldn't have been more than a few minutes at most."

"You think perhaps it was as much as five minutes?"

"Perhaps."

"Ten minutes?"

"Perhaps."

"Fifteen minutes?"

"I consider it very unlikely. Actually I think death occurred within a matter of two or three minutes."

"And which bullet wound caused death?"

"Oh, Your Honor," Fraser said, getting to his feet, "I object to this type of cross-examination. The questions have already been asked and answered."

"They've been asked," Mason said, "but they haven't been answered."

"Furthermore, it's incompetent, irrelevant and immaterial. It doesn't make any difference," Fraser went on.

Judge Keyser said, "I'd like to hear from counsel if he feels the questions are pertinent or relevant to any particular point."

"I think it is very important to find out how the victim died, when the victim died and what caused the death of the victim. I think that's important in any murder case," Mason said.

"But where an assailant fired two bullets, does it make any difference which bullet was fired first or which wound was the one which produced death?" Judge Keyser asked.

"How do *we* know that the assailant fired two bullets?" Mason asked.

Judge Keyser looked at Mason with an expression of swift surprise. "Are you contending there were two assailants?" he asked.

"Frankly, I don't know," Mason said. "I am contending at the moment, as the legal representative of this defendant, that I have the right to find out *all* the facts in the case."

"The objection is overruled," Judge Keyser said.

Dr. Calvert said angrily, "Let me make this statement to the Court and counsel. There were two bullets. One of the bullets actually penetrated a portion of the heart. I consider that bullet produced almost instantaneous death. The other bullet was a little to the left. It missed the heart but would have been fatal within a few minutes . . . that is, that's my opinion."

"All right," Mason said. "Let's call the bullet that missed the heart bullet number one and the bullet which penetrated a portion of the heart bullet number two. Which was fired first?"

"I don't know."

"I submit that it's incompetent, irrelevant and immaterial," Fraser said. "This is simply a case of an attorney trying to grasp desperately at the straw of some technicality."

Judge Keyser shook his head. "I think there is an interesting point here. I don't know what the other evidence will show, but if counsel is pursuing this lead with some definite objective in mind, it is manifestly unfair to deprive the defendant of the right of a searching cross-examination. Therefore, I will overrule the objection."

"Which bullet caused death, Doctor?"

"I don't know. It depends upon the sequence in which the bullets were fired."

"If," Mason said, "the bullet we have referred to as bullet number two was fired first and bullet number one was fired after an interval of as much as three minutes, you would assume that bullet number one was fired into a dead body. Is that correct?"

"If you want to assume anything like that, I would say yes."

"If bullet number one was fired first, it would have been how long before death intervened?"

"My best opinion would be three to five minutes."

"But it could have been as much as ten minutes?"

"Yes."

"Now, suppose that after bullet number one was fired and, assuming that it was fired first, bullet number two was fired almost immediately, then death actually occurred from bullet number two."

"I would so assume if we accept those premises."

"Both bullet number one and bullet number two were recovered?"

"That's right. Both of them were taken from the body."

"And what did you do with them?"

"I personally gave them to Alexander Redfield, the ballistics expert."

"And what did you tell him when you gave him the bullets?"

"That they were the bullets taken from the body of Nadine Ellis."

"You had identified the body by that time?"

"It had been identified so that I could make that statement to Mr. Redfield."

"You gave him both bullets?"

"Yes."

"Did you mark them in any way?"

"I made a small secret mark on the bullets, yes."

"So that you can identify them?"

"Yes."

Mason said, "I assume that the prosecution has the bullets here and that they will shortly be introduced in evidence. I think that Dr. Calvert should identify the bullets at this time."

"We can identify them," Fraser said, "by having the witness Redfield testify that the bullets he produces are the ones he received from Dr. Calvert."

"I would like to connect up every link in the chain," Mason said. "I think I have a right to do so."

Fraser said angrily, "If the Court please, I was warned that I would encounter just these badgering tactics from counsel. After all, this is only a preliminary examination, and I am not going to be trapped into making a big production of it."

"I'm not making a big production of it," Mason said. "I am simply asking that the witness produce the bullets that he mentioned in his testimony. He stated he recovered them from the body of Nadine Ellis. I want to see those bullets."

"I think counsel is within his rights," Judge Keyser said. "Certainly you intend to produce the bullets within a few minutes, Mr. Deputy District Attorney."

"I do," Fraser said, "but I want to put on my case in my own way and not have the defense attorney tell me how I'm going to do it."

"Come, come," Judge Keyser said. "Apparently it doesn't make any difference. If you have the bullets here, why not produce them? Is there any reason why they can't be produced or why you are reluctant to produce them?"

"No, Your Honor."

"Let the witness identify them, then."

Fraser, with poor grace, turned to Alexander Redfield, the ballistics expert who was seated directly behind him, and accepted a glass test tube from Redfield. He approached the witness stand and handed this test tube to the doctor.

"I hand you two bullets, Doctor. I'll ask you to look at them and state whether or not they are the bullets you took from the body of the decedent."

Dr. Calvert took a magnifying glass from his pocket, inspected the bullets through the glass test tube, then nodded slowly. "These are the bullets," he said. "They both have my secret mark on them."

"What is your secret mark?" Mason asked. "Where is it?"

"I prefer to keep it secret," Dr. Calvert said. "It is a very small mark that I make and it serves to identify the bullets which I recover in the course of my autopsies."

"Then you use the same mark on all of your bullets?" Mason asked.

"That's right."

"Why?"

"So I can identify them. So that they are not to be confused with bullets that are recovered by some of the other autopsy surgeons. In that way I know my own work."

"I see," Mason said. "You use the same mark on all bullets you recover?"

"That's what I said, yes!" Dr. Calvert snapped.

"Then may I ask how many bullets you recover in the course of a year from bodies in connection with your own autopsies?"

"I don't know. It isn't a standard amount. It varies, depending on the number of autopsies, the number of homicides by shooting, and various other factors."

"Do you recover as many as fifty bullets a year?"

"Not on an average, no, sir."

"As many as twenty-five?"

"I think perhaps in some years I have recovered twenty-five. I wouldn't say that was an average."

"As many as twelve?"

"Yes, I would think so."

"And the only way you have of identifying these bullets is by your secret mark?"

"That is right. That is all the identification I need."

"It may be all the identification *you* need, Doctor, but as I understand it, these two bullets are now identified simply as being bullets which you recovered, not bullets which were recovered from the body of Nadine Ellis."

"Well, I know that those are the bullets."

"How do you know?"

"I can tell by looking at them, the shape of the bullets, the caliber."

"Then why was it necessary for you to put your secret mark on them?"

"So there would be no mistake."

"The same secret mark that you put on an average of a dozen bullets a year, that you have at times put on as many as twenty-five bullets in a year?"

"Oh, Your Honor," Fraser said. "This is argumentative. The question has been asked and answered. It's simply an attempt on the part of counsel to browbeat the witness."

Judge Keyser regarded Mason thoughtfully, then turned to the witness. "Isn't there anything that you use in the line of a label or identification on these bullets that shows they are the particular bullets that were recovered in this particular case?"

"I handed them to Alexander Redfield," Dr. Calvert said. "They were in a test tube when I handed them to him, and the test tube had a number; that is, there was a piece of paper pasted on the test tube, and that test tube had a number. It was the number of the case as it was listed in our files. If that number were on this test tube, it would definitely identify the bullets as having come from that particular body."

"But that number has been removed?" Judge Keyser asked.

"Apparently it has. I notice that the label that is on the test tube now bears the handwriting of Mr. Redfield."

"Very well," Judge Keyser said. "Go ahead and resume your inquiry, Mr. Mason. I will state to the prosecutor, however, that before these bullets can be introduced in evidence, they must be connected more directly with the particular case."

"That is what I intend to do," Fraser said, "if I am only given the chance."

"Well, you'll have every opportunity," Judge Keyser snapped. "Proceed, Mr. Mason."

"Now then," Mason said, "assuming that these bullets are the bullets which you took from the body of Nadine Ellis, which bullet was fired first?"

"I've told you I don't know."

"Well, I'll put it this way," Mason said. "We referred to the bullets as bullet number one and bullet number two. Now, which of these bullets is bullet number one, as far as your testimony is concerned, and which is bullet number two?"

"I don't know."

"You don't know?"

"No."

"You didn't mark the bullets so you could distinguish them?"

"Certainly not. Both bullets came from the body. Both would have been fatal. I mean either would have been fatal. I put them in a test tube, put the code number of the case on it—which was, I believe, C-122—and personally handed the test tube to Mr. Redfield."

Redfield, who was smiling, got to his feet, started to say something, then changed his mind and sat down.

Mason said, "In other words, Doctor, the gunshot wounds in the body of Nadine Ellis showed that one wound, where the bullet actually penetrated a portion of the heart, was probably almost instantly fatal. The other inflicted a wound which would have been fatal within a few minutes. Now, you can't tell which of these bullets inflicted which wound?"

"I made no attempt to keep the bullets separate. They are both the same caliber, they were both fired from the same gun. I will state, however, that the bullet which we have referred to as bullet number two—the one which hit a portion of the heart—lodged in the spine and was somewhat flattened by the vertebra. I notice that one of these bullets is somewhat flattened, and on the strength of that I would state that in all human probability that bullet is the bullet I referred to as bullet number two—the one that hit the heart."

"Was your autopsy such that you traced each bullet as to its course?" Mason asked. "All the way through the body?"

"I traced one bullet from the point of entrance through the heart and I traced the other bullet from the point of entrance through one of the major blood vessels. I may state, however, that I did not—or perhaps I should say that I was not able—to keep the paths of the bullets completely separate because they started to converge slightly, and the deterioration of the body due to decomposition and putrefaction was such that it was virtually impossible to segregate the course of the bullets all the way through the body."

"And you can't tell which of these bullets was fired first?"

"That's right," Dr. Calvert said. And then suddenly added, in indignation, "And that, Mr. Mason, is because I am a man of medicine and not a medicine man."

"And," Mason went on urbanely, "you don't know for certain that these were the bullets that you took from the body of Mrs. Ellis. You only know that they were two bullets which you recovered in the course of your autopsy work."

"I took these two bullets from the body of Mrs. Ellis and handed them to Alexander Redfield on the evening of the twelfth," Dr. Calvert said.

"Thank you," Mason said. "That's all."

"No further questions," Fraser said. "You may be excused, Doctor. I'll call Alexander Redfield as my next witness."

Redfield, smiling slightly, came to the stand.

"Your name is Alexander Redfield, you are employed by the county as a ballistics expert and scientific investigator?" Fraser asked.

"That's right."

"Are you acquainted with Dr. Andover Calvert, the witness who just testified?"

"I am."

"Did you see him in this county on or about the twelfth of this month?"

"I did."

"Did you have any conversation with Dr. Calvert on that date?"

"I did."

"Did Dr. Calvert give you any objects on that date?"

"He did."

"What objects did he give you?"

"Two bullets."

"And what did you do with those two bullets, Mr. Redfield?"

"I put them in a test tube, sealed the test tube and marked the test tube for identification. Then I locked the test tube in a special compartment in the safe in my office."

"You made no comparison of the bullets with any test bullets?"

"Not at that date."

"When was that done?"

"Later, when I was given a weapon and asked to test fire that weapon."

"And what weapon was that?"

"That was a Smith and Wesson revolver with a two-and-a-half-inch barrel."

"Do you know the number of that gun?"

"I do. It was 133347."

"Do you have that gun?"

"I do."

"Will you produce it, please?"

Redfield reached in his brief case and pulled out the gun.

"I ask that this be marked for identification," Fraser said.

"It will be marked People's Exhibit B," Judge Keyser said.

"Now then, you received two bullets from Dr. Calvert. I will ask you if you have those bullets with you?"

"I just gave them to you."

"Here they are. Will you tell us whether or not those are the same bullets which Dr. Calvert gave you?"

"Those are the same bullets."

"How do you know?"

"They have been in my custody since the time Dr. Calvert handed them to me."

"And have remained in that test tube?"

"No, sir. I took them out of the test tube from time to time for the purpose of making comparisons and taking comparison photographs."

"Did the bullets ever leave your possession?"

"No, sir. They were in my possession from the time Dr. Calvert gave them to me until I handed them to you just a minute ago."

"I'll ask the bullets be marked for identification as People's Exhibit C," Fraser said.

"Both bullets as one exhibit?" Mason asked.

"They're in the test tube."

"I suggest that they be identified separately," Mason said. "I notice that one of the bullets is flattened on the nose of the bullet, evidently from hitting some rather solid object. The flattening is on a slant, and the edges of the bullet have been curled over. The other bullet shows little damage. I suggest that the flattened bullet be People's Exhibit C-1 and the other bullet be C-2. I will also state that in order to expedite matters I will stipulate that both the gun and the bullets may be received in evidence, which will obviate the necessity of marking them for identification now and introducing them into evidence later."

"Very well," Fraser said. "The People accept that stipulation. The bullets will go into evidence as People's Exhibit C-1 and People's Exhibit C-2."

Fraser turned to the witness. "Did you test fire this gun, People's Exhibit B?"

"I did."

"And did you compare the test bullets fired from that gun with the bullets, Exhibits C?"

"Yes."

"What did you find?"

"The bullets were fired from that gun," Redfield said. "I have photographs made through a comparison microscope which shows the bullets superimposed one upon the other and the lines of striation."

"Will you produce those photographs, please?"

Redfield produced a photograph.

"I ask that this be received in evidence as People's Exhibit D."

"No objection," Mason said.

"Cross-examine," Fraser said.

Redfield, who had been cross-examined by Mason on many occasions, turned his eyes slowly and appraisingly toward the lawyer and settled himself in the witness chair. His face showed that he intended to weigh each question carefully and not be trapped into any inadvertent admission.

"There is only one photograph," Mason said, "but there are two bullets."

"The one photograph is of bullet Exhibit C-2. Since

the other bullet was damaged and it would have been more difficult to have matched the striations, I didn't photograph that bullet."

"And you are completely satisfied that the bullets were fired from this gun which has been introduced in evidence as Exhibit B?"

"Yes. . . . Now, wait a minute. I don't think I made detailed tests of the damaged bullet. I did make detailed tests of the undamaged bullet and I made this photograph of it so there could be no question that it came from the gun, Exhibit B."

"You assumed that both bullets were fired from the same gun," Mason said.

"That's right."

"But you didn't check it?"

"I didn't check the damaged bullet to the same extent that I did the other."

"You checked it?"

"Well, now, just a moment, Mr. Mason. If you want to be painstakingly accurate about this, I am not in a position to swear that I did check both individual bullets. I know that I checked the undamaged bullet and I checked the damaged bullet to the extent that I determined they were both of the same caliber and weight and had been fired from a Smith and Wesson revolver. That can be told from the angle and pitch of the grooves. But as far as actual striations are concerned, I think I checked only the bullet which has been identified as Exhibit C-2."

"Look here," Judge Keyser said, "let's be realistic about this thing, Mr. Mason. Does this point make any actual difference in the case?"

"It does not, Your Honor," Fraser fairly shouted. "It is simply another one of defense counsel's very adroit moves which he is noted for."

"May I be heard, Your Honor?" Mason asked in a quiet voice.

Judge Keyser nodded. "You may be heard. My question was addressed to you."

"I think it is a *very* important point, if the Court please," Mason said. "I think I will be in a position to prove that if a bullet from this gun was fired into the body of Nadine Ellis, the bullet *must* have been fired after Nadine Ellis was dead.

"The defendant in this case is being tried for murder. Murder is the unlawful killing of a human being with malice aforethought. If a bullet was fired from this gun into the body of Nadine Ellis *after* she was dead, the defendant certainly isn't guilty of murder. That is, the evidence relied upon to prove her guilty of murder would prove only that she had discharged a bullet into a dead body."

"That's sheer bosh and nonsense," Fraser exclaimed heatedly. "As far as this hearing is concerned, all we need to do is to prove that Nadine Ellis was murdered, that the bullets in her body came from a gun found in the possession of the defendant."

"One of the bullets," Mason said.

"That's only a matter of expediency," Fraser said. "I will admit that the prosecution would have liked it better if the ballistics expert, Alexander Redfield, had taken the time and the trouble to have identified both bullets. But since one bullet was slightly damaged and apparently they both were fired from the same gun, he contented himself with making a positive, definite identification of only one of the bullets.

"Now, since it is only incumbent upon us to show that a crime has been committed and that there is reasonable ground to believe that the defendant committed the crime, we are quite content to introduce this gun in evidence, to introduce this bullet and rest our case."

"Now, just a minute," Judge Keyser said. "Ordinarily the Court is aware of the fact that the defense doesn't put on testimony in the preliminary hearing, and if the defense does, the Court usually disregards it unless it overwhelmingly establishes the innocence of the defendant. Courts usually feel that conflicts in evidence are to be tried in the Superior Court before a jury and that where the prosecution has made a *prima-facie* case, the Court doesn't need to look any further. However, here we have a situation where a young woman, if bound over, would probably be held in jail for some time before the case came up for trial. Her reputation would be blackened, the experience would leave a psychic scar. This Court has no intention of submitting this young woman to such an ordeal simply because of technicalities.

"If Mr. Mason assures this Court that he believes he can establish the fact that this bullet could only have been fired from this gun after death had taken place, the Court certainly feels that Mr. Redfield should identify that other bullet as having come from the same gun."

"We have no objection to that," Fraser said, "except that it simply results in a delay and newspaper notoriety, both of which are greatly desired by defense counsel."

"That will do," Judge Keyser said. "There is no occasion for personalities and, after all, if you want to be technical about it, the fault, if any, rests with the prosecution. The defense is entitled to have the scientific evidence fairly examined and fairly presented. Mr. Redfield, how long will it take you to classify that somewhat damaged bullet and show that it either came from this gun, Exhibit B, or that it did not come from that weapon?"

Redfield hesitated and said, "I am working on an emergency matter at the moment. I interrupted my work there to come to court. I can promise to have the information by late this afternoon, but I am not certain that I could have it earlier."

Judge Keyser said, "I will adjourn this matter until three-thirty this afternoon. Try and have the information by that time, Mr. Redfield. If you can't possibly have it, we will continue the case until tomorrow morning. However, I would like to dispose of the case today and I think that the information concerning this bullet is of prime importance— I take it that the prosecution has evidence that this gun, Exhibit B, was found in the possession of the defendant and there can be no question of that?"

"That is right," Fraser said.

"Well, I'm going to adjourn court until three-thirty this afternoon," Judge Keyser said. "The witness will return at that time, and counsel will be present with the defendant. The defendant is remanded to custody."

Ellen Robb dug her fingers deep into Mason's coat sleeve. "Mr. Mason, how in the world— They're crazy. I didn't shoot Nadine Ellis. I never fired that gun at all. I—"

"Just sit tight," Mason said, warning her with a glance. "Don't make any statement. Newspaper reporters may try to get you to say something. The police may question you again about that gun. Sit tight, keep quiet. And whatever you do, don't lie to me."

"I'm not lying to you."

"You have been," Mason said.

She shook her head. "If that gun fired a bullet into the body of Nadine Ellis, somebody did it before the gun came into my possession and then put it in my suitcase."

Mason studied her face searchingly. She returned his gaze with level-lidded frankness. "I cross my heart and hope to die," she said.

"That," Mason told her, "*may* not be an empty expression. If you're lying to me, the situation may be a lot more serious than you think."

Mason nodded to the policewoman to take Ellen Robb into her custody, and left the courtroom with Della Street.

CHAPTER ELEVEN

IN THE small private dining room of the restaurant where Perry Mason, Della Street and Paul Drake so frequently lunched during the noon recess, the trio seated themselves at the table.

"I don't see what makes this seem such a devastating surprise to you," Paul Drake said to Mason. "I told you quite a while ago this client of yours was no lily-white angel. I take it, she's been lying to you."

"It's more serious than that, Paul," Mason said.

"How do you mean?"

"I'll let you in on a secret," Mason said. "If that gun committed the murder, I personally am mixed in it."

"Mixed in what?"

"Mixed in the murder."

"*You* are!" Drake exclaimed incredulously.

"Call it an accessory after the fact or suppressing evidence or anything you want, Paul. I just don't believe that gun could possibly have been used in the killing."

"Nevertheless, it was," Drake said. "The evidence shows it."

Mason, his face granite-hard with concentration, paid

161

no attention to Drake's words and might not have heard him.

Drake turned to Della Street and said, "I don't get it. I've seen him skate on some awfully thin legal ice, but I've never seen him like this before."

Della Street shook her head warningly, indicating that Drake was not to pursue the subject.

Drake said, "What became of the gun that you gave me to test, Perry? That was registered in the name of George Anclitas."

"Just don't ask questions," Mason said. "Just eat your lunch."

The waiter brought in their orders, and Mason ate in thoughtful silence.

"Well," Drake said, as he pushed back his plate, "thanks for the lunch, Perry. I *have* had more cheerful meals."

Mason merely grunted in acknowledgment of Drake's remark.

"I'll get the chores done," Drake said, and left the dining room.

Della Street glanced solicitously at Perry Mason, started to say something, then checked herself.

As though reading her mind, Mason said, "I know you're wondering what's worrying me. The thing that worries me is whether the district attorney's office has baited an elaborate trap for me and I'm walking into it, or whether they have considered the case so dead open-and-shut they don't need to worry."

Della Street shook her head. "Hamilton Burger has his faults, but he's not entirely dumb. He would never consider a case, in which you were representing a defendant, a dead open-and-shut case."

"But," Mason said, "he sent this Donovan Fraser in to try the case unaided. Fraser is a young eager beaver, a relatively new trial deputy. He's anxious to win his spurs and prove himself, and he's probably a little more belligerent than he will be after he has had five more years of courtroom practice under his belt.

"Now, why did Hamilton Burger pick that particular trial deputy to oppose me? He has some veterans in the office who are remarkably good lawyers."

"Isn't Fraser a good lawyer?"

"I think he is. The point is, he's relatively inexperienced, and in this business there are some things you can learn only as the result of experience."

"That's the only reason you think he may be laying a trap for you?" Della Street asked.

"No, that's only one of the reasons," Mason said. "The thing that bothers me is that in preparing this case they have apparently taken so much for granted—and I don't think they'd do that."

"In what way?"

"For instance," Mason said, "this gun that they took from Ellen Robb is, as far as the case is concerned up to this point, simply a gun. Apparently they didn't make any effort to trace the registration of the gun. Now, I just can't understand that."

"Well, after all, they found it in her possession and they found that the test bullet matched the bullet found in Nadine Ellis' body.

"If you were district attorney, you'd call in any trial

deputy who happened to be unattached and say, 'Here's a case you *can't* lose. Regardless of the fact that Perry Mason is on the other side, you can't possibly conceive of any set of facts that would keep a judge from binding the defendant over to the Superior Court on this sort of showing."

Mason nodded.

"Well?" Della Street asked.

"I'll grant all that," Mason said, "but somehow I have a feeling that they may be laying a trap. It's almost impossible to think that they wouldn't have taken the number of the gun and tried to trace it through its various owners. Now then, if . . . if they can trace that gun to my possession, then what happens?"

"Then," she said, "you're in the soup."

"That's what I'm thinking," Mason said.

"And if you're going to get in the soup," she said, "isn't it better to become righteously indignant in court and claim that someone has doctored the evidence, that someone has substituted the bullets, that the murder simply couldn't have been committed with the weapon that was found in the possession of Ellen Robb because you, yourself, had been the one who had handed her that weapon and you had handed it to her at a time that was *after* Ellen had gone to the yacht?"

"How do we know it was after?" Mason asked.

"Why, she— I see," Della Street said.

"In other words," Mason said, "suppose Ellen is smart. Suppose she came to my office and told me a story about having gone to the yacht looking for Nadine Ellis, that she couldn't find her, that she had a fight with George Anclitas and left The Big Barn, that she found a gun in her suitcase and doesn't know what to do with it. She would tell me all this *before* Nadine Ellis had been murdered. Then, after she had given me a good story and aroused my sympathy, she'd go out and murder Nadine and—"

"Could she have done that?" Della Street asked. "Did she have the time? Remember, we had her virtually under surveillance because you had Paul Drake put operatives on the job to act as bodyguards. You felt that someone might try to cause trouble."

"That's what I'm trying to remember," Mason said. "There was an interval from the time she left our office before the bodyguards picked her up. Now then, she could have gone out to the yacht and killed Nadine Ellis during that interval. Is she a smart little babe who's taking me for a ride, or is she the victim of some sort of a diabolical frame-up? And if it's a frame-up, how the devil *could* they have worked it? How much does Hamilton Burger, the district attorney, know? How much rope is he giving me, hoping I'll hang myself, and what are my duties in this situation in view of the fact that I'm supposed to represent my client and not disclose evidence against her?"

"That," Della Street said, "is a formidable list of questions."

"And a great deal depends on getting the right answers," Mason said.

"So what do we do?" Della Street asked.

"We get in my automobile and drive around somewhere, where no one will recognize us, ask us any questions or serve us with any subpoena or other documents until just before three-thirty. Then we go to court, and no matter what happens, we stall things along so that we don't have to reach any decisions until after court adjourns for the evening. Then we have until tomorrow morning to plan a course of conduct."

Della Street nodded, pushed back her chair.

"And," Mason said, "when we get back to court at three-thirty this afternoon, *if* we should happen to find that Mr. Hamilton Burger, the district attorney himself, has entered the case, we'll know that it was an elaborate trap and that I've walked into it."

CHAPTER TWELVE

PERRY MASON carefully timed his entrance to the courtroom so that it was only a few seconds before three-thirty when he opened the swinging doors.

The bailiff, who had been watching the clock and frowning, pressed a button signaling Judge Keyser that everything was in readiness.

Two newspaper reporters hurried toward Mason. "Mr. Mason, Mr. Mason—"

The bailiff pounded a gavel. "Everybody rise," he said.

Mason walked past the reporters and stood facing the flag as Judge Keyser took his place on the bench.

Judge Keyser said, "The Court would like to get this matter finished this afternoon if it is at all possible. Now, Mr. Redfield is here and ready to take the stand?"

"Yes, Your Honor," Fraser said, looking toward the door of the witness room.

The door opened. Alexander Redfield came in, accompanied by Hamilton Burger, the district attorney.

Mason noted the significance of Burger's presence but kept his face completely without expression.

Judge Keyser, however, showed some surprise.

"You're appearing in this case, Mr. District Attorney?" he asked.

"Yes, Your Honor, in person," Hamilton Burger said.

The judge started to say something, then changed his mind, turned to Redfield, said, "Mr. Redfield, you have now had an opportunity to study that other bullet and compare it with test bullets fired from the weapon which has been introduced as People's Exhibit B. In your opinion as an expert, was that bullet fired from that weapon?"

"It was not," Alexander Redfield said.

Judge Keyser could not refrain from an involuntary ejaculation of surprise. "What!" he asked.

Redfield shook his head. "It was not fired from that weapon. It was fired from a Smith and Wesson .38-caliber revolver, but it was not fired from the weapon introduced as Exhibit B."

"But the other bullet was? The so-called second bullet?"

"That's right. The bullet in evidence as Exhibit C-1 was not fired from that weapon. The bullet in evidence as C-2 was fired from that weapon. Bearing in mind that we have simply designated those bullets as number one and two, the words first and second were only a designation used by the doctor in his testimony. It didn't indicate that the bullets were fired in that numerical sequence. Unfortunately, the bullet referred to by Dr. Calvert as the first bullet was entered in evidence as C-2 while the bullet he referred to as the second bullet became C-1 in evidence. In order to avoid further confusion, I wish to refer to each bullet specifically by its exhibit number."

Judge Keyser ran his hand along the top of his head, then looked down at Burger and over at Mason. "Does counsel on either side care to make any statement?"

Mason shook his head.

Hamilton Burger said, "We have no statement at this time, Your Honor."

"Now, just a moment," Judge Keyser said. "Let's be practical about this, Mr. District Attorney. The evidence so far shows unmistakably that a crime has been committed. There is evidence—or rather I should say there has been evidence—tending to show this defendant committed the crime. What might have been referred to as the fatal weapon was found in her possession. However, there now are certain unusual circumstances in this case.

"Because of a lapse of time and the start of putrefaction, it is impossible for the autopsy surgeon to tell which of two bullets was fired first. Either bullet could have caused death. It is impossible for the autopsy surgeon to give an estimate as to the interval of time between the firing of the first and second shot. It has been at least intimated by the defense that a part of the defense in this case will be predicated upon the assumption that one of the bullets was fired a sufficient length of time after the other bullet so that death at least could have taken place prior to the time this bullet was fired."

"I understand, Your Honor," Hamilton Burger said.

"I am assuming," Judge Keyser said, "that the position of the prosecution is that the point is immaterial as far as a preliminary hearing is concerned, that there is sufficient evidence tending to connect the defendant with the commission of the crime to result in her being bound over.

"I am forced to say that I consider this position to be well taken in the eyes of the law. However, from a practical standpoint the Court would have wished that the situation could have been cleared up. It is not a pleasant duty to bind a young woman over for trial, knowing that the interim must be spent in jail. Therefore, the Court would, for its own information, have liked to have had more light on the subject. However, if it is the position of the prosecution that technically the case calls for binding the defendant over, the Court feels that that position is probably well taken."

Mason arose and said somewhat deferentially, "I take it the Court is not precluding the defense from putting on evidence."

"Certainly not," Judge Keyser said, "but let's be realistic. With the circumstantial evidence which we have in this case, a weapon which at least could be the murder weapon, found in the possession of the defendant, you can hardly contend that the evidence doesn't at least connect the defendant sufficiently with the crime to result in an order binding her over regardless of what counter-showing you might make."

"I'm not prepared to make that concession, Your Honor," Mason said.

Hamilton Burger arose with a ponderous dignity. "May I be heard?" he asked.

"Certainly, Mr. District Attorney," Judge Keyser said, "although it seems to me that Mr. Mason has the laboring oar here."

"We are not finished with our case," the district attorney said, "and we have no intention of relying upon the evidence and the assumption as indicated by the Court. We expect to go further with our proof."

"You do?" Judge Keyser asked.

Hamilton Burger nodded.

Judge Keyser settled back on the bench. "Very well," he said. "I will state that the Court will welcome such proof. I had been hoping such proof would be adduced. That was the reason I continued the matter so we could get an opinion from Mr. Redfield. Proceed with your proof."

"I believe Mr. Mason was cross-examining the witness," Hamilton Burger said.

"That is right," Judge Keyser said. "Do you have any further questions on cross-examination, Mr. Mason?"

"I have several questions," Mason said.

"In that case," Hamilton Burger said, "I will ask permission of the Court to withdraw Mr. Redfield temporarily so that I may put on another witness who will, I believe, connect up the revolver, Exhibit B, in such a way that certain matters will be clarified. This is testimony which I am particularly anxious to introduce this afternoon."

"I have no objection," Mason said. "I would, in fact, prefer to defer my cross-examination of Mr. Redfield until this additional evidence is before the Court."

"Very well," Judge Keyser said. "So ordered. Go ahead, bring on your other witnesses, Mr. District Attorney."

Hamilton Burger said, "I call Darwin C. Gowrie to the stand."

An officer opened the door of the witness room, and Gowrie stepped into the room.

"Come forward and be sworn, Mr. Gowrie," Hamilton Burger said.

Gowrie held up his hand and was sworn.

"You are now and for some years past have been an attorney at law, practicing in the court of this state?"

"That is correct."

"I will ask you if you are acquainted with Perry Mason, the attorney for the defense?"

"I am."

"I will ask you if, on the ninth of this month, you had a conversation with Perry Mason over the telephone?"

"I did."

"At that time did Mr. Mason make some statements to you concerning certain unusual decisions in murder cases?"

"He did."

"What was the conversation?"

"Now, just a minute," Judge Keyser said. "I notice there is no objection on the part of the defense, but the Court hardly sees the relevancy of this."

"If the Court please," Hamilton Burger said, "I propose to connect this up. It is an important point in the prosecution's case which I wish to make."

"As part of a *preliminary* examination?" Judge Keyser asked.

"Exactly, Your Honor," Hamilton Burger said. "Without wishing to engage in personalities, I wish to state as an officer of this court that in the past I have felt there have been cases where defense counsel has gone far beyond the bounds of propriety in representing clients accused of crime. I may state to the Court that in several of those cases an investigation would have been made and disciplinary action quite possibly taken, only, as it happened, because of somewhat spectacular and highly dramatic developments, it turned out that the wrong person was being prosecuted for crime. Under those circumstances it was felt that an investigation would hardly be worth while.

"However, in the present case evidence is at hand which shows at least by inference *exactly* what happened, and we consider this evidence equally as important as evidence tending to connect the defendant with the commission of the crime. I may state that before we are finished with this evidence, we are going to show unmistakably a link which implicates counsel for the defense in this case, not as an attorney engaging in unethical methods, but as an actual accomplice—an accessory after the fact."

"Now, just a minute," Judge Keyser said. "That statement, Mr. District Attorney, will of course be widely publicized. The Court feels that it was unnecessary for you to make such a statement at this time."

"I merely wanted the Court to understand my position."

"Very well," Judge Keyser said, "the statement has been made now and it cannot be recalled. If the Court had had any idea of what you had in mind, the Court would have intervened and prevented the making of such statements. The Court was only asking you whether this proof was pertinent."

"It is pertinent. I wanted to show the Court how it was to be connected up."

"Very well, go ahead," Judge Keyser said. "I may state, however, Mr. District Attorney, that in the event the proof falls short of your statement, the Court will consider the making of such statement at this time as serious misconduct, perhaps amounting to a contempt of court."

"I am quite aware of the entire possibilities of the situation," Hamilton Burger said, "and I made my statement knowingly and after having given it careful thought. If I don't prove my point, I will willingly answer to charges of contempt."

"Very well, go ahead."

Hamilton Burger turned to the witness.

"Did you make notes of the conversation you had with Perry Mason?"

"Yes, sir."

"Why, may I ask?"

"Because the conversation was exceedingly unusual and very interesting as far as an attorney is concerned."

"What was the nature of that conversation?"

"Mr. Mason told me about certain legal points which were startlingly unusual and which he had investigated from time to time."

"What was the nature of the conversation in regard to those legal points?"

"Well, it came up because Mr. Mason had suggested to a client of mine that community property which had been lost in a gambling game could be recovered by the other spouse and restored to the community. It was a remarkably unusual doctrine, and I wanted to check with Mr. Mason to make certain I had not misunderstood him."

"Was there any other conversation?"

"Yes."

"Go ahead and relate the conversation."

"Well, Mr. Mason told me he hadn't been misunderstood, he confirmed a citation which certainly lays down a rather remarkable rule of law in regard to gambling."

"And then?" Hamilton Burger asked.

"Then he went on to tell me that he had a file which he kept of unusual decisions."

"Did he make a point in regard to murder?"

"Yes. He said that there were decisions to the effect that if a person fired a fatal bullet into a victim, that is, a bullet which would necessarily cause death, and then, before the victim actually expired, another individual fired a second bullet which resulted in death, the person firing the first bullet was not guilty of murder."

"Did he cite decisions?"

"He did. I made a note of those decisions because I was greatly interested."

"Now then, can you give us the time of the conversation as well as the date?"

"Yes, it happens that I can because my office keeps a note of the numbers that I call and the time consumed in conversation. I found that I was spending a great deal of my time in telephone consultations for which we were making no charge and—"

"Never mind that," Hamilton Burger said. "I am asking if you can give the exact date and the exact time, and your answer was in the affirmative. Now, will you tell us the date and the time?"

"The call was made at nine-thirty on the morning of the ninth."

"Will you please give us the references Mr. Mason gave you at that time?"

"He referred to Dempsey versus State, 83 Ark. 81, 102 S.W. 704; People versus Ah Fat, 48 Cal. 61; Duque versus State, 56 Tex. Cr. 214; 119 S.W. 687."

"Cross-examine," Hamilton Burger said to Mason.

"How did you know you were talking with me on the telephone?" Mason asked.

"I called your office number, I asked the person answering the phone to have Mr. Mason put on the line, and you came on the line."

"You recognized my voice?"

"At the time, no. I had not heard your voice. Since then I have heard your voice and know that you were the party to whom I was talking over the telephone."

"You don't know where I was when I answered that telephone—that is, you don't know whether I was in my private office, in the reception room, in the law library or where I was."

"No, sir."

"And you don't know whether I was alone or whether anyone was with me."

"No, sir, I don't know."

"That's all," Mason said. "I have no further questions."

"Call your next witness," Judge Keyser said grimly.

"Call Lieutenant Tragg," Hamilton Burger said.

Lt. Tragg emerged from the witness room and took the stand.

"You took the defendant into custody on Thursday, the eleventh, Lieutenant?"

"I did."

"You had a warrant?"

"Yes."

"A search warrant?"

"Yes."

"Did you find a revolver in her possession?"

"Yes."

"Describe it, please."

"It was a Smith and Wesson .38-caliber police model with a two-and-a-half-inch barrel, blued steel, number 133347."

"I call your attention to People's Exhibit B and ask you if you have seen that gun before."

"I have. It is the gun I found in the possession of the defendant."

"Did you find any paper in her possession?"

"I did. I found this memo taken in shorthand. I can read the shorthand notes. They say 'Murder cannot be proven if two guns used in crime inflicting equally fatal wounds at different times, Dempsey versus State, 83 Ark. 81, 102 S.W. 704; People versus Ah Fat, 48 Cal. 61; Duque versus State, 56 Tex. Cr. 214, 119 S.W. 687.' "

Hamilton Burger said, "I ask that this note be marked for identification as People's Exhibit G. I wish to keep the intervening letters free for other firearm exhibits so they may be in order. Presently I shall show this note is in the defendant's handwriting."

"No objections," Mason said.

"Cross-examine," Burger snapped.

"No questions," Mason said.

"Call Loring Crowder," Hamilton Burger said.

Once more the door of the witness room opened, and a well-groomed, rather chunky man in his late forties entered the courtroom, held up his hand, was sworn, took his seat in the witness chair, turned to Hamilton Burger.

"Your name is Loring Crowder," Hamilton Burger said. "You are engaged in the retail liquor business, Mr. Crowder?"

"That is right."

"I'm going to show you a gun, Exhibit B in this case, numbered 133347, and ask you if you have ever seen that gun before."

Crowder took the gun, turned it over, looked at the numbers, said, "May I consult a memoranda?"

"You may," Hamilton Burger said, "if you will first tell us what it is."

"It is a notebook containing the number of a gun which I purchased from the Valleyview Hardware and Sporting Goods Store."

"Go ahead, consult the notebook," Hamilton Burger said.

Crowder looked at the notebook, then at the gun, said, "This is the same gun. I bought this gun about two and a half years ago from the store mentioned. I bought it to keep in my place of business."

"And what did you do with it?"

"I gave it to a friend about a year ago."

"Who was the friend?"

Crowder said, "I gave this gun to my friend, George

Spencer Ranger. Mr. Ranger was having troubles
and—"

"Never mind that," Hamilton Burger interrupted.
"I'm just trying to trace the gun. You gave it to George
Spencer Ranger."

"That is right."

"Was it a gift or a loan?"

"It was a loan."

"And did Mr. Ranger return the gun to you?"

"No, sir, he didn't. He told me that he had given it
to—"

"Never mind what he told you. That's hearsay,"
Hamilton Burger said. "I'm simply asking you if he
gave the gun back to you."

"No, sir, he did not."

"That's all," Hamilton Burger said. "Cross-examine."

"No questions," Mason said.

"Call George Spencer Ranger," Hamilton Burger
said.

Once again an officer opened the door of the witness
room, and Ranger, a tall, loose-jointed man in his
forties with a shock of dark hair and heavy dark eyebrows, entered the courtroom.

"Hold up your right hand and be sworn," Hamilton
Burger said.

The witness was duly sworn, gave his name and address to the court reporter, seated himself on the witness chair, turned to Judge Keyser and said, "I want it
understood that I am here against my will. I have been
subpoenaed by an officer who took me into custody and

forced me to accompany him here. I am not testifying willingly."

"That doesn't make any difference at this time," Judge Keyser said. "If you were brought here in response to the process of the court, you are here and you are called as a witness. It is your duty to give your testimony."

"If the Court please," Hamilton Burger said, "this is a hostile witness. It will be necessary to ask leading questions."

"Go ahead with your examination," Judge Keyser said. "We will determine the attitude and the necessity for leading questions as we go along and if and when objection is made."

"You are acquainted with Loring Crowder?"

"I am, yes, sir."

"Did Loring Crowder lend you a Smith and Wesson revolver some time ago?"

The witness thought for a moment, then said, "Yes."

"Did you return that gun to Mr. Crowder?"

"I did not."

"Where is it now?"

"I don't know."

"What did you do with it?"

"I . . . I surrendered it."

"To whom?"

"My attorney told me it would be better to leave it with him."

"Who was your attorney?"

The witness hesitated.

"Who was it?" Hamilton Burger asked. "The court records show it. It was Perry Mason, wasn't it?"

"Yes."

"Now then, I show you a gun marked People's Exhibit B, being a Smith and Wesson revolver, number 133347, and ask you if that is the gun."

"I don't know," the witness said, giving the gun only a cursory look.

"Look at it," Hamilton Burger said. "Take it in your hand."

The witness extended his hand, looked at the gun, handed it back to Hamilton Burger, said, "I still don't know."

"All right, I'll put it this way," Hamilton Burger said. "You got a gun from Loring Crowder?"

"Yes."

"And whatever that gun was, you gave that gun to Perry Mason?"

"Yes."

"When?"

"When my case was coming up, something over six months ago."

"Did Perry Mason at any time ever give that gun back to you?"

"No."

"That was the last time you saw it, when you gave it to Perry Mason?"

"Yes."

"And the gun that you gave him was the same gun that you got from Loring Crowder?"

"Yes."

"Is there anything about this gun which is at all dissimilar to the gun which was given you by Loring Crowder?"

"I can't remember. I can't remember what that gun looked like."

"It could be this gun?"

"It could be."

"You may cross-examine," Hamilton Burger said.

"No questions," Mason said.

"Now," Hamilton Burger said, "I want to call Helman Ellis, the husband of the deceased woman."

Once more the door of the witness room was opened, and the deputy called out the name, "Helman Ellis."

Ellis entered the courtroom, glanced at Ellen Robb, hastily averted his eyes, walked over to take the oath and seated himself in the witness chair.

Hamilton Burger said, "Your name is Helman Ellis. You were the husband of Nadine Ellis? She was your wife in her lifetime?"

"Yes."

"You own the yacht on which the body was found, the *Cap's Eyes*?"

"Yes."

"When did you last see your wife alive?"

"I saw her briefly on the early morning of Wednesday, the tenth."

"Where was she?"

"She was in our house, and then I last saw her in an automobile."

"Where?"

"At our home at Rowena, in the garage."

"Did you have any conversation with her?"

"A very brief conversation."

"And of what did that conversation consist?"

"I told her I wanted to explain certain things to her.

She told me that an explanation could do no good, that things had progressed to such a point that talk would accomplish nothing."

"Then what?"

"I kept trying to patch things up with her, but I saw it was no use. I was trying to get possession of a gun she had. She told me she was going to divorce me."

"What time was that?"

"A little before six."

"Will you explain the circumstances, please?"

"The night before, that was Tuesday night, I had planned to go cruising on our yacht. She was going to accompany me. We had an argument. She pulled a gun on me and left me marooned on the yacht. She told me she was going to Arizona and kill 'my mistress.' I didn't get ashore until nine-thirty.

"After I warned Ellen, I went home and quietly let myself in. I slept on the couch without undressing. My wife latchkeyed the door and let herself in about 5:45 A.M. She had been driving our car. She left the motor running while she went to her room to get something.

"I followed her out to the car. She said she was satisfied I had tried to make her think 'my mistress,' the defendant, had gone to Arizona simply to throw her off the trail. She said she knew now where the defendant was and that I had spent the night with the defendant. She said the defendant had gone aboard our yacht in the belief I was there. She said she was going to pistol-whip the defendant so her beauty would be permanently marred."

"What did you say to that?"

"Nothing. I had never met the defendant aboard our

yacht. I knew my wife was barking up the wrong tree, so I decided to let her go, feeling she might calm down after she found out her mistake.

"She had also told me she was going to have a finger-print expert dust the cabin of the yacht to find the defendant's fingerprints. Since I felt sure there were no fingerprints of the defendant there, I felt it would be best to let my wife follow up this lead, and in that way she might convince herself her suspicions were groundless."

"Then what happened?"

"She drove off."

"And at that time she was headed for your yacht?"

"Yes."

"You never saw her alive after that?"

"No."

"Cross-examine," Burger said.

"Later on, on Wednesday, you went to my office?" Mason asked.

"Yes."

"And told me about the altercation on the yacht?"

"Yes."

"And about this subsequent meeting with your wife?"

"Yes."

"That's all," Mason said. "I have no further questions."

"Just a minute," Hamilton Burger said. "I have some questions on redirect."

Hamilton Burger arose and faced the witness. "Did you have occasion to look for your yacht, the *Cap's Eyes* later on, on Wednesday?"

"Yes."

"At what time?"

"Around noon."

"Was it at its accustomed mooring at the club?"

"No, sir, it had gone."

"When did you next see it again?"

"When the police brought it back."

"When did you next see your wife again?"

"In the morgue."

"Now, I show you a gun which was found near the hand of your wife when her body was discovered on the yacht. I note that this gun is identical in appearance with the gun which has been introduced in evidence as People's Exhibit B, number 133347. Now, I don't like to keep referring to these weapons in the record by number, so I am simply going to refer to this as the Ellis gun because it was found in the cabin of your yacht and I believe you can identify that as to ownership."

Ellis said, "I can, yes, sir. That gun was given to me by George Anclitas."

"And what did you do with it? Did you carry it?"

"No, sir, I did not. I kept it aboard the yacht for personal protection."

"Your wife knew it was there?"

"Yes."

"Where was it customarily kept?"

"In a drawer in the cabin."

"Do you know if your wife had this gun on Tuesday? Was that the gun you referred to when you testified your wife pulled a gun?"

"Yes, sir."

Hamilton Burger said, "We ask that this gun be

marked for identification as People's Exhibit E, Your Honor. We will not offer to introduce it in evidence at this time, because that offer should properly come after positive identification is made as to this being the gun that was found in the cabin of the yacht, the *Cap's Eyes.*"

"Very well," Judge Keyser said, "the gun will be marked for identification only."

"I don't think I have any further questions at this time," Hamilton Burger said, "but I notice it is nearing the hour of adjournment. My next witness, George Anclitas, is here under subpoena. He is a businessman, proprietor of an establishment in Rowena, which has several businesses combined under one management, a motel, a trout pool, a swimming pool, a night club and a parlor where legalized games are played. It is a great hardship for Mr. Anclitas to be here, and I ask permission of the Court to withdraw this witness and put Mr. Anclitas on the stand at this time.

"The testimony of Mr. Anclitas will be brief, and in this way we can finish with him this afternoon so he won't have to return tomorrow."

Judge Keyser looked inquiringly at Perry Mason. "Does the defense wish to object?" he asked.

"No objection," Mason said. "It is quite all right as far as I am concerned."

"Call George Anclitas."

The deputy opened the door of the witness room. George Anclitas emerged.

Helman Ellis, leaving the witness stand, walked in front of Ellen Robb, smiled reassuringly and returned to the witness room.

George Anclitas, his head held high, stalked to the witness stand with the stiff-backed gait of a marching soldier, turned with almost military precision, held up his hand, took the oath and seated himself.

"Your name is George Anclitas? You are one of the owners of The Big Barn in Rowena?" Hamilton Burger asked.

"Yes, sir."

"Do you know the defendant?"

"Yes, sir."

"Was she in your employ?"

"Yes, sir."

"For how long?"

"Some four or five months."

"And what were her duties?"

"She sang songs, sold cigars and cigarettes when necessary and did various odd jobs."

"When did the employment terminate?"

"She left on the evening of the ninth."

"Why did she leave?"

"I fired her."

"Why?"

Judge Keyser said, "Of course, this is preliminary but unless it's connected up I don't see its relevancy, particularly in view of the fact that the answer might tend to be an appraisal of the character of the defendant through hostile eyes."

"I think it's pertinent. I think it will be connected up, Your Honor," Hamilton Burger said.

"No objection from the defense," Mason said. "Let him go right ahead."

"Answer the question," Hamilton Burger said.

"She was bringing too much notoriety to the place. She was having an affair with Helman Ellis, and Mrs. Ellis got on to it—"

"Now, just a minute, just a minute," Judge Keyser said. "This witness is obviously testifying to hearsay now."

"I think perhaps these are conclusions of the witness, based upon his own personal observations, however," Hamilton Burger said.

"I think it's hearsay," Judge Keyser said. "Let *me* ask the witness a couple of questions. How do you know the defendant was having an affair with Helman Ellis?"

"Because I caught them."

"You caught them?"

"Well, they were embracing."

"How do you know that Mrs. Ellis knew about it?"

"Because she made a scene with the defendant, Ellen Robb."

"Were you there?"

"I was there."

Judge Keyser glanced down at Perry Mason, a puzzled frown creasing his forehead. "Very well," he said, "go ahead."

"Now then, did you give Helman Ellis a gun?"

"I did."

"What kind of a gun?"

"A Smith and Wesson, .38-caliber, two-and-a-half-inch barrel."

"I will show you a gun marked for identification as People's Exhibit E and ask you if that is the gun."

Anclitas looked at the gun, said, "That's the one."

"How long ago did you give him this gun?"

"About six weeks ago."

"Cross-examine," Hamilton Burger said.

Mason said, "Before embarking upon this cross-ex-amination, Your Honor, I would like to ask whether test bullets from this gun marked Exhibit E were compared with the fatal bullet number one taken from the body of the decedent."

Judge Keyser nodded his head. "That seems a logical question. Were they so compared, Mr. District Attorney?"

"Certainly not," Hamilton Burger snapped.

"Why not?" Judge Keyser asked.

"Why should they be? This gun, Exhibit E, was fired *at* the assailant. A bullet from this gun was found embedded in the woodwork of the cabin near the door. It had only been fired once."

"Nevertheless," Judge Keyser said, "in view of the fact that it is now apparent that there is one bullet which can't be accounted for—at least we can't account for the gun which fired it—it would seem that there should be a ballistics test made of this weapon. I should think that would have been done as a matter of routine."

"At the time," Hamilton Burger said, "we were under the impression both of the fatal bullets had been fired from the gun which was in the possession of the defendant, the gun Exhibit B."

"I can readily understand that," Judge Keyser said, "but it certainly seems to me there should be a comparison of the other bullet, the slightly damaged bullet, with test bullets fired from this gun."

"Yes, Your Honor."

"It is now becoming apparent that we can't close this case today. I would suggest that the ballistics expert make such an examination before court convenes tomorrow morning."

"Yes, Your Honor," Hamilton Burger said.

"Now go ahead with your cross-examination, Mr. Mason."

Mason said, "There was an altercation with the defendant prior to her discharge?"

"I don't know what you mean, an altercation," Anclitas said. "She attacked me."

"In what way?"

"Striking and clawing."

"And you hit her?"

"I defended myself."

"You hit her?"

"I tell you, I defended myself."

"You hit her?"

"What was I supposed to do, stand there and let my face get clawed? I tried to keep her off."

"You hit her?"

"All right, I hit her!" Anclitas shouted.

"Thank you," Mason said. "I believe you hit her in the eye."

"I don't know where I hit her. I popped her one."

"You saw her with a black eye?"

"I saw her with a black eye."

"And you have been sued for seventy-five hundred dollars actual and punitive damages because of this assault you made on the defendant?"

"I object, Your Honor," Hamilton Burger said.

"That's not proper cross-examination. It's incompetent, irrelevant and immaterial."

Judge Keyser, plainly interested, leaned forward to study George Anclitas. "The objection is overruled," he said. "It goes to show the bias of the witness."

"Answer the question," Mason said.

"All right, so I'm getting sued. Any lawyer can file a suit. She hasn't collected anything and she isn't going to."

"You propose to see to it that she doesn't collect?"

"That's exactly right. You just slapped a nuisance value suit on me, hoping I'd compromise. I've got news for you, Mr. Mason. You ain't going to get a dime."

"And as a result you don't like me?" Mason asked.

"Since you asked me the question and since I'm under oath," Anclitas said, "I don't like any part of you. I don't like the ground you walk on."

"Now then," Mason said, "you took one look at this gun and said that was the gun you had given Helman Ellis."

"That's right."

"You didn't look at the number?"

"I didn't need to. I know the gun."

"What do you know about it?"

"Look," Anclitas said, "my partner bought four guns, Mr. Mason. He bought them all at once. He bought them from the Rowena Hunting and Fishing Store. He brought them to the place of business and gave them to me."

"Do you know the numbers?"

"Why should I know the numbers?" Anclitas asked

in disgust. "I should go around carrying gun numbers in my head!"

"The guns were all alike?" Mason asked.

"All alike. It was a special order."

"Your partner went in and picked them up?"

"I placed the order, and then after the manager of the store told me the guns were in, I sent Slim Marcus down to pick them up."

"The guns were all identical in appearance?"

"That's right."

"Then how can you tell that this was the gun you gave Helman Ellis? How do you distinguish it from any of the other guns if you didn't look at the number?"

"Because I know the gun."

"How do you know it?" Mason asked. "What is distinctive about it? What differentiates it from any of the other guns?"

"Well, for one thing, this particular gun has a little nick on the front sight."

"Anything else?"

"I don't think so."

"Where are the other three guns?"

"I have them."

"Where?"

"At my place of business, naturally. I don't carry three guns with me, one in each hip pocket and one in the side coat pocket," Anclitas said sarcastically.

"If the Court please," Mason said, "I see it is approaching the hour of the afternoon adjournment. I would like to have the witness instructed to return to court tomorrow morning and bring those guns with him."

Hamilton Burger, his face flushed with indignation, was on his feet.

"Here we go again, Your Honor, a typical Perry Mason trick. It's a well-known fact that when Mason gets in a case he starts digging up guns out of anywhere and everywhere. He gets them in the case and juggles them all around and gets everybody confused. Those three guns that George Anclitas has have nothing more to do with this case than the stock of guns in the gun display counter in the Rowena Hunting and Fishing Store."

"I'm inclined to agree with the district attorney," Judge Keyser said. "I fail to see where they have any bearing in this case."

Mason said, "The witness has identified the gun that he gave Helman Ellis by stating that it had a slight nick in the front sight. There were no other marks of identification."

"Well, that one mark of identification is all he needs under the circumstances," Hamilton Burger blazed.

Mason abruptly pushed the gun into the district attorney's hands. "All right," he said, "if that's the way you feel about it, point out the nick in the front sight so the Court can see it."

Hamilton Burger shouted, "Point it out yourself! I'm not taking orders from you!"

"Then perhaps we'll let the witness point it out," Mason said. "I only suggested you do it because you were so positive that this mark of identification was sufficient. I will hand the gun to the witness and ask him to point out the identifying mark on the front sight."

Mason turned to Anclitas. "Perhaps, Mr. Anclitas, you'll be good enough to leave the witness stand, step up here and point out the notch or nick on the front sight to the Court and to the district attorney."

"He can point it out to the Court," Hamilton Burger said. "He doesn't need to point it out to the district attorney. The district attorney knows what gun this is. The district attorney does want to state to the Court, however, that the greatest care should be taken to see that these tags marking the guns as Exhibits are not switched. At the moment, defense counsel has two guns in this case, and if he's given the faintest opportunity—"

"That will do," Judge Keyser interrupted coldly. "There is no occasion for such statements. The witness will step forward and point out the nick on the front sight of the gun to the Court."

Anclitas came forward, said, "It isn't so much of a nick, really, just a place where the metal was scraped. We had an argument about whether a manicurist's nail file was hard enough to cut steel, and I drew the edge of the file along here. I—"

Abruptly Anclitas stopped, looked at the gun, then turned the gun over, held it to the light and said, "Well, I guess it wore off. It wasn't a deep cut in the metal, just a place where we'd sort of cut through the bluing on the steel."

Judge Keyser leaned forward. "But I don't see *any* place where the bluing has been cut through."

"Neither do I," Anclitas admitted.

"Yet," Perry Mason said, "this was the only mark of

identification on which you said you relied in swearing
under oath that this was the gun you had given Helman
Ellis."

"Well, it was found in his boat, wasn't it?"

"The question is," Mason said, "how *you* can be
sure."

Anclitas turned the gun over and over in his hand.
"Well," he said, "I'm certain, that's all. I just know this
is the gun but . . . well, I don't seem to see the place
where the nail file left a mark on the front sight."

Mason, feeling his way cautiously, said, "Now, let me
see if I understand you, Mr. Anclitas. You bought four
guns at one time?"

"That's right."

"And one of those guns you gave to Helman Ellis?"

"I've already said so half a dozen times."

"And there was a dispute as to whether an ordinary
manicurist's nail file was hard enough to leave a mark
on a gun barrel?"

"Yes, sir."

"And was a bet made on that?"

"Yes, sir."

"With whom?"

"With my partner, Slim Marcus."

"How much was the bet?"

"Fifty dollars."

"Do you remember how the subject came up?"

"Oh, Your Honor," Hamilton Burger said, "this is
completely incompetent, irrelevant and immaterial. It's
not proper cross-examination. Counsel is quite obviously simply trying to prolong proceedings past the

hour of adjournment, hoping that during the evening he can think of some more questions to ask Mr. Anclitas.

"I have already pointed out that it would be inconvenient for Mr. Anclitas to return to—"

Judge Keyser interrupted. "We still have a few minutes, Mr. District Attorney. The question of the identification of this gun having been opened up, and the witness having stated that he identified it solely from the mark of a manicurist's nail file left in the front sight, I certainly think counsel is within his rights. The objection is overruled. Answer the question, Mr. Anclitas."

"Well," Anclitas said, "we were talking about the different guns and I suggested they should be marked, that we had four guns and there was no way of telling one from the other unless we looked at the numbers. So I suggested we file little marks on the barrel of the guns; one mark on one gun, two on the next, three on the next and four on the other.

"Slim Marcus, my partner, thought it was a good idea, but we couldn't find a file so I said we'd go over to the barbershop and borrow a nail file from the manicurist, and he said a nail file wasn't hard enough to cut the barrel of a gun. I got in an argument about it and bet him fifty dollars."

"So what happened?" Mason asked.

"So we took the gun, went over to the barbershop, borrowed the manicurist's file, made the mark on the front sight of the gun, and I collected fifty dollars."

"Thereafter was your idea carried out, of marking each of the guns?"

"No. Slim was mad over losing the bet and thought

that I had framed the whole deal. He accused me of having experimented in advance of making the bet."

"Now, you state that this gun which had the mark on the front sight was the one that you gave Helman Ellis?"

"I certainly thought it was."

"What were the circumstances?"

"Well, after we had this bet I was carrying the gun back to the bar. It was a gun we kept underneath the bar just below the cash register so that in case of a holdup we could protect ourselves.

"Helman Ellis was standing there by the bar and saw me carrying the gun and wanted to know if I had been trying to make a collection from some customer who didn't want to pay or something of the sort—he made some joke about it, and one thing led to another and he started admiring the gun and finally I gave it to him. I felt it would be good business. Helman Ellis was becoming a regular customer and—well, I make no secret of it, I wanted to cultivate him."

"Why?" Mason asked.

"Because," Anclitas said angrily, "I'm running a place of business and I make my profit by having customers."

"Then in your mind there is no question whatever but that the weapon you gave Helman Ellis was the one that had the file mark on the front sight?"

"That's right."

"Yet you don't find this mark on the front sight here now, and therefore I take it you wish to change your statement that this was the gun you gave Helman Ellis?"

"I'm not changing anything," Anclitas said sullenly.

"That's the gun that was found on the Ellis boat; it's the gun I gave Ellis."

"But the distinguishing mark is no longer on the front sight."

"It may have worn off."

"You had no other means of identifying the gun?"

"Just by its appearance."

"When you testified, you gave as your sole reason for identifying the gun—"

"Your Honor," Hamilton Burger interrupted, "this question has been asked and answered half a dozen times. The witness has given his best opinion. We now know the facts. We aren't going to gain anything by having counsel carry on an argument with this witness. I—"

A deputy who had hurried into the courtroom moved up to Hamilton Burger and tugged at his coat sleeve.

Burger turned in annoyance, saw the expression on the deputy's face, said to the judge, "Just a moment, please, Your Honor. May I be indulged for just a few minutes? Apparently a matter of some importance has arisen."

Burger engaged in a whispered conference with the deputy. At first Burger's face showed complete incredulity, then surprise, then as the deputy continued to whisper forcefully, a slow grin began to appear on the district attorney's face.

Abruptly he nodded to the deputy, turned to the Court.

"If the Court please," he said, "a matter of transcendent importance has arisen in this case. I am going to call Perry Mason to the stand as my next witness."

"You can't do that," Judge Keyser said, then at the expression on Hamilton Burger's face, said, "unless, of course, there is some factual matter which can be cleared up by defense counsel. But certainly defense counsel is hardly qualified as a witness to appear against his client."

"As it happens, Your Honor," Hamilton Burger said, "and in order to explain the reason for my action, it seems that one Maurice Halstead, a very competent fire-arms expert engaged in ballistic examinations, was given a gun by Perry Mason's representative and was asked to fire several test bullets from that gun.

"When it appeared that there was some question about the two bullets in this case having been fired from different guns, Mr. Halstead communicated with my office to state that, while he wished to protect his relations with his client, he did not wish to be put in the position of concealing evidence. He asked that Mr. Red-field, the ballistics expert who has already testified in this case, make a confidential examination of the test bullets. If they had not been fired from the murder weapon, he asked that Mr. Redfield say nothing about the matter. If, on the other hand, they had been so fired and therefore were evidence, Maurice Halstead did not care to be put in the position of suppressing evidence."

Burger turned to Perry Mason and said significantly, "It is unfortunate that all persons are not actuated by such high standards of professional conduct."

Judge Keyser, plainly interested, was leaning forward. "Go on, Mr. District Attorney. Kindly avoid personalities. Make any statement that you wish to the

Court, since this is a case being tried without a jury."

"The test bullets fired from the gun given Maurice Halstead by Perry Mason are an undoubted match with the bullet which we have referred to as bullet number two in this case, the one which previously we had been unable to identify.

"We now have a situation, Your Honor, where it appears that one fatal bullet was fired from a weapon which was in the possession of Perry Mason, that the second bullet—which *may* have been fired some time after death—was fired from a gun which had been in the custody of Mr. Perry Mason.

"The inference is obvious. The defendant in this case came to Perry Mason with a gun which had fired a fatal bullet into the body of Nadine Ellis. I won't at this time make any accusations, but it seems that that gun very mysteriously left the possession of the defendant and that the defendant was given a gun which could only have been given her by her counsel, Perry Mason. And it is at least an inference that she was instructed to return to the scene of the crime and fire a second bullet from that gun into the body of the victim.

"This, coming at a time when counsel had recently been investigating the law concerning two persons firing fatal shots into a body, certainly tells its own story.

"It is one thing for counsel to advise a person accused of crime and try to protect the rights of that person, but it is quite another thing for an attorney to become an accessory to murder.

"Counsel has been under suspicion before. This time by a fortunate circumstance the evidence exists which has—"

"That will do, Mr. District Attorney," Judge Keyser interrupted. "You will make no statements about counsel. If you have any matter to take before the Grievance Committee of the Bar Association, you may do so. If you wish to subpoena counsel to appear before the grand jury and have the grand jury investigate the question of whether counsel has become an accessory after the fact, you also have that privilege.

"In this court you are confined to discussing the relevancy of evidence. However, I will state that the statement you have made is certainly ample foundation to enable you to call Mr. Mason to the stand.

"Mr. Mason will take the stand and be sworn as a witness on behalf of the prosecution."

"Just a moment, Your Honor," Mason said, his face granite hard. "Regardless of what the district attorney may wish to prove by me, the fact remains that I am representing the defendant in this case and am entitled to conduct this case in an orderly manner. The witness, George Anclitas, is being cross-examined by me. The witness was called out of order on the statement of the district attorney that it would work a great hardship on him to be forced to return tomorrow. I insist on concluding my cross-examination of the witness."

"And I submit, if the Court please," Hamilton Burger said angrily, "that this is simply an excuse to stall for time. Counsel has actually completed his cross-examination. Any questions he may ask from now on will be purely repetitious."

"It would seem that the examination had reached a logical conclusion," Judge Keyser said. "The Court will state it does not intend to have this cross-examination unduly prolonged. However, counsel is certainly within his rights. The witness Anclitas was put on out of order on the representation of the district attorney that it would work a great hardship on him to have to return tomorrow. Counsel is entitled to complete his cross-examination before any other witness is called, particularly in view of the fact that this witness was put on out of order at the request of the district attorney."

Hamilton Burger yielded the point with poor grace. "I serve notice here and now," he said, "that I am going to insist this cross-examination be conducted within the strict rules of evidence and not used as an excuse to prolong this case."

"Very well," Judge Keyser said, "proceed with your questions, Mr. Mason."

"You are positive that the gun you gave Helman Ellis was the one that you had personally marked with a manicurist's nail file?" Mason asked.

"Objected to as already asked and answered and not proper cross-examination," Hamilton Burger said.

"Sustained," Judge Keyser snapped.

"When this gun was handed to you by the district attorney," Mason said, "when was the last time prior to that occasion that you had seen the weapon?"

"Objected to as already asked and answered and not proper cross-examination."

"Overruled."

"Answer the question," Mason said.

"When I gave the gun to Helman Ellis."

"You're satisfied it's the same gun?"

"Objected to as repetitious, as already asked and answered."

"Sustained."

"You don't know the various numbers on the four guns which you purchased?"

"Objected to as incompetent, irrelevant and immaterial; not proper cross-examination, already asked and answered," Burger said.

"The objection is sustained," Judge Keyser ruled.

"Do you now, or did you at the time you gave the weapon to Helman Ellis, know the number of that weapon?"

"Objected to as incompetent, irrelevant and immaterial; not proper cross-examination."

"The objection is overruled."

"No, I didn't know the number of that particular gun," Anclitas said. "I didn't look at it. I told you all I know. I gave him the gun. That's all I know."

"Have you had occasion to examine the other three guns remaining in your possession?" Mason asked.

"Objected to. Not proper cross-examination," Hamilton Burger said.

"Overruled."

"No, I haven't examined them."

"I would suggest," Mason said, "that during the evening adjournment you examine these guns carefully and see if any one of those three guns does have a mark on the front sight—a mark made by a nail file such as you have described."

"That's counsel's suggestion," Hamilton Burger said, "but you don't have to act on it. I submit to the Court that this witness has given his evidence to the best of his ability."

"There may, however, have been a confusion in the

mind of the witness as to the sequence of events," Judge
Keyser said. "I think it is established that he gave *a* gun
to Helman Ellis. The gun found near the body of Nadine Ellis was a gun which had been sold to George
Anclitas or his associate, Wilton Marcus. The Court is
not very greatly impressed by any of these questions
concerning the mark on the front sight. It is quite apparent that the witness made a perfectly natural mistake in regard to the sequence of events, and unless it
can be shown that there is some significance which is
not presently apparent, the Court is not impressed by
the absence of a file mark on the front sight. If, however, it should appear that such a mark *is* on the front
sight of one of the three guns remaining in the possession of this witness, it might clarify the situation simply
by showing that there was a natural mistake.

"However the Court fails to see where it affects the
issues in this case other than, perhaps, to lay a foundation for cross-examining the witness when the matter
reaches the Superior Court."

"Now then," Mason said, "I want to account for each
one of these weapons. You purchased four weapons. I
want to know where you kept them."

"Your Honor," Hamilton Burger said, "may I object, may I *please* object? This is not proper cross-
examination. If counsel is permitted to go into the
location of each of these four weapons and cross-examine the witness as to how he knows they're the same
weapons, how he knows they were at a certain place at
a certain time, this whole situation will become completely interminable. Counsel is very apparently stalling for time, and time is running out. It is now only

a few minutes before the hour of the evening adjournment."

"Nevertheless," Judge Keyser said, "while the Court intends to be very strict in enforcing the rules of evidence and of cross-examination, the Court is not going to deprive the defendant of her rights simply because a situation has arisen in which defense counsel may well wish for time in order to prepare himself.

"The Court wishes to point out to the prosecutor that if the prosecutor had called Perry Mason to the stand without making this statement in open court, there would have been no opportunity for what the district attorney refers to as stalling."

"I thought I was within my rights in calling him," Hamilton Burger admitted somewhat sheepishly. "I had forgotten that technically he hadn't concluded his cross-examination of George Anclitas."

"That," Judge Keyser said coldly, "was your mistake, not the mistake of the Court. The Court wants to be fair in the matter. The Court will admit that in the face of statements made which apparently have been checked by the prosecutors, the circumstantial evidence indicates a situation of the utmost gravity. The Court will state further that the Court is going to get at the bottom of this and, while the Court intends to permit a reasonable cross-examination of this witness, the Court does not intend to have it unduly prolonged and the Court has now made up its mind that in the event it becomes necessary to take an evening adjournment, the Court is going to have a night session so that this matter can be disposed of without a delay which might tend to prejudice the rights of the parties.

"Now then, Mr. Mason, proceed with your cross-examination. The witness will answer the question. The objection is overruled."

"Will the court reporter read the question?" Mason asked.

The court reporter consulted his records, read the question to the witness: "Now then, I want to account for each one of these weapons. You purchased four weapons. I want to know where you kept them."

"We kept one gun by the cash register at the bar," Anclitas said. "We had one by the registration desk in the motel, and one was in the gaming room."

"You mean the gambling room?" Mason asked.

"I mean the gaming room."

"Where was the other?"

"The other was an extra. Sometimes I carried it when I was taking some money home with me. Sometimes I didn't. It was just sort of hanging around and—well, I guess you could call it an extra. That's why I gave it to Ellis."

"Did you endeavor to keep these guns separate in any way?" Mason asked. "Did you have any designation, either on the gun or on the holster?"

"There wasn't any holster—just the gun lying there where a person could grab it quick if he had to."

"And there was no attempt to designate them? That is, to differentiate one from the other?"

"Only this time that I told you about when we thought we would put some marks on them and then changed our minds."

"Within the last month," Mason said, "have you had any trouble over locating these guns? Has there been any element of confusion at any time within the last month?"

"None whatever," Anclitas said.

"Has one of the guns at any time been missing from its accustomed place?"

"Not that I know of."

"You state that you sometimes carried one of these weapons when you were carrying a large amount of money."

"That's right."

"Does any other person, or did any other person, carry one of those weapons under similar conditions?"

"My partner, Slim, carried one."

"Anyone else?"

"No one else. . . . Now, wait a minute. I think one of the hat-check girls who sometimes stayed at her mother's house and had to go home late at night, carried one for a couple of nights. I stopped her as soon as I found out what she was doing."

"You mean she carried one with her while she was on the job?"

"No, no. She had to take a bus and sometimes when she'd get off—around one or two o'clock in the morning—she was nervous about walking the six blocks to the place where she caught the bus and while she was waiting there. She tried to time her departure so she could leave and catch the bus right on the nose but she didn't dare miss the bus so she had to leave a little early to give herself a margin and sometimes the bus would be a little late. She had an embarrassing experience one night with an exhibitionist and . . . well, she just started borrowing one of the guns to take in her purse."

"Without telling you anything about it?"

"That's right."

"How did you find out about it?"

"She left her purse in the washroom. The attendant didn't know whose purse it was and took it to the office. I opened it to look for identification and found it was this girl's purse and a gun was in it. It looked like one of our guns, and I called her in the office and asked her about it, and then she admitted that she'd borrowed one from behind the counter."

"And you put a stop to it?"

"Sure I put a stop to it. She didn't have any permit to carry the gun in the first place, and in the second place suppose *we'd* been held up and the men behind the bar had reached down for the gun and there wouldn't have been any gun there?"

"But she brought the gun back whenever she took it?"

"Objected to as calling for a conclusion of the witness, as calling for hearsay evidence and not being proper cross-examination. It is incompetent, irrelevant and immaterial," Burger said.

"The objection is sustained," Judge Keyser ruled.

"What is the name of this young woman who borrowed the gun on occasion?"

"She's the hat-check girl."

"What's her name?"

"Sadie Bradford."

"Were there any witnesses present when you gave this gun to Helman Ellis?"

"Only my partner, Slim Marcus."

"And you state that Slim Marcus on occasion carried one of the guns?"

"Objected to as already asked and answered," Hamilton Burger said.

"Sustained," Judge Keyser snapped.

"And aside from this one file mark on the front sight of the gun which you think you gave Ellis, there were no identifying marks on any of the guns. Is that right?"

"Objected to as already asked and answered. Incompetent, irrelevant and immaterial. Not proper cross-examination," Burger said.

"Sustained," Judge Keyser snapped.

Mason glanced at the clock. "I have no further questions of this witness," he said.

Hamilton Burger was instantly on his feet. "Call Perry Mason as a witness for the prosecution."

"Take the stand, Mr. Mason," Judge Keyser said.

"Just a moment, Your Honor," Mason said. "I think counsel is forgetting, and perhaps the Court has overlooked the fact, that when Anclitas was put on the witness stand at the request of the district attorney, who wanted to eliminate the necessity of further attendance by Mr. Anclitas, the witness Helman Ellis was on the stand."

"I had concluded my examination of Mr. Ellis," Hamilton Burger said.

"I don't think the record so shows," Mason said. "I think instead the record shows that you said you thought you would have no more questions of that witness at that time."

"All right, I'll announce now, then, that I have concluded with that witness and I ask Mr. Mason to take the stand."

"Just a minute," Mason said. "I haven't had an opportunity to examine Mr. Ellis on re-cross-examination. If you have concluded your redirect examination I want to cross-examine him."

"You don't have anything to cross-examine him about," Hamilton Burger exploded. "All he testified to on redirect was that he had been given a gun by George Anclitas and he kept it on the yacht."

"I want to cross-examine him on that," Mason said.

"And I want you on the witness stand before you've had a chance to concoct any alibi," Hamilton Burger shouted.

"It is your contention that I am to be deprived of my right to cross-examine Mr. Ellis?"

Hamilton Burger took a deep breath. "Very well," he said, "I'll stipulate that the entire testimony of Helman Ellis may go out. I'll withdraw him as a witness. I'll strike all of his evidence out of the record."

"I won't agree to that," Mason said. "I won't so stipulate."

"Why not?"

"Because I want to cross-examine him."

Hamilton Burger glowered at Mason, then turned toward the Court.

Judge Keyser said, "It is past the hour of the evening adjournment by some minutes, Mr. Burger. I can appreciate the prosecutor's position, but the fact remains that the defense attorney has the right to cross-examine all witnesses called by the prosecution.

"Because I have some commitments and pre-trial

conferences at this time and because I know some of the officers of the court have engagements, I am going to adjourn court at this time but I am going to reconvene at eight o'clock tonight. We are going to have an evening session. I think under the circumstances the prosecution is entitled to have its case presented expeditiously."

"The defense objects," Mason said. "It is inconvenient for me personally, and I feel that the defendant is being deprived of her rights."

Judge Keyser shook his head. "I'm not going to permit any technicalities to stand in the way of getting this matter disposed of. The Court will take a recess until eight o'clock this evening, at which time all persons under subpoena in this case will return to the courtroom.

"Court's adjourned."

CHAPTER THIRTEEN

MASON PACED the office floor in frowning concentration.

Della Street presided over an electric coffee percolator. A paper bag of doughnuts was on the office desk.

From time to time Mason would stop, take a few sips from a cup of coffee and munch on a doughnut.

"You're going to need something more nourishing than that," Della Street said anxiously. "Let me go down to the restaurant and get you a ham sandwich or a hamburger or—"

Mason motioned her to silence with a wave of his hand, once more resumed his pacing of the floor.

After nearly a minute he said absentmindedly, "Thanks, Della." And then after some two minutes added, "I've got to think."

"Can I help by asking questions?"

"Try it," Mason said. "No, wait a minute. *I'll* ask *you* the questions. You give me the answers. Let's see if I can detect anything wrong."

She nodded.

Mason whirled abruptly, stood facing her with his feet spread apart, his shoulders squared, his manner

one that he sometimes used in cross-examining a witness.

"That gun Ellen Robb had," he said, "was locked in
our safe from the time Ellen Robb entered the office
until we returned it with one exception—when Drake
took it to the ballistics expert. Now then, how could a
bullet from that gun be in Nadine Ellis' body unless
Ellen Robb fired it there?"

"It couldn't," Della Street said. "The time has come,
Chief, when you've got to throw your client overboard.
She's committed murder and she's lied to you."

"Now then," Mason went on without noticing Della
Street's answer, "I took a gun out of my safe, a gun that
we'll call the Loring Crowder gun. She put that gun in
her purse. A bullet from *that* gun was *also* found in the
body of Nadine Ellis. *How* did it get there?"

"The bullet was fired from the gun," Della Street
said, "that's how it got there," and then added quickly,
"not that I'm trying to be facetious, Chief. I'm just
pointing out that the striation marks on the bullets
show that it was fired from that gun. We have to face
facts and we may as well face them now."

"All right," Mason said, "it was fired from that gun.
Who fired it?"

"Ellen Robb *had* to fire it."

Mason said, "One thing we know for a fact and that
is, the bullets couldn't have been fired simultaneously.
They must have been fired after a very considerable
time interval, probably an interval of hours. That's one
thing *we* know that the police and the district attorney
don't know. We have that much of an advantage."

"Why is it an advantage?" Della Street asked.

"Because we know something about sequence. We know that the bullet from the Crowder gun must have been fired into Nadine Ellis' dead body. Now then, once we establish that, Della, I'm not tied up with anything except being an accessory to having fired a bullet into a dead body. That's perhaps a misdemeanor—I haven't looked it up. Certainly it isn't homicide of any sort or an attempt to commit homicide."

Della Street nodded.

"On the other hand," Mason said, "I'm hoist by my own petard. Here I have been talking about this freak decision that holds that it's not murder to fire a bullet that would prove fatal into the body of a victim, if some independent agency fires another bullet into the victim and that second bullet results in death. I am assuming, of course, that the first person could be charged with assault with intent to commit murder. However, because I dug out these decisions, no one is going to believe anything *I* may say. The sequence is too, too damning. It looks as if I had tried to save a client by legal skulduggery and the juggling of evidence."

Della Street said, "Ellen Robb was sitting right here in the office when you were talking on the telephone with Darwin C. Gowrie, the attorney for Nadine Ellis. She heard you tell all about the subtle distinction in the decisions. She made notes in shorthand. You weren't advising her, you were advising Gowrie.

"Let's assume Ellen is a very smart young woman. She had killed Nadine Ellis with one shot fired from the gun which she said she had found in her baggage. When you juggled guns on her she knew it, and she took advantage of your attempt to aid her by taking the second gun—the Crowder gun which you had substituted in place of the gun she had when she entered the office—and went out and fired a second bullet into the body of Nadine Ellis."

Mason suddenly snapped his fingers. "We're overlooking one thing," he said. "We may have the time element *all* cockeyed."

"How come?" she asked.

"Suppose," Mason said, "the bullet from the Anclitas gun was fired into Nadine Ellis' body *after* the bullet from the Crowder gun?"

"It couldn't have been," Della Street said.

"Why not?"

"Because that gun was locked in our safe after you gave the Crowder gun to Ellen Robb."

"No, it wasn't," Mason said. "There's one very suspicious circumstance about that gun which we're overlooking. We took it down to Anclitas' place and planted it in the women's room."

Della Street's eyes became animated.

"Suppose we do have the order of the bullet wounds reversed," she exclaimed. "Suppose the first bullet was from the Crowder gun. Then the second bullet must have been from the Anclitas gun."

Mason nodded.

"Then you mean *after* the gun was returned to the powder room, George Anclitas took the gun, went out and fired a second shot into the dead body of Nadine Ellis?"

Mason nodded.

Della Street's eyes were sparking now. "That would account for the fact that he said nothing about having found the gun in the powder room. He must have missed it and must have had a pretty good idea of what had happened."

"What had happened?" Mason asked.

"That Ellen Robb had killed Nadine Ellis with it."

"But if this theory is correct," Mason said, "she wasn't killed with that gun. She was killed with the Crowder gun."

"All right," Della Street said, "we won't try to figure out how George knew Nadine Ellis was dead. But he did, for reasons of his own, take that gun, go out and fire another bullet into the dead body of Nadine Ellis."

"Now, wait a minute," Mason said. "You say he went out and did it. Remember that Nadine Ellis was out on a yacht and, figuring the dry fuel tank, the fact that the fuel tank had been filled when Helman Ellis and his wife were planning to take a cruise, the location of the boat, the yacht must have been out at sea for some time, and it would have been a physical impossibility for Anclitas to have taken the gun after we returned it, found the yacht and fired the second bullet. But if that had happened, the marks I made in the barrel with the etching tool would show up. Redfield would have noticed them."

"Then," Della Street said, suddenly discouraged, "it *must* have been done before, and your client has to be the one who did it."

Mason shook his head. "I'm still fighting for my client, Della."

Della Street said, "She's a millstone around your neck. You'd better cut her loose and start swimming. After all, you acted in good faith. You thought that

Anclitas had planted a gun in her things and was going to accuse her of stealing that gun. You wanted to cross him up."

Mason nodded. "I wanted to handle the situation in such a dramatic manner that we would teach George Anclitas a lesson," he said. "You can see how my unorthodox tactics backfired."

"But can't you explain what you were trying to do when you get on the witness stand?"

"Sure, I can explain," Mason said, "but no one is going to believe me. Bear in mind that I had previously pointed out that when two independent agencies fired bullets into a body, only the person firing the last shot was guilty of murder, provided the first shot hadn't proven instantly fatal.

"The circumstantial evidence certainly indicates that Ellen Robb came to me, that she told me she had killed Nadine Ellis, that I told her to give me the gun, that I gave her another gun and told her to go out and fire another shot into the body of Nadine Ellis, that I intended to use my trick defense. Also that I then went back and planted the gun in George Anclitas' place of business hoping that he would make a commotion about it and I could involve him in the murder."

"Well, what *are* you going to do?" Della Street asked.

"I wish I knew," Mason said. "All I know is, I'm going to go down fighting and I'm not going to throw my client overboard."

"Not even to save your own skin?"

Mason shook his head.

"You'll be disbarred."

"All right then," Mason said. "I'll find some other

line of work. I'm not going to betray a client. That's
final."

"Not even to tell the true facts?"

"I'll have to tell the true *facts*," Mason said. "I can
keep them from finding out what my client told me.
Any conversations we had are privileged communica-
tions. As my secretary you share in the professional
privilege. They can't make me tell anything that my
client said for the purpose of getting me to take the
case or any advice that I gave her."

"But they can ask you if you substituted guns?" Della
Street asked.

"There," Mason said, "I'm stuck. Unless I refuse to
answer on the ground that to do so would incriminate
me."

"Well, why not do that? They can't prove anything
except by inference."

Paul Drake's code knock sounded on the exit door of
Mason's private office, and Mason nodded to Della
Street. "Let Paul in, Della. Let's see what he knows, if
anything."

Della Street opened the door.

Paul Drake, looking as lugubrious as a poker player
who has failed to fill a straight which was open at both
ends, sized up the situation, said, "Hi, folks," walked
over to the paper bag, abstracted a doughnut and accepted the cup of coffee that Della Street handed him.

"Well?" Mason asked.

Drake shook his head. "This is the end of the road,
Perry."

"What do you know?" Mason asked.

"This time you have a client who really and truly

lied to you. She's in it up to her beautiful eyebrows and she's dragged you in it with her."

"How come?" Mason asked.

Drake said, "She and Helman Ellis were really ga-ga. Anclitas is telling the truth."

"Go on," Mason said, as Drake paused as though groping for the right words in which to go on.

"You remember," Drake said, "when Ellen Robb came to you after she had been thrown out of The Big Barn and had the shiner?"

Mason nodded.

"She told you she had taken a taxi to the Surf and Sea Motel and you told her to go back there?"

Again Mason nodded.

"Well," Drake said, "when she first went to the Surf and Sea Motel, it was to meet Helman Ellis."

Mason resumed pacing the floor. "How long was Ellis there?" he asked Drake.

"About half an hour."

Suddenly Mason shook his head. "That doesn't mean necessarily that my client was lying," he said. "It means that Helman Ellis was following her."

Drake said, "This is the part that hurts, Perry. He wasn't following her. He arrived before she did."

"What?"

"That's right."

"How do you know?"

"My operative talked with the man who runs the place. Now that Ellen Robb has been arrested, he's beginning to think back in his own mind, trying to recall things that would indicate either that Ellen was an innocent young woman who is being framed or that she was guilty. He's naturally interested in the whole situation and he remembered that before Ellen Robb showed up on Tuesday night, a car drove up to the motel, turned in at the entrance, circled through the grounds and then went out, as though the driver might have been looking for someone. At first he thought the man was going to register and ask for a room, so when the car slowed down, this manager jotted down the license number on a scratch pad."

"The license number?" Mason asked.

"That's right," Drake said. "You know the way they register in motels. The man writes down his name and address and the make and model of his car and the license number.

"Nine people out of ten forget the license number and it's something of a nuisance because the manager has to go out and look at the license plate and jot down the number. So this fellow keeps a pad of scratch paper by the desk, and when a car drives in, there's a powerful light shining on the car from the porch of the office. The manager automatically jots down the license number and then when the people register he doesn't have to go out and look at the license number in case they've forgotten it. And in case they give him a phony license number, he knows it immediately and can be on his guard."

"Go on," Mason said.

"Well, the manager jotted down the guy's license number. Then the fellow didn't come in to ask for a room but turned around, drove out front and parked. So the manager tore off the sheet of paper containing the license number, crumpled it and started to put it in the wastebasket. Then he thought perhaps the man was waiting for a woman companion to show up so he smoothed the piece of paper out again and put it in his desk drawer.

"Well, about ten minutes later Ellen Robb showed up in a taxi. The manager took her registration and assigned her to a cabin."

"And then he saw Ellis come and join her?" Mason asked.

"No, he didn't," Drake said, "but he did see Ellis get out of the car and walk up to the motel, apparently going in to call on somebody, and the manager *assumed* it was Ellen Robb, the unescorted woman who had registered."

"And so the manager did what?" Mason asked.

"Did nothing," Drake said. "After all, motels aren't conducted along the lines of young women's seminaries, and the manager isn't in any position to censor a young woman's callers. If he tried to do that, he'd be involved in more damage suits than you could shake a stick at, and the motel would be out of business in about two weeks. Motel managers have to take things as they come. All they watch out for is that people don't get noisy and make a nuisance out of themselves or that some woman doesn't move in and start soliciting. Even in that event they're pretty cautious, but there are certain things that give them a tip-off in cases of that sort. That type of woman usually has a certain appearance that a manager can detect, and they almost invariably work in pairs."

"All right, give me the rest of it," Mason said. "How bad is it?"

"Plenty bad," Drake said, "and the worst of it is, my man is the one who uncovered it."

"What do you mean?"

"Well, he was trying to dig up something that would help so he went down to the manager of the motel and started talking with him and asking him questions about Ellen Robb. You see, we got a bodyguard for her, Perry, but there was almost a full day before the bodyguard got there and—well, if anything phony had been pulled, that was when it must have been pulled, so my man started asking questions about what had happened when Ellen Robb registered and what had happened right afterwards, whether she had any visitors.

"So then the motel manager recalled this man and—"

"Get a good look at him?" Mason asked.

"Apparently a hell of a good look," Drake said. "The fellow walked right past the light which shines out from the office, and the manager described the guy. The description fits Helman Ellis to a T. Moreover, after my man got to asking questions, the fellow remembered that he'd smoothed out this crumpled sheet of paper with the license number on it and had put it in the drawer of the desk. Then the next day he put in some timetables and some memos and he wondered if that crumpled piece of paper might not still be in there.

"So sure enough, he dug into the drawer and pulled out that crumpled piece of paper. There's one break in the case."

"What's that?" Mason asked.

"My man pretended that the incident didn't have any particular importance and managed to get possession of that crumpled piece of paper. We've checked the license number. It's the number of Helman Ellis' automobile."

"That little tramp!" Della Street said bitterly. "Double-crossing us like that!"

Mason said, "She swore up and down there was nothing between her and Ellis, that she hadn't seen him since before that final blowup at The Big Barn Tuesday night."

"I take it," Drake said dryly, "that leaves you behind the eight ball."

"Just as far behind the eight ball as you can get," Mason said. "Now I *know* my client was lying and that puts me in the position of being an accomplice."

"Perry," Drake asked, "did you actually substitute guns?"

Mason said, "I don't need any rehearsal, Paul."

"What do you mean?"

"Hamilton Burger is going to pour the questions at me and I'll be busy answering them then. If you want to know what happened, listen to me on the witness stand."

"If you *did*," Drake said, "the murder must have been committed during the period between—"

Mason suddenly snapped his fingers. "Wait a minute, Paul. What's the time element in this thing?"

"What do you mean?" Drake asked.

Mason said, "Our office work sheets show the time that Ellen Robb left the office. Now then, I'll tell you this much, Paul. If a bullet was fired into the body of

Nadine Ellis from the gun which Ellen Robb had with her when she was arrested, it had to be fired during the interval of time between the hour she left the office here, Wednesday morning, and the time she showed up at the Surf and Sea Motel. So let's check the time element there."

"What good will that do?" Drake asked. "You *know* she had the opportunity because she did it. There must have been sufficient time for the murder to have been committed because she *did* go to the yacht and she *did* fire the bullet from that gun—if the district attorney's theory is right and you switched guns on her—and I take it that the theory is right."

"Take any theory you want to," Mason said. "I'm not making any admissions—not yet."

"Well, I can give you the time she checked in at the motel," Drake said. "It was at eleven-fifty, Tuesday night."

Mason nodded to Della Street. "Let's get our work sheets, Della. Let's see what time she left the office."

Della Street opened the date book to the date, ran down the page of the date book and said, "She arrived here at nine-twenty on the morning of Wednesday the tenth and left at nine-forty-five."

Mason said, "Mrs. Ellis was alive Wednesday morning. Her husband saw her early that morning."

"She couldn't have committed the crime after seven on Wednesday evening," Drake said, "because we had a bodyguard on the job. She was virtually under surveillance. Moreover, she went to the motel in a taxicab Tuesday night. Wednesday morning she went out before the manager saw her. Presumably she went to the bus station, took a bus and then a cab to your office. She left your office, took a bus back to Costa Mesa and then a taxi to the motel.

"We've traced her on the journey back to Costa Mesa and there's no question of the time schedule there. The manager is certain she didn't leave the motel again Wednesday afternoon, and then our bodyguards were on the job.

"So she must have killed Mrs. Ellis on the yacht between 6:00 A.M. Wednesday when the evidence shows Mrs. Ellis left for the yacht, and the time she would have had to have taken a bus to get to your office Wednesday morning."

"Provided she took a bus," Mason said. "She could have used taxicabs, and stopped by the yacht club long enough to have committed the murder and then gone to my office."

Drake said, "Ten to one, Perry, that's exactly what she did, and Hamilton Burger is going to come up with the cabdrivers who will identify her."

Mason was thoughtful. "You had men watching the unit of the motel. You were guarding against people who might have tried to hurt her, but she wasn't under surveillance."

Drake shook his head. "There was only one door in that motel unit, Perry. My men were watching to see that no one went in who might intend to make trouble and, by the same sign, they can also be sure that no one went out."

"Your men are thoroughly dependable?" Mason asked.

"The best."

"And they keep records?"

"Just like your own time records," Drake said.

"The men didn't leave for anything?"

"Not a thing," Drake said. "There were two men on the job. When one of them would go to report or powder his nose, the other man would be there waiting. You told me you wanted a one-hundred per cent job of bodyguarding and you got a one-hundred per cent job of bodyguarding."

"And when I went out there," Mason said. "I told you to dismiss the bodyguards."

"You told me to dismiss the bodyguards, but Mrs. Ellis was dead by that time—that was shortly before Ellen Robb was arrested."

A slow smile twitched at the corners of Paul Drake's mouth. "Perhaps," he said, "you can get Hamilton Burger's theory fouled up on the time element but . . ." He let his voice trail into silence, then shrugged his shoulders.

"Exactly," Mason said. "Your mind has run up against the fact that the proof is mathematical. The bullet was fired from that gun. If I gave her that gun, Paul, she fired the bullet from it after I gave it to her. And she simply had to have had time to fire the bullet, regardless of *when* she fired the bullet."

"But if Nadine Ellis was dead at the time the second bullet was fired," Drake said, "the crime is simply that of desecrating a corpse. That's only a misdemeanor. It may not be that."

"You're forgetting the implications," Mason said. "If she knew where the body was and if she went and fired a second bullet into it, it was because she had committed the murder and was taking advantage of this legal technicality she overheard me discuss over the telephone."

Mason looked at his wrist watch, sighed, and said, "Well, this is the end of a perfect day, Paul. We're going to have to leave for court in order to be there at eight o'clock. As long as I can find some way to cross-examine Ellis, I can stall off the fatal blow, but the minute I quit asking him questions Burger will call me as a witness and then I'm all washed up—and the worst of it is Judge Keyser knows exactly what the score is and doesn't intend to let me stall. I've got to use all my ingenuity to prolong this case until I can figure out some way of keeping off that witness stand."

Mason helped Della Street on with her coat, switched off the lights.

As they went out the door Paul Drake said, "I know now how a fellow feels when they come to get him on the day of the execution and start leading him along the last mile to the gas chamber."

"Nice feeling, isn't it?" Della Street said.

Mason might not have heard them. His eyes thoughtful, he walked toward the elevators with the same steady rhythm that had marked his pacing of the office floor.

CHAPTER FOURTEEN

JUDGE KEYSER surveyed the crowded courtroom with stern eyes as he stood at the bench. Then he seated himself, and the bailiff said, "Be seated."

Hamilton Burger arose. "Your Honor," he said, "pursuant to the understanding and the demand of defense counsel, George Anclitas has here in this brief case the three weapons from his place of business.

"I wish to submit to the Court that one of these guns which have been produced is of some significant evidentiary value in the case, because it now appears that one of these guns fired the other bullet which was taken from the body of Nadine Ellis.

"If the Court please, since there is no jury here, I am going to state to the Court certain facts in connection with these guns.

"We have in evidence the gun which was found in the yacht, the *Cap's Eyes*. This gun was the one which was purchased by George Anclitas' partner and given to Helman Ellis by George Anclitas. We will call this the Ellis gun. It is Exhibit E in this case.

"We also have the revolver, Exhibit B, which was found in the possession of the defendant.

"Now, just in order to keep the records straight, I wish to state that during the recess the ballistics expert, Alexander Redfield, fired test bullets from the three guns which were in the possession of George Anclitas. This was done for the purpose of protecting our interests in the case. It is a well-known fact that when he is defending a client in a murder case Mr. Perry Mason can juggle guns around so that the Court, the witnesses and the issues become confused. We don't want that to happen in this case.

"Now then I will state that, to the surprise of the prosecution, it turns out that one of these guns in the possession of George Anclitas *did* fire the bullet which was recovered from the body of Nadine Ellis and which bullet is in evidence as People's Exhibit C-1.

"Despite the fact the barrel has since been defaced, we are in a position to show that this is the same gun which was submitted to Maurice Halstead for test purposes, that it was in the possession of Mr. Perry Mason; that is, it was given to Maurice Halstead by Paul Drake, a detective employed by Perry Mason in this case.

"This gives us three weapons which are either involved in the case or which will be involved in the case. That leaves two more weapons which are not involved in any way in the case, and I now suggest that the Court make an order releasing George Anclitas from further attendance and releasing him from any obligation in response to a defense *subpoena duces tecum* to bring those guns into court.

"We have a total of three revolvers here, and I propose to see that those revolvers are kept separate and described in such a way that there can be no confusion.

I certainly don't want to have any more weapons brought into the case. I am making this statement, not as evidence, but simply in order to apprise the Court of the situation and in connection with a motion asking the Court to release George Anclitas from further attendance and removing those two guns, which have nothing to do with the case, from the courtroom."

"Now, just a minute," Judge Keyser said. "The Court wants to know one thing. This gun which fired the bullet, Exhibit C-1, has a mark on the front sight where a nail file cut a groove in it?"

"Yes, Your Honor," Hamilton Burger said. "However, I will state that I am satisfied this could not have been the gun which was given to Ellis.

"I think there can be no question but that this witness was the victim of an honest mistake when he stated that this mark had been made upon the front sight of the gun which was given to Helman Ellis. We have proof of that. Helman Ellis remembers the circumstances perfectly, and I expect to show by him exactly what did happen. I had announced that I was finished with the witness so that I could call Perry Mason to the stand, but since Mason refused to stipulate the entire testimony of the witness could go out, and since the witness is in court—having merely been withdrawn from the stand so George Anclitas could take the stand—I now wish to recall the witness, Ellis, to the stand."

Judge Keyser looked meaningly at Perry Mason and said, "In view of the fact that this is only a preliminary hearing, that the Court has called for a night session in order to clear up certain matters, the Court certainly

doesn't intend to permit counsel for either side to con-
sume time with any general fishing expeditions. The
questions and answers will conform to the strict rules
of evidence.

"Now, Mr. Burger, you may proceed. Mr. Ellis, return
to the stand, please."

Hamilton Burger, glancing at the clock, looking back
at the spectators, noticing the array of newspaper reporters in the front row, smiled triumphantly and said,
"Mr. Ellis, do you recall the circumstances under which
Mr. Anclitas gave you a revolver?"

"Very clearly."

"Will you state to the Court what those circumstances
were?"

"Mr. Anclitas and his partner, W. W. Marcus, had
made a bet of some kind about a revolver. I didn't
know exactly what the bet was but I did see Slim Marcus—I beg the Court's pardon, I mean W. W. Marcus
—pay fifty dollars to George Anclitas and at that time
Mr. Anclitas was holding a gun in his hand. I admired
the gun and said that I was going to get one for purpose of protection and at that time Slim—that is, Mr.
Marcus—reached under the counter or bar and pulled
out a gun which was exactly similar and said something
to the effect that, 'We have too many guns. We might
as well give him one' and at that time George Anclitas
presented me with the gun which Mr. Marcus had
handed to me.

"That, however, was not the gun which Mr. Anclitas
had been holding in his hand when he returned from
the barbershop and beauty parlor where he and his
partner had been making a bet."

Hamilton Burger nodded and smiled at the Court. "That explains it, I think, Your Honor," he said. "I have no further questions."

"Do you have some cross-examination?" Judge Keyser asked Perry Mason.

"Yes, Your Honor."

"Please be advised that under the circumstances the Court will try to give you all reasonable latitude in cross-examination but will not countenance any tactics to gain time or any questions which may be asked for the purpose of delay," Judge Keyser said. "You may proceed with the cross-examination."

"Are you in love with the defendant in this case?" Mason asked.

"No, sir."

"Were you at any time in love with her?"

"Objected to as not proper cross-examination," Hamilton Burger said.

"Overruled," Judge Keyser announced.

"I think I was at one time. At least I was infatuated with her."

"Is it true that your wife discovered this infatuation?" Mason asked.

"Objected to as not proper cross-examination," Hamilton Burger said.

Mason said, "If the Court please, the prosecution's own witnesses have stated that there was a scene between the defendant and Nadine Ellis. I am entitled to cross-examine this witness on it."

"If the Court please," Hamilton Burger said, "of course we showed that altercation, and if counsel had wanted to cross-examine *that* witness on *that* altercation he had that right, but *this* witness has given no such testimony and therefore *this* is not proper cross-examination."

"Except insofar as it may go to show bias of the witness," Judge Keyser said, hesitating perceptibly in an attempt to be scrupulously fair.

"What has happened in the past doesn't show the bias of the witness," Hamilton Burger said. "The fact that his wife became jealous doesn't show the witness' bias. The question is, what is in the mind of the witness at the present time? What is his relation toward the defendant? What are his thoughts? What are his feelings? His bias? His prejudice? Or his lack of bias or prejudice?"

"And I submit, if the Court please," Mason said, "that the only proper way to show that is not by asking the witness how he feels but by showing the relationship which has existed between the parties."

"I think that is correct," Judge Keyser said, "but I will not permit a report of an account of an altercation between the decedent and the defendant by way of cross-examination at this time and of this witness."

"I'll reframe the question," Mason said.

Mason turned to the witness. "At a time when your wife and the defendant had an altercation over you, and accusations were made by your wife, were you present and did you take any part in the altercation?"

"Same objection," Hamilton Burger said.

"This question is permissible," Judge Keyser said.

"I make the further objection that it assumes a fact not in evidence."

"But it is in evidence," Judge Keyser said, "not by

this witness but by your own witnesses. The objection is overruled. Answer the question."

"I took no part," Ellis said.

"Did you see the defendant on the eighth of this month?"

"Yes, sir."

"At The Big Barn where she was working?"

"Yes, sir."

"Were you present when she was discharged on Tuesday, the ninth?"

"No, sir."

"Did you see her that same night after she had been discharged?"

"I saw her before she was discharged."

"That isn't the question. Did you see her afterwards?"

"I . . . I don't remember."

"Let's see if we can refresh your memory," Mason said. "The defendant went to the Surf and Sea Motel in Costa Mesa. Did you go there?"

"Yes, that's right. I did."

"And saw her there?"

"Very briefly."

"When did you next see her?"

"I don't remember. I think . . . I don't think I saw her after that until she had been arrested."

"You don't remember?"

"I can't say positively, no, sir."

"This was a girl with whom you had been infatuated and yet you can't remember whether you saw her or not?"

"Sure I saw her but it was after she had been arrested. I can't remember. I saw her so many times that it was difficult to keep them straight."

"You remember seeing her at the Surf and Sea Motel?"

"Yes, sir."

"That was on the night of Tuesday, the ninth of this month?"

"Yes, sir."

"How long did you see her on that occasion?"

"About ten or fifteen minutes."

"Where did you go after you left the defendant that night?"

"Objected to as incompetent, irrelevant and not proper cross-examination," Hamilton Burger said. "This witness is not on trial."

"I have a right to test his recollection," Mason said.

"You're trying to test his recollection in regard to matters which have absolutely nothing to do with the case," Hamilton Burger said. "If you start following every move made by this witness over the period of time from Tuesday, the ninth, until the body of his wife was discovered, you'll have this court sitting here all night inquiring into matters which have absolutely nothing to do with the case."

"The objection is sustained," Judge Keyser said.

"Did your wife tell you that she had been advised by her attorney that in case two bullets were fired into a body by two persons acting independently that only the person firing the bullet which actually resulted in death was guilty of murder?" Mason asked.

"Objected to as incompetent, irrelevant and immaterial, calling for hearsay, not proper cross-examination," Hamilton Burger said.

"Sustained," Judge Keyser snapped.

"You were at The Big Barn on the night of Tuesday, the ninth?"

"Yes."

"All right," Mason said, "I'm going to put it to you directly. Didn't you at that time take possession of one of the guns in The Big Barn? Now remember, you're under oath."

"What do you mean by 'take possession'?"

"I'm asking you," Mason said, "if you didn't arrange with Sadie Bradford to pick up one of the guns and turn it over to you."

"Just a moment, Your Honor," Hamilton Burger said. "This is getting far afield. This is not proper cross-examination. It is—"

Judge Keyser, leaning forward looking at the witness's face, said suddenly, "I think it is. The Court wants an answer to that question. Did you or did you not, Mr. Ellis?"

The witness shifted his position once more, moistened his lips with the tip of his tongue, said finally, "Yes, I did."

"And," Mason said, "didn't you kill your wife with that gun? Then didn't you arrange with Sadie Bradford to put that gun in the baggage of this defendant while the defendant was in the powder room? Thereafter didn't the defendant tell you that she had consulted me? Didn't you therefore on Wednesday morning ex-

amine the gun which was in the defendant's possession
and find that it was not the gun that you had planted?
Didn't you thereupon surreptitiously remove the gun
the defendant had in her baggage on Wednesday, go
down to your yacht and fire another bullet from that
gun into the dead body of your wife? Then didn't you
surreptitiously return that gun to the defendant's bag?
Didn't you do all of this without her knowledge before
bodyguards had been employed to protect the defendant, all the time assuring her of your great love and
devotion and telling her that you would arrange to
marry her as soon as the necessary arrangements could
be made, but swearing her to complete and utter se-
crecy?"

"Your Honor, Your Honor," Hamilton Burger
shouted, "this is the height of absurdity! This is the
most fantastic, preposterous idea ever promulgated by
counsel in an attempt to save his own skin! It is—"

"It is," Judge Keyser interrupted in low, level tones,
"a question which certainly tends to show the bias of
the witness. Under the circumstances I am going to permit it. The witness will answer the question."

White to the lips, Helman Ellis said, "I did not."

There was a sudden commotion in the rear of the
courtroom.

The young woman who came marching determin-
edly forward said, "I see it all now. That's *exactly* what
he did! He used me as a cat's-paw. I want to surrender
and turn state's evidence."

The bailiff started to pound for silence. One of the
officers jumped up to grab the woman, but Judge Key-

ser restrained the officer with his hand, said, "Silence," to the bailiff, turned to the woman and said, "Who are you?"

"I'm Sadie Bradford, the hat-check girl," she said. "I realize now exactly what he did. He used me for an accomplice."

Judge Keyser looked at Perry Mason. The puzzled perplexity in his eyes slowly changed to grudging admiration. "I think," he said, "the Court will, of its own motion, continue this matter until tomorrow morning at ten o'clock, and I suggest that the district attorney endeavor to unscramble this situation before court convenes tomorrow."

"I insist upon calling Perry Mason as a witness tonight, and in connection with this preliminary examination," Hamilton Burger shouted.

Judge Keyser smiled at him. "I think, Mr. District Attorney, that on sober second thought you will be glad that you didn't call Mr. Mason. Court has adjourned."

Judge Keyser got up and left the bench.

Mason continued to stand. His facial expression gave no indication of his inner thoughts.

Newspaper reporters, swarming through the gate in the mahogany rail, pelted him with questions. Photographers exploded flash bulbs.

"No comment," Mason said. "I will reserve any statement until after tomorrow morning at ten o'clock."

CHAPTER FIFTEEN

A WEARY HAMILTON BURGER arose, tried to ignore the crowded courtroom and addressed himself to Judge Keyser.

"If the Court please," he said, "the prosecution moves for the dismissal of the case against Ellen Robb, and in making that motion the prosecution feels it only fair to state to the Court that Helman Ellis has given a signed confession, that Helman Ellis was to some extent infatuated with Ellen Robb. He was also, however, having an affair with Sadie Bradford, the young woman who doubled as hat-check girl and as attendant in the ladies' powder room. Ellis is an opportunist, and he was no longer interested in his wife.

"It is true that George Anclitas gave Helman Ellis a gun. This gun was kept in Ellis' house. According to Helman Ellis' confession, he secured possession of one of the other guns which was kept behind the bar in The Big Barn for protection against holdups. On Tuesday evening Helman Ellis shot his wife with this gun while they were aboard his yacht, the *Cap's Eyes*. In order to make it appear that his wife had been defending herself against an assailant, he took the gun which George

Anclitas had given him and, after he had murdered his wife, fired a shot into the woodwork near the cabin door, then cocked the gun again and left the cocked and loaded revolver by the dead body of his wife, near her right hand.

"Helman Ellis then returned to The Big Barn, saw the defendant, and also saw his friend, Sadie Bradford. He persuaded Sadie Bradford to plant the gun with which the murder had been committed in the baggage of Ellen Robb, hoping that it would remain there until it was discovered by the police. Sadie Bradford had no knowledge of the murder. Ellis persuaded her to plant the gun because he said he wanted to have Ellen Robb discharged so he could terminate an affair with her.

"Later on, through his friend Sadie Bradford, Ellis learned of the altercation which had resulted in the discharge of Ellen Robb and learned that Ellen Robb had telephoned the Surf and Sea Motel for a reservation, stating that she intended to go there for the night. Helman Ellis immediately drove to the motel, waited for Ellen to arrive, and then under the guise of his great affection for her and his desire to help her, first convinced himself that the gun had indeed been planted in Ellen's baggage and then persuaded Ellen that she must under no circumstances admit that she had seen him that evening at the motel or that there was anything between them.

"Thereafter, according to his confession which we now have reason to accept at its face value, Helman Ellis left the motel, drove directly to the yacht club, loosened the yacht from its mooring, drifted with the tide until he was able to start the motors without anyone at the yacht club knowing the boat had been cast loose. He then took the boat to Catalina Island and caught the morning plane back to the mainland.

"Knowing that Ellen Robb planned to call on Perry Mason, he made it a point to see her after she had left Mason's office. He walked with her to the place where she was to take the bus to Costa Mesa and got her to describe in detail her visit to Perry Mason's office.

"When Ellen Robb had told him that Mason had told her to keep the gun in her possession and had done nothing about it, Ellis became suspicious and got Ellen to show him the gun which she was then carrying in her purse.

"We now come to the interesting part of Helman Ellis' confession which was designed to completely baffle the investigators. The gun which George An- clitas had given to Helman Ellis was not the gun that had the scratch on the front sight. But the gun with which the murder had been committed, and which had been planted in the bag of Ellen Robb, did have that scratch on the front sight. Ellis had a shrewd suspicion that perhaps Mason in an attempt to protect his client had substituted guns, giving her an entirely different gun, and when he inspected the gun which Ellen Robb showed him, he was convinced that this was the case because that gun did not have a scratch on the front sight.

"Ellis persuaded Ellen Robb that it would be dan- gerous for her to carry the gun which was then in her purse, on the bus. He said that she might be appre- hended for carrying a concealed weapon. He said that Mr. Mason had undoubtedly given her the right advice and that she should return the gun to the bag where she had found it, but that it would be better if *she* did not carry that gun in her purse since she had no permit. He therefore volunteered to take possession of the gun and return it to her possession later on in the day so that she could then put it back in the bag where she had found it. But he persuaded her that under no circumstances must she tell anyone of his intercession in the matter or of his interest.

"He then explained to Ellen Robb that he had some business matters to attend to, left her at the bus station, drove at once to an air field where he rented a plane, since he has a flier's license, and flew to Catalina Island. There he again sought out the yacht, unlocked the cabin door, fired a shot from this second gun into the dead body of his wife, locked the cabin door of the yacht, sailed it around to the other side of the island, tied it up to a convenient rock, pointed the yacht out to sea, locked the steering gear in position, started the motor, then untied the doubled rope and let the yacht head out to sea. He then returned to the place where he had left his rented airplane, flew back to Los Angeles, went to the office of Perry Mason and persuaded Perry Mason that Ellen Robb was in danger of attack from Nadine Ellis—knowing that Mason would in all probability hire bodyguards to protect his client.

"Thereafter Ellis, according to his confession, drove to the Surf and Sea Motel, entering the place through a driveway back of the alley where he would not be noticed. He explained to Ellen Robb that he had done her a great favor in bringing the gun back to her but that she must never mention his connection with the matter.

He swore his undying love and affection for her and promised her that they would be married when he could arrange with his wife to get a divorce.

"Again according to the confession of Ellis, which apparently is true, he did not know about the pro-scribed area for small boats off Catalina Island. He thought that his yacht would sail out into the ocean until the fuel tanks were exhausted, that then it would probably be capsized during some storm, and sink. He knew that the boat was hardly seaworthy. If, however, anything happened and the boat *was* discovered, he knew that the body of his wife would contain a bullet fired from a gun which was in the possession of Ellen Robb. And he felt certain that by having arranged the crime as he did, he could give himself a perfect alibi.

"Now then, if the Court please, that is the gist of the confession of Helman Ellis. I feel it my duty as an offi-cer of the court to disclose that confession at this time in connection with a motion to dismiss the case against Ellen Robb. I feel that she has been victimized and I wish to make this statement so that the facts can be made public."

Judge Keyser regarded Hamilton Burger thought-fully. Then his eyes shifted to Perry Mason. "The Court still doesn't understand how it happened that the gun which was originally placed in the defendant's baggage was returned to the possession of George Anclitas."

Hamilton Burger said wearily, "It seems that Sadie Bradford, while working as attendant in the women's powder room, found this gun on the floor of the powder room at a time when she had momentarily stepped to the door to talk with Helman Ellis. She feels certain that Helman Ellis had placed the gun on the floor, and that when she opened the powder-room door, she had kicked the gun into position under one of the wash-bowls. She knows that the gun was not there when she stepped to the door. There was no one in the powder room at the time. When she returned from her conver-sation with Mr. Ellis, the gun was lying there under the washbowl. She therefore picked it up and returned it to its place under the bar, feeling that in so doing she was following the wishes of Helman Ellis.

"The perplexing point is that Helman Ellis, while confessing the murder, still insists that he had nothing to do with returning that gun to the washroom. How-ever, under the circumstances and in view of the fact that the powder room is ventilated entirely by fans and has no windows, that there is no door to the powder room except the one door where the witness, Sadie Bradford, was standing, it would seem that for some reason which I confess I can't understand at the time, Helman Ellis is continuing to lie about returning that gun—and for the life of me," Hamilton Burger blurted, "I can't see why he would lie about it unless it was in an attempt to involve Perry Mason as counsel for the defense.

"It now appears that Perry Mason acted unconven-tionally but not illegally. Having been advised that a gun had been planted in a suitcase in the defendant's possession, he had test bullets fired from that gun and gave them to a ballistics expert for checking. In doing this he was quite probably within his rights."

"I still don't see how the Crowder gun could have

been placed in the purse of Ellen Robb unless it was done by her counsel."

"May I address the Court, Your Honor?" Mason asked.

"Certainly, Mr. Mason."

"When my client came to my office and stated that someone had planted a gun in her suitcase, I desired an opportunity to examine that gun," Mason said. "I felt that I was well within my rights in so doing, particularly in view of the fact that there was no indication that any crime had been committed at that time. I substituted a gun from my office in such a way that the defendant would not know there had been any substitution of guns.

"I feel that any attorney who is confident that someone has attempted to involve his client by planting stolen property in her possession is entitled to take such steps to see to it that in any search of his client's possessions designed to produce that stolen property, the property recovered may not necessarily be the property which was deliberately planted in the possession of the client."

"So far so good," Judge Keyser said. "The Court is inclined to agree with you there, although it is certainly an unconventional procedure. The proper procedure would have been to report to the police."

"That is a matter of expediency and depends upon the circumstances," Perry Mason said.

"However, as to all the rest of this," Judge Keyser said, "with all of this manipulation of weapons and the fact that it appears a murder had been committed with the weapon which apparently had been planted in the baggage of your client, Mr. Mason, how do you account for subsequent events?"

"I don't think *I* have to account for them," Mason said. "I have exonerated my client, I have exposed a murderer. If my methods were unconventional, they were at least effective."

Judge Keyser smiled.

Hamilton Burger, his face somewhat red, said, "If there was any possible opportunity for Perry Mason to have been in any way connected with the return of that weapon to the powder room in The Big Barn, I would feel differently about it. As it is, I have only the word of a confessed murderer and his accomplice as to what happened and I am satisfied that regardless of the truth of what has been told me, the situation as disclosed by Sadie Bradford, who has now become a state's witness, is such that it would have been impossible for Perry Mason to have placed that gun where it was found. I feel Helman Ellis entertains a bitter hatred for Perry Mason because of the way Mason interfered with his well-laid plans for murdering his wife. In some way Ellis secured possession of that gun and returned it to the women's powder room, hoping to involve Mr. Mason.

"Quite obviously, Mr. Mason, who must have acted very unconventionally if not illegally, is not going to betray the confidences of his client. Since my own witnesses say Mr. Ellis must have had that gun in his possession and returned it to the washroom, and since the only witness against Perry Mason is now a self-confessed murderer with a vindictive hatred of counsel, and since it appears counsel's client is innocent, I am convinced that whatever happened it would be impossible to proceed against Perry Mason. If I did so, moreover, I would be questioning the integrity of one of the prosecution's own witnesses and weakening my case against Helman Ellis, who, incidentally, has now repudiated his confession and insists that it was obtained by coercion and promises of immunity."

Perry Mason said, "If the prosecutor is satisfied that it was impossible for *me* to have returned that gun, I certainly am not one to contradict him."

Judge Keyser gave the matter long and earnest thought, then finally shook his head. "This is a situation," he said, "which completely baffles the Court. However, it is now quite apparent that in view of the circumstances as disclosed by the prosecutor, whatever counsel did to protect his client who was completely innocent of any wrongdoing, resulted not only in the acquittal of an innocent person but the detection and arrest of the guilty person.

"Under those circumstances it seems that there is nothing for the Court to do except . . . dismiss the case against Ellen Robb, release her from custody, and take a recess."

Judge Keyser arose from the bench, started toward his chambers, paused, glanced thoughtfully at Perry Mason, shook his head and then hurried on into chambers.

Hamilton Burger, surrounded by reporters anxious to learn the details of Ellis' confession, had no chance to exchange any comments with Perry Mason, and Perry Mason, winking at Della Street, took advantage of the confusion to hurry from the courtroom.

"How in the world did you know?" Della Street asked him as they descended in the elevator.

"Because," Mason said, "it was the only thing that could have happened. From the time Ellen Robb got that gun from me she didn't have time to find the yacht, fire a bullet into the body of Nadine Ellis and return to the Surf and Sea Motel. Remember that Drake traced her movements from the bus depot to the motel.

"The only thing that *could* have happened was that the boat with the body of Nadine Ellis must have been taken to sea in two installments. First, a night cruise to some isolated cove in Catalina; then, in the second stage, being pointed out to sea and left to run out of fuel. The only place I could think of where the yacht could have made such a two-stage cruise was by stopping at Catalina and, quite obviously, Ellen Robb had no opportunity to get to Catalina on at least two different occasions.

"Moreover, once I stopped to think of it, I realized that the gun which was found in the cabin with Nadine Ellis must have been planted there after Mrs. Ellis had been killed. One shot had been fired from that gun, and the gun, fully cocked, was lying on the cabin floor near her hand.

"When a person tries to do accurate shooting with a double-action gun, he quite frequently pulls back the hammer so as to work the mechanism with a simple pull of the trigger, but when one is trying for rapid shots at close range, there is no time to cock the gun manually. Almost invariably, under such circumstances, a person uses the double-action mechanism and in so doing it would be impossible for the gun to have been fully cocked after the first shot had been fired. Therefore I began to suspect the gun had been a plant and if it had been planted, then the bullet fired into the woodwork of the cabin was designed to throw us off the trail.

"After that it was simple, once I realized that the bullet from the Anclitas gun must have been fired first. That meant that Mrs. Ellis must have been dead when I handed Ellen Robb the other gun. Then the yacht must have started to Catalina Island before Ellen Robb came to my office. This meant Helman Ellis must have been lying about that whole conversation he claimed he had with his wife on Wednesday morning. For one thing, the Ellises had only one car, and the evidence that Helman drove it to Ellen's motel Tuesday night precluded the possibility that Mrs. Ellis had driven it to Phoenix Tuesday evening. Once I started on that chain of reasoning, I knew what *must* have happened."

"But how did you know the bullet from the Anclitas gun was the *first* bullet?"

"Because I marked the barrel with an etching tool before it left our possession, and the bullet recovered from the body of Mrs. Ellis didn't show those marks which would have been on it if it had been fired after I marked the barrel with the etching tool."

"Well," Della Street said, "you certainly had your back to the wall that time. Is this going to teach you not to take chances on behalf of your clients in the future?"

Mason grinned and shook his head. "It's simply going to teach me to practice the art of concentration," he said. "I never thought as fast or as hard in my life as I did from the time court adjourned yesterday afternoon until I threw the crucial question at Helman Ellis in cross-examination last night.

"When I left that courtroom, I felt as though I had been put through a wringer."

Della Street looked up at him with admiration in her eyes. "Yet during all of that time," she said, "you never wavered in your loyalty to your client, despite the fact that you were virtually certain she had lied to you."

Mason heaved a sigh. "Della," he said, "whenever I waver in my loyalty to a client, do me a favor. Just close up the office, get some paint remover and erase the words ATTORNEY AT LAW from the door of the reception room."

THE CASE
OF THE
BLONDE
BONANZA

FOREWORD

FROM time to time, paying tribute to outstanding leaders in the field of legal medicine, I have dedicated my books by appropriate forewords.

This book, however, is not dedicated to one individual but to a group of men.

As one who has had much to do with crime and with the trial of criminal cases, I have learned to appreciate the value of scientific investigation and of the impartial devotion to truth which characterizes the true expert.

The professional witness who uses his technical qualifications as a springboard by which he can inject himself into a partisan position in a legal controversy is an old-fashioned carry-over from a bygone day.

The modern expert witness regards the facts with scientific objectivity. He states the reasons for his opinions with concise logic and is the first to admit any fact which may be opposed to his opinion or which may seem to be opposed to it.

I have watched the American Academy of Forensic Sciences grow from an idea in the brain of my friend, the late Dr. R. B. H. Gradwohl, to its present position of dignified power.

It is my hope that the public will learn to appreciate the importance of legal medicine, of the scientific methods of crime detection, and will learn to distrust the old-fashioned witness who testifies under the guise of an expert but is actually a professional partisan.

The scientific witness of today is interested only in finding the truth. He recites the facts as they exist, his opinion is impartial, and his voice unpartisan.

And because the American Academy of Forensic Sciences has done so much to bring all this about, I respectfully dedicate this book to:

THE AMERICAN ACADEMY OF FORENSIC SCIENCES.

Erle Stanley Gardner

CHAPTER ONE

BECAUSE DELLA STREET, Perry Mason's confidential secretary, was spending a two-week vacation with an aunt who lived at Bolero Beach, the lawyer, having consulted with a client in San Diego, drove by on the way home. Since it was Saturday, and a beautiful day, a little persuasion on Della Street's part, plus a dinner invitation from Aunt Mae, caused the lawyer to stop over at the Bolero Hotel.

"Moreover," Della Street had pointed out, "you can then drive me back on Monday morning."

"Is this a pitch to get a ride back," Mason asked, "or a scheme on the part of you and Mae to get me to take a vacation?"

"Both," she retorted. "Any lawyer who gets so busy he regards a Saturday afternoon and a Sunday as being a vacation needs to be taken in hand. Aunt Mae has promised one of her chicken and dumpling dinners, the beach will be thronged with bathing beauties, and I have, moreover, a mystery."

"You won't need the mystery," Mason said. "Surf,

sand, sunshine, bathing beauties, and one of Mae's chicken-dumpling dinners make the law business seem drab and uninviting, the air of the office stale and the perusal of law books a chore. I'll stay over."

"Then," she said, her eyes twinkling, "you're not interested in the mystery."

"I didn't say that," Mason said. "I said you had already established the proper inducement. The mystery is the frosting on the cake—not essential but delightful."

"Put on your trunks and meet me on the beach in half an hour," she said, "and I'll introduce you to the mystery."

"It's animate?"

"It's animate."

"Two legs or four?"

"Two—and wait until you see them."

"I'll be there in twenty minutes," Mason promised, and actually made it in eighteen.

He found Della Street stretched out on the sand under the shade of a beach umbrella.

"And now?" he asked, surveying her sun-tanned figure approvingly.

"She should be along any minute now," Della Street said. "It's almost noon. . . . Are you hungry?"

"Ravenous," he said, "but in view of Mae's promise of chicken and dumplings I want to restrain my appetite for the time being."

"I'm afraid," she said, "you're going to *have* to eat something— Wait a minute, here she comes now."

Della Street indicated a curveaceous blonde walking

slowly down the strip of wet sand at the margin of the waves.

"See it?" she asked.

"Every visible inch of it," Mason said.

"Did I misjudge the legs?"

"Second most beautiful pair on the beach. I presume the mystery is, why does she always walk alone?"

"That's only one of the mysteries. Would you like to leave our things here and follow her?"

"Are they safe?"

"It's a private beach and *I* haven't had any trouble. Terry-cloth robes, sandals and reading material seem to remain in place."

"Let's go," Mason said.

"The young woman in question," Della Street said, "is wending her way to the lunchroom."

"And we follow?"

"We follow. It's a snack bar and open-air lunchroom for bathers. You can get very good food."

"And how do we pay for it?" Mason asked, looking down at his bathing trunks.

"If you're registered at the hotel, you sign a chit. If you're not registered, but are a member of the beach club, you can also sign."

"You promised to *introduce* me to the mystery," Mason said, as they moved toward the lunchroom.

"Notice," she said, "that I promised to introduce you to the mystery—not to the young woman."

"There's a distinction?"

"Very much so. Like that between the *corpus delicti* and the corpse. As you have pointed out so many times, the average individual thinks that the *corpus delicti* in a murder case is the corpse. Actually, the expression, if I remember your statements correctly, relates to the body of the *crime* rather than the body of the *victim*."

"And so," Mason said, "I take it I am introduced only to the mystery and not to the body to which the mystery pertains."

"From this point on," Della Street said, as they entered the lunchroom, "you're on your own. However, I may point out that during the whole ten days I have been watching her she has remained unescorted. This is indicative of the fact she is not easy."

"And of what does the mystery consist?" Mason asked.

"What do you think of her figure?"

"I believe the expression," Mason said, "is well-stacked."

"You would gather that perhaps she was fighting a weight problem?"

"One would say that weight and whistles were her two major problems in life."

"All right," Della Street said, "she's seated in that booth over there. If you'll sit in this one, you can look across and see what she orders. You won't believe it," she warned.

Mason and Della Street ordered toasted baked ham sandwiches and coffee, settled back on the waterproof cushions, and, after a few minutes' wait, saw the voluptuous blonde in the booth across the way being served with what seemed to be a glass of milk.

"That certainly seems abstemious enough," Mason said.

"For your information," Della Street said, "that is a glass of half milk and half cream. I bribed the information from the waitress—and you haven't seen anything yet."

The blonde in the bathing suit slowly drank the contents of the glass. Then the waitress brought her a sizzling steak, French fried potatoes and a salad, followed by apple pie alamode and two candy bars.

"I presume the candy bars are to keep her from getting hungry until tea time," Mason said.

"You don't know the half of it," Della Street said. "She'll be back here at about four o'clock for tea. She'll have a chocolate sundae and a piece of rich cake. Her tea will consist of a chocolate malted milk."

Mason cocked a quizzical eyebrow. "You seem to have taken an undue interest."

"Undue!" she exclaimed, "I'm fascinated! I told you I bribed the waitress. They're talking about it in the kitchen. The help have totaled the calories consumed each day and the result is what would be referred to in Hollywood as supercolossal."

"It takes that to keep the figure at its proper level?" Mason asked.

"Level is not exactly the word," she said. "The figure is noticeably growing. But wait until she signs the chit and leaves the booth—then see what she does."

The blonde finished with her dessert, signed the check, picked up the two candy bars, and walked toward the entrance. On the way, she detoured long enough to stand on a pair of scales which had a huge dial with a rotating hand.

Della Street said, "That's nearly five pounds in the last eight days."

"You've been watching?"

"I've been watching and marveling. The girl seems to be making a desperate, deadly, determined effort to put on weight, and she's carrying plenty already."

"How long has this been going on, Miss Sherlock Holmes?" Mason asked.

"For about two weeks, according to the waitress."

"This information was readily volunteered?" Mason asked.

"In return for a five-dollar tip."

Mason said musingly, "It's a situation that's worth looking into."

"You've certainly looked the situation over," Della Street said, as the blonde went through the door.

"And what does she do now?" Mason asked.

"She has a beach umbrella and she lies down, dozes and reads."

"No exercise?"

"Oh, yes—enough exercise to give her a healthy appetite. And while your untrained masculine eye may not appreciate the fact, Mr. Perry Mason, her bathing suit is being stretched to the limit. It was tight enough to begin with, and now it seems to be about to burst—in both directions."

"You've told your Aunt Mae about this?" Mason asked.

"I discussed it with her two or three times, and Mae came down with me yesterday to see it for herself."

"Mae doesn't know her?" Mason asked.

Della Street said thoughtfully, "I think she does, Perry. She had a smug smile on her face. She kept her dark glasses on while we were in the booth and sat back under my umbrella. I think she was trying to keep the blonde from seeing and recognizing her."

"But Mae didn't admit anything?"

"Nothing. She's been busy planning the details of the chicken-dumpling feed with all of the fixings."

Mason signed the chit for their meal, said, "There must be a gag tied in with it somewhere, some sort of a publicity stunt."

"I know," Della Street said, "but what in the world *could* it be?"

"She is always alone?"

"She keeps away from all of the beach wolves. And that," Della Street announced, "is rather difficult."

"I take it," Mason said, "that you haven't been entirely successful."

"Perhaps," she said, "I haven't tried quite so determinedly. However, I let everyone know I was keeping Saturday and Sunday wide open for you."

"Evidently you felt sure you could persuade me to stay over," Mason said.

She smiled. "Let's put it this way, Mr. Perry Mason. I felt certain that if you didn't stay over I wouldn't have a completely disastrous afternoon or a danceless evening."

Mason said musingly, "Apple pie alamode . . . chocolate malted milk . . . there simply has to be a catch in it somewhere, Della—and there's an irresistible body meeting an immovable bathing suit. Something is bound to happen."

"We could, of course, open a branch office here at the beach."

"I'm afraid our clients wouldn't come that far, Della."

"Well," Della Street predicted, "a bathing suit can only stretch so far."

CHAPTER TWO

MAE KIRBY greeted Perry Mason affectionately. "It seems that I almost never see you," she said, "and you're keeping Della on the go all the time."

Mason said, "I know, Mae. Time passes faster than we realize. I keep going from one case to another."

"At breakneck speed," she said. "You'd better slow down. Flesh and blood can't stand that pace. Come on in. Here's someone who wants to meet you."

Della Street stood in the doorway, smiling at Mason and then giving him a quick wink as Mae led him into the room. She said, "Dianne Alder, this is Perry Mason."

The young woman who was standing by the window was the same blonde whom Mason and Della Street had been watching earlier in the day.

She gave Mason her hand and a dazzling smile. "I'm absolutely thrilled," she said. "This is a wonderful privilege. I've heard about you so much and read about you, and to think of actually meeting you! It was so thoughtful of Mrs. Kirby to invite me over."

Mason glanced swiftly at Della Street, received a slight shake of the head from Della and then said, "You flatter me, Miss Alder. The pleasure is mine."

Dianne Alder said, "I've seen your secretary on the beach several times in the last week but had no idea who she was or I'd have been bold enough to introduce myself. She's beautiful enough to make everyone think she's—"

"Come, come," Della Street interrupted. "You're making us all too vain, Dianne."

Mae Kirby said, "Now we're going to have one nice dry Martini and then we're going to have dinner— chicken and dumplings."

Dianne Alder said, "I've heard of Mrs. Kirby's chicken and dumplings. They're almost as famous as Perry Mason."

"You're looking forward to them?" Della Street asked.

"Am I looking forward to them? I'm simply ravenous!"

Mason and Della Street exchanged glances.

It wasn't until after the cocktails and just before sitting down to dinner that Mason was able to jockey Della Street into a corner for a hurried confidential conversation.

"What is this?" he asked. "Some sort of a trap or frame-up?"

"I don't think so," she said. "It was just a surprise Aunt Mae was planning for us. She knew that I was interested and evidently she's known Dianne for some time. She invited her to come over for dinner and meet you.

"Usually Aunt Mae is very considerate. She knows there are lots of people here who are dying to meet you, and when you're here for dinner she never invites anyone else. This time is the exception."

"Found out anything?" Mason asked.

Della shook her head and was on the point of saying something when Mae said, "Come on now, you two. You're either talking business or making love, and you shouldn't do either on an empty stomach. Come on in here and sit down. You sit there, Perry, and Della, you sit over here. Dianne can sit next to me."

Thirty minutes later when they had finished with their hot mince pie and coffee, Della Street said, "Well, it was wonderful, Aunt Mae, but I'm afraid I've put on a pound and a half."

"So have I—at least I hope I have," Dianne said. Mason raised his eyebrows.

There was silence for a moment and then Della Street said, "You *hope* you have?"

"Yes, I'm trying to gain weight."

Della Street glanced at the front of the girl's dress and Dianne laughed somewhat awkwardly. "It's something I can't discuss," she said. "I know how you feel. You think I don't need it, but actually I . . . well, I have to put on another four pounds."

"What are you going to do," Della Street asked, "take up wrestling?— No, no, I didn't mean it that way, Dianne. I just wondered, the way you said it, you sounded as though you were trying to make a definite weight."

"But I am."

Mason raised his brows in a silent question.

She flushed slightly and said, "I don't know how the subject came up. I— Oh, skip it."

"Of course," Della Street said, "we don't want to pry, but now you certainly have aroused our curiosity, and I know my boss well enough to know that when his curiosity is once aroused it gnaws at his consciousness like termites in a building. You'd better tell us—that is, if it isn't too confidential."

"Well," Dianne said, "it's confidential in a way—that is, I'm not supposed to talk about it. But I know that Mrs. Kirby can be just as close-lipped as anyone. That's one thing about her, she never does gossip—and for the rest of it, I'm talking to an attorney and his secretary."

"Go ahead," Della Street invited.

"Well," Dianne said, "the truth of the matter is I'm going to model a new style."

"A new style?" Della Street asked, as Dianne broke off to laugh self-consciously.

"It sounds absolutely absurd," she said, "but I'm getting paid to put on weight and . . . well, that's all there is to it."

"Now, wait a minute," Della Street said. "Let's see if I get this straight. You're being paid money to put on more weight?"

"Twelve pounds from the time I started."

"Within a time limit?"

"Yes."

"And someone is paying you for it?"

"Yes. Some designers. The— Oh, I know it sounds silly and . . . I don't know how I got started on this. It— Well, anyway, some style designers feel that there has been too great a tendency to take off weight, that everyone is fighting weight and it isn't natural and that people would be a lot happier and feel a lot better if they didn't keep so diet conscious, if they were free to eat what they wanted.

"Of course there are people who are simply fat, and my sponsors don't want that. They have been looking for some time for a young woman who is—well, as they expressed it, firmly fleshed, who could put on enough weight to wear certain styles they wanted to bring out. They're going to photograph me and put me on television. Well, that's it. I'm to be a new sort of model, start a trend.

"You know how it is in the fashion shows. Some slender model who concentrates on being willowy and svelte comes out modeling a dress. But the women who are sitting there looking at that dress are nearly all of them twenty to thirty pounds heavier than the model.

"My sponsors have had me examined by a physician and they feel that I can keep my waist measurement and my carriage and still put on twelve to fifteen pounds and—well, they're going to try and make curves stylish. . . . Oh, why did I get started on this?"

Dianne suddenly covered her scarlet face with her hands and said, "I feel so horribly self-conscious."

"Not at all," Mason said, "you interest me a lot. I think there's a good deal to this. You mentioned your sponsors, some style company?"

"Frankly," she said, "I don't know who the sponsors are. I'm dealing through an agency . . . and I'm under contract not to discuss what I'm doing with anyone."

"I see," Mason said thoughtfully.

"Are you putting weight on?" Della Street asked.

"Heavens, yes! I've had to count calories for the last five years and now I'm just reveling in having everything I want. Now I've built up my appetite to a point where I just can't resist food. I'm going to make the weight all right but the hard part is whether I can shut off the supply of food when I've made the weight. I'm afraid I'm going to overshoot the mark."

Mason said, "You certainly have the figure to make women curve-conscious and sell clothes."

"Well, of course," she said, "that's what's at the back of it. They want to sell clothes. They feel that the average woman is simply sick and tired of starving herself and that I can make—that is, that *they* can make a new trend in styles if they can find the right model."

"I think they've found her," Mason said. And raising his coffee cup, smiled at the highly embarrassed Dianne Alder and said, "Here's to success!"

Fifteen minutes later, however, when Mason was able to get Della Street to one side, he said, "Della, there's something terribly fishy about this whole business with Dianne Alder. She says she has a contract. Apparently it's a written contract. She seems to be a very nice girl. I would dislike very much to see her victimized. I'm going to make my excuses and leave. See if you can get a heart-to-heart, woman-to-woman talk with her and find out more about that contract. You've been around law offices long enough to be able to spot the joker if you can get a look at it."

"If she's getting money for putting on weight," Della Street said wistfully, "she's living an ideal existence."

"Until someone jerks the rug out from under her," Mason said, "and leaves her with all those curves."

Della Street smiled. "I know how easy and rapid it is to put it on and how very slow and painful the process is of taking it off—but what in the world could anybody want with her— Well, you know, I mean *why* would anyone make a contract of that sort?"

Mason said, "Since she's a friend of your Aunt Mae, it might be a good plan to find out."

CHAPTER THREE

IT WAS NINE O'CLOCK the next morning when Mason's phone rang.

"Are you decent?" Della Street asked.

"Fully clothed and in my right mind," Mason said. "Where are you?"

"I'm down in the lobby."

"What gives?"

"The contract."

"What contract? Oh, you mean with Dianne Alder?"

"Yes."

"You know what it's all about?"

"I've done better than that. I have her copy with me."

"Good," Mason said. "Come on up. I'll meet you at the elevator."

Mason met Della and asked, "Have you had breakfast?"

"No. You?"

Mason shook his head.

"I'm famished," she said.

"Come on in," Mason told her, "and we'll have some

sent up to the suite and eat it out on the balcony over-looking the ocean."

The lawyer called room service and placed an order for a ham steak, two orders of fried eggs, a big pot of coffee and toast.

Della Street, walking over to the full-length mirror, surveyed herself critically. "I'm afraid," she said, "I'm being inspired by the example of Dianne Alder and am about to go overboard."

"That breakfast won't be fattening," Mason said.

"Hush," she told him. "I've been at the point where I've even been counting the calories in a glass of drinking water. And now, inspired by the example of Dianne getting paid for putting on weight, I feel that you should supplement that order with sweet rolls and hash-brown potatoes."

"Shall I?" Mason asked, reaching for the phone.

"Heavens, no!" she exclaimed. "Here, read this contract and prepare to lose a secretary. Why didn't someone tell me about this sooner?"

"Inspired?" Mason asked.

"To quote a famous phrase," Della Street said, "it's nice work if you can get it. I'm thinking of getting it. Eat all you want and get paid for it. Have a guaranteed income. Be free from worries so you can put on weight in the right places."

"What," Mason asked, "are the right places?"

"The places that meet the masculine eye," she said.

Mason settled in his chair, glanced through the contract, frowned, started reading it more carefully.

By the time the room service waiter arrived with the

table and the breakfast order, Mason had completed a study of the contract.

Della Street waited until after the table had been set on the balcony, the waiter had left the room, and Mason had taken the first sip of his coffee.

"Well?" she asked.

Mason said, "That's the damnedest contract I've ever read."

"I thought you'd be interested in it."

"The strange thing," Mason said, "is that on its face the contract seems so completely reasonable; in fact, so utterly benevolent. The party of the first part agrees that Dianne may fear she will have trouble getting secretarial employment if she puts on weight, and recognizes the fact that as of the time the contract is signed she is gainfully employed as a secretary in a law office at a salary of five thousand, two hundred dollars a year.

"Since the party of the first part desires that she shall give up that employment and devote herself exclusively to her work as a model, it is guaranteed that she will receive an income of one hundred dollars a week, payable each Saturday morning.

"On the other hand, Dianne, as party of the second part, agrees to put on twelve pounds within a period of ten weeks, to resign her position immediately on the signing of the contract, and loaf on the beach, getting as much of a sun tan as possible.

"It is agreed that she will pose in bikini bathing suits as the party of the first part may desire, but she shall not be required to pose in the nude. And if she wishes,

at the time of posing in a bikini bathing suit, she may
have a woman companion present as her chaperon.

"Now," Mason went on, "comes the peculiar part of
the contract. It is stated that the parties contemplate
that Dianne's total income may greatly exceed the sum
of fifty-two hundred dollars a year; that the fifty-two
hundred dollars is a minimum guarantee made by the
party of the first part; and Dianne is entitled to have
that and to keep that income without dividing it. If,
however, her income exceeds that amount, she is to
share it fifty-fifty with the party of the first part. And,
since the party of the first part is taking a calculated
risk, it is agreed that Dianne's gross income shall be
computed for the purposes of the division as any money
she may receive from any source whatever during the
life of the contract.

"The contract is to exist for two years, and the party
of the first part has the right of renewing it for an additional two years. And, at the expiration of that time, a
further right of renewal for another two years.

"During all of the time the contract is in effect any
and all monies received from any source whatever by
the party of the second part other than the hundred-a-
week guarantee are deemed to be gross income which
shall be divided equally, whether such income comes
from modeling, lecturing on health, posing, television,
movies or from any other source whatever, including
prizes in beauty contests, gifts from admirers or otherwise; inheritances, bequests, devices or otherwise; and
it is recited that the party of the first part having guar-

anteed her income for the life of the contract, and having made plans to put her in the public eye, and to give her opportunities to greatly increase her income, is entitled to one-half of her gross income regardless of the source, and/or whether it is directly or indirectly the result of his efforts on her behalf or of the publicity resulting from his efforts under the contract."

Mason picked up his knife and fork, divided the ham steak in half, put a piece on Della Street's plate, one on his own, and gave his attention to the ham and eggs.

"Well?" Della Street asked.

"Dianne is a nice girl," Mason said.

"She has a striking figure," Della Street said.

Mason nodded.

"She might be described as whistle bait," Della Street went on.

"Well?" Mason asked.

"Do you suppose the party of the first part is completely unaware of these things?"

Mason said, "In the course of my legal career I've seen quite a few approaches. I've never seen one quite like this, if that's what the party of the first part has in mind."

"In the course of my secretarial career," Della Street said demurely, "I've seen them *all*, but this is a new one."

"According to the letter of that contract," Mason said, "if Dianne Alder should meet a millionaire, receive a gift of a hundred thousand dollars and should then marry, or if her husband should die and leave her the million dollars, the party of the first part would be entitled to fifty per cent."

"Marrying a million dollars is not one of the normal occupational hazards of a legal secretary in a relatively small beach town," Della Street said.

Suddenly Mason snapped his fingers.

"You've got it?" Della Street asked.

"I have *an* explanation," Mason said. "I don't know whether it's *the* explanation but it's quite an explanation."

"What?" Della Street asked. "This thing has me completely baffled."

Mason said, "Let us suppose that the party of the first part, this Harrison T. Boring, whoever he may be, is acquainted with some very wealthy and rather eccentric person—some person who is quite impressionable as far as a certain type of voluptuous blonde beauty is concerned.

"Let us further suppose Boring has been scouting around, looking for just the girl he wants. He's been spending the summer on the beaches, looking them over in bathing suits. He's picked Dianne as being nearest to type, but she is perhaps slightly lacking in curves."

"Wait a minute," Della Street interjected. "If Dianne's lacking in curves, I'm a reincarnated beanpole."

"I know, I know," Mason said, brushing her levity aside. "But this individual has particular and rather peculiar tastes. He's very wealthy and he likes young women with lots of corn-fed beauty, not fat but, as Dianne expressed it, 'firm fleshed.'"

"Probably some old goat," Della Street said, her eyes narrowing.

"Sure, why not?" Mason said. "Perhaps some rich old codger who is trying to turn back the hands of the clock. Perhaps he had a love affair with a blonde who was exceptionally voluptuous and yet at the same time had the frank, blue-eyed gaze that characterizes Dianne.

"So Boring makes a contract with Dianne. He gets her to put on weight. He gets her to follow his instructions to the letter. At the proper time he introduces her to this pigeon he has all picked out, and from there on Boring takes charge.

"Any one of several things can happen. Either the pigeon becomes involved with Dianne, in which event Boring acts as the blackmailing mastermind who manipulates the shakedown, or the man lavishes Dianne with gifts, or perhaps, if Boring manipulates it right, the parties commit matrimony."

"And then," Della Street asked, "Boring would be getting fifty per cent of Dianne's housekeeping allowance? After all, marriage can be rather disillusioning under certain circumstances."

"Then," Mason said, "comes the proviso that any money she receives within the time limit of the contract, whether by inheritance, descent, bequest or devise, is considered part of her gross income. Boring arranges that the wealthy husband leads a short but happy life, and Dianne comes into her inheritance with Boring standing around with a carving knife ready to slice off his share."

Della Street thought that over for a moment. "Well, what do you know," she said.

"And that," Mason said, "explains the peculiar optional extension provisions of the contract. It can run for two years, four years or six years at the option of the party of the first part. Quite evidently he *hopes* that the matter will be all concluded with the two-year period, but in the event it isn't and the husband should be more resistant than he anticipates, he can renew the contract for another two years, and if the husband still manages to survive the perils of existence for that four-year period, he can still renew for another two years."

"And where," Della Street asked, "would that leave Dianne Alder? Do you suppose he would plan to have her convicted of the murder?"

"No, no, not that," Mason said. "He couldn't afford to."

"Why not?"

"Because," Mason pointed out, "a murderer can't inherit from his victim. Therefore Boring has to manipulate things in such a way that the wealthy husband dies what seems to be a natural death. Or, if murdered, that some other person has to be the murderer. Dianne, as the bereaved widow, steps into an inheritance of a few million dollars, and Boring, as the person who brought Dianne into the public eye and thereby arranged for the meeting with her future husband, produces his contract and wants a fifty-fifty split."

"With that much involved, wouldn't the contract be contested on the grounds of public policy, undue influence and a lot of other things?"

"Sure it would," Mason said, "but with that much involved and with a contract of this sort in the background, Dianne would make a settlement. If she became a wealthy widow with social possibilities ahead of her, she would hardly want to have this chapter of her career brought into the open; the diet, the putting on weight, the deliberate entrapment of her husband, and all the rest of it."

"In other words," Della Street said, "Harrison T. Boring walked down the beaches looking for a precise type of feminine beauty. When his eyes lit on Dianne, he recognized her as a potential bonanza."

"Bear in mind," Mason said thoughtfully, "that there are certain other things. Dianne has the build of a strip-tease dancer but essentially has the background of a darn nice girl. Those are the things on which Harrison T. Boring wants to capitalize, and I may point out that the combination is not very easy to come by.

"Usually a girl with Dianne's physical attributes has developed an attitude of sophistication, a certain degree of worldly wisdom, and the unmistakable earmarks of experience, whereas Dianne is essentially shy, self-conscious, easily embarrassed, slightly naïve and delightfully easy on the eyes."

"I see that Dianne has impressed you by her good points," Della Street said.

Mason's eyes were level-lidded with concentration. "What has Dianne told you about Boring, anything?"

"Very little. She knows very little.

"Dianne was a legal secretary. She was, of course, conscious of her figure. She was also conscious of the fact that if her waist should expand, the rest of her figure would be damaged. So she did a lot of swimming and walking. She would quit work at five o'clock during the summer afternoons, then, taking advantage of daylight saving time, get into her swimming suit, come down on the beach and walk and swim."

"Unescorted?" Mason asked.

"She tried to be. She wanted exercise. The average man who wanted to swim with her wasn't particularly keen on that sort of exercise; in fact, very few of them could keep up with her. She walked and ran and swam and, of course, acquired a delightful sun tan.

"Since women of that build like to admire themselves in the nude in front of mirrors, and are painfully conscious of the white streaks which mar the smooth sun tan where convention decrees a minimum of clothing should be worn, Dianne supplemented her weekday swimming parties by lying in the nude in a sun bath she had constructed in the privacy of the back yard.

"About three weeks before this contract was signed she noticed that she was being stared at rather persistently and finally followed by a man whom she describes as being in his thirties, with keen eyes and a dignified, distinguished manner. He looked like an actor."

"And what happened?"

"Nothing at first. Dianne is accustomed to attracting attention. She's accustomed to having men try to make passes at her and she takes all of that in her stride.

"Then one day Boring approached her and said he had a business proposition he'd like to discuss with her and she told him to get lost. He said that this was purely legitimate; that it had to do with the possibility of her getting gainful employment in Hollywood and was she interested.

"Naturally, Dianne was interested. So Boring gave her this story about a new trend in fashion, about the fact that women were becoming neurotic by paying too much attention to slim figures; that one of the most popular actresses, with women, was Mae West; that if Mae West had only started a new type of dress style it would have gone over like a house afire; that nature didn't intend women to have thin figures after they had reached maturity as women.

"Dianne said he was very convincing and of course the offer he made was quite attractive.

"All Dianne had to do was to put on weight and put in a lot of time training so that the flesh she put on was firm flesh and not fat. Boring was very insistent about that."

"All right," Mason said, "she signed the contract. Did she get any advice on it? She was working for lawyers and—"

"No, she didn't," Della Street interjected. "Boring was particularly insistent that she keep the entire matter completely confidential, that no one should know about it; that under no circumstances was she to mention the reason why she was resigning from her secretarial position.

"Boring explained that he wanted to have this new style of his so highly personalized that women would become aware of Dianne's beauty before they realized that they were being given a new style. Boring said that women were very resistant to new styles until they became a vogue and then they fell all over themselves falling in line.

"Boring has ideas for Dianne to attract a lot of public attention and then he is going to have her put on a series of health lectures. He's going to give her scripts that she is to follow, speeches she is to make, explaining that nature intended a woman to have curves and that men really like women with curves; that the slim, neurotic models are an artificial by-product of the dress designer's art.

"Boring told her that he could set the country afire with the right kind of approach to this thing and that all women would throw diets out of the window, start putting on weight and would only be anxious to have the weight firm flesh instead of bulging fat; that he intended to open up a series of Dianne Alder studios for healthful figures and charming curves."

Mason said, "Hang it! The guy could be right at that, Della."

"It would be a job," Della said. "Something you wouldn't want to gamble a hundred dollars a week on."

"It depends," Mason said. "The stakes are big enough. . . . All right, now what happened after the contract was signed? Did Boring insist that she become cuddly with him?"

"That is the strange part," Della Street said. "Dianne rather felt that that would be a part of the contract and was rather hesitant about it until finally Boring, discovering the reason for her hesitancy, told her that once she signed the contract she would see very little of him;

that he was going to be busy in Hollywood, New York and Paris, laying the foundations for this new type of promotion. So finally Dianne signed the contract.

"She hasn't seen Boring since but she hears from him on the telephone. Every once in a while he will call her and from the nature of the conversation Dianne knows that he is keeping a close watch on what she is doing."

"Now, that's interesting," Mason said.

"Dianne finds it rather disconcerting."

"How does she receive her hundred dollars, Della?" Mason asked.

"Every Saturday morning there is an envelope in the mail with a check. The checks are signed by the Hollywood Talent Scout Modeling Agency, per Harrison T. Boring, president."

"Well," Mason said, "I don't like to give up a good murder mystery before it's even got off the ground, Della, but there's just a chance this whole idea may be on the up-and-up. Boring's idea sounds pretty far-fetched and fishy when it's written in the cold phraseology of a contract, but the more you think of his explanation, the more plausible it sounds.

"I was hoping that we were on the track of a potential murder before the potential corpse had really walked into the danger zone. I had visions of waiting until Harrison T. Boring had introduced Dianne to his millionaire pigeon and then stepping into the picture in a way that would cause Mr. Boring a maximum of embarrassment and perhaps feathering Dianne Alder's nest."

"As to the latter," Della Street said, "we have to remember that every time Dianne's nest gets two feathers, Boring gets one of them."

"That's what the contract says," Mason observed, "but sometimes things don't work out that way. . . . Well, Della, I guess we'll have to give Mr. Harrison T. Boring the benefit of the doubt and you can return Dianne's contract to her. But we'll sort of keep an eye on her."

"Yes," Della Street said, "I thought you would want to do that."

Mason looked at her sharply but found nothing other than an expression of innocence on her face.

Abruptly the telephone rang. Della Street picked up the instrument.

"Hello," she said in a low voice. "This is Mr. Mason's suite."

Dianne Alder's voice came over the phone in a rush of words.

"Oh, Della, I'm glad I caught you!— Your Aunt told me where to find you.— Della, I have to have that contract back right away. I'm sorry I let you have it and I hope you didn't say anything about it to anybody."

"Why?" Della asked.

"Because . . . well, because I guess I shouldn't have let it out of my possession. There's a proviso in the contract that I'm to do everything I can to avoid premature publicity and— Gosh, Della, I guess I made a booboo even letting you have it or talking about the arrangement. You're the only one I've told anything at all about it. Mr. Boring impressed on me that if I started telling even my closest friends, the friends would tell their friends, the newspapers would get hold of it and make a feature story that would result in what he called premature publicity.

"He said that when they got ready to unveil the new models they'd give me a lot of publicity. That was when I was to go on television and they were going to arrange for a movie test, but nothing must be done until they were ready. They said they didn't want irresponsible reporters to skim the cream off their campaign."

"Do you want me to mail the contract?" Della Street asked.

"If it's all right with you, I'll run up and get it."

"Where are you now?"

"I'm at a drugstore only about three blocks from the hotel."

"Come on up," Della Street said.

She cradled the phone, turned to Perry Mason and caught the interest in his eye.

"Dianne?" Mason asked.

"That's right."

"Wants the contract back?"

"Yes."

Mason resumed his contemplative study of the ceiling. "Is she coming up to get the contract, Della?"

"Yes."

"What caused her sudden concern, Della?"

"She didn't say."

"When she comes," Mason said, "invite her in. I want to talk with her."

Mason lit a cigarette, watched the smoke curl upward.

At length he said, "I have become more than a little curious about Harrison T. Boring. He may be smarter than I thought."

The lawyer lapsed into silence, remained thoughtful until the chimes sounded and Della Street opened the door.

Dianne Alder said, "I won't come in, Della, thanks. Just hand me the papers and I'll be on my way."

"Come on in," Mason invited.

She stood on the threshold as Della Street opened the door wide. "Oh, thank you, Mr. Mason. Thank you so much, but I won't disturb you, I'll just run on."

"Come in, I'd like to talk with you."

"I . . ."

Mason indicated a chair.

Reluctantly, apparently not knowing how to avoid the lawyer's invitation without giving offense, Dianne Alder came in and said, "Actually I'm in a hurry and I . . . I didn't want to disturb you. I let Della look over my contract. She was interested and . . . well, I wanted to be sure that it was good. You see, I'm depending a lot on that contract."

"You have dependents?" Mason asked.

"No longer. Mother died over six months ago."

"Leave you any estate?" Mason asked casually.

"Heavens, no. She left a will leaving everything to me, but there wasn't anything to leave. *I* was supporting *her*. That's why I had to keep on with a steady job. I had thought some of—well, moving to the city but Mother liked it here and I didn't want to leave her, and it's too far to commute."

"Father living?"

"No. He died when I was ten years old. Really, Mr. Mason, I don't like to intrude on your time, and I—well . . . someone is waiting for me."

"I see," Mason said, and nodded to Della Street. "Better give her the contract, Della."

Dianne took the contract, thanked Della Street, gave Mason a timid hand, said, "Thank you so much, Mr. Mason. It's been such a pleasure meeting you," and then, turning, walked rapidly out of the door and all but ran down the corridor.

"Well?" Della Street said, closing the door.

Mason shook his head. "That girl needs someone to look after her."

"Isn't the contract all right?"

"Is Boring all right?" Mason asked.

"I don't know."

"He's paying one hundred dollars a week," Mason said. "He agrees to pay fifty-two hundred dollars a year. Suppose he doesn't pay it. Then what?"

"Why, he'd be liable for it, wouldn't he?"

"If he has any property," Mason said. "It hasn't been determined that he has any property. No one seems to know very much about him.

"Dianne Alder has given up a job. She's putting on weight—that's like rowing out of a bay when the tide is running out. It's mighty easy to go out but when you turn around and try to come back, you have to fight every inch of the way.

"Suppose that some Saturday morning the hundred dollars isn't forthcoming. Suppose she rings the telephone of Harrison T. Boring at the modeling agency and finds the phone has been disconnected?"

"Yes," Della Street said, "I can see where that would put Dianne in an embarrassing predicament. But, of course, if she were working at a job, the boss could tell her that he was handing her two weeks' wages and had no further need for her services."

"He could," Mason said, "but if he hired her in the first place and her services were satisfactory, he would have no particular reason to dispense with them."

"Perhaps Boring would have no reason to dispense with her services," Della Street said.

"That depends on what he was looking for in the first place," Mason pointed out. "If Dianne marries a millionaire, she has to pay over half of what she gets during a six-year period. If Boring quits paying, Dianne may have nothing but an added twelve pounds of weight and a worthless piece of paper."

Abruptly the lawyer reached a decision. "Get Paul Drake at the Drake Detective Agency, Della."

Della Street said, "Here we go again."

"We do, for a fact," Mason said. "This thing has aroused my curiosity. As an attorney I don't like to stand with my hands in my pockets and watch Dianne being taken for a ride.

"I know I'm getting the cart before the horse, but I'll bet odds that before we get finished Dianne will be asking for our help. When she does, I want to be one jump ahead of Boring instead of one jump behind."

Della Street said archly, "Would you be so solicitous of her welfare if she were flat-chested?"

Mason grinned. "Frankly, Della, I don't know. But I *think* my motivation at the moment is one of extreme curiosity, plus a desire to give Boring a lesson about picking on credulous young women."

"All right," she said, "I'll call Paul. He usually comes into the office around this time on Sundays to check up on the reports made by his various operatives over Friday and Saturday."

Della Street put through the call. After a few moments she said, "Hello, Paul. . . . The boss wants to talk with you."

Mason moved over to the telephone. "Hi, Paul. I have a job for you. A gentleman by the name of Harrison T. Boring. He has a business. It's called the Hollywood Talent Scout Modeling Agency. It's a Hollywood address and that's all I know for sure."

"What about him?" Drake asked.

"Get a line on him," Mason said, "and I'm particularly interested in knowing if he is cultivating some millionaire who has a penchant for young women. If you find any millionaires in the guy's background, I'd like to know about them.

"And it's very important that he has no inkling of the fact he's being investigated."

"Okay," Drake said, "I'll get a line on him."

"Here's another angle of the same picture," Mason said. "Dianne Alder, about twenty-four, with lots of this and that and these and those, blonde, blue-eyed, with lots and lots of figure. Living here at Bolero Beach. Mother died six months ago. Father died when she was ten years old. Worked as a secretary for a law firm. I'm interested in her. She's been living here for some time and it shouldn't be too difficult to get her background. What I am particularly interested in at the moment is finding out whether she's being kept under surveillance."

"May I ask who your client is?" Drake said. "I'd like to get the picture in proper perspective."

"I'm the client," Mason said. "Get your men started."

When Mason had hung up the telephone, Della Street said, "You think she's under surveillance, Perry?"

"I'm just wondering," Mason said. "I'd like to know if someone knew she'd been talking with us and had delivered a warning. She seemed rather disturbed about something. If anyone is playing games, I want to find out about it and if I'm going to be asked to sit in on the game I want to draw cards.

"Comment?"

Della Street smiled. "*No* comment, but I still wonder what would happen if she'd been flat-chested."

CHAPTER FOUR

PERRY MASON had a court hearing set for Monday morning. The hearing ran over until midafternoon and it was not until three-thirty that the lawyer reached his office.

Della Street said, "Paul has a preliminary report on your friend, Harrison T. Boring."

"Good," Mason said.

"I'll tell him you're here and he'll give you the low-down."

Della Street put through the call and a few moments later Paul Drake's code knock sounded on the door of Mason's private office.

Della Street opened the door and let him in.

"Hi, Beautiful," he said. "You certainly are a dish with all that beautiful sun tan."

"You haven't seen it all," she said demurely.

Mason said, "She gave *me* an overdose of sun just sitting out on the beach, looking at Dianne Alder. Wait until you see *her*, Paul."

"I understand from my operatives," Drake said, "that Dianne is quite somebody."

"She certainly cuts a figure," Della Street said.

"She's a nice kid, Paul," Mason said, "and I'm afraid that she's being victimized. What have you found out?"

"Well, of course, Dianne is an open book," Drake said. "My operatives quietly nosed around down there at Bolero Beach. She worked for a firm of attorneys, Corning, Chester and Corning. She hadn't been there too long. She hasn't had too much legal experience but she's an expert typist and shorthand operator. The point is, everyone likes her. The members of the partnership liked her, the clients liked her, and the other two stenographers liked her.

"Then something came along and she quit, but she didn't tell them why she was quitting. She quit almost overnight, simply giving them two weeks' notice.

"She'd been supporting her mother, who had been helpless for some eighteen months prior to her death. It had taken every cent the girl could earn and scrape together to pay the expenses of nursing. She'd work in the office daytimes and then come home and take over the job of being night nurse. It was quite a physical strain and quite a financial drain."

"No one knew why she had quit?" Mason asked.

"No. She was rather mysterious about the whole thing, simply said she was going to take life a little easier, that she had been working very hard and had been under quite a strain. People who knew what she had been through sympathized with her and were glad to see her relaxing a bit.

"One of the girls in the office thought that Dianne was going to get married but didn't want anyone to know about it. She got that impression simply because of the manner in which Dianne parried questions about what she was going to do and whether she had another job lined up.

"Dianne's father was drowned when she was about ten years old. He and another fellow went off on a trip to Catalina and like all of these inexperienced guys who start off with outboard motors and open boats, they simply didn't realize the problems they were going to encounter. They ran into head winds apparently; ran out of gas, drifted around for a while and finally capsized. The Coast Guard found the overturned boat."

"Bodies?" Mason asked.

"The body of the other man was found, but George Alder's body was never found. That caused complications. At the time there was quite a bit of property, but his affairs were more or less involved and there was a delay due to the fact that the body wasn't found. However, after a while the court accepted circumstantial evidence that the man had died, and the property, which was community property, went to the wife. She tried to straighten it out so she could salvage something but there were too many complications. And I guess by the time she got through meeting obligations and working out equities, the estate didn't amount to much.

"The mother worked as a secretary for a while and got Dianne through school and then through business college. For a while they both worked and got along pretty well financially. Then the mother had to quit work and finally became ill and was a heavy drag on Dianne during the last years of her life.

"Now then, we start in on Harrison T. Boring and there's a different story. Just as it was easy to find out about Dianne, it's hard to find out anything about Boring. The guy has a small account in a Hollywood bank. You can't find out much about it, of course, from the bank, but I did find out that he had references from Riverside, California. I started investigating around Riverside and picked up Boring's back trail there. Boring was in business but no one knew what business. He didn't have an office. He had an apartment and a telephone. He had an account at one of the banks, but the bank either didn't know anything about what he did for a living or wouldn't tell.

"However, we finally ran the guy to earth but we haven't been on the job long enough yet to tell you very much about him. Right at the moment he's somewhere in Hollywood. The place where he has desk space can evidently reach him on the phone whenever it's necessary.

"There's a phone listing under the name of the Hollywood Talent Scout Modeling Agency. It's the same number that's shared by all the clients, and the place where desk space is rented and where mail is answered.

"You wanted to find out about any millionaires in his background. There may be one. Boring has had some business dealings with a George D. Winlock. It's just business, but I don't know the nature of the business.

"Winlock is one of the big shots in Riverside, but he's

very shy and retiring, very hard to see; handles most of his business through secretaries and attorneys; has a few close friends and spends quite a bit of his time aboard his yacht which he keeps at Santa Barbara."

"Did you make any attempt to run down Winlock?"

"Not yet. I don't know very much about him. He drifted into Riverside, went to work as a real estate salesman, worked hard and was fairly successful. Then he took an option on some property out at Palm Springs, peddled the property, made a neat profit on the deal, picked up more property and within a few years was buying and selling property right and left. The guy apparently has an uncanny ability to know places that are going up in value.

"Of course, today the desert is booming. Air conditioning has made it possible to live comfortably the year around, and the pure air and dry climate have been responsible for attracting lots of people with a corresponding increase in real estate prices.

"Winlock got right in on the ground floor of the desert boom, and as fast as he could make a dollar he spread it out over just as much desert property as he could tie up. At one time he was spread out pretty thin and was pretty much in debt. Now he's cashing in. He's paid off his obligations and has become quite wealthy."

"Married?" Mason asked.

"Married to a woman who has been married before and who has a grown son, Marvin Harvey Palmer.

"That's just about all I can tell you on short notice."

"When did Winlock come to Riverside?" Mason asked.

"I didn't get the date. It was around fifteen years ago."

Mason drummed with his fingers on the edge of the desk, looked up and said, "See what you can find out about Winlock, Paul."

Drake said, "What do you want me to do, Perry? Shall I put a man on Winlock?"

"Not at the moment," Mason said. "Boring yes, but Winlock, no."

"I already have a man working on Boring," Drake said. "He's in Hollywood at the moment and I've got a man ready to tail him as soon as contact can be made. I can put a round-the-clock tail on him if that's what you want."

"Probably the one man is sufficient at the moment," Mason said. "The point is that he mustn't get suspicious. I don't want him to feel anyone is taking an interest in him.

"What about the Hollywood Talent Scout Modeling Agency, Paul? Did you get anything on it?"

"It's just a letterhead business," Drake said. "The address is at one of those answering-service places where they have a telephone, a secretary and a business address that serves a dozen or so companies. The whole thing is handled by one woman who rents an office and then subrents desk space and gives a telephone-answering, mail-forwarding service."

"Okay, Paul," Mason said. "Stay with it until you find out what it's all about. Remember that technically I don't have any client. I'm doing this on my own so don't get your neck stuck out."

"Will do," Drake said and went out in a rush, slamming the door behind him.

Drake had been out of the office less than ten minutes when the phone rang and Della Street relayed the message from the receptionist. "Dianne Alder is in the office," she reported.

Mason's frown suddenly lightened into a smile. "Well, how about that?" he said. "She's taken the bait and now someone has jerked the line and she's feeling the hook. Go bring her in, Della."

Della Street nodded, hurried through the door to the reception room and was back in a few moments with an apologetic Dianne Alder.

"Mr. Mason," she said, "I know I shouldn't intrude on you without an appointment and I feel just terrible about what happened yesterday; but . . . well, the bottom has dropped out of everything and I just *had* to find out what to do."

"What's happened?" Mason asked.

"A letter," she said, "sent registered mail, with a return receipt demanded."

"You signed the receipt?"

She nodded.

"And the letter is from Boring?" Mason asked.

Again she nodded.

"Telling you that your contract was at an end?"

She said, "Not exactly. You'd better read it."

She took a letter from an envelope, unfolded the paper and handed it to Mason.

Mason read the letter aloud for the benefit of Della Street.

"My dear Miss Alder: I know that as a very attractive young woman you realize the instability of styles and the vagaries of the style designers.

"A few weeks ago when we approached you with the idea of creating a new trend, we felt that there were very great possibilities in the idea; and, what is more to the point, we had a wealthy backer who agreed with us.

"Now, unfortunately, there has been a change in certain trends which has caused our backer to become decidedly cool to the whole idea and we ourselves now recognize the first indications of a potentially adverse trend.

"Under the circumstances, realizing that you are making great sacrifices in order to put on weight which may be difficult to take off, knowing that you have given up a good job and feeling that you can very readily either return to that position or secure one equally advantageous, we are reluctantly compelled to notify you that we are unable to go ahead with further payments under the contract.

"If you wish to keep yourself available and there should be a change in the trend, we will keep you in mind as our first choice but we feel it would be unfair to you to fail to notify you of what is happening and the fact that we will be unable to continue the weekly payments in the nature of a guarantee.

"Sincerely yours, Hollywood Talent Scout Modeling Agency, per Harrison T. Boring, President."

Mason studied the letter thoughtfully for a moment, then said, "May I see the envelope, please, Dianne?"

She handed him the envelope and Mason studied the postmark.

"You received your money Saturday morning?" he asked.

She nodded.

"And this letter was postmarked Saturday morning. Would you mind telling me why you were so anxious to get your contract back yesterday, Dianne?"

"Because I realized that I was not supposed to give out any information about what I was doing and—"

"And someone telephoned you or reminded you of that clause in your contract?"

"No, it was just something that I remembered Mr. Boring had said."

"What?"

"Well, you know I had been working as secretary for a firm of attorneys and he told me that he not only didn't want any publicity in connection with the contract, and that I wasn't to talk to anyone about it, but he mentioned particularly that he didn't want me to have any attorney friend looking it over, and if I took it to an attorney it would be a very serious breach of confidence."

"I see," Mason said.

"So after I let Della take the contract I suddenly realized that if she should show it to you, I would have been violating his instructions and the provisions of the contract. Tell me, Mr. Mason, do you suppose there's any chance that he knew what I was doing? That is, that I'd seen you Saturday and that I'd let Della Street look at the contract and—"

Mason interrupted by shaking his head. "This letter is postmarked eleven-thirty Saturday morning," he said.

"Oh, yes, that's right. I . . . I guess I felt a little guilty about letting the contract out of my possession."

"Was there a letter with the check you received Saturday morning?"

"No. Just the check. They never write letters, just send me the check."

"Did you notice the postmark?"

"No, I didn't."

"Save the envelope?"

"No."

"It must have been mailed Friday night," Mason said, "if you received it Saturday morning. Now, that means that between Friday night and Saturday noon, something happened to cause Mr. Boring to change his mind."

"He probably learned of some trend in styles which—"

"Nonsense!" Mason interrupted. "He wasn't thinking about any trend in styles. That contract, Dianne, is a trap."

"What kind of a trap?"

"I don't know," Mason said, "but you will notice the way it's drawn. Boring pays you a hundred dollars a week and gets one-half of your gross income from all sources for a period of up to six years if he wants to hold the contract in force that long."

Dianne said somewhat tearfully, "Of course I didn't regard this as an option. I thought it was an absolute contract. I thought I was entitled to a hundred dollars a week for two years, at least."

"That's what the contract says," Mason said.

"Well then, what right does he have to terminate it in this way?"

"He has no right," Mason said.

"I'm so glad to hear you say so! That was the way I read the contract, but this letter sounds so—so final."

"It sounds very final," Mason said. "Very final, very businesslike, and was intended to cause you to panic."

"But what should I do, Mr. Mason?"

"Give me a dollar," Mason said.

"A dollar?"

"Yes. By way of retainer, and leave your copy of the contract with me, if you brought it."

Dianne hesitated a moment, then laughed, opened her purse and handed him a dollar and the folded contract.

"I can pay you—I can pay you for your advice, Mr. Mason."

Mason shook his head. "I'll take the dollar, which makes you my client," he said. "I'll collect the rest of it from Boring or there won't be any charge."

Mason turned to Della Street. "Let's see what we can find listed under the Hollywood Talent Scout Modeling Agency, Della."

A few moments later Della Street said, "Here they are. Hollywood three, one, five hundred."

"Give them a ring," Mason said.

Della Street put through the connection to an outside

line, her nimble fingers whirled the dial of the telephone, and a moment later she nodded to Mason.

Mason picked up his telephone and heard a feminine voice say, "Hollywood three, one, five hundred."

"Mr. Boring, please," Mason said.

"Who did you wish to speak with?"

"Mr. Boring."

"Boring?" she said. "Boring? . . . What number were you calling?"

"Hollywood three, one, five hundred."

"What? . . . Oh, yes, Mr. Boring, yes, yes. The Hollywood Talent Scout Modeling Agency. Just a moment, please. I think Mr. Boring is out of the office at the moment. Would you care to leave a message?"

"This is Perry Mason," the lawyer said. "I want him to call me on a matter of considerable importance. I'm an attorney at law and I wish to get in touch with him as soon as possible."

"I'll try and see that he gets the message just as soon as possible," the feminine voice said.

"Thank you," Mason said, and hung up.

He sat for a few moments looking speculatively at Dianne.

"Do you think there's any chance of getting something for me, Mr. Mason?"

"I don't know," Mason said. "A great deal depends on the setup of the Hollywood Talent Scout Modeling Agency. A great deal depends on whether I can find something on which to predicate a charge of fraud; or perhaps of obtaining money under false pretenses."

"False pretenses?" she asked.

Mason said, "I don't think Boring ever had the faintest idea of promoting you as a model legitimately. Whatever he had in mind for you was along entirely different lines. He didn't intend to use you to start any new styles, and my best guess is that all of this talk about finding a firm-fleshed young woman who could put on twelve pounds and still keep her curves in the right places was simply so much double-talk.

"I think the real object of the contract was to tie you up so that you would be forced to give Boring a fifty per cent share of your gross income."

"But I don't have any gross income other than the hundred dollars a week—unless, of course, I could make some because of modeling contracts and television and things of that sort."

"Exactly," Mason said. "There were outside sources of income which Boring felt would materialize. Now then, something happened between Friday night and Saturday noon to make him feel those sources of income were not going to materialize. The question is, what was it?"

"But he must have had *something* in mind, Mr. Mason. There must have been some tentative television contract or some modeling assignment or something of that sort."

"That's right," Mason said. "There was something that he had found out about; something he wanted to share in; something he was willing to put up money on so he could hold you in line. And then the idea didn't pan out."

"Well?" she asked.

Mason said, "There are two things we can do. The obvious, of course, is to get some money out of Boring by way of a settlement. The next thing is to try and find out what it was he had in mind and promote it ourselves.

"Now, I want you to listen very carefully, Dianne. When a person is a party to a contract and the other party breaks that contract, the innocent person has a choice of several remedies.

"He can either repudiate the contract or rescind it under certain circumstances, or he can continue to treat the contract as in force and ask that the other party be bound by the obligations, or he can accept the fact the other party has broken the contract and sue him for damages resulting from the breach.

"All that is in case the element of fraud does *not* enter into the contract. If fraud has been used, there are additional remedies.

"Now, I want you to be very careful to remember that as far as you are concerned the contract is at an end. There are no further obligations on your part under the contract. But we intend to hold Boring for damages because of the breach of the contract. If anyone asks you anything about the contract, you refer them to me. You simply refuse to discuss it. If anyone asks you how you are coming with your diet, or your weight-gaining program, you tell them that the person with whom you had the contract broke it and the matter is in the hands of your attorney. Can you remember that?"

She nodded.

"Where are you going now? Do you want to stay in town or go back to Bolero Beach?"

"I had intended to go back to Bolero Beach."

"You have your car?"

"Yes."

"Go on back to Bolero Beach," Mason said. "See that Della has your address and phone number and keep in touch with your telephone. I may want to reach you right away in connection with a matter of some importance.

"Now, how do you feel about a settlement?"

"In what way?"

"What would you settle for?"

"Anything I could get."

"That's all I wanted to know," Mason said. "You quit worrying about it, Dianne, and incidentally start cutting down on the sweets and developing a more sensible diet."

She smiled at him and said, "My clothes are so tight I . . . I was just about to get an entirely new wardrobe."

"I think it'll be cheaper in the long run," Mason said, "to start taking off weight."

"Yes," she said somewhat reluctantly, "I suppose so. It's going to be a long uphill struggle."

CHAPTER FIVE

It was shortly before five o'clock when Gertie rang Della Street's telephone and Della Street, taking the message, turned to Mason.

"Harrison T. Boring is in the outer office in person."

"What do you know!" Mason said.

"Do I show him in?"

"No," Mason said, "treat him like any other client. Go out, ask him if he has an appointment, get his name, address, telephone number and the nature of his business, and then show him in. In the meantime slip Gertie a note and have her call Paul Drake, tell him Boring is here and I want him shadowed from the moment he leaves."

"Suppose he won't give me his telephone number and tell me the nature of his business?"

"Throw him out," Mason said, "only be sure there's enough time for Paul to get a tail on him. He's either going to come in the way I want him to or he isn't going to come in at all. My best guess is the guy's scared."

Della Street left and was gone nearly five minutes.

When she returned she said, "I think he's scared. He gave me his name, telephone number, address, and told me that you had said you wanted to have him call you upon a matter of importance, that rather than discuss it over the telephone he had decided to call in person since he had another appointment in the vicinity."

"All right," Mason said. "Now we'll let him come in."

Della Street ushered Harrison Boring into the office.

Boring was rather distinguished-looking, with broad shoulders, sideburns, keen gray eyes, and a certain air of dignity. He was somewhere in his late thirties, slim-waisted and spare-fleshed, despite his broad shoulders. He had a close-clipped mustache which firmed his mouth.

"Good afternoon, Mr. Mason," he said. "I came to see you. You asked me to get in touch with you, and since I was here in the neighborhood on another matter I decided to come in."

"Sit down," Mason invited.

Boring accepted the seat, smiled, settled back, crossed his legs.

"Dianne Alder," Mason said.

There wasn't the faintest flicker of surprise on Boring's face.

"Oh, yes," he said. "A very nice young woman. I'm sorry the plans we had for her didn't materialize."

"You had plans?"

"Oh, yes, very definitely."

"And made a contract."

"That's right—I take it you're representing her, Mr. Mason?"

"I'm representing her."

"I'm sorry she felt that it was necessary to go to an attorney. That is the last thing I would have wanted."

"I can imagine," Mason said.

"I didn't mean it that way," Boring interposed hastily.

"I did," Mason said.

"There is nothing to be gained by consulting an attorney," Boring said, "and there is, of course, the extra time, trouble and expense involved."

"*My* time, *your* trouble, *your* expense," Mason said.

Boring's smile seemed to reflect genuine amusement. "I'm afraid, Mr. Mason, there are some things about the facts of life in Hollywood you need to understand."

"Go ahead," Mason said.

"In Hollywood," Boring said, "things are done on front, on flash, on a basis of public relations.

"When a writer or an actor gets to the end of his contract and his option isn't taken up, he immediately starts spending money. He buys a new automobile, purchases a yacht, is seen in all the expensive night spots, and lets it be known that he is at liberty but is thinking of taking a cruise to the South Seas on his yacht before he considers any new contract.

"The guy probably has just enough to make a down payment on the yacht and uses his old automobile as a down payment on the new car. He has a credit card which is good for the checks at the night spots and he's sweating in desperation, but he shows up regularly with good-looking cuties and buys expensive meals. He radiates an atmosphere of prosperity.

"During that time his public relations man is busily engaged in trying to plant stories about him and his agent is letting it be known that while his client has his heart set on a nine to twelve months vacation on his yacht in the South Seas, he *might* be persuaded to postpone the vacation long enough to take on one more job if the pay should be right.

"That's Hollywood, Mr. Mason."

"That's Hollywood," Mason said. "So what?"

"Simply, Mr. Mason, that I live in Hollywood. I work with Hollywood. I had some elaborate plans. I backed those plans up with what cash I had available and I was able to interest a backer.

"Late Friday night my backer got cold feet on the entire proposition. I hope I can get him reinterested, but I can't do it by seeming to be desperate. I have to put up a good front, I have to let it appear that the loss of his backing was merely a minor matter because I have so many other irons in the fire that I can't be bothered over just one more scheme which could have earned a few millions."

"And so?" Mason asked.

"And so," Boring said, "Dianne would have shared in my prosperity. Now she has to share in my hard luck. If the girl is willing to keep right on going, if she's willing to develop her curves and try to glamorize herself in every way possible, I am hoping that the deal can be reinstated."

"How soon?"

"Within a matter of weeks—perhaps of days."

"You mean you hope the backer will change his mind?"

· "Yes."

"Do you have any assurance that he will?"

"I think I can— Well, I'll be perfectly frank, Mr. Mason. I think I can guarantee that he'll come around."

"If you're so certain of it, then keep up your payments to Dianne Alder."

"I can't do it."

"Why?"

"I haven't the money."

Mason said, "We're not interested in your hard luck. You made a definite contract. For your information, upon a breach of that contract my client could elect to take any one of certain remedies.

"She has elected to consider your repudiation of the contract as a breach of the contractual relationship and a termination of all future liability on her part under the contract. She will hold you for whatever damages she has sustained."

"Well, I sympathize with her," Boring said. "If I were in a position to do so, I'd write her a check for her damages right now, Mr. Mason. I don't try to disclaim my responsibility in the least. I am simply pointing out to you that I am a promoter, I am an idea man. I had this idea and I had it sold. Something happened to unsell my backer. I think I can get him sold again. If I can't, I can get another backer. But every dollar that I have goes into keeping up the type of background that goes with the line of work I'm in. My entire stock-in-trade

310 ERLE STANLEY GARDNER

is kept in my showcases. I don't have any shelves. I don't have any reserve supplies."

"And you're trying to tell me you don't have any money?" Mason asked.

"Exactly."

Mason regarded the man thoughtfully. "You're a salesman."

"That's right."

"A promoter."

"That's right."

"You sell ideas on the strength of your personality."

"Right."

"So," Mason said, "instead of talking with me over the telephone, instead of referring me to your attorney, you came here personally to put on your most convincing manner and persuade me that you had no cash and therefore it would be useless for my client to start suit."

"Correct again, Mr. Mason."

"Do you have an attorney?"

"No."

"You'd better get one."

"Why?"

"Because I'm going to make you pay for what you've done to Dianne Alder."

"You can't get blood out of a turnip, Mr. Mason."

"No," Mason said, "but you can get sugar out of a beet —if you know how—and in the process you raise hell with the beet."

Boring regarded him speculatively.

"Therefore," Mason said, "I would suggest that you

get an attorney and I'll discuss the situation with him
rather than with you."

"I don't have an attorney, I don't have any money to
hire an attorney, and I'm not going to get one. With all
due respect to you, Mr. Mason, you're not going to get a
thin dime out of me; at least, as long as you act this
way."

"Was there some other way you had in mind?" Mason
asked.

"Frankly, there was."

"Let's hear it."

"My idea is just as good as it ever was. Sooner or later
I'm going to get another backer. When I do, Dianne will
be sitting on Easy Street. I tell you, Mr. Mason, the idea
is sound. People are tired of starving their personalities
along with their bodies.

"You let some well-nourished, firm-fleshed, clear-eyed
model come along that has lots of figure, and we'll start
a style change overnight."

"I'm not an expert on women's styles," Mason said.
"I try to be an expert on law. I'm protecting my client's
legal interests."

"Go ahead and protect them."

"All right," Mason said. "My client has a claim of
damages against you for whatever that may be worth.
We won't argue about that now. My client also has the
right to consider your repudiation of the contract as a
termination of all future liability on her part."

"I am not a lawyer, Mr. Mason, but that would seem
to be fair."

"Therefore," Mason said, "regardless of what else may be done, you have no further claims on Dianne Alder or on her earnings."

"I'd like to see the situation left in *status quo*," Boring said.

"*Status quo* calls for the payment of a hundred dollars a week."

"I can't do it."

"Then there isn't any *status quo*."

Boring held out his hand to Mason with a gesture of complete friendship. "Thank you, Mr. Mason, for giving me your time. I'm glad we had this talk. Dianne is a nice girl. You do whatever you can to protect her interests, but I just wanted to let you know that trying to collect from me would simply be throwing good money after bad."

Boring kept talking while he was shaking hands. "If I ever get any money of my own, Mason, you won't need to sue me for it because I'd back this idea of mine with every cent I had. It's a red-hot idea and I know it's going to pay off. I realize that the situation is a little discouraging at the moment as far as Dianne is concerned, but I know that sooner or later my idea is going across. I feel in my bones that within a few short months Dianne will be the toast of the town."

"Let's be very careful," Mason said, moving Boring toward the exit door, "that the toast doesn't get burnt."

"I can assure you, Mr. Mason, with every ounce of sincerity I possess, that I have her best interests at heart."

"That's fine," Mason said, "and you can be assured that I have them at heart."

Mason held the exit door open for Boring, who smiled affably then turned and walked down the corridor.

Mason turned to Della Street as the door closed. "You got Paul Drake?" he asked.

"That's right. He'll be under surveillance from the time he leaves the building. One of Drake's operatives will probably be in the elevator with him as he goes down."

Mason grinned.

"Quite a promoter," Della Street said.

Mason nodded. "That damned contract," he said. "What about it?"

"I wish I knew what Boring was after. I wish I knew the reason he drew up that contract in the first place."

"You don't believe his story about a new type of model and—"

Mason interrupted to say, "Della, I don't believe one single damn thing about that guy. As far as I'm concerned, even his mustache could be false— Get me that contract, will you, Della? I want to study it once more."

Della Street brought him the file jacket. Mason took out the contract and read it carefully.

"Any clues?" Della Street asked.

Mason shook his head. "I can't figure it out. It's . . ." Suddenly he stopped talking.

"Yes?" Della Street prompted.

"Well, I'll be damned!" Mason said.

"What?" Della Street asked.

"The red herring is what fooled me," Mason said.

"And what's the red herring?"

"The avoirdupois, the diet, the twelve pounds in ten weeks, the curves."

"That wasn't the real object of the contract?" Della Street asked.

"Hell, no," Mason said. "That was the window dressing. That was the red herring."

"All right, go ahead," she said. "I'm still in the dark."

"Take that out of the contract," Mason said, "and what do you have left? We've seen these contracts before, Della."

"I don't get it."

"The missing-heir racket," Mason said.

Della Street's eyes widened.

Mason said, "Somebody dies and leaves a substantial estate, but no relatives. No one takes any great interest in the estate at the moment except the public administrator.

"Then these sharpshooters swoop down on the situation. They start feverishly running down all the information they can get on the decendent. They find that some relatives are living in distant parts, relatives who have entirely lost track of the family connection.

"So these sharpshooters contact the individual potential heirs and say, 'Look here. If we can uncover some property for you which you didn't know anything at all about, will you give us half of it? We'll pay all the expenses, furnish all the attorneys' fees out of our share. All you have to do is to accept your half free and clear of all expenses of collection.' "

"But who's the relative in this case?" Della Street asked. "Dianne's family is pretty well accounted for.

Her father died, and all of the estate, such as it was, was distributed to her mother, and then her mother died, leaving everything to Dianne."

"There could be property inherited from the more remote relatives," Mason pointed out. "That's where these sharpies make their money."

"Then why would he quit making the payments to her and forfeit all right to her share of the money?"

"Either because he found out she wasn't entitled to it," Mason said, "or because he's found another angle he can play to greater advantage."

"And if he has?" Della Street asked.

"Then," Mason said, "it's up to us to find out what he's doing, block his play and get the inheritance for Dianne, all without paying him one thin dime."

"Won't that be quite a job?" Della Street asked.

"It'll be a terrific job," Mason said. "We're going to have to get hold of Dianne and start asking her about her family on her father's side and her mother's side, her cousins, aunts, second cousins, uncles and all the rest of it. Then we've got to start running down each person to find out where they're located, when they died, how they died, where they died, what estate was probated and all the rest of it.

"There is, however, one method of short-cutting the job."

"What's that?"

"By shadowing Boring, checking back on where he's been, what he's been doing, and, if possible, with whom he's corresponding—and that's a job for Paul so we'll let Paul wrestle with it until he gets a lead.

"Come on, Della, let's close up the office and forget about business for a change. We may as well call it a day."

Della Street nodded.

Mason opened the exit door, started to go out, suddenly paused and said, "Della, there's someone rattling the knob of the door of the reception office—would you mind slipping out and telling him that we're closing up and see if we can make an appointment with this man for tomorrow."

A few moments later she was back in the office. "You may want to see this man, Chief," she said.

"Who is it?"

"His name is Montrose Foster and he wants to talk to you about Harrison T. Boring."

"Well, well!" Mason said, grinning. "Under the circumstances, Della, I guess we'll postpone closing the office until we've talked with Mr. Montrose Foster, following which we could, if so desired, dine uptown and perhaps invite Paul Drake to go to dinner with us.

"Bring him in."

Within a few seconds, Della Street was back with a wiry, thin-faced individual whose close-set, black, beady eyes were restlessly active. He had high cheekbones, a very prominent pointed nose, quick, nervous mannerisms and rapid enunciation.

"How do you do, Mr. Mason, how do you do?" he said, "I recognize you from your photographs. I've always wanted to meet you.

"Tops in the field, that's what you are, sir, tops in the field. It's a pleasure to meet the champion."

"What can I do for you?" Mason asked, sizing the man up with good-natured appraisal.

"Perhaps we can do something for each other, Mr. Mason. I'll put it that way."

"Well, sit down," Mason said. "It's after hours and we were just closing up. However, if you'll be brief, we can make a preliminary exploration of the situation."

"My interest is in Harrison T. Boring," Foster said, "and I have an idea that you're interested in him."

"And if so?" Mason asked.

"I think we could pool our information, Mr. Mason. I think I could be of some assistance to you and you might be of some assistance to me."

"Where do we begin?" Mason asked.

"I happen to know—and never mind how I happen to know it—that you left word for Harrison Boring to get in touch with you. I happen to know that Mr. Boring picked up that message and in place of calling you on the telephone as apparently you wished him to do, came here in person. I happen to know that he left here only a short time ago. And, if you'll forgive me, that was the reason I was so persistently trying to attract attention by knocking at the door of your reception room. I felt certain you were still here."

"I see," Mason said.

"Now then," Foster went on, "if you'll let me have the name of your client, Mr. Mason, I think I can perhaps be of help to you."

"And why do you wish the name of my client?"

"I'm simply checking, Mr. Mason, to make certain that I'm on the right track."

Mason's eyes narrowed slightly. "I fail to see what good it would do to divulge the name of my client. If, of course, you wish to tell me anything about Boring, I'm ready to listen."

"Boring," Foster said, "is an opportunist, a very shrewd character, very shrewd."

"Unscrupulous?" Mason asked.

"I didn't *say* that," Foster said.

"May I ask how you know so much about him?"

"The man worked for me for a period of two years."

"In what capacity?" Mason asked.

"He was a—well, you might say an investigator."

"And what is your line of work?" Mason asked.

Foster became elaborately casual. "I have several activities, Mr. Mason. I am a man of somewhat diverse interests."

"The principal one of which," Mason said, making a shot in the dark, "is locating missing heirs. Is that right?"

Foster was visibly shaken. "Oh," he said, somewhat crestfallen, "you know about that, do you?"

"Let's put it this way, I surmised it."

"And why did you surmise that, may I ask?"

"The fact that you were so interested in the name of my client, Mr. Foster."

Foster said somewhat sheepishly, "I may have been a little abrupt but, after all, I was trying to help *you*, Mr. Mason. That was what I primarily had in mind."

"And at the same time, helping yourself to a piece of cake," Mason said. "Let's see if I can reconstruct the situation. You're running an agency for the location of lost heirs. Boring was working for you. All of a sudden he resigned his position and started quietly investigating something on his own.

"You felt certain that this was some information he had uncovered in the course of his employment and something on which he was going to capitalize to his own advantage. You have been making every effort to find out what the estate is, and who the missing heir is, and hope you can get the information before Boring signs anyone up on a contract."

Montrose Foster seemed to grow smaller by the second as Mason was talking.

"Well," he said at length, "I guess you've either found out all there is to know or else you got Boring in such a position you were able to turn him inside out."

"What was the matter on which Boring was working when he quit you?" Mason said. "Perhaps that would be a clue."

"That's a clue and a very nice one," Foster said, "and it's a very nice question, Mr. Mason, but I'm afraid we've reached a point where we're going to have to trade. You give me the name of the client and I'll give you the name of the estate on which Boring was working."

Mason thought things over for a moment, then slowly shook his head.

"It might save you a lot of time," Foster said pleadingly.

"That's all right," Mason told him. "I'll spend the time."

"It will cost a lot of money."

"I have the money."

"You give me the name of your client," Foster said, "and if that client hasn't already signed up with Boring, I'll run down the matter for twenty-five per cent. Surely, Mr. Mason, you can't expect anything better than that. Our usual fee is fifty per cent and that's in cases which don't involve a great deal of work."

"Well," Mason said, "I'll take your offer under advisement."

"There isn't time, Mr. Mason. This is a matter of considerable urgency."

Mason said, "I don't do any horse-trading until I've seen the horse I'm trading for."

"I've put my cards on the table."

"No, you haven't. You haven't told me anything about yourself except to confess that the information you've been able to uncover has not been anything on which you could capitalize."

"All right, all right," Foster said. "You're too smart for me, Mr. Mason. You keep reading my mind, so to speak. I *will* put the cards on the table. If I could find the name of the heir, I'd start running it down from the other end and then I'd find it. As it is, you're quite correct in assuming that I haven't been able to get any satisfaction from checking over the estates which Boring was investigating."

"And you've talked with Boring?" Mason asked. "Offered to pool your information? Offered him a larger commission than you customarily granted?"

"Yes. He laughed at me."

"And then what happened?"

"Then I'm afraid I lost my temper. I told him what I thought of him in no uncertain terms."

"And what were the no uncertain terms?"

"The man is a liar, a cheat, a sneak, a double-crosser, a back-stabber and entirely unscrupulous. He puts up a good front but he's nothing more than a con man. He worked for me, let me carry him during all the lean times, then just as soon as he stumbled onto something juicy he manipulated things so he could put the whole deal in his pocket and walk off with it."

Mason flashed Della Street a quick glance. "I take it you didn't have him tied up under contract. Therefore, there wasn't any reason why he couldn't quit his employment and go to work on his own, so I can't see why you're so bitter."

"This wasn't something he did on his own, Mason. Don't you understand? This was something he uncovered while he was working for me. I was paying him a salary and a commission and he stumbled onto this thing and then, instead of being loyal to his employer and his employment, he sent me a letter of resignation and started developing it himself."

"If you don't know what it was," Mason asked, "how do you know it was something he uncovered as a part of his employment?"

"Now look," Foster said, "you're pumping me for a lot of information. I know what you're doing, but I have no choice except to ride along in the hope that you will see the advantages of co-operating with me."

"I'm afraid," Mason said, "I don't see those advantages clearly, at least at the present."

"Well, think them over," Foster said. "You let me know the name of your client and I'll start chasing down the thing from that angle. I have facilities for that sort of investigative work. That's my specialty."

"And then you'll want half of what my client gets?" Mason asked.

"I told you I'll make a deal with you, Mason. I'll take twenty-five per cent and I'll do all the work. You can take twenty-five per cent as your fee and then your client will get the other half. Is that fair?"

"No."

"What's unfair about it?"

"If I don't do any of the work," Mason said, "I shouldn't charge my client twenty-five per cent of the inheritance."

"Well, you've got to live," Foster said.

"With myself," Mason pointed out, smiling.

"Oh, all right, all right. Think it over," Foster said. "You're going to be doing business with me sooner or later anyway."

"How so?"

"Because I'm going to find out what Boring is working on if it takes my last cent. I'm going to see to it that he doesn't profit by his double-crossing."

"That's a very natural attitude for you to take," Mason said, "if you want to spend the effort and money."

"I've got the time, I've got the money, I'll make the effort," Foster said. "Think my proposition over, Mr. Mason. Here's one of my cards. I'm located in Riverside. *You* can reach me on the phone at any time, day or night. Call the office during the daytime, and the night number is my residence."

"Thanks a lot," Mason said. "I'll think it over."

As Della Street held the corridor door open for Montrose Foster, he twisted his head with a quick, terrier-like motion, wreathed his face into a smile and hurried out into the corridor.

The door slowly closed behind him and Della Street turned to Mason.

"The plot thickens," she said.

"The plot," Mason said, frowning thoughtfully, "develops lumps similar to what my friend, on a camping trip, called Thousand Island gravy."

"Well?" she asked.

"Let's start taking stock of the situation," he said. "Foster was the brains behind a lost heirs organization. He dug out the cases and carried the financial burden. Boring, with his impressive manner and his dignified approach, was the contact man.

"Now then, if any unusual case had been uncovered, if any information had been turned up, one would think Foster would have been the man to do it, not Boring."

"I see your point," Della Street said.

"Yet Boring is the one who turns up the case and despite the fact that Foster had been directing his activities, Foster doesn't have a single lead as to what the case is. So now Foster is desperately trying to find out who the heir is and start backtracking from that angle."

"Well," Della Street said, "it's a tribute to your thinking that you figured it out this far, largely from studying the contract."

"*I'm* not handing myself any bouquets," Mason said. "I should have figured it out sooner. . . . Now then, Foster is evidently having Boring shadowed."

"Otherwise he wouldn't have known he came here?" Mason nodded.

"And we're having Boring shadowed," Della Street said.

"Shadows on shadows," Mason told her. "Come on, Della, we're going to have dinner on the office expense account and think things over. Then I'll drive you home."

"Cocktails?" Della Street asked, with a smile.

"The works," Mason said. "Somehow I feel like celebrating. I love to get into a situation where everyone is trying to double-cross everyone else."

"What about Dianne? Do we talk with her and tell her what we have discovered?"

"Not yet," Mason said. "We do a little thinking first; in fact, we do a lot of thinking."

CHAPTER SIX

A ROUTINE COURT HEARING on Tuesday morning developed into a legal battle which ran over into the afternoon and it was three-thirty that afternoon before Mason checked in at his office.

"Hello, Della," the lawyer said. "What's new?"

"Mostly routine," she said. "How did the court hearing go?"

Mason grinned. "Things were looking pretty black and then the attorney on the other side started arguing with the judge over a minor point and the argument progressed to a point where there was considerable heat on both sides. By the time the hearing was finished the judge decided it our way."

"And what did you do?" she asked, with exaggerated innocence. "I suppose you just stood there with your hands in your pockets while the attorney and the judge were arguing."

"I tried to act the part of a peacemaker," Mason said. "I poured oil on the troubled flames."

Della Street laughed. "I'll bet you did just that."

"What's new with our case involving the curvaceous blonde, Della?"

"There seems to be a lot of activity centering in Riverside," she said. "Paul Drake reports that Harrison Boring has gone to Riverside. He is now registered in the Restawhile Motel and is in Unit 10.

"Drake's man also reports that Boring is being shadowed by another agency."

"You mean he's wearing two tails and doesn't know about either one?" Mason asked.

"Apparently not," Della Street said. "Of course, under the circumstances Drake's man is being *most* discreet and is relying as much as possible on electronic shadowing devices which send out audible signals to the car following. He thinks the other agency is using contact observation with no electronic shadowing. So far, Boring apparently isn't suspicious. Paul says the man is hurrying around, covering a lot of territory."

Mason settled back in his swivel chair. "Hurrying around, eh?" he said musingly.

"Here's the mail," Della Street said, sliding a stack of letters across Mason's desk.

Mason picked up the top letter, started to read it, put it down, then pushed the pile of mail to one side, sat for more than a minute in thoughtful silence.

"Something?" Della Street asked.

"I'm toying with an idea," Mason said, "and hang it, the more I think of it, the more plausible it seems."

"Want to talk it out or let it incubate?" she asked.

"I think I'd like to talk it out," Mason said, "and let's see if it isn't logical. Boring was working on lost heirs, obscure estates. Yet when Foster tried to back-track his activities, he couldn't find anything. Neverthe-less, Foster is a pretty thoroughgoing chap and he has the inside track. In the first place, he knows all the rou-tine methods of investigation and in the second place he knew exactly where Boring had been and what activi-ties he had engaged in. Yet nothing that he has been able to uncover gives any clue to what triggered Boring's break with him."

Della Street, knowing that Mason was simply think-ing out loud, sat thoughtfully attentive, furnishing him with a silent audience.

"So suddenly Harrison T. Boring comes to Dianne Alder," Mason said, "and ties her up on a contract, but the contract is so disguised that neither she nor anyone else who might look at the contract would tumble to the fact that it was a lost heir's contract; the sugar-coating disguised the pill to such an extent that the whole thing looked like a piece of candy."

Della Street merely nodded.

"Now then," Mason went on, "Montrose Foster. Re-gardless of the fact that he's a little terrier, but no one's dummy, he begins to think that perhaps he should start working on the case from the other end and is anxious to find out who Boring has been seeing."

Again Della Street nodded.

"He is having Boring shadowed. He undoubtedly knows that Boring is seeing Winlock. But Winlock doesn't seem to be the solution to the problem, at least as far as Foster is concerned.

"Now, that's where we're one step ahead of Montrose

Foster. We know that whatever lead Harrison Boring
may have uncovered, he followed it to Dianne Alder.
Dianne Alder is the target in the case, the pot of gold at
the end of the rainbow."

Mason was silent for a few seconds, then he said, "Yet,
having found Dianne Alder and having tied her up,
Boring suddenly lets her go.

"Now, why?"

Della Street merely sat looking at him, making no
comment.

"The reason is, of course," Mason said, "that the advantage Boring intended to get from his contract with
Dianne—and that must have been a considerable advantage for him to put out a hundred dollars a week—has
been superseded by something much more profitable to
Harrison Boring."

"Such as what?" Della Street asked.

"Blackmail."

"Blackmail!" she exclaimed.

"That's right," Mason said. "He started out on a missing heir's contract and he suddenly shifted to blackmail.
That is about the only explanation that would account
for his going to all that trouble to sign Dianne up on a
missing heir's contract and then suddenly drop her."

"But why would blackmail tie in with missing heirs?"
she asked.

"Because," Mason said, "we've been looking at the
whole picture backwards. There aren't any missing
heirs."

"But I thought you just said Dianne was a missing
heir."

"We may have started in with that idea," Mason said, "but it's a false premise and that's why we aren't getting anywhere, and that's why Montrose Foster isn't getting anywhere. Dianne Alder isn't a missing heir; this is a case of a missing testator."

"What do you mean?"

"Dianne's father was killed some fourteen years ago, drowned accidentally while boating in the channel, but his body was never found."

"Then, you mean . . . ?"

"I mean," Mason said, "that his body wasn't found because he wasn't dead. He was rescued in some way and decided to leave the impression that he was dead. He went out and began life all over and probably amassed something of a fortune.

"He probably was tired of his home life, wanted to disappear the way many men do, but never had the opportunity until that boating accident."

"So then?" Della Street asked, with sudden excitement.

"So then," Mason said, "we start looking for a wealthy man—someone who has no background beyond fourteen years ago, someone who couldn't divorce his wife because he was supposed to be dead, someone who has since remarried, someone who is exceedingly vulnerable, therefore, to blackmail.

"Dianne, as his daughter, would have a claim which could be enforced."

"But didn't Dianne's mother take all of the estate?" Della Street asked.

"All that she knew about," Mason said. "All the es-

tate that Dianne's father left *at the time of his disappearance*. But technically he was still married to Dianne's mother. Technically anything that he acquired
after his disappearance and before the death of Dianne's
mother was community property."

"Then," Della Street said, with sudden excitement,
"the key to the whole thing is George D. Winlock."

"Exactly," Mason said. "Winlock, the wealthy man
whom Harrison Boring is cultivating at the moment;
Winlock, the real estate speculator who showed up in
Riverside about fourteen years ago as a salesman, who
started plunging in real estate, became wealthy, and is
now one of the town's leading citizens; Winlock, who
has a high social position, a wife who really isn't a wife.
. . . No wonder Boring was willing to let Dianne off the
hook! He had landed a bigger fish."

"I take it," Della Street said, "that we go to Riverside."

Mason grinned. "Get your things packed, Della. Put
in some notebooks and pencils. We go to Riverside."

"And we see George D. Winlock?"

"We make some very careful investigations," Mason
said, "and we are very, very careful indeed not to upset
any apple carts, not to make any accusations, not to
jump to any false conclusions, but very definitely we see
George D. Winlock."

"And when we see him?"

"We see him as Dianne Alder's attorney, and the min-
ute we do that I think you will find that Harrison T.
Boring's blackmail has been dried up at the source.
And, since Boring has repudiated his contract with Di-

anne, whatever we can get for her by way of a settlement will be pure velvet to her.

"How long will it take you to get some things packed,
Della?"

She smiled. "Five minutes. I've been through this
same thing so often that I'm now keeping an overnight
bag in the coat closet."

CHAPTER SEVEN

SID NYE, Paul Drake's right-hand man, was waiting for Perry Mason when he and Della Street arrived at the colorful Mission Inn Hotel in Riverside.

"Hello, Sid," Mason said, shaking hands. "You know Della Street. What's new?"

"Something I want to talk over with you," Nye said. "I talked with Paul on the phone and he said you were on your way up here and should be here any minute."

Della Street filled out the registration cards, and Mason, Nye and Della were shown up to the lawyer's suite. Mason ordered a round of drinks, and Nye, settling himself comfortably in the chair, said, "The fat seems to be in the fire."

"Just what happened?" Mason asked.

"I don't know all of the ramifications of the case," Nye said, "but it seems that you were having a Harrison T. Boring shadowed."

"That's right. What happened?"

"Apparently he got wise that he was being tailed, but

it wasn't our fault. There was another man following him, and Boring first became suspicious because the other man was using contact shadowing."

"Go ahead," Mason said.

"You remember Moose Dillard?" Nye asked.

Mason frowned, then said, "Oh, yes. I place him now. The big fellow that I represented when he was in a jam over losing his license."

"That's right. That was when he lost his temper and flattened a politician who was calling him names. Personally I think the politician had it coming to him, but that's neither here nor there. The guy had political influence and Dillard has a hell of a temper. Anyway, Moose Dillard was tailing Boring. He put an electronic bug on Boring's car so the tailing could be done without giving Boring any cause for alarm, and there's no reason on earth Boring should have known he was being shadowed if it hadn't been for this other man using contact methods.

"Well, Boring spotted the other shadow and started out to ditch him, and did a good job of it. That other shadow was left way back in Hollywood somewhere, but it made Boring shadow conscious.

"Of course, with our electronic tailing devices, Moose Dillard had no trouble. Anyhow, when a guy once gets suspicious, Dillard is such a big guy it's hard to forget him. A tail should be an inconspicuous fellow who can mingle with the crowd, and Dillard has always had a little trouble fading out because of his build, but he's the best automobile tail in the business. He's a genius at handling a car. He wraps those big hands of his

334 ERLE STANLEY GARDNER

around the steering wheel and the car seems to be a part of him."

Mason nodded. "What happened?"

"Well, Boring decided to come back to Riverside. I don't know what it was, probably a telephone conversation he had with someone. Anyway, he was in Hollywood, then he threw a suitcase into his car and started out at high speed. He cut figure eights and lost the other shadow. Dillard kept on his tail. After they hit the freeway, Dillard kept pretty well in the background, relying on the electronic device to keep him posted."

"And what happened?"

"Boring went to Winlock's office, then to the Restawhile Motel here and registered in Unit 10. Dillard waited awhile, then registered and got Unit Number 5, which is across the way from Unit 10 and would give a pretty good view of Boring's place.

"Now, here's the peculiar thing: Dillard checked in and drew the curtains across the window but left just a little crack in the curtain so he could see out, and after a while he saw Boring come out, cross over directly to Dillard's automobile, open the door and start prowling around."

"What did Dillard do?"

"He sat tight. He said he was inclined to go out and grab the guy by the collar and give him a good shaking but he remembered the trouble he'd been in before, so he just sat in there and took it."

"What was Boring looking for?"

"Presumably he was suspicious of Dillard and wanted

to find out something about the registration of the automobile."

"Did he learn anything?"

"That's anybody's guess. The registration is in the name of Paul Drake as an individual and, of course, in order to comply with California law there's a certificate of registration in a cellophane window strapped to the steering post."

"So Dillard sat tight?"

"Dillard sat tight but he's afraid he's been spotted and he wants instructions."

Mason thought for a minute, then said, "Tell him to stay right there in the unit and keep his eye on the unit where Boring is staying. I want to know everyone who comes to see Boring and I want to know what time Boring goes out."

"But suppose Boring does go out. Does Dillard try to shadow him?"

"No," Mason said. "It would be too dangerous under the circumstances. He'd be spotted even if he was using an electronic shadowing device. He'll just have to sit tight."

"The guy hasn't had any dinner," Nye said. "He's a big guy and he gets hungry."

"Well, I don't want to take a chance on letting him go out, at any rate while Boring is there. Do you folks have a good woman operative up here?"

"Not up here but we could probably get one. What do you want?"

"A good-looking woman could go into Dillard's apart-

ment looking as though she were some married woman
on a surreptitious date and probably smuggle Dillard
in something to eat. It wouldn't be what he wants, but
she could get some hamburgers and a Thermos jug of
coffee and carry them in. Then if Boring is turning the
tables on Dillard and keeping an eye on Dillard's apartment, the fact that this woman goes in there with just
the right furtive attitude will probably reassure Boring
and, at the same time, give Dillard something to eat."

"Can do," Nye said. "But it will take a couple of
hours."

"Anything else new?" Mason asked.

"That seems to be it at the moment, but probably
you'd better call Paul, let him know that you're here
and that you and I have been in touch—or would you
rather I just reported to Paul?"

"No, I'll call him," Mason said. "Get him on the
phone, Della."

Mason turned back to Nye and said, "Sit back and re-
lax and tell me something about George Winlock, because I'm going to talk with the guy."

"There isn't much to tell. He's a chap who came here
about fourteen years ago and got a job as a real estate
salesman. He was a hard worker and a good salesman.
He made a couple of big commissions; then he had a
chance to tie up some property that he thought was
good subdivision property and instead of simply taking
a listing on it he took an option—paid every cent he had
for a ninety-day option, then got busy and peddled it
for a hundred thousand profit. From that time on he
started pyramiding. The guy has brains, all right, and

he's a shrewd operator. But he keeps pretty much in the background."

"What about his wife?"

"She's inclined to be just a little snooty; puts on airs, is just a little bit patronizing as far as the local society is concerned, and while they kowtow to her because of her social position, I have a feeling she wouldn't win any popularity contests if there was a secret ballot, but she'd probably be elected Queen of the May if the feminine voters had to stand up and be counted."

"What about her son?"

"Marvin Harvey Palmer is one of those things," Nye said. "We're getting too many of them. He apparently feels that there's never going to be the slightest necessity for him to do any work and he doesn't intend to try. He's an addict for sports cars, a devil with the women, has been picked up a couple of times for drunk driving, but has managed to square the rap somewhere along the line, and— Oh, hell, Perry, you know the picture."

Della Street said, "Here's Paul Drake on the line, Chief."

Mason crossed over to the telephone.

Drake said, "Hello, Perry. I'm going to give you a description of a man and you can tell me if it means anything to you."

"Go ahead."

"Five-foot eight or nine; weight about a hundred and thirty-five pounds, bony shoulders; high cheekbones; very dark but rather small eyes, and a pointed nose that's quite prominent. He's in his late thirties or early forties, quick-moving, nervous—"

"You are describing Mr. Montrose Foster," Mason interrupted. "He's the president of Missing Heirs and Lost Estates, Incorporated, and he called on me trying to pump me for information. Harrison Boring worked for him before branching out on his own."

"He's found Dianne Alder."

"The hell he has."

"That's right."

"How did he find her?"

"I'm darned if I know, Perry. He nosed her out some way. The guy probably is pretty smart. He seems to be a fast worker.

"I think he traced Harrison Boring to Bolero Beach and when he got to inquiring around Bolero Beach he found out that Boring was interested in Dianne Alder.

"Now, it's anybody's guess whether Foster did a little snooping around and found out what Boring's deal with Dianne was, and took it from there; or whether he decided to work fast and go shake Dianne down and see what she'd tell him.

"One thing is certain. Dianne became very much upset as a result of his visit, and shortly after he left, Dianne got her car and drove off in a rush."

"You're not having her tailed?" Mason asked.

"No. You didn't tell me to. As it happened, the Bolero Beach operative who was nosing around on Boring's back track happened to learn that this character with the pointed nose had been making inquiries about Boring, and so he tried to pick the guy up. He ran into him just as Foster was leaving Dianne's apartment. Then

Dianne came out within about ten minutes, jumped in her car and took off in a hurry."

"How long ago?"

"An hour or an hour and a half."

Mason said, "Your man, Moose Dillard, who was shadowing Boring, seems to have attracted Boring's attention. Boring detected the other tail he was wearing and then spotted Dillard when Dillard registered in the Restawhile Motel. He went over to take a look at Dillard's automobile. That car is registered in your name."

"So I understand," Drake said. "I have a report on it. What are you going to do about Dillard?"

"I'm talking with Sid Nye now," Mason said. "Sid is in my suite here in the hotel. I told him to have Dillard stay put. We'll get some woman operative to look as though she's keeping a motel date with him, and take some sandwiches and a Thermos jug of coffee in to him. He can, of course, get a line on anyone who comes to see Boring there at the motel but his efficiency is pretty much impaired as far as we're concerned."

"How about putting another shadow on Boring?"

"I don't know," Mason said. "I don't think it's going to be necessary. I've decided to cut the Gordian knot by getting in touch with the man about whom this whole thing revolves."

"Who's that?"

"George D. Winlock."

"Winlock!" Drake said.

"Right."

"You've decided he's the one Dianne was picked out for?"

"No. I'm approaching the problem from another angle, Paul. I've come to the conclusion Winlock holds the key to the entire situation."

"Can you discuss it over the phone?"

"No," Mason said. "I'll have to quarterback it from here, Paul."

"Okay," Drake said. "You're on the ground up there and Nye is in charge of the forces up there. You just go ahead and tell Sid what you want done. . . . Do you want my men on the job down there in Bolero Beach any more?"

"No, call them off," Mason said. "I'll tell Sid what to do."

As Mason hung up the phone, Sid said, "Well, I'll get busy and get some good-looking gal lined up who can take some dinner in to Dillard. Dillard has a phone in his room and can call out, but we have to play it easy because the line goes through a switchboard there at the motel and there's always the chance the manager may be listening in."

"Where can I reach you if I should want you in a hurry?" Mason asked.

"The best way is through the office of the Tri-Counties Detective Agency. They're our correspondents up here and we co-operate with them down at our end of the line and they handle things up here."

"Okay," Mason said. "I'll be in touch with you."

"You're going to see this man Winlock?"

"I'm going to try to."

"He's a pretty shrewd operator," Nye said. "He plays them close to his chest."

Mason nodded to Della Street. "See if you can get him on the line, Della."

"Maybe I'd better wait here until you find out what's cooking," Nye said.

Della Street consulted the telephone book, put through the call and nodded to Perry Mason. "Mr. Winlock," she said, "this is the secretary of Mr. Perry Mason, an attorney of Los Angeles. Mr. Mason would like to talk with you. Will you hold the phone just a moment, please?"

Mason took the phone which Della Street extended to him, said, "Hello, Mr. Winlock. Perry Mason talking."

Winlock's voice was cold and cautious. "I've heard of you, Mr. Mason," he said. "And I have seen you. I was in the courthouse very briefly one time when you were trying a case up here in Riverside."

"I see," Mason said. "I would like to have a few minutes of your time, Mr. Winlock."

"When?"

"At the earliest possible moment."

"Can you tell me what it's about?"

"It's about a matter which concerns you personally, and which I think it would be unwise to discuss over the telephone even in general terms."

"Where are you now?"

"I'm at the Mission Inn."

"I have an important meeting a little later on, Mr. Mason, but I can give you thirty minutes if you could come out right away."

"I'll be there within ten minutes," Mason promised.

"Thank you. Do you know where I live?"

"I have the address," Mason said. "I'll rely on a cab-driver to get me there."

Mason hung up the telephone, said to Della Street, "You're going to have to hold the fort, Della. Keep in touch with things and I'll let you know as soon as I leave Winlock's."

Nye said, "I'll drive you out, Perry. I know where the place is. I can drive you out and wait until you finish your interview and drive you back."

Mason hesitated a minute, then said, "Okay, do that, if you will, Sid. It will save a few minutes and those few minutes may be precious. I want all the time I can have with Winlock."

CHAPTER EIGHT

GEORGE D. WINLOCK's HOUSE was an imposing structure on a scenic knoll.

Nye parked the car in front of the door and said, "I'll wait."

"Okay," Mason said. "I shouldn't be very long."

Mason ran up the steps to the porch, pressed the pearl button, heard the muted chimes in the interior of the house and almost instantly the door was opened by a young man in his late teens or early twenties who regarded Mason with insolent appraisal.

"Yeah?" he asked.

"I am Perry Mason," the lawyer said. "I have an appointment with George Winlock."

"C'mon in," the young man said.

Mason followed him into a reception hallway. The young man gestured toward a door on the right. "George," he yelled. "C'mon down."

He turned to Mason and said, "Go on in there."

Having said that, the young man turned his back, walked through a curtained doorway and disappeared.

343

Mason went through the door indicated and found himself in a large room which was evidently used for entertaining purposes. In addition to the arrangement of chairs around the table in the center of the room and in front of the fireplace, there were enough chairs along the sides to seat a dozen guests.

Mason was standing, looking around, when a tall, thin individual in the early fifties, wearing dark glasses entered the room. He came forward with an air of quiet dignity, extended his hand and said, "How do you do, Mr. Mason? I'm George Winlock."

Mason shook hands and said, "I'm sorry to disturb you outside of office hours but it is a matter which I considered to be of some importance."

"I would certainly trust your judgment as to the importance of the matter," Winlock said.

Mason studied the man thoughtfully. "The matter is personal and it's rather embarrassing for me to bring it up."

"Under those circumstances," Winlock said, "if you will be seated right here in this chair, Mr. Mason, I'll take this one and we'll start right in without any preliminaries. I have an appointment later on and my experience has been that those things which may prove embarrassing are best disposed of by going right to the heart of the matter and not beating around the bush."

Mason said, "Before seeking this interview, Mr. Winlock, I tried to find out something about your background."

"That," Winlock said, "would be simply a matter of good business judgment. I frequently do the same thing.

If I am going to submit a proposition to someone, I like to know something about his background, his likes and dislikes."

"And," Mason went on, "I found you had enjoyed a very successful career here in Riverside over the past fourteen years."

Winlock merely inclined his head in a grave gesture of dignified assent.

"But," Mason said, "I couldn't find out anything at all about you before you came to Riverside."

Winlock said quietly, "I have been here for fourteen years, Mr. Mason. I think that if you have any business matter to take up with me, you can certainly find out enough about me in connection with my activities over that period to enable you to form a pretty good impression as to my likes and dislikes and my tastes."

"That is quite true," Mason said, "but the matter that I have to take up with you is such that I would have liked to have known about your earlier background."

"Perhaps if you'll tell me what the matter is," Winlock said, "it won't be necessary to take up so much of the limited time at our disposal searching into my background."

"Very well," Mason said. "Do you know a Dianne Alder?"

"Alder, Alder," Winlock said, pursing his lips thoughtfully. "Now, it's difficult to answer that question, Mr. Mason, because my business interests are very complex and I have quite an involved social life here. I don't have too good a memory for names, offhand, and usually when a matter of that sort comes up I have to refer the inquiry to my secretary who keeps an alphabetical list of names that are important to me. . . . May I ask if this person you mention, this Dianne Alder, is a client of yours?"

"She is," Mason said.

"An interest which pivots about the affairs of some other client?" Winlock asked.

Mason laughed and said, "Now you're cross-examining me, Mr. Winlock."

"Is there any reason why I shouldn't?"

"If you are not acquainted with Dianne Alder, there is no reason why you should," Mason said.

"And if I am acquainted with this person?"

"Then," Mason said, "a great deal depends upon the nature of that knowledge—or, to put it another way, on the measure of the association."

"Are you implying in any way that there has been an undue intimacy?" Winlock asked coldly.

"I am not implying any such thing," Mason said. "I am simply trying to get a plain answer to a simple question as to whether you know Dianne Alder."

"I'm afraid I'm not in a position to answer that question definitely at the moment, Mason. I might be able to let you know later on."

"Put it this way," Mason said. "The name means nothing to you at this time? You wouldn't know whether you were acquainted with her unless you had your secretary look it up on an alphabetical index?"

"I didn't exactly say that," Winlock said. "I told you generally something about my background in regard to people and names and then I asked you some questions which I consider very pertinent as to the nature and extent of your interest in ascertaining my knowledge or lack of it as far as the party in question is concerned."

"All right," Mason said, "I'll stop sparring with you, Mr. Winlock, and start putting cards on the table. Dianne Alder's father disappeared fourteen years ago. He was presumed to have been drowned. Now then, is there any possibility that prior to the time you came to Riverside there was a period in your life where you suffered from amnesia? Is it possible that, as a result of some injury or otherwise, you are not able to recall the circumstances of your life prior to arriving in Riverside? Is it possible that you could have had a family and perhaps a daughter and that your memory has become a blank as to such matters?

"Now, I am putting that in the form of a question, Mr. Winlock. I am not making it as a statement, I am not making it as an accusation, I am not making it as a suggestion. I am simply putting it in the form of a question because I am interested in the answer. If the answer is no, then the interview is terminated as far as I am concerned."

"You are acting upon the assumption that Dianne Alder may be my natural daughter?" Winlock asked.

"I am making no such statement, no such suggestion, and am acting upon no such assumption," Mason said. "I am simply asking you if, prior to the time you arrived in Riverside, there is any possibility that there is a hiatus in your memory due to amnesia, traumatic or otherwise."

Winlock got to his feet. "I'm sorry to disappoint you,

Mr. Mason, but there is no hiatus in my memory. I have never been bothered with amnesia and I remember my past life perfectly in all its details.

"I believe that answers your question, and, as you remarked, an answer of this sort would terminate the interview as far as you are concerned."

"That is quite correct," Mason said, getting to his feet. "I just wanted to be certain, that's all."

"And may I ask why you came to me with this question?" Winlock asked, as he started escorting Mason to the door.

"Because," Mason said, "if there had been any possibility of such a situation existing, I might have been in a position to have spared you a great deal of embarrassment and trouble."

"I see," Winlock said, hesitating somewhat in his stride.

Mason stopped, faced the other man. "One more question," he said. "Do you know a Harrison T. Boring who is at the moment registered in Unit 10 at the Restawhile Motel?"

"Boring . . . Boring," Winlock said, frowning. "Now, there again, Mr. Mason, I'm going to have to point out to you that one of my pet peeves is having someone pull a name out of a hat and say, 'Do you know this person or that person?' My business affairs are rather complex and—"

"I know, I know," Mason interrupted, "and your social life is not by any means simple. Buf if you know Harrison T. Boring in the way that you would know him if my surmise is correct, you wouldn't need to ask your secretary to look up his name on an alphabetical list."

"And just what is your surmise, Mr. Mason?"

"My surmise," Mason said, "is that regardless of whom he may be contacting, Harrison Boring tied Dianne Alder up in a contract by which he was in a position to collect a full fifty per cent of any gross income from any source whatever which Dianne might receive during the period of the next few years. He then dropped Dianne and repudiated the contract, indicating he had opened up a more lucrative market for any knowledge he might have."

Winlock stood very stiff and very still. Then said, at length, "You know that he made such a contract?"

"Yes."

"May I ask the source of your information, Mr. Mason?"

"I've seen the contract and know of its subsequent repudiation. If, therefore, you are not being frank with me, Mr. Winlock, you should realize what the repudiation of Dianne's contract means. It means that Boring feels he could get *more* than half of what Dianne is entitled to. This means he has opened up a new source of income which he intends to use to the limit."

"I think," Winlock said, "you had better come back here and sit down, Mr. Mason. The situation is a little more complex than I had anticipated."

Winlock walked back to the chair he had just vacated, seated himself and indicated that Mason was to seat himself in the other chair.

Mason sat down and waited.

There was a long period of silence.

At length Mason took out his cigarette case, offered one to Winlock, who shook his head.

"Mind if *I* smoke?" Mason asked.

"Go right ahead. There's an ash tray there on the table."

Mason lit the cigarette.

Winlock said, after a moment, "What you have just told me, Mr. Mason, is very much of a shock to me."

Mason said nothing.

"All right," Winlock said. "I see that you are starting an investigation, Mr. Mason, and I may as well forestall some of the results of that investigation. I had hoped that it never would be necessary for me to tell anyone the things I am going to tell you.

"My true name is George Alder. I was married to Eunice Alder. A little over fourteen years ago I started for Catalina Island in an open boat with an outboard motor. The boat ran out of fuel when we encountered head winds and heavy tide currents. We drifted about for a while, then a storm came up and the boat capsized. The accident happened at night. I am a good swimmer. I tried to keep in touch with my companion, but lost him in the darkness. I managed to keep myself afloat for some two hours. Then, as it was getting daylight, I saw a boat approaching. I managed to wave and shout and finally got the attention of one of the girls on the boat. She called out to the man at the wheel and the boat veered over and picked me up.

"I was near exhaustion.

"My married life had not been happy. My wife, Eunice, and I had, as it turned out, very little in common other than the first rush of passion which had brought about the marriage. When that wore off and we settled down to a day-by-day relationship, we became mutually dissatisfied. She evidenced that dissatisfaction by finding fault with just about everything I did. If I drove a car, I was driving either too fast or too slow. If I reached a decision, she always questioned the decision.

"I evidenced my dissatisfaction by staying away from home a great deal and in the course of time developed other emotional interests.

"During the long hours I was swimming I felt that the situation was hopeless. I reviewed my past life. I realized that I should have separated from her while she was still young enough to have attracted some other man. An attempt to sacrifice both of our lives simply in order to furnish a home to a young daughter was, in my opinion, poor judgment."

"It's difficult to judge a matter of that sort," Mason said, "because the judgment is usually made in connection with the selfish interests of the person considering the situation."

"Meaning that you don't agree with me?" Winlock said.

"Meaning that I was merely making a marginal comment," Mason said. "However, all that is in the past. If you want to justify your course of conduct I'm very glad to listen to you, but I feel that in view of what you have said we're getting to a point where time is short."

"Exactly," Winlock said. "I'll put it this way. The boat that picked me up was headed for Catalina. I explained to them that I had been on a somewhat drunken party on another boat; that I had made a wager that I could swim to Catalina before the boat got there and had been drunk enough and foolish enough to plunge overboard to try it and the others had let me go, with a lot of jeering and facetious comments.

"I told my rescuers that I had a responsible position and that I certainly couldn't afford any publicity. So they fitted me out with clothes, which I agreed to return, and put me ashore at Catalina and said nothing about it.

"Now then, recently Harrison T. Boring found out in some way what had happened and that I was actually George Alder."

"And he has been asking money?"

"He has been paid money," Winlock said. "I gave him four separate payments, all of which represented blackmail. Boring came to Riverside in order to collect yet another payment. This time it was a very substantial payment and it was represented to me it would be a final payment."

"How much?" Mason asked.

"Ten thousand dollars in cash," Winlock said.

"Can you afford blackmail of that sort?" Mason asked.

"I can't afford not to pay blackmail. This man is in a position to wipe me out. Because I didn't dare to answer the questions in connection with the vital statistics required on a marriage license, I persuaded my present wife that there were reasons why I didn't want to go through with another marriage and, because she was a divorced woman and the interlocutory degree had not

become final, we simply announced to our friends that
we had run away and had been married in Nevada over
a week end.

"I may state that at that time the circle of my friends
was much more limited than is the case at the present
time, and what we did—or rather, what we said we had
done—attracted very little attention. There was, I believe, a small article in the society column of the local
newspaper."

"But how do you feel about Dianne?" Mason asked.
"You simply walked out of her life. You deprived her
of a father, you never let her know—"

"I *couldn't* let her know," Winlock said. "I had to
make a clean break. There was no other way out of it.
However, I may state that I have kept in touch with Dianne without her knowing anything at all about it. If
she ever had any real need for money, I'd have seen that
she had it.

"She had a very good job as a secretary with Corning,
Chester and Corning of Bolero Beach. She has perhaps
no realization of just how she secured that job. If it
hadn't been for the influence of a firm of attorneys here
in Riverside, who, in turn, were indebted to me, I doubt
very much that Dianne would have secured such a good
job so early in her career.

"However, that's neither here nor there. I am not
trying to justify myself to you, Mr. Mason. I am simply
pointing out that your statement to me is a great shock,
because it is now apparent that Boring is not interested
in a lump sum settlement as he told me, but plans to
bleed me white.

"This would kill my wife. To have a scandal come out at this particular time, to have it appear our relationship was illicit, to lose her social prestige— Well, I can't even bear to think of it."

"Your wife has a son by another marriage?"

"That's right. And as far as he is concerned, I— Well, I am not talking about him. If something happened that would— If that young man had to go out and stand on his two feet— Oh, well, that's neither here nor there. There's no use discussing it."

Mason said, "May I ask what Boring told you when he solicited this last ten-thousand-dollar cash payment?"

Winlock shrugged his shoulders. "Probably it would be an old story to you," he said. "The man rang me up. He told me that he was sincerely repentant; that he was just being a common blackmailer; that it was ruining his character and making a crook and a sneak of him; that he had an opportunity to engage in legitimate business; that he needed ten thousand dollars as operating capital; that if he could get this in one lump sum, he could invest it in such a way that he could have an assured income and that I would never hear from him again.

"He promised me that if I got him this one ten-thousand-dollar payment, that that would be the last; that he would, as he expressed it, go straight from that point on. That I would have the satisfaction of knowing I had straightened him out at the same time that I was relieving myself of the possibility of any further payments."

"You believed him?" Mason asked.

"I paid him the ten thousand dollars," Winlock said dryly. "I had no choice in the matter."

"The line of patter Boring handed you," Mason said, "is just about standard with a certain type of blackmailer."

"What are *you* going to do?" Winlock asked.

"I don't know," Mason told him. "Remember, I am representing your daughter, but that she has no suspicion of the true facts in the case—as yet. As her attorney, I will tell her. Now, what do *you* intend to do?"

"There is only one thing I can do," Winlock said. "I must throw myself on Dianne's mercy. I must ask her to accept financial restitution and leave my wife with her social position intact. That would be all I could hope for."

"But if you could come to terms with Dianne, what are you going to do about Boring?" Mason asked.

Winlock's shoulders slumped. "I wish I knew," he said simply. "And now, Mr. Mason, I simply *must* keep my other appointment."

Mason shook hands. "I'm sorry to bring you bad news."

"I had it coming," Winlock said, and escorted him to the door.

"Situation coming to a head?" Sid Nye asked, as Mason opened the door and jumped in the car beside him.

"The situation is coming to a boil," Mason said, "and I think it's going to be advantageous to take some further steps in the interests of justice."

"Such as what?" Nye asked.

"Such as scaring the living hell out of a blackmailer,"

Mason told him. "Let's go to the hotel. We'll talk with Paul Drake, find out if he knows anything, get in touch with Della Street, and then set the stage for one hell of a fight."

Nye grinned. "I take it your interview with Winlock was satisfactory?"

"It opened up possibilities," Mason said.

Nye said, "A kid went tearing out of here in a sports car seven or eight minutes ago, and a dame who is a knockout drove out just a minute or two ago. That mean anything?"

Mason was thoughtful as Nye started the automobile. "I think it does," he said at length.

CHAPTER NINE

SID NYE drove Mason to the Mission Inn, said, "Well, I'll go on about my business, Perry, and check up on what's happening. I'll keep in touch with you. You're going to be at the hotel?"

"As far as I know," Mason told him.

"Okay, I'll do a little checking. If you need me, you can get me at the Tri-Counties Detective Agency. I'll be there."

"Okay, thanks a lot," Mason said. He watched Nye drive away, then entered the hotel and went up to his suite.

"Well, Della," he asked, "how about dinner?"

"I was hoping you'd think of that," she said, "but I have news for you."

"What?"

"Dianne is here."

"Where?"

"Somewhere in Riverside. I told her she'd better come up here and wait for you but she was all worked up."

"What did she want?"

"Montrose Foster has been in touch with her all right."

"And upset her?"

"I'll say it upset her. He told her the facts of life."

"Such as what?"

"That Boring was only trying to get something out of her for his own good. He asked her if Boring had got her to sign anything, and she said he had, and he wanted to see the contract but she didn't give him any satisfaction."

"Then what?"

"Then Foster started trying to pump her about her family, trying to find out something on which he could capitalize and trying to keep Dianne in the dark. You'll never guess the one he finally lit on."

"What?"

"The good old stand-by," Della Street said. "White slavery. Dianne has read enough about that and seen enough about it in Hollywood pictures so she fell for it, hook, line, and sinker. Foster told her that Boring was just grooming her for immoral purposes, that before he got done with her he'd have her where she couldn't fight back, and that she'd wind up as a dope fiend, a physical, moral wreck. He told her that whatever contract she signed it was entered into under false pretenses; that she should repudiate the contract immediately; that Boring was a fly-by-night; that he was strictly no good; that he was an opportunist; that he'd get her to give up her job, lose contact with her friends; get her in his

power with a few hundred dollars and then lower the
boom."

"And Dianne fell for it?"

"She's so upset she hardly knows what she's doing.
She didn't tell him about Boring terminating the contract."

"How did she know that we were here?"

"That apparently was more or less of an accident.
She came here on her own and heard someone talking
in the lobby about Perry Mason, the attorney, being
registered here in the hotel. So she telephoned from a
drugstore."

"But why did she come to Riverside in the first place,
Della?"

"She knows Boring is here. She asked me if I
thought she should confront him and demand an explanation. She said she wanted to let him know he'd
have to give her back that copy of the contract he had
with her signature on it. She is so worked up now she
seems to think that the contract is an agreement to fat-
ten herself up and go to South America to lead an immoral life. The poor kid is hysterical. I tried to talk to
her but she wouldn't let the words get through. I told
her to come here at once."

"Did she say she would?"

"She didn't say anything except what a mess she'd be
in if Boring let anyone know she'd signed a contract to
become a quote white slave unquote."

"Well," Mason said, "under the circumstances, I
think we should stay here in the suite until Dianne

shows up. Did she tell Foster anything about her father?"

"Apparently," Della Street said, "Foster is overlooking the obvious. He was trying to get Dianne to talk about her family, about her father's brothers and sisters, about her mother's relatives. He's looking for some distant tie-in, some obscure relative she has lost track of who could have died and left her a fortune that no one knows about.

"How did you come out with Winlock? Any luck?"

"We hit pay dirt, Della."

"Then, Dianne is his daughter?"

"Yes. She's his daughter and she's a blackmailer's bonanza."

"What are you going to do?" she asked.

"Throw some of *my* weight around," Mason said. "I have three objectives. First, to safeguard Dianne's interests; second, to keep Foster from finding out the facts; third, to scare the living hell out of a blackmailer so he'll become a fugitive from justice."

"And then what?" Della Street asked.

"Boring has taken ten thousand dollars blackmail money. I don't know whether we can prove it so it will stand up in court, but he undoubtedly has the ten thousand dollars in cash in his possession. He can't explain how he got it.

"Winlock is sitting on the edge of a volcano. I don't know just what he's worth but I imagine we can make a deal with him by which Dianne can get at least a half million dollars in return for not blowing the whistle—

but before we make any settlement with Winlock, we'll find out just how much is involved. I think when Dianne knows the facts, she'll be inclined to be charitable, but there's the emotional shock which has to be cushioned."

"When will she know the facts?" Della Street asked.

"Just as soon as I see her," Mason said. "She's my client. I'm her attorney. My knowledge is her knowledge. I can tell her what I know in confidence and then we'll work out the best course of action, but I have her emotions to consider."

"We were," Della Street reminded him, "talking about dinner."

"I think they have excellent room service here," Mason said. "We'll have a big porterhouse steak, with baked potatoes and sour cream, tomato and avocado salad, Thousand Island dressing, and—"

"Heavens!" Della Street said. "Are you trying to make a Dianne Alder out of me? Am *I* supposed to put on twelve pounds?"

Mason said, "You're working for a fiend in human form. I'm fattening you up for the South American market."

"My resistance has turned to putty," Della Street said. "I'm unable to resist the thought of savory food. . . . Suppose Dianne comes in while we're waiting or while we're eating?"

"That's the idea of the big porterhouse steak," Mason said. "We'll have it big enough so we can put in an extra plate and feed Dianne."

"If you're going to feed her," Della Street said,

"you'd better order a double chocolate malted milk and some mince pie alamode on the side."

"And if Dianne shouldn't show up?" Mason asked. "I suppose you could—"

Della Street threw up her hands. "Don't do it," she said. "I might not be able to resist."

Mason looked at his watch. "Well," he said, "I think Dianne will probably be in. Ring the registration desk and see if she's here or has a reservation, Della, and get room service and have the food sent up here in forty-five minutes."

Della Street inquired for Dianne Alder, found out that she was not registered at the hotel, contacted room service and ordered the meal.

While they were waiting, Mason put through a call to Paul Drake. "Anything new at your end, Paul?"

"Things have simmered down here."

"Dianne is up here," Mason said. "Sit right there in your office. Things are coming to a head. You can have some hamburgers sent in."

"Have a heart, Perry. I was taking soda bicarbonate all afternoon."

"Well," Mason said, "on second thought, Paul, you may as well go out, but be back inside of an hour and leave word with the office where you can be reached. I've seen Winlock and now I know all the answers."

"You mean he admitted—"

"I mean we're okay," Mason said, "but I can't discuss it."

"How long do you want my men on the job up there, Perry?"

"Until I tell you to quit. I think we're about at the end of the case now—at least this phase of it—but our friend, Dillard, is anchored there at the motel. Evidently Boring has him spotted and is getting pretty suspicious."

"What are you going to do with Boring?"

"After I've seen Dianne," Mason said, "I'm going down and have a heart-to-heart talk with Boring."

"You mean the party is going to get rough?"

"I mean the party is going to get *very* rough."

"Can you handle him, Perry?"

"I can handle him. I never saw any blackmailer yet I couldn't handle. I'm going to put him in such a position that he'll consider himself a fugitive from justice, and if his conscience makes him resort to flight and concealment of his identity, I don't see how I can be expected to do anything about that."

"Certainly not," Drake said. "You'll be a paragon of righteous virtue. I'm on my way, Perry. I'll leave word in the office where I can be reached, but don't call me until I've wrapped myself around the outside of a steak and French fried potatoes."

"Better make it a baked potato," Mason said, "or you'll be eating bicarbonate again. Be good, Paul."

The lawyer hung up, looked at his watch, said, "I wish Dianne would show up. I want to have *all* the reins in my hand before I start driving."

It was, however, twenty minutes later that there was a timid knock at the door of the suite.

Mason nodded to Della Street. "Dianne," he said.

Della went over and opened the door.

Dianne Alder stood on the threshold.

"Come in, Dianne," Della Street said. "He's here."

Dianne followed her into the room, gave Mason a forced smile, said, "Oh, I'm *so* glad."

"Sit down," Mason said. "We have a nice steak coming up and you look to me as though you could use a drink."

"I could use two of them," she said.

"All in, eh?" Mason asked.

She nodded.

Mason said, "Look, Dianne, let's get certain things straightened out. You've paid me a retainer. I'm your attorney. We have a confidential relationship. Anything you tell me is in confidence; anything that I learn which could affect you in any way, I tell you. I'm obligated to. Do you understand?"

"Yes."

"Now, you're in for a shock," Mason told her. "You're going to have some information which is going to hit you right where you live. . . . What do you want to drink?"

"Is brandy all right?"

"No," Mason said. "That's not the kind of a before-dinner drink you should have—you want a Manhattan or a Martini."

"I don't think I want anything to eat."

Mason said, "What's the matter, Dianne? Something seems to be bothering you. Suppose you start by telling me a few things. Why did you come to Riverside in such a rush?"

"I . . . I wanted to see somebody."

"Who?"

"Mr. Boring."

"You knew he was up here?"

"Yes."

"How did you know?"

"Someone told me."

"Who?"

"A man who knows him very well. Someone he used to work for."

"Montrose Foster?"

"Yes."

"What else did Foster tell you?"

"That I've been a little fool, that Mr. Boring was just trying to take advantage of me and that the contract about using me for a model was all just eyewash; that what he really had in mind was something altogether different."

Mason regarded her thoughtfully, said, "Did he tell you what it was, Dianne?"

"White slavery."

Mason crossed over and put a hand on her shoulder. "Look, Dianne," he said, "this has been a rough day as far as you're concerned. You've had some shocks and you're going to have some more shocks. You've been seeing too many movies. Now quit worrying about Boring. Leave him to me."

The telephone rang.

Mason nodded to Della Street, again turned to Dianne. "Look, Dianne, you're shaking like a leaf. What's the trouble?"

She started to cry.

Della Street, on the telephone, said, "I'll get him right away, Sid."

She nodded to Mason. "Sid Nye. Says it's important."

Mason hurried across to the telephone, picked up the instrument, said, "Yes, Sid. What is it?"

"I don't know," Nye said, "but I've had a call from Moose Dillard. It was a peculiar call."

"What was it?"

"He said, 'Sid, do you know who is talking?' and I recognized his voice and said yes, and he said, 'Hey Rube' and hung up."

"Just that?" Mason asked.

"Just that. Just *Hey Rube.* He worked for a circus at one time. You can figure what that means."

"Where are you now?"

"At the Tri-Counties."

"How long will it take you to get down to the front of the Mission Inn?"

"About two minutes."

"I'll be there," Mason said.

The lawyer hung up the telephone, turned to Della Street. "Della," he said, "tell Dianne the story. Break it to her easy, one woman to another. When the food comes up, give her some food and put a piece of steak aside for me. I may be back in time to get it. I may not."

"Two Martinis for Dianne?" Della Street asked.

Mason shifted his eyes to Dianne.

She met his gaze for a moment, then lowered her eyes.

Mason whirled to Della Street. "Not a damn one," he said, "and she's not to talk with anyone until I get back. Understand? Not anyone!"

Mason made a dash for the door.

CHAPTER TEN

Sid Nye picked Mason up in front of the Mission Inn.

"What do you make of it, Sid?"

"It's a jam of some sort. Moose isn't one to lose his head in a situation of that kind. Evidently something's happened and he didn't dare say anything over the phone because the call probably went through the switchboard at the motel. He evidently wanted to use something that I'd understand and other people wouldn't. Moose is quite a character. He had a circus background and he knew I'd understand Hey Rube."

"That means a free-for-all fight?" Mason asked.

"Not exactly. It means that all the carnival people gather together against the outsiders. It may or may not mean a clem, but it means you start knocking anything or anybody out of your way and—well, it's just a good old rallying battle cry."

Nye was piloting the car with deft skill through the traffic.

"Then Dillard needs help?"

"He sure as hell does," Nye said. "It could be almost

367

anything. It means he's in a hell of a jam and wants us
to get there."

"Well," Mason said, "it suits me all right. I'm due to
have a little talk with Harrison T. Boring as of now."

"It's a talk he'll like?" Nye asked, grinning.

Mason said, "It's a talk which will, I hope, give Mr.
Boring an entirely new series of ideas and perhaps a
complete change of environment."

Nye swung the car down a side street, suddenly slowed,
said, "That's a police car in front of the place, Perry."

"What number is Dillard in?" Mason asked.

"Number 5."

"All right," Mason said, "drive right up to Number 5.
If Dillard is in trouble, we'll be right there. If the police car is there for someone else, we'll pay no attention
but go into Dillard's place."

Nye swung into the entrance of the motel, found a
parking place, switched off headlights and ignition,
looked to Mason for instructions.

"Right into Number 5," Mason said.

The lawyer and Nye converged on the door of Number 5.

"Try the knob," Mason said in an undertone.

Nye was reaching for the knob when the door opened.

There were no lights on inside the unit. The big lum-
bering individual who hulked in the doorway said in a
husky voice, "Come on in."

"No lights?" Nye asked.

"No lights," Dillard said, and closed the door behind
them. "Don't stumble over anything. Your eyes'll get
accustomed to the darkness in a minute. I'm sitting here

at the window with the curtains parted so I can get a line on what's happening."

"What is happening?"

"I don't know. The police are there now, and the ambulance left just a few minutes ago."

"The ambulance?" Nye said.

"That's right. They took him away."

"Who? Boring?"

"Right."

Nye said, "You know Perry Mason, Moose."

"Sure," Moose said, his hand groping for Mason's in the dark. "How are you, Mr. Mason? Haven't seen you for a while."

Then he said, by way of explanation to Nye, "Mason got me out of a jam a while back."

"I know," Nye said. "Just wanted to be sure you recognized him in the dark. Now, what's been happening out here?"

"Plenty has been happening," Dillard said, "but what it's all about is more than I know. Boring was having a convention. All sorts of people coming and going. Then the girl showed up and left in a hurry and about ten minutes after she left the cops came. I wanted to keep casing the joint and didn't want to give a tip-off to the manager. I had a hell of a time getting anyone on the phone. Whatever was happening, it took their attention off the switchboard. Finally I managed to get them to answer.— You can't get an outside line on these phones unless they connect you.— I guess I was all of five minutes jiggling that hook up and down, putting the light on and off, waiting for someone to answer."

"All right," Nye said, "they answered. "Was there anything unusual? Did they apologize or make any explanation?"

"Not a word. Someone said, 'Manager's office,' and I said, 'I want to get an outside line,' and the manger said, 'You can't dial a number from this phone. You have to give me the number and I connect you.' So I gave them the number of the Tri-Counties and asked for you. I was pretty certain they were listening on the line. I could hear breathing. So I just told you, 'Hey Rube,' and hung up. I figured that would get you here as quick as anything and I didn't want to ask you to come rushing out because I knew you'd ask questions and if I started answering questions we'd have this unit under surveillance and that might not be the thing you wanted."

"That's good thinking," Mason said. "What happened after that?"

"An ambulance came right after I hung up. They took him out on a stretcher."

"He isn't dead then," Mason said.

"It was an ambulance, not a meat wagon. I don't know what sort of a system they use here but I have an idea the ambulance means the guy's hurt."

"All right," Mason said, "let's find out what happened. Who came here?"

"I can't give you names," Dillard said. "I can give you one license number and some descriptions. That's all I have to go on at the present time."

"You were watching through the window?"

"Had the lights out and the curtains parted and a

pair of eye-glass binoculars. Those have about a two and a half power magnification; and then I've got an eight-power binocular here that is a night glass. I use it on surveillance jobs of this sort."

"All right, what can you give us?" Mason asked.

"I can't give you too much without turning the light on so I can read my notes. I made the notes in the dark."

"Tell us what you can remember."

"First rattle out of the box," Dillard said, "there was this fellow who's been prowling around Bolero Beach; a slim, fast-moving guy with a mosquito beak for a nose. . . ."

"His name's Montrose Foster," Mason said. "He's the president, whatever that means, of Missing Heirs and Lost Estates, Inc. Boring was working for him until he suddenly quit his job, and Foster thinks Boring hit some pay dirt that he didn't want to share with anyone."

"Could be," Dillard said. "Anyway, this fellow came in around eight and he was there about fifteen minutes. I've got the times marked down."

"Now, you could see all of these people all right?" Mason asked.

"Sure. There was some daylight when this man you call Foster was here. And later on there's enough light here in the parking place so I could see people well enough to identify them."

"Okay," Mason said. "Then what happened?"

"Well, for about five minutes after this man Foster left there was nothing doing. I kept thinking our man would go out to dinner but he didn't. He seemed to be waiting for someone or something. And then, around twenty minutes past eight, this kid driving a sports car showed up and boy, was he making time. He slammed that sports car into the entrance and wham! right up to Unit Number 10. He jumped out and was inside all in one motion. It was getting dark then."

"Did he knock on the door?" Mason asked.

"He knocked."

"How old was this man?"

"Around twenty-two to twenty-three; somewhere in there; driving a high-powered foreign sports model. He parked it at such an angle I couldn't get the license number."

"On a guess," Mason said, "that was Marvin Harvey Palmer.

"All right, how long did he stay?"

"Somewhere around fifteen minutes. Then he left and a woman came in, a woman about forty, and boy, was she worked up! She went in the minute the kid went out. She was just as stately as you please, and she was in there nearly ten minutes. Then she came out, and that's when the man went in. Now, this man had been waiting. He'd seen the woman's car and recognized it, or had seen the woman or something; anyway, he'd parked his car down at the far end of the parking place here, then he'd seen the woman's car and he'd driven out, parked his car in the street someplace and walked in and hung around in the shadows down at the far end waiting for the woman to leave. He was a dignified guy wearing dark glasses. The minute the woman left he hot-footed it across to Unit 10, banged on the door and went in and was there about five minutes. He came out and things simmered down for about ten minutes and then this blonde came in and boy, was she a knockout. . . . I got the license number on *her* car."

"Did you get a good look at her?" Mason asked.

"I'll say I got a good look at her. She parked the car and opened the door on the left-hand side and slid out from behind the steering wheel. Believe me she was in a hurry and she didn't care how she looked when she got out—she was just getting out.

"Unit 10 was on the other side of the car from her and when she opened the door and slid out she was coming right toward me. Her skirt just rolled up under her and— Boy, oh, boy, talk about legs!"

"Let's go a little higher than the legs," Mason said. "What about her face?"

"Around twenty-four or so; blonde, tall, and my God, what a figure! She really filled out her clothes."

"All right," Mason said, "this is important. Now, what time did she go in and how long was she in there?"

"She went in about ten minutes after the man left and she was in there, I guess, ten or fifteen minutes. And when she came out she was all excited. Boy, was *she* running! She made a dive for her car. This time she went in the door that was on the right-hand side and slid across the seat. She threw the car into reverse and whipped out of here in such a hurry that she forgot to turn her headlights on. I've got the time written down in my notebook."

"And after that?" Mason asked.

"After that, everything was quiet for a couple of minutes. Then the manager came down and pounded on

the door and after a while opened the door and went in.
Then she came out on the run and a few minutes after
that the police came."

"All right," Mason said. "Now, let's get this straight.
You have been watching this place ever since—what
time?"

"Ever since the guy got in here, or right after he got
in."

"You know every person who went into that motel.
You saw everyone."

"Sure, I saw them."

"There's no back entrance?"

"Just the one door. That is, we may have to check it,
but I'm sure there's just the one door because that's the
way the places are laid out . . . and Sid was going to
send someone in with some eats for me. . . . Boy, I'm
famished!"

"Never mind that," Mason said. "This blonde was in
there for how long?"

"About fifteen minutes."

"And she was the last one in?"

"That's right. This guy was hurt. If it was a fist fight,
it was the man. If it was a shot or a stab, it could have
been the girl—probably was, because she was the last
one in."

Mason took Nye to one side, said in a low voice, "We'll
peg the first man definitely as Montrose Foster. We'll
peg the next man tentatively as Marvin Harvey Palmer,
and the third visitor could have been Mrs. Winlock.
Then the man with the dark glasses we can be pretty

certain was George Winlock. . . . What time did we leave the Winlock residence, Sid?"

"Right around eight-twenty-five," Nye said.

"And it's how far from the Winlock residence here?"

"Not over five minutes if you're driving in a hurry. Both the motel here and the Winlock residence are on the same side of town."

"All right," Mason said. "As soon as we left the place, George Winlock jumped in his automobile and drove here. He found his wife's car parked out in front.

"Now, if that second visitor was Marvin Harvey Palmer, he must have left the house to come out here a short time *before* we left the house. You told me a sports car left the place."

Nye said, "Would it be in order to ask if your interview with George Winlock exploded a bombshell?"

"It exploded a bombshell," Mason said.

"All right," Nye said, "the answer is simple. The room was bugged. The kid found out what was going on and wanted to beat everybody to the punch, so he came tearing out here."

"Then what happened?" Mason asked.

"Then the wife followed. She was ready to start at about the same time but she wanted to put on her face and take the shine off her nose.

"Her husband left immediately after we did. He drove out here and—well, that's it."

They moved over to join Dillard.

"Whatever happened," Dillard repeated, "is the result of what the blonde did."

"Now, wait a minute," Mason told him. "You're getting out of orbit, Dillard. The blonde in all probability is my client."

"Oh-oh," Dillard said.

"It's one thing for you to say what time she came and what time she left," Mason went on, "but it's quite another thing to have you making any big fat surmises as to what happened while she was in that cabin."

"I'm sorry," Dillard apologized, "I guess I spoke out of turn, but—well, the way I looked at it, there was no other way of figuring it."

"There may be another way of looking at it," Mason said. "Let's suppose that this young man tried to get something from Boring and got a little rough. He left Boring lying unconscious on the floor. The woman could have been the boy's mother. She went in and found the man lying on the floor, dying. She also found some weapon that tied the crime in with her son. She paused long enough to straighten certain things up, remove certain bits of evidence, including the weapon; then she took off.

"The man could have been her husband. He was waiting for her to come out so he could go in. He'd spotted her car as soon as he drove up."

"And the minute he spotted the car," Nye said, "he knew that the room in his house had been bugged and that his wife had been listening in on whatever conversation it was that you had with him."

"Well," Mason said, "let's suppose that the boy *had* hit Boring with the butt of a revolver, and that his mother found Boring unconscious and got out; then the husband, coming in as soon as his wife had left, found the man in a dying condition. He looked around just long enough to make certain his wife hadn't left any clues that would indicate she had been there—that meant *he* could have been the one who picked up the revolver—and then *he* got out."

Dillard asked, "Have you fellows got names to put on these tags of son, mother and husband?"

"We *think* we have," Mason said. "I'm talking in terms of tags instead of names because you're going to be a witness. If you haven't heard any names, it'll be that much better for you."

Dillard said, "You fellows figure it up any way you want to. All I know is that the blonde was the last one in the room. If she's your client, I'm not going to start guessing what she was doing in there for fifteen minutes, but you know what the police are going to think. You may sell your idea to a jury, but the police won't buy it. They'll feel that if she found the man lying on the floor badly injured or dying, she wouldn't have stuck around for fifteen minutes."

Nye said, "Let me ask you a straight question, Dillard. Do you ever lose pages out of your notebook?"

"Not in a murder case," Dillard said. "I've been in enough trouble."

"You have, for a fact," Mason told him.

"But," Dillard went on, "I don't have to tell *all* I know if I haven't anyone to tell it to."

"What do you mean?"

"I could be hard to find."

Mason thought things over and said, "I don't think that's the answer, Dillard."

"Well, what is the answer?" Dillard asked.

"I'll be darned if I know," Mason said, "but I've got to talk with my client before the police talk with her and before the police get wise to you."

"Well, you've got to move plenty fast," Dillard said, "because the police are going to get wise to me."

"How do you figure that out?"

"I checked in here right after Boring. I got the place across the parking lot where I could have a good view of his unit."

"You say you got it?" Mason asked.

"That's right."

"How did you get it?"

"I asked for it."

"Oh-oh," Nye said. "That *is* going to put the fat in the fire."

"Why did you ask for it?" Mason inquired.

"Because I didn't want to sit out there in my car. That's too damn conspicuous. I wanted a place where I could look across the parking place. I asked the manager what she had and she told me she had several vacancies and I asked for Number 5. I asked if it was vacant and she said it was and I said I wanted it."

"Did she ask you why?"

"She didn't *ask* anything but she looked me over a couple of times and once she begins to put two and two together, she's going to tell the police about me. They'll ask her if there was anything unusual and she'll say no, and then they'll ask her about other tenants and if anybody checked in about the same time that Boring did, or a little after he did, and then she'll remember me and then the police will start talking to me if I'm around. Or, if I'm not around, they'll check the registration card for the license number on the automobile, find it's in the name of Paul Drake, and then they'll want to see me."

Mason said to Nye, "I've got to go talk with my client right away. Dillard, you can sit here in the dark and I'll give you a ring if I need to."

"Remember one thing," Dillard told him. "If you should give me a ring *after* the police have asked questions of the manager, somebody will be listening in on the line."

Mason said, "I usually act on the assumption someone *is* listening in on the line."

"If I don't hear from you, then what?" Dillard asked.

"Get out as best you can," Mason said. "On second thought, it might be a good plan to get out of here right now. . . . You haven't had any supper?"

"That's right. They said a dame would bring me some sandwiches."

Nye snapped his fingers. "I've got to contact the agency and head her off. If she should come walking in here right now, it *would* cause trouble."

"Why not go get something to eat?" Mason asked Dillard. "There's no use keeping Unit 10 under surveillance now. The police will have it blocked off and probably will have a detective spending the night in there, just to see if any telephone calls come in."

"Okay," Dillard said, "I'll go to dinner."

"We'll go out together," Nye said. "I'll take Mason to the hotel and come back and get you."

"I have my car here, you know," Dillard said.

"Then we'll take both cars," Nye told him. "I'll take Mason to the hotel and I'll have to head off that woman operative with the sandwiches and coffee."

Mason nodded. "On our way, Sid."

CHAPTER ELEVEN

DELLA STREET said, "We saved it for you, Chief, but it's all cold. I didn't dare to keep it in the warming oven for fear it would be too well done."

"That's all right," Mason said. "I'll eat it cold."

"Oh, no," Della Street protested. "Let's have another hot one sent up. I'll—"

"There may not be time," Mason said. "You didn't each much, Dianne."

"I didn't— Somehow I don't seem to be hungry."

"A little different from the way you were when I first met you," Mason said.

"Yes, I—"

"Something happened to change the picture?" Mason asked conversationally, seating himself and cutting off a piece of the steak. "You don't crave food as you feared you would?"

"I . . . I don't know. I guess I just lost my appetite."

"What did you come up here for?" Mason asked. "To Riverside?"

"Yes."

"To see Mr. Boring."

"See him?"

"Not yet. Della said to come here. I know now after listening to her, that you should be the one to do the talking."

There was silence for a minute.

Della Street said, "The coffee is hot, Chief. I kept that going over the candle flame but it isn't fresh—it will only take a few minutes to get more coffee."

Mason shook his head, said to Dianne, "Right now Boring is either at the hospital or at the morgue."

"Why?" she asked, her eyes wide. "Did something happen to him?"

"Something happened to him," Mason said.

Dianne put her hand to her throat. Her eyes got large and round.

"Something happened to him," Mason said, "while you were talking with him."

"I . . . I . . ." She started blinking back tears.

Mason said, "Now look, Dianne. You're playing a dangerous game. It can possibly trap you into a life term in a prison cell. You can't afford to lie to your lawyer. Now, tell me the truth. What happened?"

"What do you mean, what happened?"

Mason said, "You went to the Restawhile Motel. You knew that Boring was in Unit 10. You called on him. Now, did you find him lying on the floor or—"

"Lying on the floor!" she exclaimed. "What do you mean?"

"Go on," Mason said. "Tell me the truth. And don't

ever lie to me—don't ever try to lie to me again,
Dianne. If you do, I'm going to walk out on you."

She said, "All right, Mr. Mason, I'll tell you the truth.
I wanted to tell you the truth all along. I *did* see him. I
knew he was up here at the Restawhile."

"Who told you?"

"This man that told me so much about him. He told
me where I could find him. He told me that the only
thing to do was to make him give me back the other
copy of that contract; that he had deliberately tricked
me and that he didn't care a thing in the world about
whether I put on one pound or fifty; that all of that stuff
about being a model and building up my figure and all
that was just so much eyewash, that he would use that
contract to get me to go to South America and then suddenly cut me off without any funds and I'd have
to . . . to sell myself. He said that as long as Boring
had that contract with my name on it, he could ruin my
reputation any time he wanted to."

"Did you tell him Boring had terminated that contract?" Mason asked.

"No, because I felt that so-called repudiation was just
a part of the plan to get me in his power."

"What time did you see Boring?" Mason asked.

"Just before I came here."

"And did he tear up the contract?"

"He . . . gave it back to me."

"And then what?"

"Then I walked out."

"How long were you there?"

"The whole thing couldn't have been over five minutes."

"And when you left, what about it?"

"Then I came here."

"How long were you in there?"

"It couldn't have been—not over five minutes."

"You couldn't have been in there fifteen or twenty minutes?"

"Heavens, no, Mr. Mason. I don't think I was in there five minutes. Those things happen awfully fast. I don't think I was in there over two minutes. I just told him that I'd found out about him and found out about that contract and it was all a phony and I wanted to call things off and I wanted him to give me that other copy of the contract back."

"And then what?"

"And then he said that he didn't know who had been talking to me but he had my name on the dotted line and, as he said, he had me sewed up."

"And then what?"

"Mr. Mason, I've been over it. It's just the way I told you. He told me that he had me all sewed up and I told him that I knew he was a big phony, that the whole contract was a phony, that he didn't have any career as a model for me, that he just wanted to get me in his power, and he laughed and said I *was* in his power, and I told him I wasn't, that if he thought he could make me do anything that wasn't right just because of the money involved, he had two more guesses coming and that I had retained you as my lawyer and then he gave me the contract. That scared him."

Mason said, "Look, Dianne, this can be very, very serious. If you picked up a chair and clubbed him over the head while you were defending yourself, or if you used a weapon or if he tumbled and fell, all you have to do is to say so. You've got a good reputation, you can create a good impression and a jury will believe you. But if you try to tell a lie and get caught, it's going to mean you're going to be convicted of homicide; perhaps manslaughter, perhaps even second-degree murder."

She tried to meet his eyes but failed.

"Dianne," Mason said, "you're lying."

Abruptly she said, "I *have* to lie, Mr. Mason. The truth is simply too utterly devastating."

Mason said harshly, "You've wasted enough time trying to lie. You can't get away with it, Dianne. You're an amateur. You're not a good enough liar. You haven't had enough practice. Now, tell me the truth before it's too late."

"What do you mean, too late?"

"The police," Mason said. "They may be here any minute. Now, tell me the truth."

"I'm afraid you won't believe me."

"Tell me the truth," Mason said, "and get started—fast!"

"All right," she said, "I went to the motel unit and—well, I was all worked up and excited and indignant and—"

"Never mind all that," Mason said. "What did you do?"

"I went to the door and it was open just an inch or two and I could see a light on inside. I knocked and no one answered so I pushed the door open and—well, there he was, lying on the floor. The place reeked with the smell of whiskey and I thought he was dead drunk."

"You didn't hit him with anything?"

She shook her head vehemently. "Heavens, no! He was lying there. I thought he was drunk and so I looked around to try and find his signed copy of my contract."

"And you found it?"

"Yes."

"Where?"

"In a brief case."

"You took it?"

"Yes."

"Then what?"

"I bent over him and it was then I noticed that he was hurt. The whiskey wasn't on his breath, it was on his clothes."

"Then what?"

"I ran out, drove to a phone booth about three blocks down the street, called the office of the motel, told the woman who answered that the man in Unit Number 10 had been hurt, and then hung up the phone before she could ask any questions.

"Then I came up here."

"Dianne," Mason said, "you're still lying. You had to make quite a search to find that contract. You found Boring unconscious on the floor. You started looking through his baggage and through his clothes, trying to find that contract. You didn't find it until nearly fifteen minutes had passed, and you found ten thousand dollars in money and you took that along with the contract."

She shook her head. "It was just as I told you. I took the contract. I didn't see any money."

"How long were you in there?"

"I don't think it was two minutes."

"Then why did you try to lie to me at first?"

"I was afraid that— Well, I thought I could escape responsibility by making it seem that he was alive and in good health when I left and . . . well, you know, we parted friends."

"Did he make passes at you?" Mason asked.

"I tell you, he was unconscious. He was lying on the floor."

Mason said, "You're the damnedest little liar I've ever tried to help. For your information, the police are going to be able to *prove* that you were in that cabin for nearly fifteen minutes."

"I tell you, I wasn't! I didn't— Oh, Mr. Mason, won't you *please* believe me? I'm telling you the truth now. I swear to heaven that I am!"

Mason regarded her coldly.

"You're angry with me," she said. "You're not going to represent me. You—"

"I've taken your retainer," Mason said. "I'm going to represent you. Before I get done I'm going to give you a damn good spanking and see if I can whale the truth out of you.

"Now, Della has told you about the background of this thing, about your father being alive?"

She nodded tearfully.

Mason said, "You're in a mix-up and—"

The chimes sounded.

Mason frowned thoughtfully for a moment, then said to Della Street, "See who it is, Della."

Della Street opened the door.

A uniformed officer said, "You'll pardon me, but I want to talk with Miss Dianne Alder."

"What do you want of her?" Mason asked, stepping forward.

"Who are you?" the officer asked.

"I'm Perry Mason. I'm her attorney. I'm representing her on a contract over which there's been a dispute. What do you want of her?"

"We want to question her about a murder."

"Whose murder?"

"Harrison T. Boring. He was fatally injured earlier this evening. We want to ask Dianne Alder if she knows anything that would help us."

"Do you folks think she's in any way responsible?" Mason asked.

"We don't know," the officer said. "We're trying to piece together what did happen."

"And why do you want to talk with Dianne Alder?"

"We have a tip."

"Tips are a dime a dozen," Mason said.

"The chief sent me to bring her down to headquarters to answer questions."

"All right," Mason said, "she isn't going to headquarters. She's upset and nervous and she's had an emotional shock."

"In connection with this case?" the officer asked.

"Don't be silly," Mason said. "The emotional shock was in connection with the loss of a modeling contract which she had expected would lead to movie and television appearances. She's on the verge of hysteria."

The officer hesitated. "That may or may not be significant," he said. "I was sent to bring her in. I—"

"All right," Mason said, "you're not going to bring her in. For the time being she's not going to talk with anyone. She's going to have a strong sedative, and after she gets her emotions under control she'll talk with the chief of police, the prosecuting attorney, or anyone who wants to talk with her. Right now she isn't talking."

"That's going to put her in rather a peculiar position. It may direct suspicion to her," the officer said.

"Direct suspicion and be damned!" Mason told him. "Do you want to adopt the position that the police force of this city is inhuman enough to question an emotionally upset, half-hysterical woman at a time when she's in such an emotional state she should be under the care of a physician?"

"I'll report to the chief," the officer said. "I don't think he'll like it."

"You do that," Mason told him, "and you can tell the chief personally from me, that Dianne Alder is going to be out of circulation until tomorrow morning. She isn't going to answer questions from the newspapers, from the police, or from anyone until she has her nerves under control and has recovered completely from emotional shock."

"We could take her into custody, you know," the officer said.

"That's your right," Mason told him. "Any time you want to swear out a warrant for her arrest you go right ahead. However, you know and I know that you haven't a scintilla of evidence against her. The only reason that you're here to question her is because you've received an anonymous tip from someone who is trying to add to her troubles. For your information, Officer, this young woman has been the victim of a colossal conspiracy. She's just discovered what has happened and the emotional shock is tremendous.

"If you can assure me that you have one iota of actual evidence against her, we'll try and get a physician to quiet her nerves and then see if we can get a statement from her. But if you are acting on the strength of an anonymous tip telling you to get hold of her and question her, I'm going to tell you that that anonymous tip comes from the same individuals who have been trying to muscle in on this young woman's property rights— individuals who have played fast and loose with her emotions with absolutely no concern for the outcome.

"Now, what do you want to do?"

The officer grinned and said, "I guess you called the turn, Mr. Mason. In view of that attitude we'll wait until she's in condition to be questioned."

The officer indicated the tearful, frightened Dianne Alder. "That is Miss Alder?" he asked.

"That's Miss Alder," Mason said, "and the young woman with her is Della Street, my secretary. I'm Perry Mason, her attorney."

"You'll see she doesn't leave town?" the officer asked.

"I'll be responsible for her," Mason said.

The officer turned to Dianne. "I'm sorry, Miss Alder," he said, and left the room.

Mason said to Della Street, "Get another suite fast, Della. Get Dianne out of here. Stay in that suite with her tonight. We won't let anyone know where she is. I'll close the door to this bedroom and if anyone who calls on me here jumps to the conclusion that you and she are behind that closed bedroom door, I can't help it."

Mason turned to Dianne. "Whatever you do," he said, "don't lie. Tell the absolute truth. When you are feeling better you can tell your story in detail to Della Street, but if the police should try to question you, tell them that you aren't going to make any statement except in the presence of your attorney, and send for me. Do you understand?"

Dianne nodded.

"*I* understand," Della Street said. "Come on, Dianne, let's go."

CHAPTER TWELVE

DELLA STREET had been gone less than five minutes when Mason heard a soft code knock on the door; one rap, a pause, four quick raps, a pause, then two raps.

The lawyer made sure the door to the north bedroom of the suite was closed, then crossed the parlor, opened the corridor door and saw Sid Nye on the threshold.

"Hi," Sid said. "I just thought I'd pass the word along that the police have a tip on Dianne."

"I know they do," Mason said. "Who gave it to them?"

"Probably Montrose Foster," Nye said. "It was an anonymous tip. I also wanted to let you know that you aren't going to have anything to worry about on that time schedule."

"What do you mean?"

"Moose Dillard had a wrestling match with his conscience and decided that it wasn't necessary for him to make *any* report to the police. Of course, if they question him it's going to be another matter."

"Did he get out of the place all right?" Mason asked.

"Like a charm," Nye said.

"What happened?"

"Actually it was pretty simple. I parked my car about
a block down the street, walked up to the entrance to
the parking place, walked toward the office of the motel
as though I were going in there, then detoured around
to the side and ducked in at Number 5."

"No one saw you?"

"I'm quite certain they didn't. They gave no indication if they did."

"Then what?"

"I scouted the place, then went outside and got in
Dillard's car. He'd given me the keys to it. I started the
motor, got it warmed up, then gave a signal to Moose.
He came out and got in the car and we shot out of there
fast."

"What did you do with the room key?" Mason asked.

"Moose said he left it inside."

"Then what?"

"I rode around with Moose for a while and talked
with him. After that I had him take his car and I got my
car. Moose went on his way and I came back here."

"You say you *talked* with him."

"That's right."

"What did you talk with him about?"

"You have two guesses."

"You didn't make any suggestion that he should duck
out, did you?"

"Heavens, no. Far be it from me to make any suggestion like that—perish the thought! Of course, I pointed

out to him that if the police wanted to question him
they could, but he really didn't have any obligation to
do anything except report to Paul Drake—and he's lost
his notebook."

"*Lost* his notebook!" Mason said.

"That's right. It must have dropped from his pocket
somewhere. Of course I pointed out to him that he'd
cut rather a sorry figure if he didn't have that notebook."

"Look here, Sid, let's be frank. Did you steal that
notebook or hide it?"

"Not in that sense of the word. Dillard feels it must
have fallen out of his pocket when he was getting in his
car. He had his coat over his arm and he tossed the coat
into the car."

"Will the police find it?"

"I don't think so. I saw it when it dropped to the floor
of the car. I also have a vague recollection of seeing
something fall out when I opened the car door to let
Dillard out. I didn't pay much attention to it at the
time. I *could* go back and look in the gutter."

Mason frowned. "You can't afford to take chances
with the police in a murder case, Sid."

"Sure. I know that. On the other hand, I'm not Dillard's guardian. The guy can go to the police later on
if his conscience bothers him.

"Now, what happened in connection with this anonymous tip on Dianne? Did the police question her?" Nye
asked.

"No."

"Why?"

"I wouldn't let them."

"The police must be pretty soft here in Riverside."

"I was pretty hard," Mason said. "If they'd had any evidence, they'd have taken her in, but to drag a nice young woman down to headquarters simply on the strength of an anonymous tip is poor business from a public relations standpoint.

"Do you know where Dillard went?"

"I wouldn't have the slightest idea," Nye said, looking up at the ceiling.

"Suppose we should happen to need him? Suppose we should want to get in touch with him in a hurry?"

"Wherever he is," Nye said, "I'm quite certain he reads, or will read, the Riverside papers, and any ad that was put in the classified column would undoubtedly get his attention."

"I see," Mason said.

"Well, I must be going," Nye told him. "I have quite a few things to do and I wouldn't be too surprised if they didn't put your suite here under surveillance a little later on. It might be just as well if I kept in touch with you by telephone."

"Your calls will go through a switchboard," Mason warned.

"Oh, sure," Nye said. "I wouldn't say anything that I wouldn't want everybody to hear. Of course if I should talk to you about moose hunting, you'll know what it's all about."

"Sure," Mason said, dryly.

"And I can tell you the most likely place we could go to find a moose."

"I'm quite certain," Mason said, "that the information would be of interest to me but only in the event I should want to hunt a moose. Right now I can't imagine anything that would be further from my thoughts."

Nye grinned, said, "You know where you can reach me if you want me," and went out.

For some ten minutes Mason paced the floor thoughtfully, smoking a cigarette, his head bent forward in frowning concentration.

Then the chimes sounded on the door.

Mason crossed over and opened it.

George Winlock stood on the threshold. "May I come in?" he asked.

"Certainly," Mason said. "Come right in, sit down."

Winlock entered, seated himself, regarded Mason thoughtfully from behind the tinted lenses of his glasses.

Mason said, "You don't need to wear those now, you know."

"I've worn them for fourteen years," Winlock said. "I really do need them now."

"You had something in mind?" Mason asked.

Winlock said, "I have a problem that's bothering me."

"What is it?"

"Dianne."

"What about her?"

"I have been pretty much of a heel as far as she is concerned."

"Do you expect me to argue that point with you?"

"Frankly I do not, but I want to make some sort of settlement, some sort of restitution."

"Such as what?"

"Property."

"A girl who has been attached to her father and then is led to believe that her father is dead, and subsequently finds out that he has been alive all of the time but hasn't cared enough about her to lift his finger to get in touch with her, is apt to have lost a good deal of her filial devotion."

"I can understand that. I thought perhaps you and I could discuss the property end of the situation and then later on, perhaps, Dianne could be made to see things from my viewpoint and realize that under the circumstances there wasn't much else I could have done."

"I'm afraid that's a viewpoint that will be pretty hard for her to grasp."

"However," Winlock said, "I see no reason for airing all of this in the press."

"It will be uncovered."

"I don't think so."

"I do," Mason said. "Montrose Foster, president of the Missing Heirs and Lost Estates, Inc., is on your trail."

"Exactly."

"You knew that?" Mason asked.

"I know it now."

"You can't hush anything up with Foster nosing around, prying into the background."

"I'm not entirely certain you're right," Winlock said.

"Foster is basing his investigation upon the premise Dianne has some relative who died and left an estate in which she could share. Actually there was such a relative, a distant relative of mine, and the estate is small. I feel Foster can be handled in such a way he will go chasing off on a false trail."

"I see," Mason said.

"That leaves you," Winlock said.

"And Dianne," Mason reminded him.

"Dianne is a very considerate young woman. She isn't going to do anything that would ruin the lives of other people."

"Meaning the woman who is known as your wife?"

"Yes. I repeat, that leaves you, Mr. Mason."

"It leaves me."

"I could arrange to see that you received rather a large fee for representing Dianne, perhaps as much as a hundred thousand dollars."

"I'm representing Dianne," Mason said. "I'll do what's best for her."

"It won't be best for her to make a disclosure of my past and her relationship to me."

"How do you know it won't?"

"It would simply complicate matters and get her involved."

Mason said, "You're pretty influential here. The police have received an anonymous tip to question Dianne. You should have enough influence to get the police to disregard that anonymous tip. You don't want her questioned—now."

Winlock thought for a moment, then said, "Get her out of town."

"And then?" Mason asked.

"That's all there'll be to it."

"You can control the police investigation?"

"Within reasonable limits and indirectly, yes."

"That leaves the question of her property rights," Mason said.

"Her legal rights to any property are exceedingly nebulous."

"I don't think so," Mason said. "In this state, property acquired after marriage is community property."

"But I have been separated from my first wife for more than fourteen years."

"Forget the expression, your first wife," Mason said. "You had only one wife."

"Would that have anything to do with the subject under discussion?"

"A great deal."

"I'm afraid I fail to follow you, Mr. Mason. Eunice Alder is now dead. Property acquired during marriage is community property, but on the death of the wife that property automatically vests in the husband, subject, of course, to certain formalities. If you had approached me prior to the death of Eunice, the situation might have been very different. As matters now stand, I am quite definitely in the saddle."

"You may think you're in the saddle," Mason said, "but you're riding a bucking bronco and you can be thrown for quite a loss. Under the law the wife's interest in the community vests in the husband on her death *unless* she makes a will disposing of her interest in the community property. Your wife made such a will. Dianne is the beneficiary."

Winlock frowned thoughtfully. "How much would you want for Dianne?" he asked.

"How much have you got?"

"It depends on how it is evaluated."

"How do you evaluate it?"

"Perhaps three million, if you consider all of my equities."

"All right, what's your proposition?"

"I'll liquidate enough holdings to give Dianne five hundred thousand dollars. I will give her fifty thousand dollars in cash. I will pay her a hundred thousand dollars within ninety days. I'll pay the balance within a year."

"And in return for that?"

"In return for that I want absolute, complete silence about our relationship, about my past."

"All right," Mason said. "You're of age. You're supposed to know what you're doing. Now I'll tell you about Dianne. I'm not going to give you any answer. I'm not going to make you any proposition. I'm going to think things over and I'm going to play the cards in the way that will be in the best interests of Dianne Alder.

"If the police find out about her connection with Harrison T. Boring and question her about her business with Boring, it may well be to Dianne's advantage to disclose the relationship with you, and the whole background."

"Just so I can have the picture straight," Winlock said, "will you summarize briefly Dianne's business with Boring, just what it was?"

Mason said, "Boring found out about the relationship. He came to Dianne with a lot of legal hocus-pocus pretending he was interested in her as a model who was to appear on television and in movies in connection with the introduction of a new style in women's garments.

"Back of all that legal hocus-pocus, however, and the bait of television appearances, was the hook that he was to get one half of all of her gross income from any source, inheritance or otherwise. In return for that he was to pay her a hundred dollars a week.

"Last Saturday he sent her notice that the payments would be discontinued. That means he decided it would be better and more profitable as far as he was concerned to sink his hooks into you for blackmail rather than to let Dianne collect and then engage in litigation as to whether his contract was any good, whether it had been entered into under false pretenses, etc., etc.

"Dianne consulted me about the termination of the contract and the loss of the hundred-dollar-a-week income. She knew nothing about the reason back of the contract.

"I had my suspicions aroused because I was having Harrison Boring shadowed, and so I came to you earlier this evening. Dianne knew nothing about what I was doing. When Montrose Foster found her and convinced her that in order to protect her good name she must get the other signed copy of the contract back from Boring, she very foolishly failed to consult me but tried to take matters into her own hands."

"What did she do? Did she call on Boring?"

"I don't think I care to amplify my statement," Mason said. "However, the police are following up what apparently was an anonymous telephone tip and want to question her about Boring. They came here and tried to take her to headquarters. I refused to let her go. If they question her, it is quite possible the cat will be out of the bag. I'll do whatever will protect Dianne's best interests."

"And if they don't question her?" Winlock asked.

"Then," Mason said, "I'll take your proposition under advisement and discuss it with Dianne."

Winlock said, "Let me use the telephone, if I may."

He walked over to the telephone, called police headquarters, then after a few moments said, "Hello, this is George D. Winlock. I want to talk with Chief Preston. It's quite important that I— Oh, he is? Well, put him on, will you, please?"

There was a moment of silence, then Winlock said, "Hello, Chief? This is George Winlock. Look here, Chief, you sent someone to question a Dianne Alder at the Mission Inn. What did you want to see her about?"

Winlock was silent for nearly a minute while the telephone made harsh metallic sounds through the receiver.

Then Winlock said, "That's all it was? Just an anonymous telephone tip? . . . All right, Chief, look here. I happen to know something about Dianne Alder. Some people have been attempting to annoy her in connection with a television modeling contract which she has signed. There are matters of professional jealousy involved, and this anonymous telephone tip, I am satisfied, was inspired by reasons of personal spite and it wouldn't do the slightest good to question her but would embarrass her personally and— Well, thanks a lot, Chief. I thought I'd let you know. . . . All right, you speak to your men, will you? . . . Thanks a lot, good night."

Winlock hung up the telephone. "Does that answer your question, Mason?"

"That answers my question," Mason said.

"Get her out of town," Winlock said.

"Right at the present time," Mason said, "she's under sedation."

"Well, get her out first thing in the morning."

"Don't you want to see her?"

"She knows all about me?"

"She does now."

Winlock said, "Yes, I want to see her, but not here. The situation is too hot. I want her to return to Bolero Beach. I will get in touch with you about a meeting and talk with both you and her about a property settlement.

"In the meantime I trust that I can count on your discretion."

Mason said, "You can count on my doing what is best for Dianne's interests."

Winlock said, "Please tell her that I called, that she was under sedation, that it was therefore hardly a proper time or a proper place for me to see her. Please tell her that I am using my influence to protect her from

any disagreeable publicity, and that I would like to
have her reserve judgment about what I have done until
she has a chance to hear my side of the story.

"And you might also explain to her," Winlock went
on, "that I have interceded personally with the police
to see that she is not annoyed."

"That much I can promise you I'll do," Mason said.

Winlock extended his hand. "Thank you very much,
Mr. Mason, and good night."

"Good night," Mason said, and escorted him to the
door.

CHAPTER THIRTEEN

WINLOCK had not been gone more than three minutes when Mason heard the chimes and opened the door. A strikingly beautiful woman stood there smiling seductively.

"May I come in, Mr. Mason?" she asked. "I'm Mrs. Winlock and I knew my husband was calling on you. I waited behind some potted palms in the lobby until he had left. I want to see you privately."

"Come in," Mason invited, "and sit down."

"Thanks. I'll come in but I won't sit down. I'll tell you what I want and what I have to offer in a very few words."

"What do you have to offer?" Mason asked.

"Freedom for Dianne Alder."

"And what do you want?"

"What I want is to retain my social position, my respectability and my property interests. Is that clear enough?"

"It's clear enough," Mason said. "Now give me the

details. What makes you think Dianne Alder's freedom is at stake?"

"Don't be naïve, Mr. Mason. Dianne came to Riverside to see Boring. She saw him. She was probably the last person to see him alive."

"How do you know this?"

"The police have received an anonymous telephone tip to that effect."

"How do you know that?"

"Through a friend of mine who is in a position to know."

"You seem to know a great deal."

"Knowledge is power."

"And you want power?"

"Power and more power. I won't try to deceive you, Mr. Mason. There is a concealed microphone in our library. My son is at a romantic age. There have been times when girls have sought to blackmail him. I deemed it wise to have the house wired so conversations could be monitored."

"And so you heard my conversation with your husband this evening?"

"Every word."

"All right. Just what is your proposition?"

"If you could prove Harrison Boring was injured— fatally injured—*before* Dianne called on him, it would establish your client's innocence, would it not?"

"Presumably it would," Mason said.

"I can give you that proof."

Mason said, "Perhaps you'd better sit down, Mrs. Winlock, and we'll talk this over."

"Very well." She moved over to a chair, seated herself and crossed her knees, adjusting her skirt so that
the hemline was where it would be most effective
in showing to advantage a pair of very neat nylon-clad
legs. She settled back in the chair and smiled at Mason
with calm confidence.

"Just how would we go about proving this?" Mason
asked.

"That," she said, "is a matter of detail which we will
discuss later on. The main question is whether you
agree with me in principle that if you can establish this
matter by definite proof, I am entitled to keep my
name, my position, my respectability and the bulk of
my property."

"What else are you prepared to offer in return?"
Mason asked.

"What do you mean by the words, 'What else?' "

"What about Dianne's property rights?"

"Does she have any?"

"Yes."

"What did my husband want?"

"I think perhaps you had better discuss the matter
with him."

"Well, I will put it this way. Whatever proposition
my husband made in regard to a division of property
would be acceptable to me."

Mason said, "I'd have to know a little more about
how you intend to make this proof and I'd have to
discuss it with my client."

"Very well," she said. "Let us suppose that Harrison
T. Boring was a blackmailer, a crook and a promotor.

Let us suppose that there were wheels within wheels, that sometime during the evening he became engaged in an altercation with someone who was trying to share in the spoils and, as a result, Boring was fatally injured.

"Now then, let us suppose that my son called on Boring, found him lying injured, but made no specific examination. In fact he assumed that the man was dead drunk, and left. Let us suppose that I called on Boring, found him injured and came to the conclusion my son had been engaged in an altercation and left the place; that sometime later I phoned the manager of the motel, told her to look in on the man in Unit 10 and hung up.

"Let us assume that my husband followed me in a visit to Boring, found him injured, assumed that I had inflicted the injuries and left."

"That would require your testimony, the testimony of your husband and the testimony of your son, and you would be censured for not calling for aid as soon as you saw the injured man."

"All of that might be arranged. Tell me, what would be the penalty?"

"If your son thought the man was drunk and had reason so to believe, there would be no violation of the law. If you *knew* that a crime had been committed and failed to report it, the situation might be rather serious."

"Suppose that I also thought he was drunk?"

"That," Mason said, "would present a story which might well tax the credulity of the listener. Two coincidences of that sort would be rather too much."

"Suppose my husband should admit that he knew

the man was injured but thought I had been the one who had struck him with some weapon and that the injury was not serious, that Boring was knocked out. Would the offense be serious enough so that my husband could not be let off with probation and perhaps some admonition and rebuke from the court?"

"Remember," Mason said, "that the man died. A great deal would depend on the nature of his injuries, whether a more prompt hospitalization would have resulted in saving his life. Remember also I am Dianne's attorney and am not in a position to advise either you or your husband."

"Under those circumstances," she said, "my proposition had better remain in abeyance.

"I might also mention, Mr. Mason, something that you don't seem to have realized—that the room where Mr. Boring was found fairly reeked with the smell of whiskey."

Mason raised his eyebrows.

"I gather that you didn't know that."

"It is always dangerous to jump to conclusions," Mason said, "but I am interested in the fact that *you* noticed it."

She smiled and said, "You play them rather close to your chest, don't you, Mr. Mason?"

"At times I think it is advisable," Mason said.

Abruptly she arose. "I have told you generally what I have in mind," she said, "and you might think it over. I trust that under the circumstances Dianne will not make any rash statements which would tend to make any meeting of the minds impossible?"

"Are you suggesting," Mason asked, "that I suborn perjury?"

"Certainly not, Mr. Mason." She smiled. "Any more than I am suggesting that I commit perjury. I am simply speculating with you on what would happen under certain circumstances and whether or not it would be possible to bring a situation into existence which would cause those circumstances to be established by evidence."

"It's an interesting conjecture," Mason said. "Now will you tell me exactly what happened when you entered the motel unit rented by Harrison T. Boring?"

"I never even said I was there."

"I know you were there," Mason said.

She smiled archly and said, "Then what you don't know is what I found when I entered the room."

"Exactly."

"And under normal circumstances, when would be the first time you would discover this, Mr. Mason?"

"When you were placed on the witness stand and examined by the prosecution and I had an opportunity to cross-examine you."

"And you think you could discover the true facts by cross-examination?"

"I would try."

"It's an interesting thought," she said. "And now, Mr. Mason, having given you a brief statement as to the purpose of my visit, I am not going to let you try to trap me by any further conversation."

She arose, crossed the room with the gracious manner of royalty bestowing a favor, gave Mason her hand, smiled up into his eyes and said, "It's been a pleasure meeting you, Mr. Mason."

"I trust we will meet again," Mason said.

"Oh, I'm sure of it," she told him. "My telephone is listed in the book and you can reach me at any time. I will always be available to *your* call."

Mason watched her down the corridor, then slowly and thoughtfully closed the door.

CHAPTER FOURTEEN

AT THREE O'CLOCK in the morning Mason was awakened by the persistent ringing of his telephone.

Sleepily, he groped for the instrument, said "Hello," and heard Sid Nye's voice.

"Unlock your door. I'm coming up and don't want anyone to see me."

The connection was severed before Mason could say a word.

The lawyer rolled out of bed, went to the parlor of the suite and unlocked the door.

A few minutes later Sid Nye slipped into the room.

"You're not going to like this," he warned.

"Shoot," Mason said.

"They caught Moose Dillard, evidently nabbed him several hours ago."

"What do you mean they *caught* him?"

"He was trying to make a getaway and they nabbed him."

"How come?"

"Well, the police wanted to make a check on persons in adjoining units in the motel to see if any of them had seen or heard anything unusual. They made a door-to-door canvass and everything checked out until they came to the door of Unit 5. Then they found no one home, the door unlocked, the key on the dresser, the bed hadn't been slept in and Dillard had left the drapes slightly parted and the chair in place where he had been sitting looking across at Unit 10 with a whole ash tray full of cigarette stubs on the floor."

"Keep talking," Mason said, as Nye hesitated.

"Well, of course, we hadn't figured they'd *search* the other units, but they did. The story was there just as plain as if Dillard had left a written statement of what he'd been doing. There was the chair by the window, the drapes slightly parted, the tray full of cigarette stubs giving an indication of how long he'd been watching."

Mason nodded.

"The police checked on the license number of Dillard's automobile, found out it was registered to Paul Drake, alerted the California Highway Patrol giving them the license number of Dillard's automobile and a description of the driver. They also alerted the city police with a radio bulletin. As it happened, one of the city police picked up Dillard at a service station on the outskirts of town where he was gassing up."

"Then what happened?"

"Well, they checked on Dillard's driving license, his occupation, found he was a private detective, started asking him why he was so anxious to get out of town, and intimated that he might have a little more license trouble if he didn't co-operate.

"That was all Dillard needed. He'd been through the mill once and he didn't want any more beefs."

"So he spilled everything he knew?"

"Everything. He even took them to the place where we'd 'lost' the notebook. It was still there lying by the curb. They nailed it. Of course, that showed Dianne was the last one to see Boring alive, or presumably alive; that she had dashed out of the place, her manner showing great excitement and emotional disturbance.

"The bad thing is that Dillard insists Dianne was in the room almost fifteen minutes. The police didn't like that."

"And *I* don't like it," Mason said. "She swears she wasn't."

"Time could pass pretty fast if she was looking for something," Nye said.

"Not that fast," Mason said, frowning. "There's no chance Moose Dillard could have been mistaken?"

"Hell, no. Not on a deal like that. Moose is a little slow thinking sometimes. He's quick-tempered and he makes mistakes, but as an operative he's tops. He knows what he's doing, he keeps notes, he's a good observer and you can depend on his data."

Mason was thoughtfully silent.

"It's a hell of a mess," Sid Nye said.

"It's tough," Mason admitted, "but we're going to have to face conditions as they are and not the way we'd like to have them. You can't argue with a fact.

"Why haven't they arrested Dianne, Sid?"

"I don't know. Perhaps they're waiting for—"

The telephone rang.

Mason answered it.

Della Street said, "There's a policewoman here in the room and she has a warrant for Dianne."

"Let Dianne go with her," Mason said. "And tell Dianne not to make *any* statement except in my presence. Tell her to say *nothing—nothing*."

"I'll tell her," Della Street said.

"Stall along as much as you can, Della. I'll be down as soon as I can get some clothes on."

"Will do," she promised.

Mason started dressing, talking to Sid Nye as he hurried into his clothes.

"Sid, I want you to get out of town while the getting's good. You're not a witness to anything and therefore it won't be concealing evidence to have you hard to find. However, right at the moment I don't want the police inquiring into *my* activities after I came to Riverside."

"You don't want anyone to know you called on Winlock?"

Mason buttoned his shirt. "That's right, and I don't care about having the police know Winlock called on Boring. . . . Will Dillard be able to tell them it was Winlock, his wife and stepson who called on Boring?"

"No. He doesn't have their license numbers or names. He has the general descriptions of two of the automobiles and descriptions of the people. The only license number he has is that on Dianne's car. He can, of course, make an identification if they confront him with the persons but there's nothing that would lead them

to the Winlocks from his description; in fact, the Winlocks would be the last persons they'd suspect in a case
of this sort."

Mason fastened his belt. "And remember, in case
you're questioned, *you* don't *know* who Boring's callers
were. You've only surmised—and the same is true of
me."

Mason hurried down to Della Street's room and a
policewoman answered his knock.

"Good morning," Mason said. "I'm Perry Mason. I'm
Dianne Alder's attorney. Do I understand you're taking her into custody?"

"Yes."

"I want to talk with her."

"She isn't dressed. I'm taking her into custody. You'll
have to talk with her at headquarters."

Mason` raised his voice. "I'll talk to her through the
door. Say absolutely nothing, Dianne. Don't tell the police about your name, your past, your parents or—"

The door slammed in the lawyer's face.

Mason waited some ten minutes in the corridor until
the policewoman, accompanied by Della Street and Dianne Alder, emerged into the corridor.

"Can you take it, Dianne?" Mason asked. "Can you
keep quiet?"

Dianne nodded.

The policewoman turned on him. "I don't want lawyers addressing my prisoner," she said. "If you want to
consult with your client, you can come to the jail and
do it in a regular manner."

"What's wrong with this?" Mason asked.

"It's against my orders. If you persist I'll have to charge you with interfering with an arrest."

"Is it a crime," Mason asked, "to advise a client in the presence of an arresting officer, that if she once starts answering any questions the point at which she stops will be considered significant, but if she doesn't answer any questions at all on the advice of her counsel, and demands an immediate hearing, she is—"

"That will do," the policewoman said angrily. "You're talking to her."

"I'm talking to you."

"Well, your words are aimed at her. I'm going to ask you and Miss Street to leave now. That's an order."

Mason smiled. "My, but you're hard to get along with."

"I can be," she said angrily.

Dianne Alder dropped a pace behind so that she was looking over the officer's shoulder at Perry Mason. She raised her forefinger to her lips in a gesture of silence.

Mason bowed to the officer. "I accede to your wishes, Madam. Come on, Della."

CHAPTER FIFTEEN

CARTER LELAND, the district attorney of Riverside County, said to the magistrate, "If the Court please, this is a simple matter of a preliminary hearing. We propose to show that the defendant in this case had a business arrangement with the decedent, Harrison T. Boring; that she became convinced Boring had swindled her, that she was exceedingly indignant, that she went to the Restawhile Motel in order to see him and did see him; that she was the last person to see Boring alive and that when she left the room Boring was in a dying condition.

"That is all we need to show, in fact more than we need to show, in order to get an order binding the defendant over for trial."

"Put on your case," Judge Warren Talent said.

"My first witness is Montrose Foster," Leland announced.

Montrose Foster came forward, held up his right hand, was sworn, seated himself nervously on the witness stand.

"Your name is Montrose Foster, you reside in Riverside and have for some two years last past? You are the president of Missing Heirs and Lost Estates?"

"That is true."

"On last Tuesday, the day of the murder as charged in the complaint, did you have occasion to talk with the defendant?"

"I did."

"Where did this conversation take place?"

"At Bolero Beach."

"Did the defendant make any statement to you about her feeling toward Harrison T. Boring?"

"She did."

"What did she say?"

"She said she could kill him."

Leland turned abruptly and unexpectedly to Perry Mason. "Cross-examine," he said.

"Is that all you're going to try to bring out on direct examination?" Mason asked.

"It's enough," Leland snapped. "I don't intend to let this preliminary hearing become a three-ring circus."

Mason turned to the witness. "Did you," he asked, "say something to the defendant that was well calculated to cause her to make that statement?"

"Objected to," Leland said, "as calling for a conclusion of the witness. He can't testify as to what was in the defendant's mind or what was calculated to arouse certain emotions, but only to facts."

"Sustained," Judge Talent said. "I think you can reframe the question, Mr. Mason."

"I'll be glad to, Your Honor," Mason said, and turned

to the witness. "Did you *try* to say something that would be calculated to arouse her rage toward the defendant?"

"Why, Your Honor," Leland said, "that's exactly the same question. That's a repetition of the same question calling for a conclusion of the witness and in defiance of the ruling of the Court."

"No, it isn't," Mason said. "This question now relates to the state of mind of the witness."

"And that's completely immaterial," Leland said. Mason grinned. "You mean I can't show his bias?" Leland started to say something, caught himself.

Judge Talent smiled and said, "The question has been skillfully reframed. The objection is overruled."

"I told her certain things about Boring," Foster said.

"The question, Mr. Foster, was whether you tried to arouse her anger against Boring by what you told her."

"Very well. The answer is yes."

"You deliberately tried to arouse the defendant's anger?"

"I told you, yes."

"Did you tell her that Boring had been attempting to sell her into white slavery?"

"Well—that was her idea."

"You agreed with it?"

"I didn't disagree with it."

"At no time during the conversation did you mention that Boring's purpose in his dealings with her was one of immorality?"

"Well, she brought that subject up herself."

"And you, in your conversation, encouraged her in that belief?"

"Yes."

"And told her that Boring had deceived her in order to get her to sign an agreement which was intended to enable him to sell her into white slavery?"

"I didn't tell her that. She told me that."

"You agreed with her?"

"Yes."

"And then, after that, you told her that *was* Boring's objective?"

"All right, I did."

Mason smiled. "Now, *you* knew what Boring was after, didn't you, Mr. Foster? Didn't you tell me that Boring had located some property and an estate to which the defendant could establish title?"

"That's what he was after, yes."

"And you knew what he was after?"

"Of course I did."

"Then that was his real objective?"

"Yes."

"Therefore when you told the defendant that the purpose of Boring's contract with her was to get her in his power for other reasons, you lied to her."

"I let her deceive herself."

"Answer the question," Mason said. "When you told her that, you lied to her."

"That's objected to—it's not proper cross-examination," Leland said. "It also assumes facts not in evidence."

"Objection overruled on both counts," Judge Talent said.

"All right," Foster snapped, "I lied to her."

"You did that in order to get an advantage for yourself?"

"Yes."

"You are, then, willing to lie as a part of your everyday business transactions in order to get an advantage for yourself?"

"I didn't say that," the witness said.

"I'm asking it," Mason said.

"The answer is no."

"You don't generally lie in order to get an advantage for yourself?"

"That certainly is objectionable, Your Honor," Leland said.

"I think so. The objection is sustained," Judge Talent ruled.

"But you did tell such a lie in order to get such an advantage in *this* case," Mason said.

"Yes," the witness snapped.

"Now, on the evening of the murder, you yourself saw Harrison T. Boring at the Restawhile Motel, did you not?"

"Yes."

"And had an interview with the decedent?"

"Yes."

"Your Honor," Leland said, "the prosecution wishes to object to any testimony as to what took place at that interview. It was not brought out on direct examination, and if counsel wants to go into it, he must make this witness his own witness."

"I think it shows motivation and bias," Mason said.

"I'm inclined to agree with you," Judge Talent said.

"I think you can at least show the bias and interest of this witness, and if it appears that he himself was in contact with the decedent on the day of the murder, that may well establish an interest."

Mason turned to the witness. "Did you lie to Boring at the time you had that interview with him?"

"No."

"You didn't tell him that this defendant was going to repudiate any arrangement she might have with him, but that if Boring would let you in on the secret of what he had discovered, you would co-operate with Boring and would keep the defendant in line and you would share whatever property she was entitled to fifty-fifty—words to that effect?"

"That was generally the nature of my proposition."

"But you didn't have the defendant tied up with any agreement?"

"I felt I could secure such an agreement."

"But you told Boring you had her tied up?"

"Something of that sort."

"So you lied to Boring?"

"All right!" the witness shouted. "I lied to Boring. He lied to me and I lied to him."

"Whenever it suits your advantage, you're willing to lie?" Mason asked.

"If the Court please," Leland said, "that's the same question that has already been ruled on. I object to it."

"Sustained," Judge Talent said.

"So, on last Tuesday," Mason said, "in connection with your ordinary business activities, in two interviews you told lies in order to get an advantage for yourself."

"Same objection," Leland said. "It's the same question, Your Honor."

"I don't think it is," Judge Talent said. "It is now a specific question as to two interviews with two people. However, I'm going to sustain the objection on the ground that the question has already been asked and answered. The witness had admitted lying to each of two people on the same day."

Mason turned to the witness. "And are you lying now?"

"No."

"Would you lie if it suited your advantage?"

"Objected to as not proper cross-examination, and as argumentative," Leland said.

"Sustained," Judge Talent said.

"Did you have any physical altercation with Boring at the time you saw him?"

"I— It depends on what you mean by a physical altercation."

"Did Boring hit you?"

"No."

"Did he grab you by the coat or other garment?"

"He pushed me."

"Did he throw you out?"

"He tried to."

"But wasn't man enough to do it?"

"No."

"Because you resisted him?"

"Yes."

"And how did you resist him?"

"I poked him one."

"So," Mason said, smiling, "on the day of Boring's death, on this Tuesday evening, you went to see the decedent shortly before his death. You had lied to the defendant, you lied to Boring, you engaged in a struggle with him and you poked him. Is that right?"

"All right, that's right," Foster said.

"You had reason to believe Boring had a large sum of money on him and you demanded that he surrender a part of all of that money to you—that he divide it with you?"

"Objected to as not proper cross-examination," Leland said.

Judge Talent thought the matter over, then said, "I'm going to sustain that objection."

"*Did* you get some money from him?" Mason asked.

"Same objection."

"Same ruling."

"No further questions," Mason said.

"That's all," Leland said. "I'll call Steven Dillard as my next witness."

Moose Dillard lumbered to the stand, his huge frame seeming to sag inside of his coat. His eyes were downcast and he studiously avoided Perry Mason.

"What's your name?" Leland asked.

"Steven Dillard."

"What's your occupation?"

"I'm a detective."

"A private detective?"

"Yes, sir."

"Were you employed as such on last Tuesday?"

"Yes."

"Did you know the decedent, Harrison T. Boring?"

"I had seen him."

"When had you first seen him?"

"On Monday."

"Where?"

"Leaving Perry Mason's office."

"And what did you do with reference to following him?"

"I had put an electronic bug on his automobile."

"By that you mean an electronic device for the purpose of enabling you to follow the automobile?"

"Yes."

"Can you describe this device?"

"It is a battery-powered device which was attached to his car and which sends out signals which are received by a companion device attached to the car I was driving. By using it I didn't need to get close to the car I was tailing."

"And you thereafter shadowed Mr. Boring?"

"Yes."

"You followed him to the Restawhile Motel in Riverside?"

"Yes."

"And as a part of your shadowing operations secured a unit directly across from him?"

"That's right."

"What time did you check into that unit on last Tuesday?"

"At about six o'clock in the evening."

"Did you keep Unit 10, in which Harrison Boring was registered, under surveillance?"

"I did."

"During that evening did you see the defendant?"

"I did."

"At what time?"

"I kept some notes. May I look at those notes?"

"Those notes were made by you?"

"Yes."

"They are in your handwriting?"

"Yes."

"And were made at the time?"

"Yes."

The district attorney nodded. "You may consult the notes for the purpose of refreshing your recollection."

Dillard said, "The defendant came to his cabin at about nine o'clock and left at nine-twelve."

"Are you certain of your time, Mr. Dillard?"

"Absolutely."

"Do you know that your watch was correct?"

"It is my custom to carry an accurate watch, and when I am on a job I make it my habit to check the watch with the radio."

"Did you notice anything about the defendant's manner that would indicate emotional agitation when she left?"

"She was in a tremendous hurry. She almost ran out of the unit and around to the side of her automobile and jumped in the car."

"You recognized the defendant?"

"Yes."

"You took down the license number of the automobile she was driving?"

"Yes."

"What was it?"

"It was TNM 148."

"Did you subsequently check the registration slip on that automobile?"

"I did."

"And what name appears on that registration slip fastened to the steering post of the automobile?"

"The name of Dianne Alder."

"And after she left, who else went into the Boring cabin?"

"No one, until the manager of the motel looked in just long enough to open the door, step inside, then hurry out."

"And after that, who else came?"

"Two police officers."

"And after that, who else went in?"

"Two stretcher bearers."

"This was while the police were there?"

"Yes."

"Then, from the time the defendant left that cabin, no one else entered the cabin until the officers came. Is that right?"

"That's right."

"Cross-examine," Leland snapped to Perry Mason.

"I may have misunderstood your testimony," Mason said. "I thought you said that from the time the defendant left the cabin no one entered it until the officers entered."

"That's right."

"How about the manager of the motel? Didn't she enter?"

"Well, she just looked in and out."

"What do you mean by *looked* in."

"Opened the door and looked in."

"Did she enter the unit?"

"It depends on what you mean by enter. She stood there in the doorway."

"Did she step inside?"

"Yes."

"Did she close the door behind her?"

"I . . . I don't think so."

"You have your notebook there in which you kept track of the times?"

"Yes."

"May I see that notebook?" Mason asked.

The witness handed it over.

Mason said, "You show that a man who was driving a sports car entered the unit."

"That was earlier."

"Then another man entered the unit, a man who, according to your notes, wore dark glasses."

"Your Honor," Leland said, "if the Court please, I object to this line of interrogation. The purpose of my examination was to show only that the defendant entered the building and was the last person to see the decedent alive; that she was in there a full twelve minutes and that when she departed she was greatly agitated.

"Now then, the witness has refreshed his memory from notes made at the time. Mr. Mason is entitled to exam-

ine him on those notes only for the purpose of showing
the authenticity of the notes. He cannot go beyond the
scope of legitimate cross-examination and ask questions
about matters which were not covered in my direct examination."

"I think under the circumstances that places an undue
restriction upon the cross-examination," Judge Talent
said.

Leland remained standing. "If the Court please, I
don't want to argue with Your Honor, but this is a very
vital matter. It is possible to confuse the issues if the
door is opened on cross-examination to a lot of collateral
matters. This is only a preliminary hearing. I only need
to show that a crime was committed and that there is
reasonable ground to connect the defendant with the
commission of that crime. That is the only purpose of
this hearing and that's all I need to show."

Judge Talent turned to Mason. "Would you like to be
heard on this, Counselor?"

"I would," Mason said. "It is my contention that the
testimony of this witness is valueless without his notes. I
propose to show that his notes are inaccurate and then I
am going to move to strike out his entire evidence."

"You aren't trying at this time, by cross-examining
him about other persons who entered the unit, to do
anything other than question the validity of his notes?"

"That is the primary purpose of my examination."

"Objection overruled," Judge Talent said. "You may
certainly examine him on his notes."

"Answer the question," Mason said.

"My notes show that a man entered at eight and was

out at eight-fifteen; that another man entered at eight-twenty and was out at eight-thirty-five; that a woman entered at eight-thirty-six and was out at eight-forty-five; that a man in dark glasses entered at eight-forty-six and was out at eight-fifty; that the defendant entered at nine and was out at nine-twelve."

"When was the last time you saw the decedent?" Mason asked.

"When he entered Unit 10."

"You didn't see him personally come to the door to admit any of these people whom you have mentioned in your notes?"

"No. . . . Now, wait a minute. I did see the decedent go out to the parking lot where my car was parked and look at the registration. That was shortly after we had checked in at the motel, sometime before he had any visitors."

"I'm not asking about that at this time," Mason said, "I notice that your notes show nothing after nine-twelve."

"That's when the defendant went out."

"And your notes show nothing else?"

"That was when I quit taking notes."

"Why did you quit taking notes? Did you know the man was dead?" Mason asked.

"Oh, Your Honor, I object to that," Leland said. "That question is absurd."

"There must have been some reason the man stopped taking notes," Judge Talent said. "I think counsel is entitled to cross-examine him about his notes. The objection is overruled."

"Well, I quit taking notes when the defendant left because . . ."

"Because what?" Mason asked.

"Because you and my boss were there personally and you could see for yourself what went on."

"Oh, I see," Mason said. "Then you quit taking notes when I came to the cabin. Is that right?"

"Yes."

"And you want us to understand that your notes are accurate up to that time?"

"Yes."

"But," Mason said, "your notes don't show the arrival of the police officers. Your notes don't show the arrival of the ambulance."

"Well, I told you about them."

"But you didn't know we were going to come."

"I expected you."

"So you quit taking notes when you expected we would come."

"Well, I didn't think it was necessary to take notes on those. That wasn't why I was shadowing the man."

"And," Mason said, "your notes don't show the time the manager of the motel entered that unit, how long she was in there, or when she came out."

"Well, she just looked in and out and I didn't think that was important."

"Oh," Mason said, "you want us then to understand that your notes only show the matters that you considered important. In other words, if anyone entered the unit and you didn't think that person was important, it doesn't show in your notes."

"Well, I— All right," Dillard blurted, "I overlooked a bet there. I didn't put down the time the manager came in."

"Or the time she went out?"

"She came in and went out all at the same time."

"Came and went in the same instant?" Mason asked, feigning incredulity.

"Well, you know what I mean. She went in and—she was only in there a second and then she came running out."

"There was a telephone in the unit which you occupied?"

"Yes."

"And you mentioned that you had a boss there in Riverside?"

"A man who was above me in the organization for which I am working, yes."

"You are referring to Sidney Nye?"

"Yes."

"And you called Sidney Nye?"

"Yes."

"When?"

"Right after the manager of the motel came running out. I figured there was something wrong."

"Let's see if I can understand the floor plan of the room which you occupied. There was a bed in that room?"

"Yes."

"A chair?"

"Yes."

"There was a window looking out on the parking

place, and by sitting at that window you could look across and see the entrance to Unit 10?"

"Yes."

"And there was a telephone?"

"Yes."

"Where was the telephone?"

"By the bed."

"Now, after you saw the manager come running out, you went to the telephone and called a report in to Sid Nye, didn't you?"

"Well, I didn't report but I gave him the signal something was wrong."

"And what did you say?"

"I got him on the phone and said, 'Hey Rube.' "

"You had previously worked in a circus?"

"Yes."

"And 'Hey Rube' is a rallying cry for the circus people to unite in a fight against the outsiders?"

"Something to that effect, yes."

"Did you have any trouble in getting Sid Nye?"

"No, he answered the phone as soon as it rang."

"I asked you," Mason said, "if you had any trouble in getting Sid Nye."

"Well, yes. The manager, of course, was busy notifying the police and—"

"You don't know what the manager was doing," Mason said. "You couldn't see her, could you?"

"No."

"Then you don't know *what* she was doing."

"Well, I surmised what she was doing because I had

to sit at the phone for such a long time before anyone answered."

"You knew that the calls went through a switchboard there in the office?"

"Yes."

"And she had to connect you with an outside line?"

"I had to give her the number and she would call it."

"Now, while you were at the phone, you had your back to the window, didn't you?"

"I couldn't be in two places at the same time."

"Exactly," Mason said. "You had previously called Sid Nye, earlier in the evening, hadn't you?"

"No, I— Yes, wait a minute, I did. I told him I had been made."

"What did you mean by that?"

"I meant that the subject had become suspicious and had gone out and had looked at the registration certificate on my car."

"That was the last time you saw him?"

"Yes."

"And while he was doing that you telephoned Sid Nye?"

"No, I waited until after he'd turned his back and gone into the motel unit that he occupied."

"That was Unit Number 10?"

"Yes."

"And then you telephoned Sid Nye and told him you had been made?"

"Yes."

"Any other conversation?"

"That was about it."

"Didn't you tell him you were hungry?"

"Well, that's right. I asked him if I should go out to dinner."

"And what did he say?"

"No. He told me to sit tight. He—I think he was in your room at the time and was talking with you and relaying your instructions."

"And during that time you were at the telephone?"

"Of course I was at the phone."

"And had your back turned toward the window?"

"Yes."

"So," Mason said, "as far as your notes are concerned they are inaccurate and incomplete in that they don't show anything that happened after the defendant left the unit."

"There wasn't anything else that happened, except that the police came."

"And the manager of the motel?"

"And the manager of the motel."

"And, during the time you had your back turned while you were telephoning or trying to get a connection through the switchboard, any number of people could have come and gone."

"Well—Like I told you, Mr. Mason, I couldn't be in two places at the same time."

"So," Mason said, "as far as you know, Boring wasn't in Unit 10 at all during the time the defendant was there."

"How do you mean?"

"The decedent could have left that unit while you

were telephoning Nye to tell him that you had been made, as you expressed it, and the decedent could have again entered the unit after the manager had entered the unit and then left in a hurry, and while you were telephoning Sid Nye to say *Hey Rube*."

"All right," Dillard said, "I kept the place under surveillance but I can't be everyplace at once. Naturally when I was at the telephone I couldn't be there at the window, and when I went to the bathroom I wasn't there."

"Oh," Mason said, "then you weren't at the window *all* of the time."

"No. I did a reasonable job of surveillance and that's all you can expect."

"So your notes are inaccurate in that they don't show *every* person who came to the unit and they don't show every person who left."

"Those notes are accurate."

"They show the persons that you saw entering and the persons you saw leaving," Mason said, "but you don't know how many other people could have gone in or gone out that you didn't see."

"I'd have seen them, all right."

"But you were in the bathroom on at least one occasion?"

"Yes."

"Perhaps two?"

"Perhaps."

"And you didn't put down the time the manager of the motel was in there?"

"No."

"Or the time she left?"

"No."

"That's all," Mason said.

"If the Court please," Leland said, "I intended to let that conclude my case but under the circumstances and in view of the highly technical point raised by counsel I will call the manager of the motel.

"Mrs. Carmen Brady, will you come forward and be sworn, please?"

Mrs. Brady was sworn, identified herself as the manager of the motel.

"On Tuesday night did you have occasion to go to Unit 10?"

"I did."

"What time was this?"

"I made a note of the time. It was exactly nine-twelve."

"And what happened?"

"The telephone rang and a woman's voice said that I had better check on the man in Unit 10, that he seemed to be ill. I hung up the telephone, went to the unit and looked in and Mr. Boring was lying there on the floor. He was breathing laboriously and heavily and I dashed back and called the police."

"Cross-examine," Leland snapped at Perry Mason.

"What time did this call come in?" Mason asked.

"At twelve minutes past nine."

"You went to the unit?"

"Yes."

"How long were you in there?"

"No time at all. I opened the door and saw this man

lying on the floor and turned and dashed out and notified the police."

"At once?"

"At once."

"Did you close the door behind you when you entered
the motel unit?"

"I . . . I can't remember, Mr. Mason. I think I
started to close the door and then saw the man on the
floor and was startled and ran toward him and bent over
him and saw he was still alive and then I dashed out of
the unit and called the police."

"How do you fix the time of the call as being nine-
twelve?"

"I made a note of it."

"At the suggestion of the police?"

"Yes."

"Then you marked down the time, *not at the time the
phone call was received but at some time afterwards?*"

"Within a few minutes afterwards."

"How long afterwards?"

"Well, I called the police and told them the man was
injured, and they wanted to know how I knew and I
told them about having received a tip over the telephone, and the police officer suggested that I make a
note of the time."

"So you made a note of the time."

"Yes."

"And what time was that?"

"It was just a little after nine-thirteen."

"Then you made a note of nine-twelve, a little after
nine-thirteen?"

"Well, I thought the call had been received a minute earlier."

Mason said, "You received this call. You hung up the telephone and went at once to Unit 10?"

"Yes."

"And then went back to the motel and then picked up the telephone and called the police."

"Yes."

"How far is it from the office to the motel unit?"

"Not over seventy-five feet."

"Did the police tell you it was then nine-thirteen?"

"Not at the time, no."

"How did you fix the time?"

"By the electric clock in the office."

"And did that clock show the time as nine-thirteen?" The witness hesitated.

"Did it?" Mason asked. "Yes or no?"

"No. The clock showed the time as nine-seventeen."

"Yet you now swear it was actually nine-thirteen?"

"Yes."

"On what basis?"

"The police records show I called at nine-thirteen. Their time is accurate to the second. Later on when I checked my clock I found it was fast."

"When did you check it?"

"The next day."

"You did that after you found there was a discrepancy between your time and that on the police records?"

"Yes."

"I think that's all," Mason said. "I have no further questions."

"I'll call Dr. Powers to the stand," Leland said.

Dr. Powers took the stand.

"Did you have occasion to perform an autopsy on a body on Wednesday morning?"

"I did."

"Had you previously seen that individual?"

"I had treated him when he arrived in an ambulance at the emergency room."

"What was his condition at that time?"

"He was dying."

"When did he die?"

"About twenty minutes after his arrival."

"Do you know the cause of death?"

"A fracture of the skull. He had been hit with some blunt instrument on the back of the head."

"He was hit with a blunt instrument, Doctor?"

"As nearly as I can tell."

"There was a fracture of the skull?"

"Yes."

"And it resulted in death?"

"Yes."

"Cross-examine," Leland said.

"There was no external hemorrhage?" Perry Mason asked.

"No."

"An internal hemorrhage?"

"Yes. Within the skull there was a massive hemorrhage."

"Injuries of this sort could have been sustained by a fall, Doctor?"

"I don't think so. The portion of the skull in question

had received a very heavy blow from some heavy object."

"Such as a club?"

"Perhaps."

"A hammer?"

"I would say, more in the nature of a bar of some sort."

"Perhaps a pipe."

"Perhaps."

"Did you notice any other injuries?"

"Well, I noticed a contusion on the side of the man's face, a rather slight contusion but nevertheless a contusion."

"You mean a bruise?"

"Yes."

"Technically a traumatic ecchymosis?"

"Yes."

"Any other injuries?"

"No."

"No further questions," Mason said.

"I'll call Herbert Knox," Leland said.

Knox came forward, was sworn, identified himself as an officer, stated that he had received a radio report at nine-fifteen to go to the Restawhile Motel; that he arrived at approximately nine-eighteen, was directed to Unit 10; that he there found a man who was injured, that this was the same man who had been taken to the emergency unit and turned over to Dr. Powers, the witness who had just testified; that the man was then, in his opinion, in a dying condition and that the witness subsequently saw the body in the morgue and it was the body of the same individual he had first seen in Unit 10 at the Restawhile Motel.

"Cross-examine," Leland said.

"Did you notice the odor of whiskey in the unit?" Mason asked.

"I certainly did. Whiskey had been spilled over the clothes of the injured man. The odor was strong."

"You made an inventory of the things in the room?"

"Later on, yes."

"There was a traveling bag and some clothes?"

"Yes, a two-suiter and a traveling bag."

"Did you find any money?"

"Not in the unit, no."

"Did you at any time search the injured man for money?"

"Not until after his arrival at the hospital. I personally searched the clothes which were removed from him."

"Did you find any money?"

"A hundred and fifteen dollars and twenty-two cents in bills and coins," the officer said.

"There was no more?"

"No. He was wearing a money belt. It was empty."

"Did you search Boring's automobile?"

"Yes."

"Did you find any money?"

"No."

"As far as you know, the money which you have mentioned represented the entire cash which he had?"

"Yes."

"That's all," Mason said.

"That's our case, if the Court please," Leland said.

"We ask that the defendant be bound over for trial."

"Does the defense wish to make any showing?" Judge Talent asked. "If not, it would seem that the order should be made. This is simply a preliminary hearing and it has been established that a crime has been committed and that there is at least reasonable ground to believe the defendant is connected with the commission of the crime."

Mason said, "It is now eleven-thirty. May I ask the Court for a recess until two o'clock, at which time the defense will decide whether we wish to put on any case?"

"Very well," Judge Talent said. "We'll continue the case until two P.M. Will that give you sufficient time, Mr. Mason?"

"I think so, yes," Mason said.

After court adjourned, newspaper reporters interviewed Mason and Leland briefly.

Leland, coldly aloof, said, "I am fully familiar with counsel's reputation for turning a preliminary hearing into a major courtroom controversy. It is entirely improper and, if I may say so without criticizing my brother district attorneys, I think the reason is that some of those district attorneys have become a little gun shy of Mr. Mason. They try to put too much evidence and that gives the defense an opportunity to make a grandstand showing."

The newspaper reporter turned to Mason. "Any comment?" he asked.

Mason grinned and said, "I'll make my comment at two o'clock this afternoon," and walked out.

CHAPTER SIXTEEN

MASON, Della Street, and Paul Drake ordered lunch to be served in their suite at the Mission Inn.

The telephone rang shortly after Mason had placed the order.

Della Street nodded to Mason. "For you, Chief," she said, and then added in a low voice, "Mrs. W."

Mason took the phone, said, "Hello," and Mrs. Winlock's smooth, cool voice came floating over the line.

"Good afternoon, Mr. Mason. How did the court hearing go this morning?"

"Very much as I expected," Mason said cautiously.

"And do you want to do something that is for the best interests of your client?"

"Very much."

"If," the voice said, "you will adhere to the bargain I outlined to you, you should be able to score another triumph over the prosecution, have the defendant released and have the case thrown out of court.

"Both my son and I are in a position to testify, if necessary, that when we entered that unit the man was ly-

445

ing on the floor breathing heavily and we thought he was drunk. And I will testify that I was the one who made the phone call to the manager of the motel."

"Suppose I simply subpoena you and put you on the stand?" Mason asked.

She laughed and said, "Come, come, Mr. Mason, you're a veteran attorney. You could hardly commit a booboo of that sort. Think of what it would mean if I should state the man was alive and well when I left."

"And your price?" Mason asked.

"You know my price. Complete, utter silence about matters which will affect my property status and my social status. Good-by, Mr. Mason."

The receiver clicked at the other end of the line.

Della Street raised inquiring eyebrows.

Mason said, "Paul, you're going to have to pick up lunch somewhere along the line. I want you to go out to the Restawhile Motel. I want you to take a stop watch. I want you to get the manager to walk rapidly from the switchboard, out the front door, down to Unit 10. I want you to have her open the door, walk inside, turn around, walk back, pick up the telephone, call police headquarters and ask what time it is. See how long it takes and report to me."

"Okay," Drake said. "What time do you want me back here?"

"Call in," Mason said. "I may have something else for you. Telephone a report just as soon as you have checked the time."

"Okay," Drake said, "on my way."

Five minutes after Drake had left, the chimes in the

suite sounded, and Della Street opened the door to a very agitated George D. Winlock.

"Good afternoon," Winlock said. "May I come in?"

"Certainly. Come right in," Mason said.

Winlock looked at Della Street. "I would like very much to have a completely private conversation with you, Mr. Mason."

"You can't do it," the lawyer said. "Under the circumstances I'm not going to have any conversation with you without a witness. However, I may state that Miss Street is my confidential secretary and has been such for quite some time. You can trust to her discretion, but she'll listen to what's said and, what's more, she'll take notes."

Winlock said, "This is a very, very delicate matter, Mr. Mason. It is very personal."

"She's heard delicate matters before which have been very, very personal," Mason said.

Winlock debated the matter for a moment, then surrendered. "You leave me no choice, Mr. Mason."

"Sit down," Mason said. "Tell me what's on your mind."

Winlock said, "My wife has told you that she and her son, Marvin Harvey Palmer, are willing to testify that they were the two people who were seen entering Unit 10 between eight and nine; that at that time Boring was lying on the floor breathing heavily; that they smelled whiskey and thought he was lying there drunk; that Marvin Palmer waited for some minutes, hoping that Boring would revive so that he could talk with him; that my wife was there a much shorter period of time."

"Well?" Mason asked.

"It's not true," Winlock said, with some agitation. "Boring was in full possession of his health and his faculties when they were there."

"How do you know?"

"Because I was there after they were."

"You haven't told me," Mason said, "what was the nature of your interview with Boring."

"I told him I was going to have him arrested for blackmail, that there was no longer any opportunity to keep my relationship with Dianne secret, that you had uncovered it and that Dianne herself knew about it, that under the circumstances I was going to have him arrested in the event he wasn't out of town by morning."

"Did you ask him for the ten thousand dollars back?"

"Yes. I made him return the money."

"Without a struggle?"

"I threw a terrific scare into him. He hated to part with that money, but he didn't want to go to prison for blackmail."

Mason said, "You had given Boring ten thousand dollars in cash?"

"I had."

"At what time?"

"At about five P.M. He had stopped by my office just before closing time. He was there very briefly. I had the money ready for him."

"And from your office he went directly to the motel?"

"I believe he did. You should know. Apparently you were having him shadowed."

"That's what the detective's report said," Mason observed.

Winlock said, "I am very deeply disturbed about this thing, Mr. Mason. I cannot permit my wife to commit perjury simply in order to save our reputation. That's altogether too great a price."

"And how do you know it's perjury?"

"Because Boring was in good health when I left him."

"That's what you say," Mason said, eying Winlock narrowly, "but there's another explanation."

"What?"

"That you killed him," Mason said.

"*I* did!"

"That's right. That you went to Boring and threatened him with arrest, and Boring told you to go ahead and arrest and be damned; that you weren't going to push him around. You had an argument, hit him, inflicting fatal injuries, and removed the money you had given him as the result of his blackmail.

"In that event, your wife's testimony wouldn't be directed primarily at saving Dianne, but at saving you.

"The man was lying there dying when Dianne entered the motel unit. You were the last one to see him prior to the time Dianne saw him. The minute you state that he was alive and well when you saw him, you make yourself a murderer."

"I can't help it," Winlock said. "I am going to tell the truth. I've steeped myself in deceit as much as I am going to."

"Now then," Mason went on, "what would happen if your wife went on the stand and your stepson went on the stand and both of them swore positively that when *they* entered that unit in the motel they found Boring lying on his back, breathing heavily, with the odor of whiskey overpoweringly strong?"

"If I were put on the stand I would still tell the truth."

"Suppose you weren't put on the stand?"

Winlock got up and started pacing the floor, clenching and unclenching his hands. "God help me," he said, "I don't know what I'd do. I'd probably get out of the country where I couldn't be interviewed. I—"

"You'd get out of the country," Mason said, "because you'd be avoiding a charge of murder."

"Don't be foolish, Mr. Mason. If I had killed him, I would be only too glad to ride along with the story my wife and stepson are thinking of concocting in order to purchase Dianne's silence. I would then perjure myself and swear that the man was unconscious and apparently drunk."

Mason said, "Unless this act you're now putting on is all a part of the over-all scheme to save your own neck and to confuse me. . . . The minute you tell me that this man was alive and well when you left, you put me in a position of suborning perjury in the event I permit your wife and stepson to testify as witnesses for the defense that he was lying there in a stupor, apparently dead drunk."

"I can't help it, Mr. Mason. I've gone just as far as I'm going to along the slimy path of deceit in this thing. I've got to a point now where I can't sleep, I can't live with myself."

"And how does Mrs. Winlock feel about all this?" Mason asked.

"Unfortunately, or fortunately, as the case may be, she doesn't share my feelings. Apparently the only thing that is bothering her is the question of how to prevent this situation from being disclosed, how to prevent her social set from knowing that she has been living a life of deceit for the past fourteen years, that she hasn't been married to me at all. Her only concern is for the immediate effect on her social and financial life."

"All right," Mason said, "go home and talk it over with her. Remember this, as an attorney at law I'm obligated to do what is for the best interests of my client.

"*You* tell me that he was alive and well when you left, but your wife and your stepson tell me that he was lying there fatally injured; only, because his clothes were saturated with whiskey, they thought he was drunk.

"I'm not in a position to take your word against theirs. I have to do what's for Dianne's best interests."

Winlock said, "You can't do it, Mason. You're a reputable attorney. You can't suborn perjury."

"You think your wife is going to perjure herself?"

"I know it."

"You don't think Boring might have been putting on an act for their benefit? That he had poured whiskey over his clothes and was lying there, apparently in a stupor? That he then got up when you entered the unit and talked with you?"

"There was no odor of whiskey on his garments when I talked with him."

Mason said, "If such is the case, *you* are Boring's murderer. You have to be."

"Don't be a fool, Mason," Winlock said.

"Under those circumstances," Mason observed some-what thoughtfully, "the case would—under those circumstances—be mixed all to hell. Nobody would know what to do. It would shake this community to its foundations."

"If my wife and my stepson get on the stand and commit perjury," Winlock said, "I suppose I have no alternative but to get on the stand and tell a similar story, but I'll tell you right now, Mason, it would be a lie."

"Under those circumstances," Mason said, "*I* wouldn't call *you* as a witness. But that doesn't keep me from calling Mrs. Winlock and Marvin Harvey Palmer."

Winlock looked at Mason, then hastily averted his eyes. "I wish I knew the answer to this," he said.

"And I wish *I* did," Mason told him, eying him thoughtfully.

"I can, of course, get my wife out of the jurisdiction of the court," Winlock said.

"Sure you can," Mason said, "but I'll warn you of one thing. If I decide to put on a defense and call your wife and stepson and they're not available, I'll tell the court the conversations I have had with them and the fact that they have offered to testify. I'll insist on having the case continued until they can be called as witnesses, and you can't stay out of the jurisdiction of the court indefinitely. You have too many property interests here."

Winlock shook his head, said, "I have no alternative. I'm gripped in a vise." He walked to the door, groped for the knob and went out.

Della Street regarded Mason quizzically.

Five minutes later the telephone rang.

Della Street said, "Mrs. Winlock for you, Mr. Mason."

Mason took the receiver.

Again Mrs. Winlock's voice, almost mockingly cool, said, "Have you reached a decision yet, Mr. Mason?"

"Not yet," Mason said.

"I'll be available at my house, Mr. Mason. Give me a few minutes to get ready. My son will be with me."

"And you'll testify as you have indicated?" Mason asked.

"I'll testify as we have indicated, *provided* you will give me your word as a gentleman and an attorney that you and Dianne will preserve the secret of Dianne's relationship, and will accept the financial settlement offered by Mr. Winlock.

"Good day, Mr. Mason."

Again the phone was hung up at the other end of the line.

At that minute two waiters appeared, bringing in the luncheon.

"Well, Mr. Perry Mason," Della Street said, when the waiters had left the room, "you seem to have worked yourself into a major dilemma."

Mason nodded, toyed with the food for a few minutes, then pushed his plate aside, got up and started pacing the room.

"Know what you're going to do?" Della Street asked.

"Damn it!" Mason exploded. "The evidence points to the fact that George Winlock is the murderer."

"He has to be," Della Street said. "That is, unless Dianne is lying."

"I have to take my client's story as the truth," Mason said. "I am bound to accept her statement at face value. And yet she has to be lying about making that phone call to the manager of the motel. Mrs. Winlock must be the one who made that call. Dillard's testimony as to the time Dianne left clinches that. Dianne simply didn't have time to get to the phone and make that call.

"Now then, the significant thing is that Mrs. Winlock didn't make the call until *after* her husband had left the cabin *and* had a chance to report to her that he had frightened or forced Boring into returning the blackmail money."

"Then that leaves George D. Winlock the murderer," Della Street said.

"And he's handled things so cleverly," Mason agreed, "that if I do try to expose him as a murderer, I look like a heel. If, on the other hand, I put Mrs. Winlock and her son on the stand and let them swear to the story they've offered to tell, I get Dianne off the hook but leave myself open to a charge of suborning perjury at any time Winlock wants to lower the boom on me."

"Could this be a very shrewd, clever stunt that they jointly have carefully worked out and rehearsed?" Della Street asked.

"You're damn right it could," Mason said.

"And," she asked, "what's going to be your countermove?"

"I don't know," Mason told her. "At first I thought it was simply an offer to furnish perjured testimony and

I was going to throw the whole thing out in the alley. Now I'm not so certain that it isn't a carefully, cunningly contrived plot to hamstring my defense and put me in such a position that I don't know what actually did happen."

The lawyer resumed his pacing of the floor.

After a few minutes he said, "Of course, Della, it's not up to me to prove who did murder the guy—that's up to the prosecution. My job is to prove Dianne innocent."

"Can you do it?" she asked.

"With this testimony I could do it hands down," Mason said.

Again the telephone rang.

"Paul Drake," Della Street said.

"Hello, Perry," Paul Drake said. "I'm finished down here at the Restawhile Motel."

"What did you find out?"

"The distance to be covered is about a hundred feet each way. Moving at a fairly normal rate of speed it takes about thirty seconds each way. Moving at a rapid rate of speed, you cut that time down.

"Getting in, picking up the telephone and putting the call through accounts for seven seconds. So her testimony is approximately correct. Figure about a minute and ten seconds as the outside time limit if she did what she said she did."

"All right," Mason said, "here's something else for you, Paul. Drive down to the telephone booth three blocks down the street. Time yourself from the entrance of the motel. Call me from that booth and let

me know how long it takes until you hear my voice. I'll
be waiting here at the phone."

"Okay," Drake said, "and then I want some lunch.
I'm ravenous. I suppose you folks are sitting up there
smug and well fed."

"We're neither smug nor well fed," Mason said. "I'm
sitting on the end of a great big limb and I'm not too
certain somebody between me and the tree doesn't have
a very sharp saw.

"Get busy and see what you can find out, Paul."

Four minutes later, Paul Drake telephoned.

"Hello, Perry," he said when he had the lawyer on
the line. "It took me exactly two minutes from the time
I left the entrance of the motel to get down here, park
my car, get in the telephone booth, close the door, dial
you and get your answer."

"Hang it," Mason said. "Dianne couldn't have left
the place and placed that call, or else the time element
is all wrong."

Drake said dryly, "She was the last person to see Harrison Boring alive. You may be able to mix Dillard up
on the time element but that's all it's going to amount
to, just a technicality. The facts speak for themselves."

"Of course," Mason said into the telephone, almost
musingly, "the time Dianne left can be checked with
physical facts. The time she entered is fixed only by
Dillard's watch.

"Just suppose he made the mistake of setting his
watch not by the radio but by the clock there in the
motel office."

"Would it help if you could show that?" Drake asked.

"Anything would help," Mason said. "That is, anything that clarifies the situation."

"Or confuses it," Drake said dryly. "I'm going to get some lunch."

Mason hung up the telephone, turned to Della Street. "Two minutes," he said.

"And that throws Dillard's time off about four minutes?"

"Something like that."

Della Street said, "He was looking at his watch in the dark and he *could* have misread the hands."

"It's vital as far as Dianne is concerned," Mason said.

"Of course," she pointed out, "it opens up some question of doubt, but after all she was in there at least ten minutes, even if Dillard did make a mistake."

"She says she wasn't," Mason said.

"But," Della Street pointed out, "she admits she remained long enough to search for and find the contract. She was only estimating the time."

Mason said, "The thing that annoys me is the smooth assurance of this district attorney who acts on the assumption that this is just a simple routine matter of another preliminary hearing in another murder case and there's no reason on earth why he shouldn't have it all buttoned up inside of half a day."

"But," Della Street said, "the *main* problem is whether Winlock is lying, whether the whole family isn't protecting the stepson, or who struck the fatal blow and when. After all, Dillard's time discrepancies are minor matters."

Mason said, "I have in my hand an opportunity to introduce testimony that will throw the district attorney's case out of the window, get Dianne in the clear and at the same time get a property settlement for her running into a very substantial figure.

"If I do that, Winlock is either going to claim I was guilty of suborning perjury—or at least is in a position to do so any time he chooses to lower the boom."

"What will happen if you *don't* do it?" Della Street asked.

"Then," Mason said, "Dianne is going to get bound over on a murder charge. She'll be in jail awaiting trial, she'll come up before a jury; by that time Mrs. Winlock will have withdrawn her offer and sworn she never made it. It will be the word of Dianne against a lot of circumstantial evidence and against the evidence of a man who has a great deal of influence in the community, George D. Winlock.

"Then I'll spring a dramatic surprise that Winlock is the girl's father and is testifying against her to protect himself. I'll make a high-pressure plea to the jury —and in all probability they'll convict Dianne of manslaughter rather than murder. That's about the best I can hope to accomplish. That's the price of trying to be ethical. To hell with it."

Della Street, realizing the nature of the crisis which confronted the lawyer, watched him in worried silence.

CHAPTER SEVENTEEN

JUDGE TALENT said, "This is the time heretofore fixed for resumption of the hearing in the case of the People of the State of California versus Dianne Alder. You were to let the Court know at this time whether you wish to put on a defense, Mr. Mason."

Mason said, "If the Court please, this is not a simple matter. There are complications which I am not in a position to disclose but which nevertheless cause the defense some concern as to the best course to pursue."

District Attorney Leland was on his feet. "If the Court please, the defense has had all the time they asked for and I object to granting any further time."

"I am not asking for further time," Mason said, "but I would like to clarify one matter in regard to the time element. I would like to ask a few more questions on cross-examination of the witness, Steven Dillard."

"Is there any objection?" Judge Talent asked Leland.

"There is lots of objection, Your Honor. This man, Dillard, is actually a hostile witness. He is in the employ of defense counsel. He gave his testimony reluc-

tantly and he gave it so that he shaded everything he
could in favor of the defense. The cross-examination
was completed, my case was closed, and I object to having counsel try these tactics of recalling a witness for
further cross-examination. It's irregular."

"The matter rests in the discretion of the Court,"
Judge Talent said. "Would you like to amplify your
statement, Mr. Mason?"

"I would, if the Court please. Dillard stated that the
defendant was in the unit from nine o'clock to nine-
twelve. Yet the records will show that the police were
notified at nine-thirteen, which would indicate that the
manager of the motel must have been in there at least
by nine-twelve. The manager of the motel, in turn, was
notified by some woman over the telephone that—"

"You don't need to go any further, Mr. Mason. The
Court is interested in the proper administration of justice. Your request will be granted. Mr. Dillard, resume
the stand, please."

Dillard once more came to the stand.

Mason said, "I would like to have you consult your
notes in regard to the time element, Mr. Dillard. I
would ask the district attorney for the notes which you
state you kept at the time."

The district attorney grudgingly passed over the
notebook.

Mason stood beside Dillard. "These figures are
scrawls, rather than figures," he said. "How do you explain that?"

"I was sitting there at the window and I took notes
in the dark. I didn't want to turn on the light."

"Now, you were also looking at your wrist watch in the dark in order to determine the time, were you not?"

"My wrist watch has luminous hands."

"Is there any chance you could have missed the time by five minutes?"

"Certainly not. I could see the dial very clearly."

"Could you have missed it by two minutes?"

"No."

"By one minute?"

"Well, I'll put it this way, Mr. Mason. I couldn't see the second hand, but I could see the hour hand and the minute hand and I might—I just might—have made a mistake of half or three-quarters of a minute; I don't think as much as a full minute."

Mason said, "If Dianne left that unit, got in her car, drove to a telephone, called the manager of the motel; if the manager of the motel had then gone down to the unit to look for herself and then returned and called the police, it is obvious that the police couldn't have received the call by nine-thirteen if Dianne had left the unit at nine-twelve."

Dillard said nothing.

"Now, I notice that while the other figures are in the nature of scrawls," Mason said, "the words 'blonde enters cabin' with the license number of her automobile, TNM 148 and the hour 9:00, are written very neatly. And the words, 'blonde leaves unit' with the figure 9:12 P.M. are also written very neatly. Can you explain that?"

"Well, I . . . I guess perhaps I had moved over to where the light was better."

"Then," Mason said, "you didn't write those figures down *at the time* the defendant left the cabin. Perhaps you wrote them down later."

"No, I wrote them at about that time."

"At *about* that time, or at that time?"

"At that time."

"Your Honor," Leland said, "this is no longer legitimate cross-examination. The question has been asked and answered, and counsel is now attempting to argue with the witness and browbeat him."

Judge Talent said, "There is rather a peculiar situation here. May I ask counsel if it is the contention of the defense that the defendant actually was the person who put through the telephone call to the manager of the motel, suggesting that there was something wrong with the occupant of Unit 10?"

Mason said, "I feel that without jeopardizing the interests of the defendant, I can answer that question by saying that it may appear the call was made by her or by someone else and the time element may be the determining factor."

"She couldn't have made that call," Leland said. "It had to have been someone else, and counsel is trying to take advantage of this peculiar situation in the time element to give his client a chance to claim she made the call."

Mason, studying the notebook which had been kept by Dillard, apparently paid no attention to the objection.

"Mr. Mason," Judge Talent said, "an objection has been made. Do you wish to argue it?"

"No, Your Honor."

"I think the question has been asked and answered. I will sustain the objection."

Mason turned to Dillard. "All right, I'll ask you another question which has *not* been asked and answered, Mr. Dillard. Isn't it a fact that you made this entry about the defendant entering the cabin with the license number of her automobile, and putting down the time that she left the cabin, *before the defendant left the cabin?* And while you were sitting at a desk under a reading lamp where you could write these figures neatly and concisely?"

Dillard hesitated, then said, "No."

"And isn't it a further fact," Mason said, "that you are notoriously hot-tempered; that after the man with dark glasses left Unit 10, the decedent, Harrison T. Boring, who had caught you peeking through the parted curtain, came over to your unit, threatened you, and you lost your temper and hit him; that the blow knocked him down; that he hit his head on a stone and lay still; that you, realizing that you had seriously injured the man, picked him up, took him over to his own unit, opened the door, dropped him on the floor, poured whiskey over him, returned to your unit and while you were debating what you were going to do next, saw the defendant enter the unit rented by Boring; that you thereupon quit watching the unit, debating what you were going to do to save your own skin, that while you were debating the matter you heard the defendant's car start and heard her drive off; that while you were still debating what to do, you heard the police arrive; that you at a time somewhat later wrote a synthetic record of the defendant's visit, approximating the time of her arrival and estimating the time of her departure, and then called your superior, Sid Nye, and asked that he come to your assistance?"

Leland got to his feet with a supercilious smile. "Oh, Your Honor," he said, "this is altogether too absurd. This . . ."

The district attorney suddenly broke off at the expression on the judge's face. Judge Talent was leaning forward from the bench, looking down at Moose Dillard.

The big man on the stand was clenching and unclenching his huge hands. His facial muscles were twisting in the manner of a grown man who wants to cry and has forgotten how.

Dillard wiped his forehead with the back of his hand.

"You'd better answer that question, Mr. Dillard," the judge said somewhat sternly, "and answer it truthfully."

"All right," Dillard said. "That's the way it happened. I clobbered the guy. Only, I didn't knock him down, he was standin' in the door of my unit calling me names and he made a pass at me. I beat him to the punch and clobbered him.

"The blow knocked him back and his head struck against the corner post on the porch and he slumped to the ground.

"I didn't know he'd been hurt too bad, but I'd been in enough trouble. I picked the guy up and carried him back to Unit 10 and dumped some whiskey over him.

Then I saw he was badly hurt. I went back and tried to figure what to do and I saw this girl come in."

"The defendant?" Judge Talent asked.

"That's right. I didn't put down the time or anything. I went back over to the desk and sat there with my head in my hands. I heard her drive away and then after a while I heard the cops come and I knew I was in a spot.

"I called Sid Nye and told him 'Hey Rube.' He'd been in carnival life and I'd been in the circus. I knew that would get me reinforcements. I intended to tell him what had happened, but he brought Perry Mason down with him and then I knew I was in a real jam.

"Before they came, I faked that entry in the book. I just wanted to get the girl's visit down and I didn't know what time she came or what time she left so I approximated it.

"Then I *did* want to get out of town. I didn't intend to do anything that would put this girl in a jam. I just wanted to save my own neck."

Judge Talent looked at Leland.

The prosecutor stood for a moment, his facial expresson indicating the confusion of his mind. Then he slowly seated himself as though his leg muscles had lost the strength to support him.

Judge Talent turned to Mason. "Would you mind telling the Court how you deduced what happened, Mr. Mason? Obviously it just occurred to you."

Mason said, "If the Court please, I had only to realize my client was telling the truth to appreciate the fact that something had to be wrong with the testimony of this witness. I then started searching for a possible ex-

planation. When I saw the neat way the entry of Dianne's visit had been made, I knew it hadn't been written in the dark.

"When I saw the letters, P.M. after the time, I knew
the entry had been faked. No detective making notes on
a night stake-out would write P.M. after the hour.

"I reproach myself for not seeing it sooner."

"On the other hand," Judge Talent said, "the Court
compliments you on a masterly cross-examination and
on your quick thinking."

The judge turned to the prosecutor.

"The case against the defendant is dismissed, and I
think we had better take the witness, Dillard, into custody for perjury and a suspicion of homicide; although
I have a feeling that he is probably telling the truth
and the actual blow was struck in self-defense.

"Court's adjourned."

CHAPTER EIGHTEEN

MASON, Della Street, Paul Drake and Dianne Alder sat in the bedroom of Mason's suite at the hotel.

Della Street said, "I can't hold off the press much longer, Chief. They're milling around there in the living room and it's taking more than cocktails to hold them in line. They want information."

Mason looked at Dianne. "What do we do, Dianne?"

Dianne took a deep breath. "As far as my father is concerned, he has repudiated me. I loved him at one time. I feel very fond of him now, but I recognize his weaknesses.

"As far as the woman who is living with him is concerned, she is a woman. She has problems of her own. She has built up a social position here and I don't want to sweep that out from under her."

Again she took a deep breath, then smiled at Mason. "I'm returning to Bolero Beach," she said. "I came up here as Dianne Alder, a model, and I'm going back to Bolero Beach as Dianne Alder.

"You can make whatever settlement you want to with my . . . my father."

"You don't want to see him?"

She blinked back tears. "He doesn't want to see me," she said, "and I can realize that it's dangerous for him to do so. I have no desire to wipe out the happiness of other people."

Mason nodded to Della Street. "That does it," he said. "We'll go out and give the reporters a statement."

THE CASE
OF THE
HORRIFIED
HEIRS

FOREWORD

A HEAVY rain in Scotland had swollen the streams. As one of them subsided, a small bundle was left by the receding waters.

This bundle contained human flesh.

A search revealed more bundles. Some of them were found days apart. Apparently, many of them had been thrown from a bridge into the turbulent flood waters.

Nearly a month after the first discoveries, a left foot was found on the roadside some distance from the stream bed. Nearly a week later, a right forearm with hand was discovered.

All of the recoveries were, of course, in a state of advanced decomposition.

When the pieces were assembled, it was found there were two heads which had been mutilated by removal of eyes, ears, nose, lips and skin. All teeth had been extracted.

It was apparent that a skilled hand had deliberately butchered two human beings in an attempt to make identification humanly impossible.

While visiting in Glasgow, I was privileged to discuss this case with the distinguished medicolegal expert whose work contributed so much to a solution of the murders.

This man is John Glaister, D. Sc., M.D., F.R.S.E. He is learned in the law and in medical science, being a barrister as well as a doctor of science and of medicine. His academic honors, the positions he has held in his long and distinguished career, would make this brief note too long for available space, should I attempt to enumerate them.

Suffice it to say he helped make medicological history by his work in this baffling murder case. The distinguishing features of the bodies were "reconstructed" by scientific methods. Brilliant deduction determined the general neighborhood where the victims had lived, and shrewd detective work resulted in apprehending the murderer.

My friend Professor Glaister is the author of *Medical Jurisprudence and Toxicology* (E. & S. Livingstone, Ltd., Edinburgh & London; 11th Edition), one of the most comprehensive and authoritative books in the field. Those who wish to learn more of the puzzling murder case mentioned, and the scientific methods used to identify the bodies and apprehend the murderer, will find an account of the case in that book.

Professor Glaister is a dedicated man. His is an honored name in his profession. He has contributed much to a science which protects the living by making the dead reveal their secrets. He is a dignified, impartial man, devoid of bias, devoted to finding out the truth, regardless of where the chips may fall.

And so, I dedicate this book to my friend

JOHN GLAISTER, D. Sc., M.D., F.R.S.E.

ERLE STANLEY GARDNER

CHAPTER ONE

MURDER is not perpetrated in a vacuum. It is a product of greed, avarice, hate, revenge, or perhaps fear. As a splashing stone sends ripples to the farthest edges of the pond, murder affects the lives of many people.

Early morning sunlight percolated through the window of a private room in the Phillips Memorial Hospital.

Traffic noises in the street which had been hushed to a low hum during the night began to swell in volume. The steps of nurses in the corridors increased in tempo, indicating an increase in the work load.

Patients were being washed, temperatures taken, blood samples collected; then the breakfast trays came rolling along, the faint aroma of coffee and oatmeal seeped into the corridors, as if apologetically asking permission to push aside the aura of antiseptic severity, promising that the intrusion would be only temporary.

Nurses holding sterile hypodermic syringes hurried into the rooms of surgery patients, giving the preliminary quieting drug which would allay apprehensions and pave the way for the anesthetic.

Lauretta Trent sat up in bed and smiled wanly at the nurse.

473

"I feel better," she proclaimed in a weak voice.

"Doctor promised to look in this morning right after surgery," the nurse told her, smiling reassuringly.

"He said I could go home?" the patient asked eagerly.

"You'll have to ask him about that," the nurse said. "But you're going to have to watch your diet for a while. This last upset was very, very bad indeed."

Lauretta sighed. "I wish I knew what was causing them. I've tried to be careful. I must be developing some sort of an allergy."

CHAPTER TWO

OUT AT the Trent residence, set in its spacious grounds reminiscent of a bygone era, the housekeeper was putting the finishing touches on the master bedroom.

"They say Mrs. Trent will be home today," she said to the maid. "The doctor asked her nurse, Anna Fritch, to be here and she has just arrived. She'll stay for a week or two this time."

The maid was unenthusiastic. "Just my luck. I wanted to get off this afternoon—it's something special."

It was at this moment that a pair of hands hovered briefly over the washbowl in a tiled bathroom.

A trickle of white powder descended from a phial into the bowl.

One of the hands turned on a water faucet and the white powder drained down the wastepipe.

There would be no more need for this powder. It had served its purpose.

Over the spacious house was an air of tense expectancy as various people waited: Boring Briggs, Lauretta's brother-in-law; Dianne, his wife; Gordon Kelvin, another brother-in-law; and Maxine, his wife; the housekeeper, the maid, the cook; the nurse; George Eagan, the chauffeur. Each

475

affected differently by the impending return of Lauretta Trent, they collectively managed to permeate the atmosphere with suppressed excitement.

Now that the morning surgery was over and the surgeons had changed to street clothes, there was a lull in the activities at the Phillips Memorial Hospital.

The patients who had been through surgery were in the recovery room; the first of them, recovering from the more minor operations, were beginning to trickle through the corridors, eyes closed, faces pale, covered with blankets as they were wheeled to their respective rooms.

Dr. Ferris Alton, medium height, slim-waisted despite his fifty-eight years, walked down to the private room of Lauretta Trent.

Her face lit up as the doctor opened the swinging door.

The nurse looked over her shoulder, and seeing Dr. Alton, moved swiftly to the foot of the bed, where she stood waiting at attention.

Dr. Alton smiled at his patient. "You're better this morning."

"Much, much better," she said. "Am I to go home today?"

"You're going home," Dr. Alton said, "but you're going to have your old nurse, Anna Fritch, back with you. I've arranged for her to have the adjoining bedroom. Technically, she'll be on duty twenty-four hours a day. I want her to keep an eye on you. We shouldn't have let her go after that last upset. I want her to keep an eye on your heart."

Mrs. Trent nodded.

"Now then," Dr. Alton went on, "I'm going to be frank

with you, Lauretta. This is the third gastroenteric upset in eight months. They're bad enough in themselves, but it's your heart that I'm concerned about. It won't stand these dietary indiscretions indefinitely. You're going to *have* to watch your diet."

"I know," she told him, "but there are times when the spiced food tastes so *darn* good."

He frowned at her, regarding her thoughtfully.

"I think," he said at length, "when you're more yourself we'll have a series of allergy tests. In the meantime, you're going to have to be careful. I think it's only fair to warn you that your heart may not be able to stand another of these acute disturbances."

CHAPTER THREE

THE HANDS and the powder had done their work. The way had been paved; the preliminaries were all out of the way.

Lauretta Trent's life depended upon a woman she had seen only once, a woman whose very existence she had forgotten about; and this woman, Virginia Baxter, had only a vague recollection of Lauretta Trent. She had met the older woman briefly ten years ago as a matter of routine.

If she tried, Virginia could probably have recalled the meeting but it was now entirely submerged in her mind, buried under the day-to-day experiences of a decade of routine problems.

Now Virginia was following the stream of passengers filing past the airline stewardesses.

"Goodbye."

"Bye now."

"Goodbye, sir."

"Goodbye. Nice trip."

"Thank you. Goodbye."

The passengers left the jet plane, inched their way to the broader corridors of the airport, then quickened their pace, walking down the long runway toward a huge illuminated

478

sign bearing the word, "Baggage," with an arrow pointing downward where an escalator descended to a lower level.

Virginia Baxter steadied herself by putting her right hand on the rail of the escalator.

She was carrying a top coat over her arm, and she was tired.

In her late thirties, she had retained a trim figure and a way with clothes, but she had worked hard during her life and minute crow's feet were beginning to appear at the corners of her eyes; there was just a suggestion of a faint line on each side of her nose. When she smiled, her face lit up; when it was in repose, there were times when the corners of her mouth began to sag ever so slightly.

She stepped from the escalator at the lower level and walked briskly toward the revolving platform on which the baggage would appear.

It was too early, as yet, for the baggage to make its appearance, but it was indicative of Virginia's character that she walked with nervously rapid steps, hurrying to reach the place where she would wait for several long minutes.

At length, baggage began to appear on a moving belt; the belt transported the baggage to the slowly revolving turntable.

Passengers began to pick out baggage; porters with claim checks stood by, occasionally pulling out heavy handbags and putting them on hand trucks.

The crowd began to thin out. Finally, only a few pieces of baggage were left on the turntable. The trucks had moved away. Virginia's baggage was not in sight.

She moved over to a porter. "My baggage didn't come in," she said.

"What was it, lady?" he asked.

"A single suitcase, brown, and a small oblong overnight case for cosmetics."

"Let me see your checks, please."

She handed him the baggage checks.

He said, "Before I start looking, we'd better wait and see if there's another truck coming. Sometimes there's a second section of trucks when there's an unusually large load."

Virginia waited impatiently.

After two or three minutes, more baggage showed up on the moving belt. There were four suitcases, Virginia's and two others.

"There they are now! Those two are mine," she said. "The brown one—the big one in front—and the oblong overnight bag in back."

"Okay, ma'am. I'll get them for you."

The suitcase, followed by the overnight bag, moved along the conveyor belt, then hit the slide to the revolving table. A few seconds later, the porter picked them up, compared the tags for a moment, put the bags on his hand truck and started for the door.

A man who had been standing well back came forward. "Just a moment, please," he said.

The porter looked at him. The man produced a leather folder from his side pocket and opened it, showing a gold shield. "Police," he said. "Was there some trouble about this baggage?"

"No trouble," the porter hastily assured him. "No trouble at all, sir. It just didn't come in with the first load."

"There's been some baggage trouble," the man said to Virginia Baxter. "This is your suitcase?"

"Yes."

"You're sure of it?"

"Of course. That's my suitcase and overnight bag and I gave the checks for them to the porter."

"Could you describe the contents of the suitcase?"

"Why, certainly."

"Will you please do so?"

"Well, on top there's a three-quarter-length beige coat with a brown fur collar; there's a checked skirt and—"

"That will give us enough of a description to make sure," the man said. "Would you mind opening it up just so I can look inside?"

Virginia hesitated for a moment, then said, "Well, I guess it's all right."

"Is it locked?"

"No, I just have it closed."

The man snapped back the catches.

The porter lowered the truck so the suitcase would be level.

Virginia raised the cover and then recoiled at what she saw on the inside.

Her three-quarter-length coat was there, neatly folded, just as she had left it, but on top of the coat were several transparent plastic containers and inside these containers, neatly wrapped, an assortment of small packages.

"You didn't tell me about these," the man said. "What are they?"

"I . . . I don't know. I never saw them before in my life."

As though at a signal, a man with a press camera and a flash gun materialized from behind one of the pillars.

While Virginia was still trying to compose herself, the camera was thrust up into her face and her eyes were blinded by a brilliant flash of light.

The man, working with swift efficiency, ejected the bulb from the flash gun, inserted another bulb, pulled a slide back and forth on the back of the camera, and took another picture of the open suitcase.

The porter had backed hastily away so that he was not included in the pictures.

The officer said, "I'm afraid, madam, you're going to have to come with me."

"What do you mean?"

"I'll explain it," the officer said. "Your name is Virginia Baxter?"

"Yes. Why?"

"We've had a tip on you," the officer said. "We were told that you traffick in narcotics."

The photographer took one more picture, then turned and scurried away.

Virginia said to the officer, "Why, of course, I'll come with you, if you're going to try to clear this up. I haven't the faintest idea of how that stuff got in my suitcase."

"I see," the officer said, gravely. "You'll have to come to headquarters, I'm afraid. We'll have that stuff analyzed and see exactly what it is."

"And if it should turn out to be—narcotics?"

"Then we'll have to book you."

"But that's—that's crazy!"

"Bring the bags this way," the officer said to the porter, closing the suitcase.

He opened the overnight bag, disclosing jars of cream, a manicure set, a negligee, some bottles of lotion.

"Okay," he said. "This is all right, I guess, but we'll have to look in these jars and bottles. We'll just take both bags along with us."

He escorted Virginia to a plain black sedan, had the porter hoist the suitcase and overnight bag into the rear seat, put Virginia in the seat behind him and started the motor.

"You're going to headquarters?"

"Yes."

Virginia noticed then that there was a police radio on the car. The officer picked up the microphone and said, "Special Officer Jack Andrews leaving the airport with a female suspect and a suitcase containing suspicious material to be checked. Time is 10:17 A.M."

The officer replaced the microphone on a hook, pulled away from the curb, and guided the car expertly and swiftly in the direction of headquarters.

There Virginia was placed in charge of a policewoman and kept waiting for around fifteen minutes, then an officer delivered a folded paper to the policewoman. She looked at it and said, "This way, please."

Virginia followed her to a desk. "Your right hand, please."

The policewoman took Virginia's right hand before she realized what was happening, then grasping the thumb firmly, rolled it over a big pad and placed it on a piece of paper, rolling out a fingerprint.

"Now, the next finger," she said.

"You can't fingerprint me," Virginia said, pulling back. "Why, I—"

The grip on the finger tightened. "Now, just don't make

it hard on yourself," the policewoman said. "The index finger, please."

"I refuse!— Good heavens, what have I done?" Virginia asked. "I— Why, this is a nightmare."

"You're privileged to make a telephone call," the woman said. "You can call an attorney, if you wish."

The words clicked in Virginia's mind.

"Where is a telephone directory?" she asked. "I want the office of Perry Mason."

A few moments later, Virginia had Della Street, Perry Mason's confidential secretary, on the line.

"May I speak with Perry Mason, please?"

"You'll have to tell me what it's about," Della Street said, "perhaps I can help you."

"I'm Virginia Baxter," she said. "I worked for Delano Bannock, the attorney, during his lifetime and up to his death a couple of years ago. I've seen Mr. Mason two or three times. He came to Mr. Bannock's office. He may remember me; I was the secretary and receptionist."

"I see," Della said. "What is the present problem, Miss Baxter?"

"I'm arrested for having narcotics in my possession," she said, "and I haven't the faintest idea of how they got there. I need Mr. Mason at once."

"Just a minute," Della said.

A moment later, Perry Mason's deep but well-modulated voice was on the line. "Where are you, Miss Baxter?"

"I'm at headquarters."

"Tell them to hold you right there, if they will, please," Mason said. "I'm on my way."

"Oh, thank you. Thank you so much. I . . . I just haven't any idea how this happened and—"

"Never mind trying to explain over the telephone," Mason told her. "Don't say anything to anyone except to tell them to hold you right there, that I'm on my way. How are you fixed for bail? Could you put up bail?"

"I . . . if it isn't too high. I have a little property, not much."

"I'm on my way up," Mason said. "I want to demand that you be taken before the nearest and most accessible magistrate immediately. Just sit tight."

CHAPTER FOUR

PERRY MASON invaded Virginia Baxter's nightmare and tore aside the web of unreality and terror.

"The magistrate has fixed bail at five thousand dollars," Mason said. "Can you raise that?"

"I'd have to draw out all of my checking account and withdraw money from the building and loan."

"That would be better than waiting in jail," Mason pointed out. "Now then, I want to know exactly what happened."

Virginia told him the events of the morning.

"You were on the plane, coming from where?"

"From San Francisco."

"What had you been doing in San Francisco?"

"I was visiting my aunt. I've been to see her several times lately. She's elderly, not at all well and she's all alone. She likes my visits."

"What are you doing? Are you working for a living?"

"Not steadily. I haven't been regularly employed since Mr. Bannock died. I have taken a few odd jobs."

"I take it, then, you have some income?" Mason asked.

"Yes," she said. "Mr. Bannock had no relatives, other than the one brother. He remembered me in his will. He

486

gave me a piece of real property in Hollywood that produces an income and—"

"How long had you been with Bannock?"

"Fifteen years," she said. "I started working for him
when I was twenty."

"You've been married?"

"Yes, once. It didn't take."

"Divorced?"

"No. We're separated, have been for some time."

"Friendly with your husband?"

"No."

"What's his name?"

"Colton Baxter."

"You go by the title 'Miss'?"

"Yes. I think it helps in secretarial employment."

"Now, you'd been to see your aunt. You got aboard that
plane. What about the baggage? Anything unusual about
the checking of the baggage?"

"No— Wait a minute, I had to pay excess baggage."

Mason's eyes showed swift interest. "You paid excess
baggage?"

"Yes."

"Do you have your receipt?"

"It's attached to my ticket. That's in my purse. They
took my purse away from me when I was booked."

"We'll get it back," Mason said. "Now then, you were
traveling alone?"

"Yes."

"Remember anything about the person you were seated
next to?"

"He was a man of about thirty-two or thirty-three,
rather well-dressed but— Well, now that I stop to think of

it, he was . . . well, there was something peculiar about
him. He was cold, rather crisp in his manner, not like the
ordinary passenger you encounter on those trips. It's hard
to explain what I mean."

"Would you know him if you saw him again?" Mason
asked.

"Yes, indeed."

"Could you identify him from a photograph?"

"I think so, if it's a clear photograph."

"You only had the one suitcase?" Mason asked.

"No, I had a suitcase and an overnight bag, an oblong
bag containing cosmetics."

"What became of that?"

"They took it. The suitcase came through first. The
porter picked it up and then picked up the overnight bag.
At that moment, a man stepped forward and showed me
his identification card and asked me if I had any objections
to his taking a quick look in my suitcase because there had
been some trouble. Since my baggage had been delayed
coming off the plane, I thought that was what he referred
to."

"What did you tell him?"

"I told him what was in the suitcase and that it was all
right for him to look."

"Can you remember anything more about the conversation?"

"Yes. He asked me first if that was my suitcase, and I told
him it was, and he asked me if I could establish my ownership by identifying the contents. Then I described the
contents, and he asked if it was all right to check."

Mason frowned thoughtfully, then said, almost casually,

"Your baggage, that is, the two pieces together weighed more than forty pounds?"

"Yes. They weighed forty-six pounds taken together, and I paid excess baggage on the six pounds."

"I see," Mason said thoughtfully. "You're going to have to exercise a lot of self-control, and you're in for a disagreeable experience, but perhaps we can work things out one way or another."

"What I can't understand," she said, "is where the stuff came from and how it could have been placed in my suitcase. Of course, it was late coming off the plane, but one wouldn't think anyone could tamper with it out there on the field going from the plane to the baggage counter."

"There were several places it *could* have been tampered with," Mason said. "After you checked the suitcase and before it was put on the plane, someone could have opened it.

"We don't know where it was stored aboard the plane in the baggage compartment. We don't *know* whether anyone could have tampered with it in there.

"Then, of course, when it was taken off the plane, there was this delay. That means that the suitcase was probably placed on the ground, waiting for another truck to come along to pick it up. Now, the way those planes are built, the baggage comes out on the other side from the side which has the passenger entrance. While the suitcase was there on the ground, it wouldn't have been too difficult for someone to have opened it and inserted these packages of narcotics."

"But why?" she asked.

"There," Mason said, "is the rub. Presumably someone was trafficking in narcotics. He knew there'd been a tip-off and his baggage was going to be searched, so he put the contraband in your suitcase and then had an accomplice telephone the police that the stuff would be in the suitcase of one Virginia Baxter. He must have been able to describe you, because the officer who was standing there waiting for you to claim your baggage evidently had a good description of you and had you spotted from the time he saw you come down the escalator."

Mason was thoughtful for a moment, then said, "How about your name? How did you have your suitcase marked? Was there an initial or a name painted on it, or what?"

"There's a leather baggage tag," she said, "one that straps around the ring at the handle, and it had my name typed on it, my name and address: 422 Eureka Arms Apartments."

"All right," Mason said, "we'll get you out on bail. I'm going to try and have you brought up on a preliminary hearing just as soon as possible. At least we'll make the police show their hand.

"I'm satisfied it's all some sort of a mistake and we *may* be able to get it cleaned up without much trouble, but you're going to have to put up with a lot of things."

"Tell me," she asked apprehensively, "there was a photographer there. Will there be anything in the newspapers about it?"

"A photographer?" Mason asked.

She nodded.

Mason said grimly, "Then the thing is a lot more sinister than I had at first supposed. It isn't just a simple mistake. Yes, it will be in the newspapers."

"My name, address, everything?"

"Name, address and photograph," Mason said. "Prepare

yourself for a picture showing the startled expression on your face and a caption such as: EX-LEGAL SECRETARY ACCUSED IN NARCOTICS CHARGE."

"But how could the newspaper have had a photographer there?"

"That's just the point," Mason said. "Some officers like publicity. In return for publicity, they give some friendly newspaper reporter a tip when they're going to make an arrest of some young woman who is photogenic.

"The newspapers play up the story, the officer gets his name in the paper with a favorable bit of publicity. Under these circumstances, be prepared to read that the value of the narcotics in your suitcase, at current retail prices, amounted to several thousand dollars."

Her face showed her dismay.

"And after I'm acquitted," she asked, "then what will happen?"

"Probably nothing," Mason said. "Perhaps a few lines on an inside page of a newspaper."

"I *will* be aquitted, won't I?" she asked hopefully.

Mason said, "I'm an attorney, not a fortuneteller. We'll do our best and you'll have to let it go at that."

CHAPTER FIVE

MASON escorted Virginia Baxter to a seat inside the rail of the courtroom.

"Now, don't be nervous," he said reassuringly.

She said, "That's like telling a cold person not to shiver. I can't help being nervous. I'm shaking like a leaf on the inside, if not on the outside. I feel full of butterflies."

Mason said, "This is a preliminary hearing. It is usually a matter of routine for the judge to bind a defendant over to the higher court. When he does that, he quite frequently increases the amount of bail. Sometimes he makes the bail almost prohibitive. You're going to have to face that possibility."

"I just can't raise any more bail, Mr. Mason, that's all, unless I sell my real property at a loss."

"I know," Mason said. "I'm just telling you what *may* happen. However, real property in your name will influence a judge in fixing the amount of bail."

"You don't hold out much hope of . . . getting me out on this preliminary hearing?"

"Ordinarily," Mason said, "the judge binds the defendant over if the prosecutor wants to go ahead with the case in the higher court. Sometimes, of course, we get a break.

"It's almost unheard of to put a defendant on the stand at the time of a preliminary examination, but if I think there's even a faint chance of getting the judge to dismiss the case, I'm going to put you on the stand so he can take a look at you and see the kind of a person you really are."

"That horrid newspaper story," she said, "—and that picture!"

"From the city editor's standpoint, it was a wonderful picture," Mason said. "It showed surprise and consternation on your face and, as far as your case is concerned, the picture may do you some good."

"But it blasted my reputation," she said. "My friends are avoiding me in a big way."

Mason started to say something but checked himself as the door of the judge's chambers opened.

"Stand up," Mason said.

Every person in the courtroom arose as Judge Cortland Albert took his seat at the bench, then glanced appraisingly at the defendant.

"This is the time heretofore fixed for the preliminary hearing in the case of the People versus Virginia Baxter. Are you ready to proceed?"

"Ready for the defendant," Mason said.

Jerry Caswell, one of the younger trial deputies who was frequently sent in to handle preliminary hearings and who was eagerly trying to make a record which would attract the attention of his superiors, was on his feet.

"The prosecution," he announced dramatically, "is *always* ready!"

He waited a moment, then seated himself.

"Call your first witness," Judge Albert said.

Caswell called the porter from the airport.

"Are you acquainted with the defendant?"

"Yes, sir. I saw her."

"On the seventeenth of this month?"

"Yes, sir."

"You are one of the porters at the airport?"

"Yes, sir."

"And you make a living from transporting baggage?"

"Yes, sir."

"Now, did the defendant, on the seventeenth of this month, indicate to you a suitcase?"

"She did. Yes, sir."

"Would you know that suitcase if you saw it again?"

"I would. Yes, sir."

Caswell nodded to a police officer who came forward with the suitcase.

"Is that the one?"

"Yes, sir, that's the one."

"I want that marked 'People's Exhibit A' for identification," Caswell said.

"So ordered," the judge ruled.

"And the defendant said that was her suitcase?"

"Yes, sir."

"Were you present when the suitcase was opened?"

"Yes, sir."

"What was in the suitcase when it was opened, other than clothes, if anything?"

"There were some packages done up in plastic."

"How many? Do you know?"

"I didn't count them. There was a goodly number."

"That's all," Caswell said. "Cross-examine."

"The defendant identified this suitcase as being hers?" Mason asked.

"Yes, sir."

"Did she give you a baggage check?"

"She did. Yes, sir."

"And you compared the number on the check given you by the defendant with the number on the suitcase?"

"Yes, sir."

"How many checks did the defendant give you?"

"Actually, she gave me two."

"What became of the second check?"

"That was for an overnight bag. I got that for her, too."

"And was that opened?"

"Yes, sir."

"Now, directing your attention to the suitcase, just prior to the time the suitcase was opened, was there some conversation with a person who identified himself as a police officer?"

"Yes, sir. Officer Jack Andrews showed this young woman his credentials and asked her if that was her suitcase."

"What did she say?"

"She said it was."

"And what did Andrews say?"

"He asked her if he could open it."

"No other conversation?"

"Well, that was the substance of it."

"I'm not asking you about the substance," Mason said. "I'm asking you about the conversation itself. Didn't he ask her if she was positive that was her suitcase, and if she could identify the suitcase by describing the articles that were in it?"

"Yes, sir, that's right."

"And then he asked her to open the suitcase so he could inspect those articles?"

"Yes, sir."

"And what about the overnight bag? Did he ask her to identify that?"

"He just asked her if it was hers."

"And she said it was?"

"Yes."

"And then what happened?"

"He opened it."

"That's all?"

"Well, of course, afterwards they took her away with them."

"Now, I call your attention to a photograph in an evening edition of the newspaper published on the seventeenth, and call your attention to this picture of the defendant and the suitcase."

"Objected to as incompetent, irrelevant and immaterial and not proper cross-examination," Caswell said.

"It is preliminary only and for the purpose of bringing out part of the *res gestae,*" Mason said.

"Overruled. I'll hear it," Judge Albert announced.

"Were you present when this picture was taken?"

"Yes, sir."

"Did you see the photographer?"

"Yes, sir."

"Where did he come from?"

"He was hiding behind one of the pillars."

"And when the suitcase was opened, he came out with his camera?"

"Yes, sir. He darted out from behind that pillar with his

camera all ready, and *boom—boom—boom* he took three pictures."

"And then what?"

"Then he ran away."

"If the Court please," Caswell said, "we move to strike out all this testimony about the photographer. Not only is it improper cross-examination but it is incompetent, irrelevant and immaterial. It serves no useful purpose."

"It serves a very useful purpose, if the Court please," Mason rejoined. "It shows that this was no mere casual search. It shows that the officer had planned the search and anticipated what he was going to find. He had tipped off a friendly newspaper reporter and, if the Court will read the article in this newspaper, it will be seen that the reporter endeavored to reciprocate by seeing that the officer had proper publicity in return for the favor extended."

Judge Albert smiled very slightly.

"Your Honor, I object. I object to any such statement," Caswell said.

"It is merely by way of argument," Mason said.

"An argument for what purpose?" Caswell asked.

"To show the relevancy of the testimony," Mason said. "To show that the officer was acting under some specific tip, some bit of information which had been given to him; and the defense proposes to find out what that information was and who gave it to him."

A look of fleeting dismay appeared on Caswell's features.

Judge Albert smiled and said, "I thought I appreciated the underlying purpose of the cross-examination when counsel started asking the questions. The motion to strike is denied.

"Do you have any further cross-examination, Mr. Mason?"

"No, Your Honor."

"Redirect?"

"No, Your Honor," Jerry Caswell said.

"Call your next witness."

Caswell said, "I call Detective Jack Andrews.

"What is your name?" Caswell asked after Andrews had been sworn.

"Jackman, J-A-C-K-M-A-N, Andrews. I am known generally as Jack Andrews, but Jackman is my name."

"Directing your attention to the suitcase which has been marked for identification as People's Exhibit A, when did you first see that suitcase?"

"When the defendant pointed it out to the porter who has just testified."

"And what did you do?"

"I approached her and asked her if that was her suitcase."

"And then what?"

"I asked her if she had any objection to my looking in the suitcase and she said she did not."

"And then what happened?"

"I opened the suitcase."

"And what did you find?"

"I found fifty packages of—"

"Now, just a moment," Mason interrupted. "I submit, if the Court please, this particular question has now been asked and fully answered. The witness said he found fifty packages. As to the contents of these packages, that is another matter and calls for another question."

"Very well," Caswell said. "If counsel wants to do it the

hard way, we'll do it the hard way. Now, did you take those packages into your possession?"

"I did."

"And did you take steps to ascertain what those packages were, what the substance consisted of?"

"I did."

"And what was the substance?"

"Now, just a moment," Mason said. "At this point, we interpose an objection on the ground that it is incompetent, irrelevant and immaterial; that no proper foundation has been laid; that the property was taken as the result of an illegal search and seizure, and is incompetent as evidence in this case.

"In this connection, if the Court please, I desire to ask a few questions."

"Very well, in connection with this objection which has been made, you may take the witness on *voir dire*."

"Did you have a search warrant?" Mason asked the witness.

"No, sir, there wasn't time to get a search warrant."

"You just went out there?"

"I just went out there, but I call your attention to the fact that I asked the defendant *if she had any objection to* my looking in the suitcase and she said it was all right, to go right ahead."

"Now, just a minute," Mason said. "You're relating the substance of the conversation. You're giving your conclusion as to what the conversation consisted of. Can you remember your exact words?"

"Well, those were virtually my exact words."

"Did you tell her you wanted to search her suitcase?"

"Yes."

"Now, just a minute," Mason said. "You're under oath. Did you tell her you wanted to search her suitcase, or did you ask her if she could identify the contents of the suitcase?"

"I believe I asked her if it was her suitcase and she said it was, and I asked her if she could describe the contents and she described them."

"And then you asked her if she had any objection to opening the suitcase *in order to show you the contents she had described*. Isn't that right?"

"Yes, sir."

"But you didn't tell her you wanted to *search* the suitcase?"

"No."

"She gave you no permission to search the suitcase?"

"She said it would be all right to open it."

"She gave you no permission to search the suitcase?"

"I told her I wanted to open it and she said it would be all right."

"She gave you no permission to search the suitcase?"

"Well, I guess the word 'search' wasn't mentioned."

"Exactly," Mason said. "Now, you went down to wait for this defendant at the airline terminal in response to a tip, did you not?"

"Well . . . yes."

"Who gave you that tip?"

"I'm not in a position to disclose the sources of our information."

"I think under the present rulings of the courts," Mason said, "this witness must show that he had reasonable grounds for wanting to search that suitcase, and an anonymous tip, or one from a person he didn't know,

wouldn't constitute reasonable grounds of search; therefore, the defendant is entitled to know the reasons for
which he wanted to search the suitcase."

Judge Albert frowned, turned to the witness. "Do you
refuse to disclose the name of the person giving you the
tip?"

"The tip didn't come to me," Andrews said. "It came to
one of my superiors. I was told that there had been a hot tip
and to go down to the airport, to wait for this party and see
if I could get permission to look in the suitcase. If I
couldn't, I was to keep her under surveillance until a
warrant could be obtained."

Judge Albert said, "This is an interesting situation.
Apparently, the defendant did not give anyone permission
to 'search' the suitcase but did give her consent to opening
the suitcase for the sole purpose of demonstrating the presence of certain articles. It's a peculiar situation."

"I'll get at it in still another way, if the Court please,"
Mason said. "I want to make the defendant's position plain.
We would like to get this matter cleaned up in this
preliminary hearing and not on some technicality."

Mason turned to the witness. "You took fifty packages
out of that suitcase?"

"Yes, sir."

"You have them here in court?"

"Yes, sir."

"Did you weigh them?"

"Weigh them? No, sir. We counted the packages and
made our inventory that way rather than by weight."

"Now, there was a second bag, an overnight bag?"

"Yes, sir."

"Did you ask the defendant to identify that?"

"She said it was hers. She had a claim check for it."

"And did you ask her about the contents?"

"No."

"Did you ask her if it would be all right to open it?"

"No."

"But you did open it and search it?"

"Yes. However, we found nothing significant in that overnight bag."

"You didn't ask her permission to open that bag?"

"I don't believe I did."

"You just went ahead and opened it anyway?"

"That was after I'd found this big shipment of—"

Mason held up his hand. "Never mind what it was, at this time," he said. "We'll refer to it simply as 'fifty packages.' What did you do with the overnight bag?"

"We have it here."

"Now then," Mason said, "since you don't know how much the fifty packages weighed, do you know how much the suitcase weighed without the fifty packages?"

"I do not."

"Did you know the defendant had paid excess baggage on the suitcases?"

"Yes."

"Yet you never weighed them?"

"No."

"I suggest, if the Court please, we weigh them now," Mason said.

"What is the purpose of this offer?" Judge Albert inquired.

"If," Mason said, "the scales show that these two bags, at the present time, and *without* the packages, weigh forty-six pounds, then it is conclusive evidence that someone planted whatever was in that suitcase *after it had left the possession of the defendant.*"

"I think the point is well taken," Judge Albert said. "I'm going to take a recess for ten minutes. The bailiff will have some scales brought into court and we will weigh those two suitcases."

"That doesn't necessarily mean anything," Caswell protested. "We only have the defendant's word that they weighed forty-six pounds. She has been out on bail. We don't know what has been taken from those suitcases."

"Haven't they been in the custody of the police?" Judge Albert asked.

"Yes, but there would have been no objection to her going to the suitcase to take clothes."

"*Did* she go to the suitcase and take anything?"

"I don't know, Your Honor."

"If you don't know whether she took something out, you don't know whether someone else put something in," Judge Albert snapped. "The Court will take a recess of ten minutes and we'll have scales brought in."

Mason sauntered out to a telephone booth, called the pressroom at headquarters and said, "An interesting demonstration is taking place in court in ten minutes. Judge Cortland Albert is going to weigh the evidence."

"Doesn't he always weigh the evidence?" one of the reporters asked facetiously.

"Not this way," Mason said. "He's going to weigh it with a pair of scales."

"What?"

"That's right. With a pair of scales in ten minutes. You'd better be up here. You might get something good."

"What department?" the reporter asked.

Mason told him.

"We'll be up," the man said. "Hold it off a little if you can."

"I can't," Mason told him. "As soon as the judge gets the scales in, he's going to reconvene court. He thinks he can do it within ten minutes and I think he can, too. The bailiff is getting the scales."

Mason hung up.

CHAPTER SIX

MASON, standing beside Virginia Baxter, said, "I'm gambling everything on the fact that you're telling the truth. If you're lying, you're going to get hurt."

"I'm not lying, Mr. Mason."

Mason said, "Ordinarily, at the time of arrest, there would be a dramatic picture on the front page showing an ex-legal secretary smuggling dope. Dismissal of the charges at a preliminary hearing would rate about five or six lines buried somewhere in the inner pages of the paper.

"What I'm trying to do is to make this thing so dramatic that it will be a big story in itself. If you're telling the truth, we'll vindicate your name in such a way that everyone who read the original article and remembered it will read this one and remember that you were acquitted of the charge.

"But if you're lying, this test is going to crucify you."

"Mr. Mason, I'm telling you the absolute truth. Why in the world would I want to peddle dope, or get mixed up in it in any way?"

Mason grinned and said, "I don't ask myself all those questions usually; I just say, 'This girl is my client and, as such, she has to be right. At least, I'm going to act on that assumption.'"

The bailiff and two deputies appeared trundling a platform scale, taken from the jail building and used to weigh prisoners at the time they were booked.

The bailiff vanished into Judge Albert's chambers to report.

The swinging doors of the courtroom were pushed open as half a dozen reporters accompanied by photographers entered the courtroom.

One of the reporters approached Mason. "Would you and your client pose by the scales?" he asked.

"I won't," Mason said. "My client will, but I think you will have to wait until court is adjourned—and by that time, there's just a chance Judge Albert might pose with you."

"Why won't you pose?" the reporter asked.

"It's not supposed to be ethical," Mason said.

The reporter's face flushed with anger. "That's the bar association for you," he said. "Appointing committees, trying to get better public relations, and then trying to hide behind a false front of legal ethics.

"When will you lawyers learn that public relations simply means taking the public into partnership and letting newspaper readers look over your shoulders and see what you're doing?

"Any time the lawyers are too stuffy or too afraid to let the public know what they're doing, they're going to have poor public relations."

Mason grinned and said, "Calm down, buddy. I'm not stopping you from looking over my shoulder, I'm simply stopping you from looking at my face with a camera and flashlight. That's supposed to be unethical advertising—not that I give a damn, but I'm leaning over backwards.

However, as far as the story is concerned, why the hell do you suppose I went to all the trouble of setting this up?"

The angry reporter looked at him, then his face softened in a grin. "I guess you're right at that," he said. "Is the judge actually going to weigh the evidence?"

"Going to weigh the physical evidence," Mason said.

"Cripes, what a story!" the reporter commented, just as the door from chambers opened and the bailiff said, "Everybody stand up."

The audience arose, and Judge Albert entered the courtroom, noticing, with a touch of amusement and some surprise, the manner in which the courtroom, which had been almost empty, had now filled up nearly to capacity with spectators from the various county offices, newspaper reporters and photographers.

"People versus Virginia Baxter," he said. "Are we ready to proceed?"

"Ready, Your Honor," Caswell said.

"Ready for the defendant," Mason announced.

Detective Jack Andrews was on the stand and the evidence was about to be weighed. "You have scales, Mr. Bailiff?"

"Yes, Your Honor."

"Check them, please, and see if they are accurate. Put them on zero and watch the beam."

The bailiff checked the scales.

"All right," Judge Albert directed, "now, let's have the suitcase and the overnight bag put on the scales."

The clerk took the two bags which had been marked for identification, placed them on the scales and carefully adjusted the beam until it balanced, then stood back.

"Exactly forty-six and one-quarter pounds, Your Honor," the bailiff announced.

There was a moment of tense, dramatic silence and then someone applauded.

Judge Albert frowned and said, "We'll have no demonstrations, please. Now, does the defendant have the airplane ticket and the receipt for the excess baggage?"

"We have, Your Honor," Mason said, handing the ticket and the receipt to Judge Albert.

Judge Albert frowned at the assistant prosecutor. "How much does the material weigh that was taken out of the bags?"

"I don't know, Your Honor. As the witness Andrews testified, it was counted by packages and not weighed."

"All right, let's weigh it," Judge Albert said. "You have it here in court?"

"Yes, Your Honor."

The bailiff started to remove the baggage from the scales.

Mason said, "If the Court please, I would prefer to have these articles simply placed on top of the bags while they are on the scales and we will then see how much it increases the weight."

"Very well," Judge Albert ruled. "It's just as easy one way as the other, perhaps a little more dramatic and, therefore, a little more convincing to have it done as counsel suggests."

Officer Andrews produced a bag with the cellophane-wrapped packages and, taking the packages from the bag, placed them on top of the suitcases.

The arm of the scale quivered, then went upwards.

The bailiff adjusted the sliding weight.

"One pound and three-quarters, Your Honor," he announced.

Judge Albert glanced at the prosecutor, then at Andrews. "Does the prosecution have any explanation for this?" he asked.

"No, Your Honor," Jerry Caswell said. "We feel that the material was found in the defendant's suitcase and therefore that she's responsible for it. After all, there was nothing to prevent her adding this material after the baggage had been weighed. She could have done it as easily as anyone else could have done it."

"Not so easy," Judge Albert said. "When the suitcases are checked on an airline, they're weighed on the scale at the time the passenger checks in, and the ticket clerk then takes them from the scale and sends them out to the airline.

"As far as this Court is concerned, the evidence is convincing and the case is dismissed."

Judge Albert stood up, looked down at the courtroom where people were still coming in through the doors and said, with a slight smile, "Court is adjourned."

One of the reporters rushed forward. "Your Honor, would you consider posing in front of the scale? We want to get a story and a picture, and we'd like to have some human interest."

Judge Albert hesitated.

"No objection whatever on the part of the defendant," Mason announced in a loud voice.

Judge Albert looked at Jerry Caswell.

Caswell avoided his glance.

Judge Albert smiled. "Well, if you want to have human interest, you'd better have the defendant standing beside me and pointing out that it's her baggage that's being weighed."

The reporters and photographers gathered around the scales.

"And let it appear that these pictures were taken after court had adjourned," Judge Albert said. "I've always been broadminded about publicity photographs in my court, although I know there are judges who object. However, I am not entirely unaware of the fact that when this defendant was arrested, the story was given a great deal of publicity and it seems to me only fair to see that her exoneration should also be accompanied by a reasonable amount of publicity."

Judge Albert took his position in front of the scales and beckoned to Virginia to come and stand at his side.

Mason escorted the nervous defendant up to a position beside the judge.

"Come on and get in this picture, Mason," Judge Albert invited.

"I think I'd better not," Mason said. "That will make the picture look posed and artificial and it may not be in the best taste from the standpoint of legal ethics; but the picture of you 'weighing the evidence' will attract a lot of attention."

Judge Albert nodded, said to Virginia, "Now, Miss Baxter, if you'll just look at the beam on the scales here, I'll bend over and be adjusting it— No, no, don't look at the camera, look at the scales. Turn a little if you want to so you can get your best angle for the camera."

Judge Albert put a hand on her shoulder, bent over and moved the balancing weight back and forth on the beam, and gleeful photographers exploded flash bulbs in rapid succession.

Judge Albert straightened, looked at Mason, then beckoned to the district attorney and led the two attorneys out of earshot of the reporters.

"There's something very fishy about this case," Judge Albert said. "I would suggest, Mr. Caswell, that you check very carefully on the person who gave you this information, or rather misinformation which resulted in a search of that suitcase."

The prosecutor said hotly, "That person has always been on the up-and-up with us; his information has been reliable."

"Well, it wasn't reliable in this case," Judge Albert said.

"I'm not so certain about that," Caswell retorted. "After all, it's not entirely impossible that the bags could have been tampered with."

"I think they were," Judge Albert said bitingly, "but *I* think the tampering occurred after the bag was checked by Miss Baxter and before it was taken off the revolving rack.

"After all, this Court wasn't born yesterday and after you see defendants coming and going, day in and day out, you have an opportunity to learn something about human nature. This young woman isn't a dope pusher."

"And after you've seen Perry Mason pull grandstand after grandstand," Caswell rejoined, "you learn something about dramatics. This scene the Court has just participated in is going to give aid and comfort to a lot of persons who don't wish law enforcement any good."

"Law enforcement had better become more efficient then," Judge Albert snapped. "There was no objection to calling photographers to photograph this young woman when her suitcase was opened, and heaven knows how much harm was done her at that time. I only hope there will be enough publicity in connection with the events of the last hour to more than offset the unfavorable publicity which was given her at the time of her arrest."

"Well, don't worry," Caswell said bitterly, "this picture will go out over the wire services and make about a third of the papers in the United States."

"Let's hope it does," Judge Albert said, and turning on his heel, headed for chambers.

Caswell walked away without a word to Mason.

Mason rejoined Virginia Baxter. "Want to go in the witness room where we can sit down and talk for a minute?" Mason asked.

"Anything," she said. "Anything, Mr. Mason."

"I just want a word with you," Mason said.

He led her into the witness room, held a chair for her, sat down opposite her and said, "Now look, who would have it in for you?"

"You mean to try and frame me on a narcotics charge?"

"Yes."

"Heavens, I don't know."

"Your husband?"

"He was very bitter."

"Why?"

"I wouldn't give him a divorce."

"Why not?"

"He was a sneak, a liar and a cheat. He was carrying on with another woman all the time I was working my head off trying to help us get ahead.

"He even dipped into the joint account we had in order

to help finance a car for this woman; then they had the unmitigated gall to tell me that people couldn't control their emotions, that a man would fall in love and he'd fall out of love and there was nothing that could be done about it."

"How long ago was this?"

"About a year."

"And you didn't give him his freedom?"

"No."

"You're still married?"

"Yes."

"How long since you've seen him?"

"Not since that big blowup, but he has called me up on the phone once or twice and asked if I had changed my mind."

"And why haven't you changed your mind?" Mason asked.

"Because I'm not going to let them play fast and loose with me that way."

Mason said, "All right, you're going to remain married to him. What advantage will that be to you?"

"It won't be any advantage to me but it will keep them from taking advantage of me."

"In other words, anything that will be a detriment to the pair of them will be to your advantage. Is that the way you feel?"

"Well, something like that."

Mason regarded her steadily. "Is that the way you want to feel?"

"I . . . I just wanted to gouge her eyes out. I wanted to hurt her in every way I could."

Mason shook his head. "There's no percentage in that,

Virginia. Ring him up and tell him that you've decided to let him have a divorce, that you'll file the divorce action—there's nothing in your religion against it, is there?"

"No."

"No children?"

"No."

Mason spread his hands in a little gesture. "There you are," he said. "You have a future, too, you know."

"I . . . I—"

"Meaning you've met someone in whom you're interested?" Mason asked.

"I . . . I have met lots of people and, for the most part, I have been plenty sour on men."

"But lately you've met one who seems to be different?"

She laughed nervously. "Must you cross-examine me now?" she asked.

Mason said, "Whenever you've made a mistake in life, the best thing to do is to wipe the slate clean and put that mistake behind you.

"However, what I wanted to talk to you about was the fact that someone is trying to put you in a position where you'll be discredited.

"I don't know who it is, but it's some person who has a certain amount of ingenuity and, apparently, some underworld connections.

"That person has struck once. You've avoided the trap, but other traps can be set and that person can strike again. I don't like it and if there's any possibility it's your husband, I'd like to eliminate him from the picture.

"There is, of course, the woman with whom your husband was in love and with whom, I presume, he is now living.

"Do you know her? Do you know anything about her background?"

"Not a thing. I know her name and that's just about all. My husband was very careful that I didn't learn too much about her."

"All right," Mason said, "here's my suggestion. File for a divorce on the ground of desertion or cruelty. Leave her name out of it, get it over with and get your freedom; and if there is anything out of the ordinary that happens within the next few days, anything suspicious, any anonymous telephone calls, anything that seems strange, call me immediately."

Mason patted her shoulder and said, "You're free now."

"But what do I do about your fee, Mr. Mason?"

Mason said, "Send me a check for a hundred dollars when you get around to it and find it convenient, but don't worry about it."

CHAPTER SEVEN

THERE had been a dearth of news the night before and as a result the story about "weighing" the evidence had been given considerable prominence.

Virginia Baxter read the papers with a growing sense of relief. The reporters had sensed that she had been framed and had done their best to see that her vindication was featured as top news.

The newspaper photographers, thoroughgoing professionals, had done an excellent job with their cameras, while Judge Albert, leaning over the scales, had placed a steadying and paternal hand on Virginia's shoulder.

It has been truthfully said that one picture tells more than ten thousand words, and in this case, the jurist's attitude left no doubt of his faith in Virginia Baxter's innocence.

The headlines in one of the newspapers read, FORMER LEGAL SECRETARY VINDICATED IN DOPE CASE.

One article made much of the fact that she had formerly been employed in a law office. While that office had in reality done little trial work, specializing in estate matters, the reporter had taken poetic license and had written that while Virginia Baxter had been working on criminal cases which Delano Bannock was defending, it probably had never occurred to her in even her wildest dreams that the time would come when she herself would stand before the bar of justice accused of a serious crime.

It was from an article in another evening paper that Virginia received a shock.

The reporter had done some background investigation and the article stated that Colton Baxter, estranged husband of Virginia Baxter, was, by coincidence, an employee of the very airline which had checked the suitcase to its destination. He was not immediately available for comment.

Virginia read that twice, then impulsively reached for the telephone and called Mason's office. Suddenly, realizing the hour, she was about to hang up when, to her surprise, she heard Della Street's voice on the line.

"Oh, I'm so sorry. I didn't realize how late it was. This is Virginia Baxter. I read something in the paper that startled me and . . . I never thought about it being so long after five."

"Do you want to talk with Mr. Mason?" Della Street asked. "Just a minute and I'll connect you. I think he wants to talk with you, too."

A moment later, Mason's voice said, "Hello, Virginia. I suppose you've read the papers and learned that your husband was located by one of the reporters."

"Yes, yes, Mr. Mason. That makes it just as clear as day. Don't you see what happened? Colton planted that stuff in my suitcase and then tipped off the newspapers. If I had been convicted, he could then have had perfect grounds for divorce. He'd claim that I had been a dope fiend all the time we were married; that I had been dealing in dope and that he had left me because of that."

"So," Mason said, "what do you want to do?"

"I want to have him arrested."

"You can't arrest him without proof," Mason said. "All you have so far is surmise."

"How much would it cost to get proof?"

"You'd have to employ a private detective and he'd charge you probably a minimum of fifty dollars a day and expenses, and then the chances are he'd be unable to get anything except more grounds for surmise."

"I have a little money. I'd . . . I'd spend it in order to catch him—"

"Not through me, you wouldn't," Mason interrupted. "As a client of mine I wouldn't let you spend that amount of money for that purpose. Even if you got some evidence it would only leave you exactly where you are now, with good grounds for divorce.

"Why don't you just wash your hands of that man; get rid of him, dissolve the marriage and begin all over again.

"If you had religious reasons for not getting a divorce, I would probably handle it in another way, but you're going to get a divorce sooner or later and—"

"I don't want to give him that satisfaction."

"Why?"

"That's what he's wanted all along, a divorce."

Mason said, "You're not doing yourself a particle of good. All you're doing is some real or fancied harm to your husband. For all you know you may be playing into his hands right now."

"What do you mean?"

"He's playing around with this other woman," Mason said. "He keeps telling her that if he could ever get a divorce he'd marry her, but you won't give him a divorce. The woman knows all this is true.

"But suppose you give him a divorce, then he's in a position where he is not only free to marry this woman, but he has to do it to make good on his promises. He may not really want to marry her.

"It may be that your husband is in exactly the position he wants to be in."

"I had never thought of it that way," she said, slowly, but then added quickly, "Then why did he plant the dope in my suitcase?"

"If he did, it was probably because he wanted to have you thoroughly discredited," Mason said. "Yours was one of those marriages that has been dissolved in hatred. You'd better quit looking back over your shoulder, turn around and face the future."

"Well, I—I'll sleep on it and let you know in the morning."

"Do that," Mason said.

"I'm sorry I disturbed you at this hour."

"Not at all. We were working on some briefs here in the office, and after I read that statement in the paper, I thought you might be calling, so I told Della to plug in an outside line.

"You're in the clear now, stop worrying."

"Thank you," she said, and hung up.

The phone had hardly been cradled when there was a buzz at the door of her apartment.

Virginia crossed over and opened the door a few inches.

The man who stood in the doorway was somewhere

around forty-five years of age, with dark wavy hair, a close-clipped mustache and intense obsidian black eyes.

"You're Mrs. Baxter?" he asked.

"Yes."

"I'm very sorry to bother you at this time, Mrs. Baxter. I know how you must be feeling, but I come to you on a matter of some importance."

"What is it?" she asked, still keeping the chain on the door.

"My name," he told her, "is George Menard—I read about you in the paper. I don't like to bring up a disagreeable subject, but of course you know that the news of your trial has been in all the papers."

"Well?" she asked.

"I noticed in the paper that you had been the secretary of Delano Bannock, an attorney, during his lifetime."

"That's right."

"Mr. Bannock died several years ago, I believe."

"That also is correct."

"I am trying to find out what was done with his files," the man said.

"Why?"

"Frankly, I want to locate a paper."

"What sort of a paper?"

"A carbon copy of an agreement which Mr. Bannock drew up for me. I've lost the original and I don't want the other party to the agreement to know it. There are certain things that I have to do under that agreement and while I think I can remember what they are, it would be an enormous help if I could locate a carbon copy."

She shook her head. "I'm afraid I can't help you."

"You were employed by him at the time of his death?"

"Yes."

"What happened to the office furniture and all that?"

"Why, the office was closed up. There was no reason for the estate to go on paying rent."

"But what happened to the office furniture?"

"I believe it was sold."

The man frowned. "To whom was it sold? You know who bought the desks, filing cases, chairs?"

"No, they were sold to some second-hand office furniture outfit. I kept the typewriter I had been using. Everything else was sold."

"Filing cases and everything?"

"Everything."

"What happened to the old papers?"

"They were destroyed— No, wait a minute, wait a minute. I remember talking with his brother and telling him that the papers should be kept. I remember now, I wanted him to keep the filing cases intact."

"The brother?"

"That's right. Julian Bannock. He was the sole heir. There weren't any other relatives. The estate was a small one.

"You see, Delano Bannock was one of those devoted attorneys who was more interested in doing a job than in getting a fee. He worked literally day and night. He had no wife or family and he spent four or five evenings a week in his office, working until ten or eleven o'clock. But the modern idea of keeping track of time by the hour just never occurred to him. He would put in hours and hours on some little agreement that had a point that interested him and then he'd make only a moderate charge. The result was that he didn't leave much of an estate."

"What about the fees that were due him at the time of his death?"

"I wouldn't know about that, but it's very well known that the estates of professional men have a lot of trouble with outstanding accounts."

"And where could I find Julian Bannock?"

"I don't know," she said.

"Do you know where he lived?"

"Someplace in the San Joaquin Valley, I think."

"Could you find out where?"

"I *might* be able to."

Virginia Baxter had been sizing up the man and finally unlatched the door chain. "Won't you come in?" she invited. "I think perhaps I can consult an old diary. I have been keeping diaries for years—" She laughed nervously— "not the romantic type, you understand, but business diaries that contain little comments about when I went to work at a certain place and how long I worked there, events of the day, when I received raises in salary and things of that sort.

"I know that I made some entries at the time of Mr. Bannock's death—oh, wait a minute, I remember now, Julian Bannock lived near Bakersfield."

"Do you know if he still lives there?"

"No, I don't. I remember now that he came down driving a pickup. The files were loaded into the pickup. I remember that after the files were loaded, I felt that my responsibility was ended. I turned the keys over to the brother."

"Bakersfield?" Menard said.

"That's right. Now, if you can tell me something about your agreement, perhaps I can remember about it. Mr.

Bannock had a one-man office and I did all of the typing."

"It was an agreement with a man named Smith," Menard said.

"What was the nature of the agreement?"

"Oh, it involved a lot of complicated things about the sale of a machine shop. You see, I'm interested, or was interested, in machinery and thought for a while I'd go into the machinery business, but— Well, it's a long story."

"What are you doing now?" she asked.

Menard's eyes suddenly shifted. "I'm sort of free-lancing," he said, "buying and selling."

"Real estate?" she asked.

"Oh, anything," he said.

"You live here in the city?"

He laughed, obviously ill at ease. "I keep going from place to place—you know how it is when a person is looking for bargains."

Virginia said, "I see. Well, I'm sorry I can't help you any more than I have."

She stood up and moved toward the door.

Menard accepted the dismissal.

"Thank you so much," he said, and walked out.

Virginia watched him to the elevator then, when the door of the cage had slid shut, took to the stairs and raced down them.

She was in time to see him jump into a dark-colored car which had been parked in the only vacant parking space at the curb, a space directly beside a fireplug.

She tried to get the license number but was unable to get it all, because of the speed with which the driver whipped out into the street and drove away.

Her eyes focused on a distinctive zero as the first of the

numbers and she had a somewhat vague impression that
the last figure of the license was a two.

The car she thought was an Oldsmobile, perhaps two to
four years old, but here again she couldn't be certain. The
man gunned the car into speed and drove away fast.

Virginia returned to her apartment, went into her bedroom, pulled out a suitcase, started rummaging through
her diaries. She found the address of Julian Bannock in
Bakersfield, an R.F.D. box and a notation in parentheses,
"no telephone."

Then her phone rang. A woman said, "I found your
name in the telephone directory. I just wanted to call you
to tell you how glad I am that you beat that horrible frame-
up."

"Thank you very much," Virginia said.

"I'm a stranger to you," the woman went on, "but I
wanted you to know how I felt."

Within the next hour there were five more calls, including one from a man who was obviously drunk and certainly
offensive, and another from a woman who wanted a willing
ear to hear about *her* case.

Finally, Virginia ignored the telephone, which continued to ring, until she went out to dinner.

The next morning she asked the telephone company to
change her number and give her an unlisted one.

CHAPTER EIGHT

Virginia found she couldn't entirely get the matter of those papers off her mind.

After all, Julian Bannock had been a rancher. He and his brother had not been particularly close, and Julian was interested only in liquidating everything in the estate and getting rid of it just as rapidly as possible.

Virginia knew there had been many important probate proceedings and agreements, but after she had turned the key over to Julian Bannock, she had paid no more attention to the estate.

But the thought of those files left her vaguely uneasy, and there had been a false note about George Menard. He had seemed all right until she had asked him about himself, then he had suddenly become evasive. She felt sure he had been lying about his background.

After all, she felt something of a responsibility for those files.

She called Information to try to place a call to Julian Bannock at Bakersfield and was informed he still had no telephone.

She tried to forget the matter and couldn't. Suppose Menard was up to something tricky.

She wanted to find out about his car registration but

didn't know how to go about it without consulting Perry
Mason, and she felt she had bothered him too much
already.

She determined to drive out to Bakersfield and talk
things over with Julian Bannock.

She left at daylight, made inquiries at Bakersfield, and
found that Julian Bannock lived some ten miles out of the
city.

She located his mailbox, drove in for some three
hundred yards, came to a yard with a barn, several sheds, a
house, shade trees and a variety of farming implements—
tractors, cultivators, hayrakes, disks—stored more or less
haphazardly in the yard.

A dog ran barking to the car, and Julian Bannock came
out.

Despite the fact she had only seen him in his "dressed
up" clothes, she recognized him instantly in his coveralls
and work shirt.

"Hello!" he said.

"Hello, Mr. Bannock. Remember me? I'm Virginia
Baxter. I was your brother's secretary."

"Oh, yes," he said, his voice cordial. "Sure. I knew I'd
seen you before somewhere. Well, come on in. We'll fix
you up a breakfast, eggs from our own yard, and maybe
you'd like some homemade bread and preserves—fruit
right off our own trees here."

"That would be wonderful," she said, "but I wanted to
talk with you about a few things."

"What?"

"Those papers that you took," she said. "Those filing
cases. Where do you have them?"

He grinned at her. "Oh, I sold all those quite a while ago."

"Not the files?"

"Well, I told the fellow to take everything. The stuff was cluttering up a lot of room here and— You know what? Mice were getting in those papers. They'd get up in there and start chewing on the papers to make nests."

"But what actually became of the *papers?* Did the man who bought the files—"

"Oh, the papers! No, they're here. The man who bought the filing cases wouldn't take the papers. He dumped the papers all out. He said the papers made the files too heavy to carry."

"And you burned them up?"

"No, I tied them up in bundles with binder twine. I guess the mice are getting in there pretty bad—you know the way it is around a ranch, you have a barn and mice live in the barn.

"We've got a couple of cats now that have been keeping things down pretty well, but—"

"Would it be all right to take a look?" she said. "I'd just like to see about some of the old papers."

"Funny thing," he said, "that you'd be worrying about those. There was a fellow here yesterday."

"There was?"

"That's right."

"A man about forty-five?" she asked. "With very intense black eyes and a small stubby mustache? He wanted—"

Julian Bannock interrupted her by shaking his head. "No," he said, "this was a fellow around fifty-five but he had bluish sort of eyes and was sort of light-complected.

"This fellow's name was Smith. He wanted to find some agreement or other."

"And what did you do?"

"I told him where the papers were, told him to look around and help himself if he wanted. I was busy and he seemed a mighty nice fellow."

"Did he find what he wanted?"

Julian Bannock shook his head. "He said that things were too much of a mess for him to unscramble. He said he didn't know anything about the files. If he could get hold of the key to the filing system, he thought he could maybe find the paper he wanted.

"He asked me if I knew anything about how the files were classified and I told him I didn't."

"It was all handled according to numbers," Virginia said. "General classifications. For instance, number one to a thousand was personal correspondence. Number one thousand to three thousand represented contracts. Three thousand to five thousand, probate. Five thousand to six thousand, wills. Six thousand to eight thousand, agreements. Eight thousand to ten thousand, real estate transactions."

"Well, I didn't disturb anything. I put all that stuff in packages and tied them up with binder twine."

"Could we take a look?" Virginia asked.

"Why, sure."

Julian Bannock led the way into the relative coolness of the barn, redolent with the clean smell of hay.

"Used to keep this barn pretty full of hay," he said, "and had quite a storage problem. Lately, I've been selling the hay because I haven't been doing much feeding. Used to have a little dairy business, but they've got so many headaches now that the small dairyman has too much of a problem; too much work; too many regulations.

"The real big dairies are handling things now with mechanical milkers, feeders and all that sort of thing—I didn't get too much for those filing cases, either. Could have kept the stuff in the cases, I guess, but I don't know what anybody'd want with all that stuff—thought some of pitching it all out and burning it up, but you talked so much about the files, I thought I'd keep them."

"Well, of course, that was some time ago," Virginia said. "As time passes, those files cease to have quite as much importance."

"Well, here we are, over here. This used to be a tractor shed, but I got room to put these— Well, *what* do you know!"

Bannock stopped in surprise before the litter of papers strewn all over the floor.

"Looks like that fellow left a hell of a mess," he said angrily.

Virginia looked in dismay at the piles of paper.

The man who had been in there had evidently cut the binder twine that had held the papers in different classifications and had pawed through everything looking for the paper he wanted, throwing the other papers helter-skelter into a pile which had spread out into an area some six feet in diameter at the bottom and some four feet high.

Virginia, looking at the carbon copies now ragged at the edges from the gnawing of mice, thinking of the care she had taken with those papers when she had typed them, felt like crying.

Julian Bannock, slow to anger, but with a steadily mounting temper, said. "Well, by gosh, I'd like to tell that fellow Smith a thing or two!"

He bent down and picked up a piece of binder twine. "Cut through slick and clean with a sharp knife," he said. "Somebody'd ought to take that man and teach him a few manners."

Virginia, studying the pile of papers, said, "He must have been in a terrific hurry. He was looking for something and he didn't have time to untie the twine, look at each package, and then tie them up again. He simply took his knife, cut the twine, looked hurriedly for what he wanted; then when he didn't find it, he threw the rest of the papers over on the pile."

Julian said thoughtfully, "You can see that all right. I'm kicking myself for not keeping an eye on him."

"How long was he here?" Virginia asked.

"Now, that I can't tell you. I let him in the barn, showed him where the things were and then left."

Virginia reached a sudden decision. "Where is the nearest telephone?" she asked.

"Well, one of the neighbors has one and he's real accommodating," Julian said. "He lives about two miles down the road."

"I want to make a long distance call," she said, "and . . . I guess it's better not to let anyone hear what I'm saying. I'll go on in to Bakersfield and put in the call from a booth there. I'll be back after a while with some big cartons. I'm going to put those papers in the cartons and then we'll keep them someplace where they're safe."

"Okay," he said, "I'll give you a hand when it comes to

putting them in. Do you think I should stack them up now and—"

"No," she said, "there's still some semblance of order. A good many of the classifications are still segregated. Somewhere there's a master book which gives the numbers and an index. That is, it was here.

"If you don't mind, I'd like to stop at one of the supermarkets and get some big cartons; then come back and try and put this stuff together again so it makes some sort of sense."

"Well, now," he said, "if you want to do it, that's fine with me, but it's a lot of work to go through and it's pretty dusty in here. You're all dressed up neat as a pin and—"

"Don't worry," she said, "I'm going to get some blue jeans and a blouse in town. If you don't mind, I'll change my clothes when I get back and get to work."

"Sure thing," he said, "we'll give you a place to change in the house, and a chance to take a bath when you're finished. This is going to be pretty dusty."

"I know it is," she said, laughing, "but us ranchers have to get used to a little dust now and then."

He grinned at her, thrust out his hand and shook hands.

"You're all right," he announced.

Virginia returned to her car, drove to Bakersfield and called Perry Mason, just as the lawyer was reaching his office.

"You wanted me to tell you if anything unusual happened," she said, "and this is unusual enough, but I just can't understand the significance."

"Go ahead," Mason said, "tell me what it is."

"You'll probably laugh and think my imagination is

working overtime. There's probably no way on earth it can be connected with anything but— Well, here's what happened."

She told him about Bannock, the papers, about the man who had called on her, his description and a general but somewhat vague description of the automobile in which he had driven away. "A model about two to four years old, I would guess. I think it was an Oldsmobile," she said. "The first figure of the license number was a zero. I tried to get it but he drove away very fast."

"Where was he parked?" Mason asked. "Could you see the parking place from which he drove his car? That might tell us how long he'd been waiting. I presume parking places right in front of your apartment house are hard to find."

"I'll say they are!" she exclaimed. "But this man didn't have any trouble. He parked right in front of the fireplug."

"Then he hadn't been there very long," Mason said. "That means he must have followed you home rather than been there waiting. I would think the police would check that fireplug space rather often."

"They do! I had a friend who parked just long enough to leave a parcel, yet she got a parking ticket. It wasn't over a minute."

"You think the first number on the license plate was a zero?" Mason asked.

"Yes, I'm quite certain of that, and I *think* the last number was a two, but I'm not at all certain of that."

"You're in Bakersfield now?" Mason asked.

"Yes. I went out to Mr. Bannock's brother's place to check with him and found that someone had been out there; gone through all the files."

"What do you mean by 'going through them'?" Mason
asked.

She described the files.

Mason's voice became crisp with authority.

"Now, this is important, Virginia. You say the files were
all cut open?"

"Yes."

"Every single bundle?"

"Yes."

"And their contents spread out?"

"Yes."

"No single bundle was intact?"

"No."

"You're sure of that?"

"Why, yes. Why is it important, Mr. Mason?"

"Because," Mason said, "it indicates a strong probability
that the person who is searching didn't find what he was
looking for.

"In other words, if you're looking for a particular paper
and you're in a hurry, you cut open bundle after bundle of
papers until you find the one you want; then you shove it
in your pocket and get away from there fast. That would
leave some bundles that hadn't been cut open.

"But if, on the other hand, *all* of the bundles are cut
open, it's a pretty good indication that the person didn't
find what he was looking for."

"I never thought of that," she said.

"You're going back to Julian Bannock's?"

"Yes, I'm taking some cardboard cartons and am going
back and I'll try to make some semblance of order out of
those files."

"All right," Mason said, "by the time you get back there,

we'll find out something about your man who is interested in the files. . . . Now, tell me, Virginia, what about wills?"

"What do you mean?"

"When Bannock would prepare a will it would usually be executed there in the office?"

"Yes."

"Who would be the subscribing witnesses?"

"Oh, I see what you mean. He would usually sign as one of the subscribing witnesses and I would sign as the other witness."

"And you had a classification of various wills? In other words, you had a file number designating wills that you had executed in the office?"

"Oh, yes, I see what you mean now. Files numbered five thousand to six thousand were wills."

"All right," Mason said, "when you go back take a look at the five to six thousand 'will' file. See how intact it is. Tie that file up and bring it here just as fast as you can make it."

"Why that file in particular?" she asked.

Mason said, "Bannock has been dead for a few years. Most of the agreements and things that he had drawn would no longer be important, but if some relative wanted to find out what was in a certain will—"

"I get you," she interrupted excitedly. "Why didn't *I* think of that. Of course, that's what it is."

"Don't jump to conclusions," Mason warned. "This is just a thought, but I think we'd better take precautions."

"I'm going right back," she promised, "and I'll keep that file of wills with me. I'll leave the other papers for a later trip."

Mason said, "If anything else happens that is in any way

out of the ordinary, give me a ring. In the meantime, I'm going to find out something about this visitor of yours."

Virginia promised to report anything new that happened; hung up the telephone; went to a supermarket, secured two cartons and then returned to Julian Bannock's place.

She found Bannock apprehensive.

"What's the matter?" she asked. "Did something else happen about those files?"

"You hadn't been gone five minutes," he said, "when a fellow showed up here who fitted the description you had given me of the man you thought was here. He was in his late forties or early fifties, had a mustache and eyes that were so dark you couldn't see any expression in them. It was like looking at a pair of black, polished stones."

"That was the man all right," she said. "What did he want?"

"Said *his* name was Smith, and he asked about my brother's files."

"What did you do?"

"I told him that we weren't letting people look at those files. He said it was important and I told him that he could sit right here and wait; that my brother's secretary was going to be here in an hour or so and that he could wait for her."

"What happened?"

"That gave him a jolt—knowing that you were coming here. He said he couldn't wait."

"Were you able to get his license number?" she asked eagerly.

"No, I wasn't," Julian said, "because he'd plastered mud all over it. There's a place up here where irrigating water sometimes runs over the road and there was quite a puddle up there that he'd gone through, but it wasn't mud that would cover a license number. I think he'd got out and deliberately plastered mud on the license."

"Well," Virginia said, "I'm going to get at those files, tie them up again and I think I'd better take some of them with me, if you have no objection."

"Take them all if you want," he said. "I can't be here all the time and if there's anything important in those papers, people could sneak in while I'm out in the fields someplace and get hold of them."

She asked, "Have you ever heard of Perry Mason, the attorney?"

"I'll say I have. I've read a lot about him."

"Well," Virginia said, "he's my lawyer. He's advising me, and I'm going to get in touch with him and do exactly as he says.

"I was going to clean up all these files and put them in boxes, but I don't have time now. I'm just grabbing this file with these numbers—let's look around and see if there are any more of these files here that have numbers between five thousand and six thousand."

Virginia scooped up a number of filing jackets that were all together and had numbers between five and six thousand. Then she and Julian made a hasty search for any other papers numbered within those brackets.

"They seem to have been all together in that bunch," Julian said.

"All right," Virginia told him. "Now, I'm going to rush these in to Mr. Mason's office. I want to get in there before lunch, if possible. Will you do the best you can to see that these others aren't disturbed while I'm gone?"

"You want me to put them in boxes?" Julian asked. "I'm sort of busy this time of year, what with irrigation and—"

"No," she said, "just leave them the way they are, if you can. But put a lock on the door—you know, a padlock. Try to keep anyone from coming in the barn.

"If anyone should try to get in, be sure to get his license number and make him give you proof of his identity. Ask to see his driving license."

"Will do," Julian said, grinning. "You don't want to go in the house and change into jeans and blouse?"

"No, there isn't time. I'm on my way. I hope I didn't get too dusty. Goodbye."

"Goodbye, ma'am," he said, and then added, "I know how much my brother thought of you and I guess he sure was a good judge of character."

She flashed him a smile, jumped in her car, placed the carton with the five-to-six thousand classification in the back seat, and took off.

CHAPTER NINE

IT WAS shortly after noon when Virginia reached Perry Mason's office.

Gertie, the receptionist, said, "Hello, Miss Baxter, they're expecting you, but I'd better give them a buzz and let them know you're here."

Gertie buzzed the phone, and a moment later Della Street came out and said, "Right this way, Virginia. We have some news for you."

Virginia followed Della Street into Mason's private office to find the lawyer frowning thoughtfully, "We've traced your mysterious visitor, Virginia," Mason said. "The one who gave you the name of George Menard. We traced him through his parking at the fireplug. We went through all the parking tickets issued by the officer who patrols that district. There were three fireplug parking tickets. One of them was for a license number ODT 062. That car is registered to a man whose description is very similar to that of the man who called on you."

"Who is he?"

"His real name is George Eagan, and he is employed as a chauffeur for Lauretta Trent. So we did a little checking and—"

"Lauretta Trent?" Virginia exclaimed.

"You know her?" Mason asked.

"Why, we did some legal work for her and— Why, yes, I'm quite certain we made at least one will for her. I have rather a vague memory that it was an unusual will. The relatives were given rather small amounts, all things considered, and there was an outsider who got the bulk of the estate. It may have been a nurse—or a doctor. Heavens! It *could* have been the chauffeur!"

Mason said, "We've found out some rather interesting things."

"About the chauffeur?"

"About Lauretta Trent. She has recently had three attacks of so-called food poisoning. The hospital records describe them as gastroenteric upsets."

Virginia said, "I've got all the old copies of wills locked in my car down in the parking lot, Mr. Mason, if it would help any. . . ."

"It will help a lot," Mason said. "I'm going to introduce you to Paul Drake, our detective. He handles all our investigative work; he's head of the Drake Detective Agency, which is on this floor— Give him a ring, will you please, Della?"

Della Street asked Gertie for an outside line. Her fingers flew over the dial. After a moment, she said, "Paul, Della. Perry would like to have you come to the office right away, if you can."

Della smiled and hung up. "He'll be here within a matter of seconds."

And it was only a matter of seconds before Paul Drake's code knock sounded on the door.

Della opened the door and let him in.

"Paul," Mason said, "this is Virginia Baxter. You probably don't know it but she's the client whom I've been representing and is the reason you have been doing this investigative work."

"I see," Drake said, smiling at Virginia. "Pleased to meet you, Miss Baxter."

Mason said, "She has some papers locked in her car down in the parking lot. Could you help her bring them up?"

"How heavy?" Drake asked. "Do I need anyone to help me?"

"Oh, no," she said, "it's a bundle of papers probably twenty inches thick. But one man can lift them."

"Let's go," Drake said.

"There's one more thing I wanted to tell you, Mr. Mason," Virginia said. "While I was away from Julian Bannock's ranch, or farm, or whatever you call it, and telephoning you and getting ready to go back and get those papers, this man showed up at the ranch."

"What man?"

"The one who called on me. Eagan, you say he is, the chauffeur for Mrs. Trent."

"And what did he want?"

"He wanted to look at some of the old files of Delano Bannock. Julian—that's the brother—told him to wait, that I was going to be back there within a few minutes."

"And what happened?"

"The man jumped in his car and drove off, going fast."

"I see," Mason said, and nodded to Drake. "Let's get those papers, Paul."

Drake accompanied Virginia to the parking lot. She unlocked her car. Drake picked up the files in the cardboard carton, hoisted the carton to his shoulder and they returned to Mason's office.

Mason said, "Let's look at the file listed under 'T' and see what you have. Let's see, you have 'T-1,' 'T-2,' 'T-3,' 'T-4,' 'T-5'; just what do those mean?"

"That's the way I kept the wills under 'T.' 'T-1' would be the first five letters of the alphabet. In other words, 'T-A,' 'T-B,' 'T-C,' 'T-D,' 'T-E'; then, 'T-2' would be the next five letters."

"I see," Mason said. "Well, let's look under the 'T-4' and see if we can find any papers relating to Lauretta Trent."

Mason spread the files out on the desk and Mason, Della Street, Paul Drake and Virginia Baxter started rapidly going through the files.

"Well," Mason said, after a few minutes' search, "apparently we have a lot of copies of wills here, but no copy of a will made for Lauretta Trent."

"But we did her work, we made at least one will for her," Virginia said.

"And," Mason said, "George Eagan was making inquiries as to the location of the carbon copies of Delano Bannock's files, and George Eagan is Lauretta Trent's chauffeur."

Mason turned to Paul Drake, "What hospital was Lauretta Trent in when she had her so-called digestive upsets?"

"Phillips Memorial Hospital," Drake said.

Mason nodded to the phone, "Get them on the line, please, Della."

Della Street asked for an outside line, got a number and whirled the dial. A moment later she nodded to Mason.

Mason picked up the phone, "Phillips Memorial Hospital?" he asked.

"Yes."

"This is Perry Mason, the attorney," the lawyer said. "I would like to get some information on one of your patients."

"I'm sorry we can't give information about our patients."

"Well, this is just a routine matter of record," Mason said casually. "The patient is Lauretta Trent. You had her in the hospital on three occasions within the last several months and all I'm interested in is finding out the name of her physician."

"Just a moment, we can give you that information."

"I'll hold the phone, if I may," Mason said.

A moment later the voice said, "The physician was Dr. Ferris Alton. He's in the Randwell Building."

"Thank you," Mason said.

The lawyer hung up, turned to Della Street, "Let's see if we can get Dr. Alton's nurse."

"His nurse?"

"Yes," Mason said, "I'd like to talk with Dr. Alton, but I think I'll have to speak with his nurse, personally, before we can get him on the line. After all, this is probably the beginning of a busy afternoon for a doctor. He probably sees a lot of office patients in the afternoon, does operating in the morning and makes hospital visits after that."

Della Street got the number; asked Gertie in the outer office for an outside line, dialed the number and again nodded to Perry Mason.

Mason picked up the telephone, said, "How do you do? This is Perry Mason, an attorney. I know that Dr. Alton is very busy and that this is just before the busiest time of the afternoon, but it is quite important that I speak with him briefly concerning a matter which may affect a patient of his."

"*Perry* Mason, the lawyer?" the feminine voice asked.

"That's right."

"Oh, I'm quite sure he'd want to talk with you personally. He's busy at the moment, but I'll interrupt him and— Can you hang on to the line for a few moments?"

"I'll be glad to," Mason said.

There was a period of silence. Then a tired, slightly impatient voice said, "Yes, this is Dr. Ferris Alton talking."

"Perry Mason, the attorney," the lawyer told him. "I wanted to ask you a few questions about a patient of yours."

"What sort of questions, and who is the patient?"

"Lauretta Trent," Mason said. "You've had her hospitalized several times within the last few months."

"Well?" Dr. Alton asked, and this time the note of impatience was quite apparent in his voice.

"Can you tell me the nature of the malady?"

"I can not!" Dr. Alton snapped.

"Very well, then," Mason said. "I can perhaps tell you something which will be of interest. I have reason to believe that Lauretta Trent made a will; that this will was executed in the office of an attorney by the name of Delano Bannock; that the attorney is now deceased; that persons are interested in surreptitiously obtaining a copy of that will; that some of the persons associated with Lauretta Trent may be taking an active interest in a search of this kind.

"Now then, I am asking you this. Are you completely satisfied with your diagnosis in the case of Lauretta Trent?"

"Certainly. Otherwise I wouldn't have discharged her."

"I understand, generally," Mason said, "that she had a gastroenteric disturbance."

"Well, what of it?"

"And," Mason said, "I have before me several of the authorities on forensic medicine and toxicology. I find that it is generally agreed that cases of arsenic poisoning are seldom diagnosed by the attending physician, since the symptoms are those of a gastroenteric disturbance."

"You're crazy," Dr. Alton said.

"Therefore," Mason went on, "I think you will understand my position when I ask you if there were abdominal cramps, cramps in the calves of the legs, a burning sensation in the stomach and—"

"Good God!" Dr. Alton interrupted.

Mason ceased talking, waiting for the doctor to say something.

There was a long period of silence over the phone.

"No one would possibly want to poison Lauretta Trent," Dr. Alton said.

"How do *you* know?" Mason asked.

There was another period of silence.

"What's your interest in this matter?" Dr. Alton asked at length.

"My interest is purely incidental," Mason said. "I can assure you that while I am representing a client, that client has no interests adverse to those of Lauretta Trent and there is no reason why you could not make any statement to me that you can make without disclosing a privileged professional confidence."

Dr. Alton said, "You've given me something to think

about, all right, Mason. Her symptoms had a great deal in common with those of arsenic poisoning. You're *so* right, physicians who are called in on cases of this sort almost never suspect the possibilities of homicidal poisoning. The cases are almost invariably given a diagnosis of enteric disturbance."

"That," the lawyer told him, "is why I'm calling you."

"Do you have some suggestions?" Dr. Alton asked.

"Yes," Mason said. "I would suggest that you get a sample of her hair pulled out by the roots, if possible. And, if possible, some cuttings of the fingernails. Let's have them analyzed for arsenic and see if we get a positive reaction.

"In the meantime, I would suggest that you try not to alarm your patient, but take steps to see that she is put upon a restricted diet which is enforced by special round-the-clock nurses—in other words, a rigid dietary supervision.

"I take it the patient is in such a financial position that the expense can be justified?"

"Of course," Dr. Alton said. ". . . My Lord, she has a heart condition which can't stand too many of these upsets. I warned her, the last one. I thought it was dietary indiscretion. She has a weakness for highly spiced Mexican food with considerable garlic— That would be almost a perfect disguise for a dose of arsenic— Mason, how long are you going to be in your office?"

"I'll be here all afternoon," Mason said, "and if you need me after office hours, you can get me through the Drake Detective Agency. Ask for Paul Drake. The offices are in the same building where I have my offices and are on the same floor."

"You'll be hearing from me," Dr. Alton said. "In the meantime, I'm going to make arrangements right away to insure that nothing else questionable will happen."

"Please bear in mind that we must try to keep from making any accusations or any statements which will alarm your patient until we're certain," Mason said.

"I understand, I understand," Alton said sharply. "Damn it, Mason, I've been practicing medicine for thirty-five years— My God, man, you've given me a jolt. . . . Classic symptoms of arsenic poisoning and I never suspected a thing—you'll be hearing from me. Goodbye."

The connection was sharply terminated.

Mason said to Virginia, "I don't like to restrict your liberties, Virginia, but I want you to be where I can reach you. Go to your apartment and stay there. Report every single thing out of the ordinary. I'll have my phone so you can get to me at any time."

Drake frowned and said, "But they couldn't prove a will by using a copy, could they, Perry?"

"Under certain limited circumstances, yes," Mason said. "If a will is missing, the general presumption is that it was destroyed by the testator, which is equivalent to a revocation. But if, for instance, a house should catch on fire and the testator should perish in the flames, it would be generally presumed that the will was burned up at the same time and, if there could be proof that it was still in effect at the time of the fire and the testator's death, then the contents could be established by secondary evidence.

"However, that's not what I'm thinking of."

"What are you thinking of?" Drake asked.

Mason glanced at Virginia and shook his head. "I'm not prepared to say at the moment.

"Virginia, I want you to go on home. You may receive a call from this man you now know is George Eagan, Lauretta Trent's chauffeur.

"You'll remember this man told you he was George Menard.

"Now, if he calls on you, be very careful not to let on that you know who he really is. Be naïve, gullible and perhaps a little greedy. If he acts as if he wanted to make you any sort of a proposition, let him feel you are willing to listen. Then stall for time.

"Call me—or if I'm not available, Paul Drake—as soon as you can get to a phone. Let us know what the man wants."

"I'm to let him think I'm willing to play along?"

"That's right. And if you are asked to do any typing, use new carbons with each sheet of paper."

"It won't be dangerous?"

"I don't think so at the moment. Not if you don't let on you know who he really is, and if you manage to stall him long enough to get to a phone. Later on we may have to take precautions."

"All right," she promised, "I'll try."

"Good girl," Mason said. "Go on home now and phone me if anything happens."

Her laugh was nervous. "Don't worry," she said, "the very first thing that occurs out of the ordinary, I'm going to dash to a telephone."

"That's right," Mason told her. "Get Paul Drake on the line if you can't get me. His office is open twenty-four hours a day."

Della Street held the exit door open for her.

"Just be careful," Mason warned, "not to let this

chauffeur know that you have any idea who he is. Be naïve, but let him feel that if he has any proposition to make you could be tempted."

Virginia Baxter flashed him a smile and left the office.

Della Street gently closed the door.

"You think this chauffeur is going to be back?" Drake asked.

"If he didn't get what he wanted," Mason said, "he'll be back. We have two people looking for a paper, and since the paper that we *think* they're looking for doesn't seem to be in the files, the probabilities are that one of them has already found it. Therefore, the other will be back."

"Just how significant is all of this?" Drake asked.

"I'll tell you," Mason said, "when we get the samples of hair and fingernails from Lauretta Trent. A person can't rely on a copy of the will unless two things have happened."

"What two things?" Drake asked.

"First, the original will is missing. Second, the person who executed it is dead."

"You think it's that serious?" Drake asked.

"I think it's that serious," Mason said, "but my hands are tied until we get a check on that arsenic factor.

"Go back to your office, Paul, alert your telephone operator and have things in readiness so that you can have a man out at Virginia Baxter's place at a moment's notice."

CHAPTER TEN

THE MAN with the black hair, the close-clipped mustache and the black, intense eyes was waiting in a car that was parked in front of Virginia Baxter's apartment house.

Virginia spotted the car first, recognized the driver sitting there concentrating on the front door of the apartment house and breezed on by without attracting any attention.

From a service station four blocks down the street, she telephoned Mason's office.

"He's out there, waiting," she said, when she had the lawyer on the line.

"The same man who called on you before?" Mason asked.

"Yes."

"All right," Mason said, "go on home; see what he wants; make an excuse to break away if you can and call me."

"Will do," she said. "You'll probably hear from me within the next twenty or thirty minutes."

She hung up the phone, drove back to her apartment house, parked her car and entered the front door, apparently completely oblivious of the man who was seated in the parked automobile across the street.

Within a matter of minutes after she had entered her apartment house, the buzzer sounded.

She saw to it that the safety chain was on the door, then opened it to confront the intense, black eyes.

"Why, hello, Mr. Menard," she said. "Did you find what you wanted?"

The man tried to make his smile affable. "I'd like to talk with you about it. May I come in?"

She hesitated a brief instant, then said cordially, "Why, certainly," and released the chain on the door.

He entered the apartment, seated himself, said, "I'm going to put my cards on the table."

She raised her eyebrows.

"I wasn't looking for an agreement made with Smith and relating to the sale of a machine shop," he said. "I was looking for something else."

"Can you tell me what?" she asked.

"Some years ago," he said, "Mr. Bannock made at least one will for Lauretta Trent. I'm under the impression he made two wills.

"Now then, for reasons that I don't want to take the time to go into at the present time, it is highly important that we find those wills. At least, the latest one."

Virginia let her face show surprise. "But—but I don't understand. . . . Why, we only had the carbon copies. Mrs. Trent would have the original wills in her safety deposit box or somewhere."

"Not necessarily," he said.

"But what good would a copy do?"

"There are other people who are interested."

She raised her eyebrows.

"There is one person in particular who is willing to do anything to get his hands on a copy of the will. Now, I would like to lay a trap for that individual."

"How?"

"I believe you purchased the typewriter that you had used in the office?"

"Yes. That is, Mr. Bannock's brother gave it to me."

He indicated the typewriter on the desk. "It's an older model?"

"Yes. We had it in the office for years. It's an exceedingly durable make and this model is pretty well dated. When the appraiser appraised the office furniture he put a very low value on this typewriter because it was so old, and Mr. Bannock's brother told me to just keep it and forget about it."

"Then you could prepare a carbon copy of a will and date it back three or four years and we could mix that carbon copy in with the old papers that went to Mr. Bannock's brother and if anyone should happen to be snooping around through those papers looking for a copy of Lauretta Trent's will, we could fool him into relying on that copy and perhaps get him to betray himself."

"Would that do any good?" she asked.

"It might do a great deal of good. . . . I take it you'd like to help a person who was a client of Mr. Bannock's?"

Her face lit up. "Then you mean Lauretta Trent would ask me to do this herself?"

"No, there are certain reasons why Lauretta Trent couldn't request you to do it, but I can tell you it would be very much to her advantage."

"You're connected with her then in some way?"

"I am speaking for her."

"Would it be all right for me to ask the nature of the association or of your representation?"

He smiled and shook his head. "Under some circumstances," he said, "money talks."

He took a wallet from his pocket and extracted a hundred-dollar bill. He paused for a moment; then extracted another hundred-dollar bill. Then, significantly, another hundred-dollar bill and kept on until there were five one-hundred-dollar bills lying on the table.

She eyed the money thoughtfully, "We'd have to be rather careful," she said. "You know Mr. Bannock used stationery that had his name printed in the lower left-hand corner."

"I hadn't realized that," the man said.

"Fortunately, I have some of that stationery— Of course, we'd have to destroy the original and leave this as a carbon copy."

"I think you could make a good job of it," he said.

She said, "I'd have to have your assurance that it was all right, that there wasn't going to be anything fradulent connected with it."

"Oh, certainly," he said. "It's simply to trap someone who is trying to make trouble with Mrs. Trent's relatives."

She hesitated for a moment. "Could I have some time to think this over?"

"I'm afraid not, Mrs. Baxter. We're working against time and if you're going to go ahead with this we'd have to do it immediately."

"What do you mean by 'immediately'?"

"Right now," he said, indicating the typewriter.

"What do you want in this will?"

He said, "You make the usual statements about the testatrix being of sound and disposing mind and memory and state that she is a widow; that she has no children; that she has two sisters who are married; that one is Dianne, the wife of Boring Briggs; that the other is Maxine who is the wife of Gordon Kelvin.

"Then go on and state that you have recently become convinced that your relatives are actuated by selfish interests and that, therefore, you leave your sister, Dianne, a hundred thousand dollars; that you leave your sister, Maxine, one hundred thousand dollars; that you leave your brother-in-law, Boring Briggs, ten thousand dollars; that you leave your brother-in-law, Gordon Kelvin, ten thousand dollars; that you leave your faithful and devoted chauffeur, George Eagan, who has been loyal to you throughout the years, all of the rest, residue and remainder of your estate."

Virginia Baxter said, "But I don't see what good that is going to do."

"Then," her visitor went on firmly, "you make another will which purports to have been executed just a few weeks before the date of Mr. Bannock's death. In that will you state that you leave Maxine and Gordon Kelvin one thousand dollars apiece; that you leave Boring Briggs and his wife, Dianne, one thousand dollars apiece, being satisfied that these people are actuated purely by selfish interests and have no real affection for you, and you leave all the rest, residue and remainder of the estate to your faithful and devoted chauffeur, George Eagan."

She started to say something, but he held up his hand and stopped her.

"We will plant those copies of the spurious wills in with Mr. Bannock's papers.

"I can assure you that they will be discovered by persons who are trying to find out in advance the terms of Lauretta Trent's will.

"These two documents will show that some years ago she began to doubt the sincerity of her sisters and particularly her brothers-in-law; that more recently she uncovered proof that they were simply trying to get what they could get their hands on and were actuated by purely selfish motives."

"But, don't you understand," she said, "that neither of these wills would be any good at all if— Well, I always signed and witnessed wills that were executed in the office. Mr. Bannock signed, and I signed.

"If they should call me and ask me if I signed this will as a witness, I would have to tell them that this will was completely spurious; that I prepared it only recently and—"

He interrupted her, smiling. "Why don't you just leave all that to me, Mrs. Baxter?" he asked. "Just pick up the five hundred dollars and start typing."

"I'm afraid I'd be too nervous to do anything while you were here. I'd have to work out the terms of the wills and then you could come back later."

He shook his head firmly. "I want to take these documents with me," he said, "and I haven't very much time."

Virginia Baxter hesitated, then remembering Mason's instructions, went to the drawer of the desk, picked out some of the old legal paper bearing Delano Bannock's imprint, put in new carbon paper, racheted the paper into the typewriter and started typing.

Thirty minutes later when she had finished, her visitor

pocketed the carbon copies of the two documents, said, "Now, destroy those originals, Virginia. In fact, I'll destroy them right now."

He picked up all the originals and copies, folded them and put them in his pocket.

He walked to the door, paused to nod to Virginia Baxter. "You're a good girl," he said.

She watched him until he had entered the elevator; then she slammed the door, raced for the telephone, called Mason's office and hurriedly reported what had happened.

"Do you have any copies?" Mason asked.

"Only the carbon paper," she said. "He was smart enough to take the originals as well as the copies, but I followed your suggestion and put in a fresh sheet of carbon paper with each page and he didn't notice what I was doing. You see, I prepared all the pages with the carbon paper inserts in advance, putting out a half a dozen pages on my desk at one time and taking a fresh sheet of carbon paper from the box for each page. So I have a set of carbons, and by holding them up to the light, it's easy to read what was written."

"All right," Mason said, "bring those carbon copies up to my office just as fast as you can get here."

CHAPTER ELEVEN

VIRGINIA sat across the desk from Mason, who carefully examined the pages of carbon.

He turned to Della Street. "Della," he said, "take some cardboard the size of these pages of carbon paper so the carbon paper won't get folded or wrinkled, put these in an envelope and seal the envelope."

When Della had done this, Mason said to Virginia, "Now, write your name several times across the seal."

"What's that for?"

"To show that it hasn't been steamed open or tampered with."

Mason watched her while she wrote her name.

"Now then," he said, "don't bother with your car because you won't be able to find a parking place and time is running against you.

"Take a taxicab. Rush this envelope to the post office, address it to yourself and send it by registered mail."

"Then what?" she asked.

"Now, listen very carefully," Mason said. "When this envelope is delivered to you by registered mail, don't open it. Leave it sealed just as it is."

"Oh, I see," she said, "you want to be able to show the date that I—"

556

"Exactly," Mason said.

She picked up the envelope, started for the door.

"How are you fixed for provisions in your apartment?" Mason asked.

"Why, I . . . I have butter, bread, canned goods and some meat. . . ."

"Enough to last you for twenty-four hours if necessary?"

"Yes, indeed!"

Mason said, "Mail that letter, go back to your apartment, stay there, keep the safety chain on the door. Don't admit anyone. If anyone calls to see you, tell him that you're entertaining a visitor and can't be disturbed. Then get his name and telephone me."

"Why?" she asked. "Do you think I'm in . . . in any danger?"

"I don't know," Mason said. "All I know is that there's a possibility. Someone tried to frame you and discredit you. I don't want that to happen again."

"Neither do I," she said vehemently.

"All right," Mason told her, "on your way to the post office. Then go back to your apartment and stay there."

When she had left, Della Street looked at Mason with raised eyebrows. "Why should *she* be in any danger?"

Mason said, "Figure it out for yourself. A will is made. There are two subscribing witnesses. One of them is dead. An attempt was made to put the other in a position where her testimony would have been discredited. Now, a new plan is in operation."

"But those spurious wills; they can't mean anything."

"How do you know?" Mason asked. "Suppose two more people die, then what happens?"

"What two people?" she asked.

"Lauretta Trent and Virginia Baxter. Perhaps a fire destroys the home of Lauretta Trent. Presumably the will has been destroyed in the conflagration.

"People look for the carbon copies of the wills prepared by Bannock to establish the contents of the burnt will. They find two wills. The effect of those wills is to indicate that Lauretta Trent was suspicious of her relatives and the people who surrounded her.

"Now then, Delano Bannock is dead. Suppose Virginia Baxter should also die."

Della Street blinked her eyes rapidly. "Good heavens . . . are you going to notify the police?"

"Not yet," Mason said, "but probably within a matter of hours. However, there are a lot of factors involved, and an attorney can't go around making accusations of this sort unless he has something more definite on which to base them."

"But it won't take much more?" Della Street asked.

"It will take very little more," Mason said.

CHAPTER TWELVE

IT WAS just before Mason was closing the office that Dr. Alton telephoned.

"Is it all right if I come up for just a few minutes?" Dr. Alton asked. "I've had a terrific work load this afternoon with an office full of patients and I'm just this minute getting free."

"I'll wait," Mason said.

"I'll be there within ten minutes," Dr. Alton promised.

Mason hung up the phone, turned to Della Street, "Any particular plans for this evening, Della? Can you wait with me for Dr. Alton?"

"I'll be glad to," she said.

"After that," Mason told her, "we can go out for dinner."

"Now, those words are music to a secretary's ears," she told him, "but may I remind you, you don't as yet have any retainer in this case which would cover expenses."

"We're casting bread on the waters," Mason said, "and don't let the matter of expense cramp your style. Just don't look at the right side of the menu."

"My figure," she sighed.

"Perfect," Mason said.

She smiled. "I'll go out in the outer office and wait for Dr. Alton."

"Bring him right in, as soon as he comes," Mason told her.

Della Street went to the outer office and a few minutes later returned, opening the door and saying, "Dr. Ferris Alton."

Dr. Alton came bustling forward, radiating intense nervous energy.

He grasped Mason's hand, said, "I'm very pleased indeed to meet you, Mr. Mason. I have to discuss this case with you, personally, which is the reason I'm bothering you.

"Incidentally, I have here two sterile phials containing the material you wanted, some clippings from the fingernails and some hair that has been pulled out by the roots.

"Now, I can either have this processed or you can."

"Better let me do it," Mason said. "It will attract less attention that way, and I have some connections which will give me a report within a very short time."

"Well, I'd be very glad to have you do it," Dr. Alton said, "but now that you've planted the suspicion in my mind, I have an uneasy feeling that we're going to have positive reactions; that there will be at least two areas in the hair that will show arsenic.

"The first attack took place approximately seven and a half months ago—too long a time, I'd guess, for any traces of the poison to remain. But the second was five weeks ago, and the last one about a week ago."

"Did you get a dietary history?" Mason asked.

"I wasn't utterly naïve," Dr. Alton said. "I wanted to find out if this was the result of an allergy or, as I suspected, contaminated food.

"On all occasions, she had eaten Mexican food."

"Who cooked it?" Mason asked.

"She has a chauffeur, a George Eagan, who has been with her for some time. She is very much attached to him—in a business way, of course. He is young enough—Well, I believe there's quite a discrepancy in ages . . . oh, say fifteen years or so.

"He drives her everyplace and he is the one in charge of the outdoor cooking; whenever they have a barbecue, he does the steaks and the potatoes, does the cooking and the serving, toasts the French bread and all the rest of it. I gather he's very expert.

"He's also expert in cooking; the Mexican foods I mentioned are cooked out of doors."

"Wait a minute," Mason said, "she would hardly have the Mexican food cooked just for herself. There must have been others present."

Dr. Alton said, "In getting a case history, I wasn't even suspicious of poisoning. Therefore, I asked only about what my patient had been eating. I didn't ask about others. I believe other relatives were also present. Eagan, the chauffeur, did the cooking. Apparently no one else besides Lauretta Trent had any symptoms."

"I see," Mason said.

"If it was poisoning, and I am now satisfied it was, it was done very expertly. . . . Now then, Mr. Mason, I have a responsibility to my patient. I want to keep from having any recurrence."

"I told you what to do," Mason said sharply. "Get three nurses, put them on the job around the clock."

Dr. Alton shook his head. "I am afraid that won't work."

"Why not?" Mason asked.

Dr. Alton said, "We're not dealing with a child, Mr.

Mason. We're dealing with a mature woman who likes to have her own way; who is rather arbitrary and—damn it, I've got to have some sort of an excuse to put out special dishes for her."

Mason's mouth tightened. "How many nurses are on the job now?"

"Just one . . . a nurse she has from time to time."

"And how did you get the fingernails and the hair?"

Dr. Alton said, uncomfortably, "I had to use a little subterfuge. I rang up the nurse and told her that I was going to give Mrs. Trent some medicine which might cause a temporary itching of the skin; that it was highly important that she not do any scratching and that I would like to have her nails trimmed down; that I wished she'd explain to the patient what I had in mind and what I was trying to accomplish. I also told her that I'd like to test the hair to see whether her digestive upsets had been due to an allergy caused by either a shampoo or a hair dye. I explained to the nurse that I didn't want to suggest that Mrs. Trent was coloring her hair; but that I felt there might be an allergy, particularly if she had had any itching or sore spots in her scalp and had scratched and had thereby caused an abrasion in the skin that would enable the dye materials to penetrate the bloodstream. I told the nurse to put the nail clippings and the hair in sterile phials."

Mason said, "Nurses take courses in poisons and their treatment. Do you think your nurse suspected anything?"

"Oh no, not a thing," Dr. Alton said. "I told the nurse I'd been puzzled about Mrs. Trent's case; that I couldn't believe that the disturbance resulted entirely from food poisoning but that I thought perhaps it might be a combination of things."

"She didn't give any indication that she thought your requests were unusual?" Mason asked.

"None whatever. She accepted them just as any good nurse would, without any comment. I told her to get a taxi and send the nail parings and the hair in their sterile phials to my office at once."

Mason said, "I know a laboratory which specializes in forensic medicine and toxicology that will give us a quick report on these, not a quantitative analysis, but it will show whether any arsenic is present."

"How soon can you have that?"

Mason said, "I think I can have it right after dinner, Doctor."

"I wish you'd telephone me," Dr. Alton said.

"All right," Mason told him, "but what have you done about furnishing your patient with round-the-clock protection?"

Dr. Alton's eyes shifted. "All right, Mason," he said, "I'll put it right on the line. You almost convinced me when you talked over the telephone, and then I became more convinced when I thought over the symptoms. But when I took time to think things over, I felt I couldn't justify taking really drastic steps pending a laboratory report; but I have taken precautionary steps which will be ample for the time being."

"What steps?" Mason asked, his voice coldly disapproving.

"I've decided that during the next few hours there won't be any element of real danger, particularly in view of the fact that this nurse, Anna Fritch, is on the job. However, I told her to see that Mrs. Trent was on a very bland diet tonight; that I intended to perform some tests and I wanted her to have nothing except soft boiled eggs and toast tonight; that I wanted the nurse to prepare both the eggs and the toast, and see that the eggs were served in the shell so that there would be no chance of too many spices being added."

"All right," Mason said, "if that's what you've done, that's what you've done. Give me your night number. I'll drop these things at the laboratory and ask for an immediate check. . . . Now, what do you propose to do if the tests are positive and show the presence of arsenic?"

This time Dr. Alton met Mason's eyes firmly. "I intend to go to the patient and tell her that she has been suffering from arsenic poisoning rather than from allergies or a digestive upset. I intend to tell her that we're going to have to take extraordinary safeguards and that, from the manner in which the symptoms developed, I have very strong suspicions that there was an attempt at homicide."

Mason said, "And I suppose you have taken into consideration that this will start a three-ring circus among relatives, authorities and people in the household. They'll call you a quack, an alarmist and accuse you of trying to alienate Lauretta Trent's affections."

"I can't help it. I have my duty as a doctor."

"All right," Mason said. "We should have that report no later than nine-thirty. The only thing that I don't agree with you on is safeguarding your patient in the meantime."

"I know, I know," Dr. Alton said. "I've debated the pros and cons with myself and I have come to the conclusion that this is the best way to handle it. I'll accept responsibility for the decision. After all, you know, it is *my* responsibility."

Mason nodded to Della Street. "All right, Della, we'll go to the laboratory, start them working on these things, and get a preliminary report at the earliest possible moment. You get Dr. Alton's night number and we'll call him just as soon as we have a report."

"And, of course," Dr. Alton said, "you'll keep things entirely confidential? You know, the police and, of course, the press. These things have a way of leaking out once they get into the hands of the police, and I know that Lauretta Trent would consider publicity—well, she'd simply hit the ceiling. It would mean the end of our professional relationship."

Mason said, "I'm in somewhat the position of being a public servant in this case, Doctor. Actually, I haven't a client. The logical client would probably be Lauretta Trent, but I certainly don't want to approach her in any way."

"You don't have to," Dr. Alton said. "The minute you find anything positive in the hair and the nails, I'm going to go to her myself and I'm going to explain to her just what you have done in the case and how valuable your assistance has been.

"In the meantime, I can assure you, on my own responsibility, that any amounts within reason you may be called upon to pay will be promptly remitted by Mrs. Trent.

"But . . ." Dr. Alton cleared his throat, "in the event your suspicions should turn out to be groundless, Mr. Mason, you are— Well, I . . . I mean to say—"

Mason grinned and interrupted him. "You mean that in the event I'm barking up the wrong tree, my costs are going to be borne exclusively by me; that I will have lost a lot of face with you."

Dr. Alton said, "You've expressed it more forcefully than I would, but very well."

Mason said, "You'll hear from me about nine or nine-thirty and then you can take it from there."

"Thank you," Dr. Alton said.

He gripped the lawyer's hand and went out.

Della Street looked at Mason speculatively, "Do you have some mental reservations about Dr. Alton?" she asked.

Mason said, "Do you know, Della, I can't help feeling what a mess it would be if Dr. Alton should be one of the beneficiaries in Lauretta Trent's will."

Della Street's eyes widened with consternation. "Good heavens," she said, "do you suppose . . . ?"

"Exactly," Mason said as her voice trailed away into silence. "And now, let's go to dinner, after stopping by the laboratory and asking for a quick preliminary report."

"And you're going to tell Dr. Alton what you find? If he's one of the beneficiaries under the will— Well, of course, under the circumstances—"

"I know," Mason said, "I'm going to tell him and then I'm going to make absolutely certain that Lauretta Trent is protected against any further so-called gastroenteric disturbances."

"That," Della Street said, "should make quite a situation."

"It will," Mason told her.

CHAPTER THIRTEEN

MASON and Della Street had a leisurely, relaxing dinner.

Della Street had left word with the laboratory to call them at the café, and the headwaiter, knowing that an important call was expected, was bustling about keeping an eye on Mason's table.

Della Street had contented herself with a small steak and baked potato, but Mason had ordered an extra-thick cut of rare prime ribs of beef, a large bottle of Guinness Stout, tossed salad and stuffed baked potato.

At length, the lawyer pushed back his plate, finished the last of his Stout, smiled across the glass at Della Street and said, "It's a real pleasure to be able to dine, to feel that we're not wasting time and yet be able to take all the time we want.

"We have the laboratory doing our analysis for us; we have Paul Drake all ready to— Oh-oh," the lawyer interrupted himself, "here comes Pierre with a telephone."

The headwaiter bustled importantly to the table, conscious of the fact that many eyes were on him as he plugged in the telephone for his distinguished guest.

"Your call, Mr. Mason," he said.

Mason picked up the telephone, said, "Mason talking."

The operator said, "Just a moment, Mr. Mason." And then Mason heard a quick, "On the line."

"Mason talking," the lawyer said.

The voice of the laboratory technician was almost mechanical as he rasped out a report.

"You wanted an analysis of nails and hair for arsenic. Both reactions were positive."

"Quantity?" Mason asked.

"It was not a quantitative analysis. I simply ran tests. However, I can state this: There are two bands of arsenic in the hair indicating a recurrent poisoning with a lapse of about four weeks in between the attacks. The nails do not give that long a sequence but do indicate the presence of arsenic."

"Can you make an analysis which would give me an idea of the quantity?" Mason asked.

"Not with the material which I have at present. I gathered that haste was imperative and I used up the material in making tests simply for the purpose of getting a reaction to the poison."

"That's fine," Mason said, "thanks a lot, just keep it under your hat."

"Anything to report to the authorities?"

"Nothing," Mason said positively. "Absolutely nothing."

The lawyer hung up the phone, scribbled the amount of a tip on a check which the headwaiter had brought him; signed his name and handed the headwaiter ten dollars.

"This is for you, Pierre. Thanks."

"Oh, thank you so much," Pierre said. "The call it was all right? It came through nicely?"

"It came through fine," Mason said.

The lawyer nodded to Della Street. They walked out of the restaurant, and Mason stopped at the telephone booth to deposit a coin and dial Dr. Alton's night number.

Mason heard the phone start ringing, and almost instantly Dr. Alton's voice said, "Yes, yes. Hello. Hello," indicating that the physician had been anxiously waiting by the telephone.

"Perry Mason talking, Doctor," the lawyer said. "The tests were both positive. The hair test indicated there had been two periods of poison ingestion about four weeks apart."

There was a long moment of stunned silence at the other end of the telephone; then Dr. Alton said, "Good God!"

Mason said, "She's *your* patient, Doctor."

Dr. Alton said, "Look, Mason, I have reason to believe that I am named as one of the beneficiaries in Lauretta Trent's will.

"This whole business is going to put me in a very embarrassing position. As soon as I make a report to Lauretta Trent, I will be castigated by the family who will insist on calling in another physician to check my diagnosis and then when that physician confirms our suspicions, the family will at least intimate that I have been trying to hurry up my inheritance."

Mason said, "You might also give a little thought to what will happen if you *don't* report what you have found out and if there should be a fourth attack during which Mrs. Trent should die."

"I've been pacing the floor thinking of that for the last hour," Dr. Alton said. "I knew that you disapproved of the extent of the precautionary measures I had taken. You

thought that I should at least have confided my suspicions
to the nurse in charge and seen that— Oh, well, that's all
water under the bridge now.

"Mason, I'm going out there. I'd like very, very much to
have you along with me when I talk with my patient. I
think I'm going to need professional reinforcements and
before I get done, I may need an attorney. I want to have
you there to substantiate the facts. I'll see that you're amply
paid by Mrs. Trent. I'll make that my responsibility."

"What's the address?" Mason asked.

"An imposing mansion on Alicia Drive, the number is
twenty-one twelve. I'm going right out there. If I should
get there first, I'll wait for you. If you get there, just park
your car at the curb on the street and wait for me.

"Actually, there's a curved driveway going up to the
front entrance, but the only place you could wait without
attracting attention would be at the curb."

"All right," Mason told him. "Della Street, my secretary,
and I are on the way out right now."

"I'll probably beat you there," Dr. Alton said. "I'll be
parked at the curb."

"Any idea of just how you are going about it?" Mason
asked.

Dr. Alton said, "I've been overly optimistic long enough.
Perhaps I should say, I've been a coward."

"You're going to tell her the whole thing?"

"Tell her the whole thing. Tell her that her life is in
danger. Tell her that I have made a mistake in diagnosis.
In short, I'm going to set off the whole chain reaction."

"You know her," Mason asked, "how will she take it?"

"I don't know her that well," Dr. Alton said.

"Haven't you been treating her for quite a while?"

"I've been her physician for years," Dr Alton said, "but I don't know her well enough to know how she'll take anything like this. No one does. She is very much of a law unto herself."

"Sounds interesting," Mason said.

"Probably interesting to you," Dr. Alton told him, "but it's disastrous as far as I'm concerned."

"Now, don't be too hard on yourself," Mason said. "Physicians don't ordinarily expect homicidal poisoning, and the records show that virtually every case of arsenical poisoning was originally diagnosed by the physician in charge as a gastroenteric disturbance of considerable magnitude."

"I know. I know," Dr. Alton said. "You can make it easy on me, but I'm not going to. I'm going to face the music."

"All right," Mason told him, "I'll meet you there."

The lawyer hung up; nodded to Della Street.

"Report to Paul Drake, Della. We're going out there. We can't let Dr. Alton face the music alone."

CHAPTER FOURTEEN

MASON found Alicia Drive without difficulty; drove slowly along until the street lights showed an imposing white mansion on high ground to the right with a curved driveway leading up to the front.

A car was parked at the curb just before the entrance to the driveway and the parking lights were on. A figure could be seen silhouetted in the driver's seat.

Mason said, "Unless I'm mistaken, that will be Dr. Alton."

The lawyer eased his car into the curb behind the other machine, and Dr. Alton almost instantly opened the door of his car and came walking back to Mason's side of the car.

"Well," Dr. Alton said, "you made good time. Let's go."

"Take both cars in the driveway?" Mason asked.

"I think so. I'll lead the way; you follow me. There's a parking place in front. That is, it's wide enough for three cars and you just leave your car behind mine."

"Let's go," Mason told him.

Dr. Alton hesitated a moment, squared his shoulders, marched grimly over to his automobile, started the motor, switched on the headlights and led the way up the curving drive.

Mason followed behind him, parked his car, walked

around to help Della out; then led her up the steps to the spacious stone landing.

Dr. Alton pressed the bell button.

Apparently Alton had expected a servant to open the door. He recoiled noticeably when a chunky, blue-eyed man in his middle fifties stood in the doorway.

"Why, hello, Doc," the man said. And then added almost instantly, "What's the matter? Anything wrong?"

Dr. Alton said with dignity, "I happened to be driving by . . . I decided to drop in to see Mrs. Trent."

The man turned speculative blue eyes on Perry Mason and Della Street.

"And these people?" he asked.

Dr. Alton, evidently upset by the meeting, apparently did not intend to perform introductions.

"They are with me," he said shortly, and started through the door.

Mason took Della Street's arm, guided her into the reception hallway, smiled affably but impersonally and started to follow Dr. Alton up a sweeping staircase.

"Hey, wait a minute!" the man said. "Hey, what is this?"

Dr. Alton turned, frowned, reached a decision. "I have asked these people—"

"Why, this is Perry Mason, the lawyer!" the man interrupted. "I've seen his picture dozens of times."

Dr. Alton, with close-clipped professional efficiency, said, "Quite right. That is Mr. Perry Mason and, in case you're interested, the young woman with him is Miss Della Street, his secretary. I want Mr. Mason to talk with Mrs. Trent."

Then, after a barely perceptible hesitation, he said, "This is Mr. Boring Briggs, a brother-in-law of my patient."

Briggs didn't even acknowledge the introduction.

"Say, what is this?" he asked. "You folks making out a will or something? What's happened? Lauretta hasn't had another one of her spells, has she?"

Dr. Alton said, "I would prefer to let Mrs. Trent give you the information, but if it will relieve your mind any, Mr. Mason is with me. Mrs. Trent didn't send for him."

"Well, don't be so crusty about it," Briggs said. "I naturally felt a little alarm. I've been out. Just got back a few minutes ago, and when I find a doctor and a lawyer coming out to the house at this hour of the night—well, I felt I was entitled to a little information, that's all."

"We'll go on up," Dr. Alton said with formal dignity. "Right this way, please."

The physician indicated the stairway with a sweep of his arm and climbed the stairs.

Mason and Della Street followed a tread behind.

Briggs stood at the foot of the stairs and watched them go up, his expression one of frowning contemplation.

Dr. Alton reached the head of the stairs, started down the corridor with long strides. Then slowed perceptibly for a moment just before coming to a door where he knocked.

A woman opened the door.

This time Dr. Alton performed the introductions. "Miss Anna Fritch," he said. "Trained nurse.

"Miss Fritch, this is Miss Della Street, Perry Mason's secretary and Mr. Perry Mason, the attorney."

Her eyes widened. "Why, how do you do? How do you do?" she said.

Dr. Alton pushed his way into the room; held the door open for Della Street and Perry Mason. "How's the patient?" he asked.

The nurse's eyes met his. She lowered her voice and said, "She's gone."

Dr. Alton's face was apprehensive. "You mean she's—"

"No, no," the nurse hastened to explain, "she is out somewhere."

Dr. Alton frowned. "I told you to take precautions about her diet and—"

"Why, certainly," the nurse said, "I put it on the chart. She had dry toast which I fixed myself on an electric toaster and two soft-boiled eggs which I cracked myself. There was no seasoning at all. I'm afraid I may have gone to extremes. I insisted she eat the eggs without salt and I told her that you didn't want her to have any seasoning tonight."

"But you didn't tell her to stay in?"

"You didn't tell me to tell her that."

"Is she driving?"

"I think George Eagan, the chauffeur, is driving her."

"How long has she been gone?"

"I don't know. I didn't even know she was going. She didn't come out through here. There's an exit door from her bedroom to the corridor. You can see for yourself."

The nurse crossed the bedroom to an adjoining bedroom and opened the door.

It was a huge bedroom with rose tapestry, indirect lighting, a king-sized bed with a telephone beside it, half a dozen comfortable chairs, an open door to a bathroom and another door leading to the corridor.

"She didn't tell you she was going out?"

"I had no idea of it."

"What time did you give her the toast and eggs?"

"About seven o'clock, and I impressed on her that you didn't want her to have anything else."

"What did she say when you told her I suspected an allergy and wanted samples of her hair and her nails?"

"She was most co-operative. She said she certainly would like to find out what was causing the trouble, that somehow she didn't think her troubles were due to what she had eaten. She suspected some sort of an allergy."

Dr. Alton said, "It's important, very important that I see her— You don't know when she'll be back?"

The nurse shook her head.

"Nor when she went out?"

"No, Doctor, it's just as I told you. I looked in on her after she had had her supper and she was gone."

"She isn't in the house?"

"No, I asked and someone said she had taken the car and gone out."

Dr. Alton walked over to the bedroom and closed the door. Then he closed the corridor door and turned to Anna Fritch.

"Did you have any clue as to why I wanted hair and nail scrapings?" he asked.

Her eyes avoided his.

"Did you?" Dr. Alton asked.

"I wondered."

"Did you suspect?"

"The request, coupled with your instructions about diet — Well, I prepared the food myself and didn't let anyone else near it."

"Then you did suspect?"

"Frankly, yes."

The door from the corridor opened, and Boring Briggs, accompanied by another man, entered the room.

"I demand to know what's going on!" Briggs said.

Dr. Alton regarded the two men with cold disdain. "I am giving instructions to the nurse."

"And you need a lawyer with you for that?" Briggs asked.

Dr. Alton said to Mason, "Mr. Mason, meet the other brother-in-law, Gordon Kelvin."

Kelvin, a tall, distinguished-looking man in his late fifties, who gave the impression of being a frustrated actor, advanced a step, bowed slightly from the waist and extended a hand with great dignity. "Pleased to meet you, Mr. Mason," he said, and then added after a moment, "and may *I* ask what you're doing here?"

Mason said, "I came to see Mrs. Trent."

"This is rather an unusual hour for a call," Kelvin said.

Mason's smile was disarming. He said, "I have been able to order my life along unconventional patterns and no longer refrain from doing what I want to do simply because it is odd, unusual, distinctive or unconventional."

The lawyer beamed at the two irate brothers-in-law.

The men exchanged glances.

"This is no occasion for levity," Kelvin said.

"I am not being facetious. I am being accurate," Mason said.

Briggs faced Dr. Alton, "Will you," he asked, "once and for all, tell us the reason for this?"

Dr. Alton hesitated for a fraction of a second, then said, "Yes, I'll tell you the reason for it. I made a wrong diagnosis on Lauretta Trent's illness."

"You did!" Briggs exclaimed in surprise.

"That's right."

"A mistaken diagnosis?" Kelvin asked.

"Exactly."

"And you admit it?"

"Yes."

Again, the men exchanged glances.

"Would you kindly tell us the real nature of the illness?" Briggs asked.

"We want to know if it's . . . serious," Kelvin supplemented.

"I dare say you do," Dr. Alton said dryly.

Briggs said, "Our wives have been out, but are expected back at any moment. They will perhaps be in a little more favorable position when it comes to . . . well . . . to getting information from you."

"Demanding an explanation," Kelvin supplemented.

"All right," Dr. Alton said angrily, "I'll give it to you. I made a mistake in diagnosis. I thought your sister-in-law was suffering from a gastroenteric disturbance induced by eating food that was tainted."

"And now you say that was not the correct diagnosis?" Briggs asked.

"No," Dr. Alton said. "It was not."

"What was the correct diagnosis?" Gordon Kelvin asked.

"Someone had deliberately given her arsenic trying to poison her," Dr. Alton said.

In the shocked silence that followed, two women came bustling into the room, two women who looked very much alike, women who spent much time and money in beauty shops and had evidently just been at one that day.

They were girdled so heavily they had an awkward stiffness of motion, their chins were held high and their hair was beautiful.

Dr. Alton said, "Mrs. Briggs and Mrs. Kelvin, Mr. Mason; and Miss Street, Mr. Mason's secretary."

Mrs. Kelvin, perhaps a few years older than her sister,

but with keen inquisitive eyes, immediately took the initiative. "What's all this about?" she asked.

Boring Briggs said, "Dr. Alton has just told us he made a mistake in diagnosing Lauretta's illness, that it wasn't food poisoning at all; it was arsenic poisoning."

"Arsenic!" Mrs. Kelvin exclaimed.

"Bosh and nonsense!" Mrs. Briggs snapped.

"He seems certain," Gordon Kelvin said, "apparently—"

"Bosh and nonsense! If the man's made one mistake, he could make two. Personally, I think Lauretta needs another doctor."

Dr. Alton said dryly, "You might speak to Lauretta about it."

Boring Briggs said. "Now, look here, is all this going to get into the newspapers?"

"Not unless you let it get into the papers," Dr. Alton said.

"You're communicating with the police?"

"Not as yet," Mason said.

There was a moment's silence.

Mason went on calmly, "To a large extent, it's up to you folks. I take it this is a situation you wouldn't want to have publicized. I can also well realize that you have received the information with feelings of mingled emotion, but we are now facing facts, and one doesn't argue with facts."

"How do *you* know they are facts?" Briggs demanded.

Mason met his eyes and said coldly, "Laboratory facts. Positive evidence."

"You can't get evidence of something that's past that way," Briggs said.

Mason said, "Something that isn't generally known is that arsenic has an affinity for fingernails and hair. Once it

gets in the system, it reaches the nails and the hair and lasts
for a long, long time. Late this afternoon, Dr. Alton had
samples taken of Lauretta Trent's hair and her fingernails.
I, personally, had an analysis made by a laboratory that is
highly competent.

"The answer was arsenic poisoning. In the hair, they
were able to trace the intervals of arsenic poisoning.

"Now then, Dr. Alton is Lauretta Trent's personal
physician. He's seen fit to disclose this information."

"Because," Dr. Alton said, "I'm trying to save the life of
my patient. I think I have treated her long enough to
understand something of her temperament. The minute I
tell her that she has been a victim of arsenic poisoning,
things are going to start happening around here."

"I'll say they are," Mrs. Briggs said. "Lauretta will hit
the ceiling."

"One dose of arsenic poisoning," Dr. Alton went on,
"may be more or less accidental; two doses indicate a deliberate attempt at homicide. Apparently, there have been
three."

His announcement was greeted with silence.

After a moment, Mrs. Kelvin said, "These tests, are they
absolute—that is, could there be any mistake?"

"They're absolute," Mason said. "There can be no
mistake."

Mrs. Briggs said, "That first time she got sick was after
she ate all that Spanish food. George cooked up the food on
the grill in the patio."

"We all had it," Mrs. Kelvin said. "That is, the first
time."

"And only Lauretta got sick," her husband pointed out.

Dr. Alton said, "Spanish food would be an ideal means of concealing an attempt at arsenic poisoning."

"That second time she got sick," Mrs. Briggs went on, "George had been doing some more outdoor cooking."

"Who is George?" Mason asked.

"George Eagan, the chauffeur," Gordon Kelvin said.

"And he doubles as a cook?" Mason asked.

"He doubles in almost anything and everything. He's with Lauretta most of the time."

"Too much of the time, if you ask me," Mrs. Kelvin snapped. "The man is positively trying to dominate her thinking."

Mason said, "Would you, by any chance, know whether he is remembered in her will?"

They exchanged shocked glances.

"Does anyone know the terms of her will?" Mason asked.

Again there were glances and a significant silence.

"Apparently," Mason said, "Delano Bannock was Lauretta Trent's attorney during his lifetime. Does anyone know if she has a will which was drawn in his office, or whether she went to some other attorney after Bannock's death?"

Kelvin said, "Lauretta jealously guards her private affairs. Perhaps she feels there is too much of her family living with her. She has become very secretive about all of her personal affairs."

"Financial affairs," Mrs. Briggs said.

"Both personal and financial," Mrs. Kelvin added.

Mason said, "I have reason to believe that the situation at the present time may be somewhat crucial."

"How did you get a sample of her hair and fingernails?" Kelvin asked.

"I instructed the nurse," Dr. Alton said.

Kelvin turned to Anna Fritch. "Did George Eagan know that you were taking samples of hair and nails?"

"She told him," Anna Fritch said. "She was bubbling over with enthusiasm that her illnesses might have been the result of an allergy. She seemed in very high spirits."

"An allergy?" Kelvin asked.

Dr. Alton said, "I explained to Nurse Fritch here that I wanted some tests made for an allergy, that there was a possibility the patient's symptoms might have been a violent and acute reaction to an allergy. I asked her to get samples of hair and nails and to explain to the patient that I was taking the nails because I was going to give her some medicine that would cause a skin irritation and I didn't want her to scratch. I also said that I thought the digestive upset she had had might have been due to an allergic reaction to a certain type of hairdressing—those things *do* happen, you know."

Kelvin said with dignity, "I think instead of standing here and becoming angry at Dr. Alton, we should give him our thanks and start doing something."

"Doing what?" Mrs. Briggs asked.

"Trying to locate Lauretta for one thing."

Mrs. Kelvin said, "She's out with that chauffeur of hers. Heaven knows where they've gone or when they'll be back. What are we going to do about trying to locate her? Call the police?"

Gordon Kelvin said, "Of course not. However, we know certain places where she might be. There are several restaurants that she frequents. There are a few friends on whom she might be calling. I would suggest that we get on the telephone and start calling, being very, very careful not to do anything which would indicate there might be any urgency in what we are trying to do."

"You two girls are probably the ones to do it. Start ringing her friends on the phone, say casually it's a little late to be calling, but that you want to speak with Lauretta.

"If it turns out Lauretta is there, take it in stride. Tell her that she's wanted home at once, that . . . that her sister isn't feeling at all well.

"Whichever sister happens to locate her can say it's the other sister who has been taken ill, and ask Lauretta to come home at once.

"In that way the chauffeur won't feel that we're suspicious of him and won't try to—well, won't try anything."

"Such as what?" Briggs asked.

"There are lots of things he could try," Mrs. Kelvin snapped.

"Well, we don't want him to get suspicious; we want him to walk right into our trap," Kelvin said.

"What trap?" Mason asked.

They looked at him for a moment, then Kelvin said, "He's the only one who could have poisoned her, don't you see?"

"No, I don't see," Mason said. "I can see grounds for suspicion but it's a long way from suspicion to actual proof. I would suggest that you be rather careful before you start talking about traps."

"I see your point," Kelvin said. "However, let's start trying to locate her and get her home. At least she'll be safe here."

"She hasn't been," Mason said.

"Well, she's going to be now!" Kelvin snapped.

"I agree with you," Dr. Alton said. "I am going to explain to her exactly what has happened; I am going to put my cards on the table, and I am going to see that she has private nurses around the clock, and that all food which she ingests is taken under the supervision of those nurses."

"Fair enough," Kelvin agreed. "I don't think anyone will object to that."

He turned to the others.

"Will they?" he asked.

Mrs. Briggs said, "Oh, stuff and nonsense! You can't put her in a virtual prison that way, or an isolation ward or something; once Dr. Alton tells her, she can be on her guard. After all, she's old enough to live her own life. She doesn't need to be isolated from all her pleasures simply because Dr. Alton said someone has tried to poison her."

Dr. Alton said angrily, "You can shorten that sentence by leaving out the words 'because Dr. Alton said' and have the sentence stand *simply because someone tried to poison her.*"

Mrs. Briggs said, "I am not accustomed to shortening my sentences."

Mason caught Dr. Alton's angry expression. "I think we'll be going, Doctor," he said.

"Well, I'm going to wait and see if they can get in touch with my patient," Dr. Alton said.

The telephone rang sharply.

"That's Lauretta calling now," Mrs. Kelvin said. "Answer it, Nurse, and then let me talk with her."

The nurse answered the phone.

"It's for Mr. Perry Mason," she said.

"Excuse me," Mason said to the others and took the phone. "Yes, hello," he said.

Virginia Baxter's voice came over the wire. "Mr. Mason, is it all right for me to see Lauretta Trent?" she asked.

Mason's eyes made a quick survey of the curious faces in the room.

"Where?" he asked.

"Up at a motel above Malibu."

"When?"

"She's overdue now. At first I thought it would be the thing to do, but after I got here I wasn't so certain."

"Where's here?"

"The motel."

"Where?"

"Here— Oh, I see what you mean. It's the Saint's Rest, and I'm in Unit Fourteen."

"Telephone there?"

"Yes. In each of the units."

"Thanks," Mason said, "I'll call back. Wait."

The lawyer hung up.

Mason nodded to Della Street, bowed to the gathering, said, "If you'll excuse us, please, we'll be going."

Dr. Alton said, "I may want to reach you later, Mr. Mason."

"Call the Drake Detective Agency," Mason said. "They're open twenty-four hours a day. They'll relay messages."

Mason started for the door.

Mrs. Briggs said, "Before you leave, Mr. Mason, I want you to know that we are absolutely horrified by what Dr. Alton has told us—and we are very much inclined to think there is more to it than appears on the surface."

Mason bowed. "You are, of course, entitled to your opinion. My only answer is to wish you a very good night."

The lawyer stood aside for Della to precede him through
the door.

CHAPTER FIFTEEN

DELLA STREET said, "I take it that call must have been important since it caused you to leave the scene of conflict."

"That call," Mason said, "was from Virginia Baxter. Evidently, Lauretta Trent has been in touch with her and has arranged a meeting at a motel called the Saint's Rest, up in the Malibu country somewhere.

"The motel has a telephone and our client is in Unit Fourteen.

"So we call her back at the first available opportunity," Mason went on. "I'm looking for a booth now, but I want to get far enough away from Lauretta Trent's house so that some of the crusading brothers-in-law won't notice me in case they should start out on a search for Lauretta."

"What do you think is going on?" Della asked.

"I don't know," Mason said, "but quite obviously there's a tie-in between the wills that were prepared in Bannock's office and the attitude of the various potential heirs."

Della said, "It's pretty convenient for the chauffeur. He inherits under the will. He does all the outdoor cooking. Lauretta Trent likes highly spiced foods and every once in a while she has a violent digestive disturbance. Perhaps nothing which would be fatal in itself, but . . . well, a violent nausea may bring on a fatal heart attack."

"Exactly," Mason commented.

"There's a service station and a phone booth down that side street," Della Street exclaimed. "I just had a glimpse of it as we drove by."

"That's for us," Mason said.

They made a U-turn, drove down the side street and into the service station.

Della entered the booth, called Information and got the number of the Saint's Rest Motel while Mason was giving instructions to the attendant to fill the car with gasoline.

Mason was just entering the phone booth when Della made the connection and asked for Unit 14.

She eased out of the booth while Mason stepped in past her and took the telephone from Della's hand.

"Hello. Virginia?" he asked when he heard his client's voice.

"Yes. Is this Mr. Mason?"

"Yes. Tell me what happened."

Virginia Baxter said, "I know that you told me to stay home, but the phone rang and it was Lauretta Trent. She asked me if I would mind meeting with her tonight to discuss a very important and very confidential matter. I told her that it would be inconvenient and that I was supposed to stay home.

"So she told me that she'd make it well worth my while. That she would pay all my expenses and give me five hundred dollars. But the understanding was I must refrain from communicating with *anyone*. Just go up there and wait for her."

"And you did?" Mason asked.

"I did. That five hundred dollars and all expenses looked as big to me as a mountain of pure gold.

"I realized I should have telephoned you but she specifically stated that I wasn't to get in touch with anyone. Not to let a single soul on earth know where I was."

"So?" Mason asked.

"So I came up here and I've been here for something over an hour and she hasn't shown up or sent me any message. I began to think about the fact that I'd let you down and so I decided to call you and tell you where I was.

"I called Paul Drake's office. They told me that you were out at Lauretta Trent's so I called there and the nurse put you on the phone."

"You hold everything," Mason said. "We're on our way out to the Saint's Rest Motel. If Lauretta Trent shows up before we get there, hold her there."

"But how can I hold her?"

"Make some excuse," Mason said. "Tell her that you have some very important information for her. If you have to, tell her that I'm on my way out.

"Tell her that you want to talk with her privately. Tell her the whole story, starting with your arrest and all about the carbon copies of the files from Delano Bannock's office."

"You think my arrest was connected with that?"

"Very much so," Mason said. "I think the idea was that you were to be put in such a position that your testimony could be discredited if it became necessary to discredit it."

"All right," she said, "I'll wait."

"Where are you?"

"I'm in my room here at the motel."

"You've been there for how long?"

"More than an hour."

"And your car?"

"It's outside in the parking lot."

"All right," Mason said, "we're coming right out."

The lawyer hung up the phone, gave his credit card to the attendant at the service station, said to Della Street, "Come on, Della, we're going to start getting things *un*scrambled."

They drove down to Santa Monica, then up along the beach where a high, angry surf was pounding on their left. Mason slowed to look for his turnoff, then took a dirt road which branched off and curled upward in a series of twisting curves.

Mason fed gas to the car and handled the wheel with deft skill, keeping well within the limits of safety, yet saving every precious second possible.

As Mason's car wound its way up the tortuous road, Della Street said, "What are you going to tell Lauretta Trent if she's there ahead of us, Perry?"

"I don't know," Mason said. "I'll have to remember that *she's* not my client."

"The chauffeur will probably be with her."

Mason nodded.

"And if he should find out that Dr. Alton has now changed his diagnosis and knows that she has been subjected to arsenic poisoning, the man could be dangerous. Lauretta Trent may never get back home."

Mason said, "If I can't talk with her privately I simply might put her in even more danger telling her about the poison. I am not under any obligation to tell Lauretta Trent anything, nor under obligation to withhold anything. I can, of course, ask her to call Dr. Alton and let him break the news to her."

"And then what?"

"Then," Mason said, "George Eagan, the chauffeur, wouldn't necessarily know anything about what has been said. But if she cares enough for him to make him a beneficiary under the will, it will probably take a lot more than a mere telephone conversation to turn her against him; and if I tell her anything, it will turn her against me."

"But Dr. Alton is also a beneficiary under the will."

"We don't know that."

"He seems to think so," she said.

Mason smiled and said, "Also he thought the first attacks were acute food poisoning. Let's see what we can do to take care of our client first. She's our main responsibility. If Lauretta Trent wants to see her, it's for a reason. Let's find out the reason and take it from there."

The road straightened out on a mesa and, within a short distance, Mason saw the lights of the motel.

"Strange place for a motel," Della Street said.

"It's for people going up to the lake for boating and for fishermen," Mason said. "There just isn't room for a motel on the main highway. It's ocean on one side and sheer bluff on the other."

Mason stopped his car in the parking place, and they walked down the long line of cabins and came to Unit 14.

He tapped on the door.

Virginia Baxter flung the door open. "My gosh, am I glad to see *you!*" she exclaimed. "Won't you come in?"

"Where's Lauretta Trent?" Mason asked.

"I haven't heard another word from her, not a word."

"But she asked you to come out here?"

"Yes."

"Why?"

"She said she had something to tell me. Something of the greatest importance to me."

"And when did this conversation take place?"

"Well, let's see . . . I left your office and went to a branch post office that wasn't too far from my apartment. I sent the letter to myself, registered mail. I had a malted milk, went to my apartment and hadn't been there more than . . . oh, an hour or an hour and a half, when the phone rang and Lauretta Trent told me who she was and asked me if I would meet her."

"Up here at this motel?"

"That's right."

"She gave you directions how to get here or did you know the place?"

"No, she told me exactly how to drive to get here and wanted me to assure her that I'd be leaving right away and wouldn't tell a soul."

"What time did she say she'd meet you?"

"She didn't give me a fixed time, but said she'd be here within an hour after I arrived."

Mason said, "You met Lauretta Trent when she was in the law office where you worked?"

"Yes."

"You were a witness to one of her wills?"

"I think there were two wills, Mr. Mason, and I can't specifically remember being a witness, but I remember drawing up the wills—that is, doing the typing—and I remember there was some peculiar provision in the wills, something about her relatives—there was something unusual about it. She didn't trust her relatives, I know that —that is, she felt they were just waiting for her to die and that their interest in her was purely selfish. I've been trying my best to think what it was that was in at least one of the wills, but somehow I just can't seem to get it clear in my mind. I have that vague recollection— You must remember that we drew lots of wills in the office."

Mason said, "Right at the moment I am not primarily concerned with whether you remember the wills but trying to find out if you remember Lauretta Trent's voice."

"Her voice? No, I wouldn't remember that. I have only a vague recollection of what she looks like, rather a tall, slender woman with hair that was turning gray . . . not a bad figure . . . you know what I mean, not heavy but . . . well-groomed."

"All right," Mason said, "you don't remember anything about her voice?"

"No."

"Then how do you know that you were talking with Lauretta Trent on the telephone?"

"Why, because she told me that— Oh . . . oh, I see."

"In other words," Mason said, "a feminine voice on the telephone told you you were listening to Lauretta Trent; that you were to come up here; that Lauretta Trent would meet you here within an hour of the time of your arrival— Now, how long have you been here?"

"Two hours—two hours and a half."

"You registered under your own name?"

"Yes, of course."

"And got this room?"

"Yes."

"And you parked your car?"

"Yes, out in the parking lot."

"Let's go take a look," Mason said.

"But why?"

"Because," Mason told her, "we're checking on everything. I don't like this. You should have followed my instructions and reported to me before you left your apartment."

"But she insisted I was not to tell anyone and that I was to get five hundred dollars and all my expenses if I followed her instructions—and, as I told you, that five hundred dollars looks particularly big to me right now."

Mason said, "She could have promised you a million just as well. If you don't get it, it doesn't make any difference how big it sounded."

Virginia led the way out into the parking lot. "It's right over— Why, that's strange. I thought I left it in that other painted oblong. I'm almost certain I did."

Mason walked over to the car. "You have a flashlight in this car?" he asked.

"No, I don't."

Mason said, "I have one in my car. I'll get it. You don't think this was the place you left the car?"

"Mr. Mason, I'm certain it was not. I remember putting the bumper right up against that stone post over there— That means I was in the parking space to the right."

"Don't touch anything," Mason said. "Stay there. I'll take a look— You've been framed once and got out of it. Perhaps we won't be so fortunate this time."

The lawyer crossed over to his car, took a flashlight from the glove compartment, returned to Virginia Baxter's car and carefully looked over the inside.

"Got your key?" he asked.

Virginia Baxter produced the key. Mason opened the

trunk, looked inside, said, "Everything seems to be in order."

He started to walk around the car, then suddenly stopped. "Hello, what's this?" he said.

"Good heavens!" she gasped, "that fender's all dented, and— Look at the front of the bumper, and there's a piece broken—"

Mason said, "Get in the car, Virginia. Start the motor."

Obediently, she jumped into the car, turned on the ignition, started the motor.

Mason said. "Go out of the exit, turn around and come in the entrance to the parking place."

Virginia Baxter switched on the headlights and said, "Only one of the headlights works."

"That's all right," Mason said, "go ahead, go out the exit, turn around and come back in through the entrance."

Mason took Della Street's arm, hurried her over to his automobile.

"You'd better get in, Della, we want this to look as plausible as possible— Get down low in the seat and brace yourself."

Virginia drove her car out of the exit, swung around in a wide loop and turned into the entrance.

Mason's car, running without headlights, made for the entrance, then swung in a swift turn just as Virginia Baxter entered.

Her headlights picked up his car. She slammed on the brakes. Tires screamed a protest. Then there was a crash and the sound of breaking glass as Mason's car hit hers.

Doors opened in the various motel units. The office door opened, and the manager came running out to stand looking at the scene of the accident. Then she came striding toward them.

"Good heavens, what happened?"

Virginia Baxter said, "You— Why, you didn't have your lights on— You didn't tell me—"

Mason said, "I goofed. I should have gone out the exit."

The manager whirled to face Perry Mason. "This is your fault," she said. "Can't you see that sign there? That says *Entrance* just as plain as day. This is the fourth accident we've had here and that's why I had those big signs put up and knocked a section of the wall down so that the *Exit* would be at the other end of the parking lot."

"I'm sorry," Mason said. "It was my fault."

The manager turned to Virginia Baxter. "Are you hurt?"

"No," she said. "Fortunately, I was going slow and I put on my brakes."

The manager turned back to Mason. "Have you been drinking?" she asked.

Mason turned half away from her. "No," he said.

"Well, I think you have—that sign there is just as plain as day— Now, let me see, dearie, you're registered here in the motel, aren't you? Unit Fourteen?"

"That's right."

"Well," she said, "if you want me as a witness you just call me any time. I'm going to call the highway patrol."

"That won't be necessary," Mason said. "It was my fault. I accept the responsibility."

"I'll say it was your fault. You've been drinking. You aren't staying here, are you?"

"I would like to see about getting a room."

"Well, we don't have any rooms left. And we don't cater

to drinking parties. You wait right here and don't try to move those cars. I'm calling the police."

The manager turned and marched back to the office.

"What in the world," Virginia Baxter asked, getting Mason to one side, "were *you* trying to do?"

"Insurance," Mason told her.

"Insurance?" she exclaimed.

"Exactly," Mason said. "Now if anyone asks you how your car got smashed up, you can tell them. Moreover, you have witnesses to prove it. You'd better go to your friend, the manager, and see if you can borrow a broom and we'll sweep this broken glass out of here; borrow a dustpan and dump it all in a trash barrel somewhere. You have one headlight and I have one headlight. It looks very much as though we're going to spend the night here unless I get busy and have a rental car delivered to me here. In which event, I'll give you a ride home."

"And our cars?" she asked.

Mason smiled and said, "After the police come, we'll try and get yours back to the parking lot. As far as mine is concerned, I think I'll have the garage tow it away."

CHAPTER SIXTEEN

HARRY AUBURN, the traffic officer who was summoned by
the manager, was very polite, very efficient and very imper-
sonal.

"How did this happen?"

"I was coming out," Mason said, "and this young woman
was coming in."

The manager said belligerently, "He flagrantly violated
the traffic rules of this parking place. There's a sign over
there that says *Exit* in letters two feet high."

Mason said nothing.

The traffic officer looked at him.

Mason said, "I will report the facts. I was driving out of
the parking place. I was coming out to the road through
this opening. The young lady was coming in."

"Didn't you see this sign *Entrance Only?*" the traffic
officer asked.

Mason said, "My insurance company has instructed me
that, in the event of any accident, I am not to say anything
that would admit liability in any way. Therefore, I will
have to advise you that I am adequately insured and that
the facts speak for themselves."

"He's been drinking," the manager said.

The officer looked inquiringly at Mason.

"I had a cocktail before dinner some two hours ago," Mason said. "I have not had anything since."

The officer went to his car, produced a rubber balloon. "Mind blowing this up?" he asked Mason.

"Certainly not," Mason said.

He blew up the rubber balloon.

The traffic officer took it over to a testing machine and, after a few minutes, returned and said. "You don't have enough alcohol to register."

"He's drunk," the manager said.

Mason smiled at her.

"Or he may be drugged," she said.

Mason handed the officer one of his cards. "You can always locate me," he said.

"I recognized you," the officer said, "and, of course, checked your name on your driving license."

"I think that's all that needs to be done here," Mason said. "I will need a tow car."

"I'll phone for one," the officer said, then moved over to his automobile, climbed into the seat, picked up the microphone of his radio and called a number.

After a while, a voice came over the radio speaker. The officer turned down the volume, raised the windows on his car so that the voice was inaudible outside of the car. He talked for some two or three minutes, then he hung up the phone and came back to Virginia Baxter.

"Where have you been this evening, Miss Baxter?" he asked.

"I drove from my apartment to the motel here."

"Make any stops along the way?"

"No."

"Where is your apartment?"

"The same address that's on my driver's license—422 Eureka Arms Apartments."

"Have any trouble along the way?" the officer asked.

"Why, no. Why do you ask?"

The officer said, "There's been a pretty bad accident down on the coast road. George Eagan, a chauffeur, was driving Mrs. Lauretta Trent, going south, when a car veered out of control, crowded the Trent car off the road, struck the rear fender, sent the car into a spin and into the ocean. Eagan escaped, but the car went over the road into the ocean. Lauretta Trent was drowned. They haven't as yet recovered her body.

"The description of the car that caused the accident matches the description of this car— You're sure *you* haven't been drinking?"

"Give her a test," Mason said.

"You any objection to taking a test?" the officer asked.

She looked at Mason with wide, frightened eyes.

"Not in the least," Mason said.

The officer didn't even turn but kept his eyes on Virginia Baxter.

"No," she said, "I'll take a test."

"Blow up this balloon," the officer said.

Virginia Baxter blew up the balloon. The officer again retired to his automobile, again talked for a while into the microphone, then returned.

"You been taking any drugs today, Miss Baxter?"

"Not today. I took a couple of aspirin last night."

"And that's all?"

"That's all."

"What time did you leave your apartment?"

"Well, let's see, it was about . . . well, probably three hours ago."

"And you came directly here?"

"Yes."

"How long have you been here?"

"You can check the time of registration," Mason suggested.

The manager said, "We don't keep a time record—only the date, but I think she's been here for . . . well, say an hour and a half anyway."

"But I've been here longer than that," Virginia said.

"Well, I'm willing to swear to an hour and a half," the manager said.

The officer looked thoughtful.

"May I ask how they got a description of the Baxter car?" Mason asked.

The officer regarded him thoughtfully, then said, "A motorist, coming along behind, saw the accident. The car turned off on the road that came up here. He got a description of the rear of the car, and a part of the license number."

"Which part?" Mason asked.

"Enough to make a pretty good identification," the officer said shortly.

Virginia Baxter suddenly burst out angrily. "All right," she said, "I've taken all I'm going to take. This is just another frame-up!

"I didn't have any accident along the road; I didn't run into Lauretta Trent's car, and as far as that chauffeur is concerned, he's a plain liar.

"He's been after me to make a forged will for Lauretta Trent and—"

"Easy, easy," Mason interrupted.

"I'm *not* going to take it easy," she stormed. "This chauffeur paid me to make a forged will. He's been planning murder and—"

"Shut up!" Mason snapped.

Virginia turned indignant eyes on him. "I don't have to keep quiet and—"

"You let me do the talking for a minute, Virginia."

The officer said, "You representing this woman?"

"I am now," Mason said.

The traffic officer went over to his automobile, picked up the microphone. This time, he left the door open so they could hear what he said.

"Auburn, at Car two-fifteen. I'm reporting from the scene of the accident at this motel.

"You can't tell a thing about the condition of this car Virginia Baxter was driving because Perry Mason slammed into it with his automobile. Apparently, Perry Mason is representing her as her attorney, and she says George Eagan, the Trent chauffeur, paid her to make a forged will and has been planning a murder.

"That's her story."

The voice that came over the intercommunicating system was loud enough for everyone to hear. It was a crisp voice, filled with authority. It said, "This is the chief investigator of the D.A.'s office. Bring that girl in for questioning. She'll probably be charged with first-degree murder. But let's get the story before Mason mixes up any more of the evidence."

"Very well, sir," the officer said.

"Start now," the crisp voice commanded, "and I mean now!"

"Shall I give her a chance to get her things and—"

The voice interrupted. "Now."

Mason said in an undertone, "This is just what I was afraid of, Virginia. You're mixed up in some sort of a plot. Now, for heaven's sake, keep quiet. Don't tell them *anything* unless I am present."

"That's going to make it look all the worse," she whispered. "They'll find that registered letter I sent myself and—"

The officer interrupted, "Right in this car, Miss Baxter, please."

"I'm certainly entitled to get my things," she said. "I—"

"Under the circumstances," the officer interrupted, "you're under arrest. If I have to, I can put handcuffs on you."

"What's going to happen with this driveway blocked?" the manager asked. She had been standing as an openmouthed spectator but had finally gotten her breath restored.

"We'll send a wrecking car," the officer said. "In the meantime, I have other things to do."

He slammed the door of the car, started the motor, skidded out of the exit, hit the highway, turned on his red light, and the manager, Della and Mason listened to the scream of his siren vanishing in the distance.

Mason surveyed the wreckage ruefully. "Well," he told Della, "we are, for the moment, immobilized. The first thing to do is to arrange for transportation."

CHAPTER SEVENTEEN

IT WAS ten o'clock in the morning. Mason paced the attorney's room at the jail impatiently.

A policewoman brought Virginia Baxter in, then discreetly withdrew out of earshot.

Mason said, "I understand you told the police everything, Virginia."

She said, "They kept after me until way late—it must have been nearly midnight."

"I know," Mason said sympathetically. "They told you that they wanted to clear you so you could go home and go to bed; that if you'd only tell them the truth they'd investigate it and, if it checked out, they'd release you immediately; that, of course, if you refused to say anything that was your privilege but, in their own minds, it would show them that you were guilty and they'd stop trying to clear you. In that event they'd go home and go to bed and leave you in jail."

Her eyes widened with surprise. "How did you know what they said?" she asked.

Mason merely smiled. "What did you tell them, Virginia?"

"I told them everything."

Mason said, "Hamilton Burger, the district attorney, and Lieutenant Tragg told me they wanted me here this morning; that they were going to ask you some questions that they thought I should hear. Now, that means something pretty devastating. They evidently have some unpleasant surprises for you.

"It also means that you finally told them you wanted to get in touch with me and they then complied with the law by putting through a call to my office."

"That's exactly what happened," she said. "I told them everything last night because they said they'd investigate and, if I was telling the truth, I could go home and go to bed.

"Right after I'd told them everything, they simply got up and said, 'Well, Virginia, we'll investigate,' and started to walk out.

"I told them that they said I could go home and go to bed, and they said, Why, of course I could, but not tonight. It would be the next night—that it would take a day to investigate."

"Then what?"

"I didn't sleep hardly a wink—being behind bars for the second time—Mr. Mason, what *is* the matter?"

"I don't know," Mason told her, "but a great deal depends on whether you've told me the truth or whether you're lying."

"Why should I lie to you?"

"I don't know," Mason said, "but you've certainly been mixed up in some bizarre adventures, if one believes your story."

"And suppose one doesn't believe it?"

"Well," Mason said, "I'm afraid the district attorney and Lieutenant Tragg of the Homicide Squad are two people who don't believe you."

"Would you expect them to?"

"Sometimes they believe people," Mason said. "They're actually trying to do a job. They're trying to do justice but of course they don't like to have unsolved homicides."

"What about the homicide?" she asked.

Mason said, "George Eagan, the chauffeur, was driving Lauretta Trent down the coast highway. They were coming south from Ventura.

"Mrs. Trent told the chauffeur that she'd tell him where to turn off, that they were going to a motel up in the mountains.

"They approached the turnoff leading up to the motel where you were waiting. So far the facts seem to indicate that Lauretta Trent was the one who telephoned you and asked you to wait for her there."

"She did, Mr. Mason. She did. I told you—"

"You don't know," Mason interrupted. "All you know is that a feminine voice told you that it was Lauretta Trent speaking and you were to go up there and wait at the motel.

"Anyway, just as the chauffeur was preparing to make the left turn, a car came up behind him fast. He swung to the right of the road so as to let the second car get by. However, that car swung over and crowded the Trent car right off the road and over the edge.

"There was an angry surf, and the chauffeur, George Eagan, knew there was deep water down there. He yelled to Mrs. Trent to jump and he flung the car door open and jumped himself. He apparently hit his head on a rock. In any event he was unconscious for some period of time.

"When he came to, there was no sign of the Trent automobile. The highway patrol was there. The highway police got a tow car, sent down divers and located the Trent car. They got grappling hooks on it, used a winch, brought it to the surface. There was no sign of Mrs. Trent, but the door on the left-hand, rear side of the car was unlocked and open. Evidently she had opened that door before the car went over the grade and rolled into the surf.

"They may never recover her body. There are treacherous currents there and a terrific undertow. Skin divers who went down there looking around had a hard time wrestling with the currents. A body could have been carried out to sea or swept down the coast. There's a terrific riptide at that point."

"But why pick on me?"

"The chauffeur got a quick look at the rear end of the car that hit him. The description matches your car. A man who was two cars behind got a look at the last two figures on the license plate and they're the same as yours."

"But I didn't leave the motel," she said.

Mason said, "They picked up some glass at the place where the car had been crowded over the road. There were fragments of a glass headlight. Then the police went up to the motel where I ran into you with my car and examined the glass up there. They found a piece that had broken out of your headlight. The broken piece fits exactly into the lens on your headlight. Then the broken piece of glass that they found down where Lauretta Trent was crowded off the road also fits into the piece of glass that came out of that same headlight. By putting the whole thing together, they have patched up the glass fragments like a jigsaw puzzle and have virtually everything. There is only one small, triangular piece of glass that is missing."

"But that chauffeur," Virginia Baxter said, "why should they believe him when he did all those things?"

"That," Mason said, "is something I don't understand myself. You told them about the chauffeur?"

"Of course."

"About his wanting to bribe you to forge a copy of the will?"

"Yes."

"And about the way you made the carbon copies and mailed them to yourself?"

"Yes. I told them everything, Mr. Mason. I realize now that I shouldn't have, but once I started talking—well, I was just . . . I was just scared stiff. I wanted so desperately to convince them and have them turn me loose."

Abruptly, the door opened. District Attorney Hamilton Burger, accompanied by Lieutenant Tragg, entered the room.

"Good morning, Virginia," Hamilton Burger said.

He turned to Perry Mason. "Hi, Perry. How's everything this morning?"

"How are you, Hamilton?" Mason said. "You going to turn my client loose?"

"I'm afraid not," Burger said.

"Why not?"

"She told us quite a story about George Eagan, the chauffeur for Lauretta Trent," Hamilton Burger said. "It was a nice story, but we don't believe it.

"Lauretta Trent's relatives told us quite a story about the chauffeur. It's a plausible story but it doesn't check out in some details. We're beginning to think that your client *may* be tied in with Lauretta Trent's relatives, trying to discredit Eagan and obscure the issues; incidentally, covering up attempts they have made at committing murder—a murder which was actually consummated by your client."

"Why, that's absurd," Virginia exclaimed. "I never met Lauretta Trent's relatives in my life."

"Perhaps," Mason said, "if you wouldn't be so hypnotized by an act put on by that chauffeur, you might have a clearer understanding of the situation."

"Well, we'll see about that," Burger said.

He stepped to the door, opened it and said to someone outside, "Come in."

The man who entered was in his forties. He had a shock of coal-black hair, dark complexion, high cheekbones, and intense black eyes.

He shifted his eyes from Hamilton Burger to look directly at Virginia Baxter, then shook his head emphatically.

"Have you ever seen this young woman before?" Burger asked the man.

"No," he said, shortly.

"There you are," Burger said, turning to Virginia.

"Well, *that's* nothing," she said. "I've never seen him before either. He looks in a general way like the Trent chauffeur, but he's not the man who called on me."

"This," Lieutenant Tragg announced dryly, "is George Eagan, the chauffeur for Lauretta Trent. . . . That's all, George, you may go now."

He turned to Mason and said, "George hit his head when he tumbled out of that automobile. He was unconscious for an undetermined length of time."

"Now, just a minute," Mason said. "Just a minute. Don't pull that stuff with me. If he's able to be out walking around and come here to identify, or fail to identify, my client, he can answer a question."

"He doesn't have to," Hamilton Burger said.

Mason ignored the district attorney's comment, said to the chauffeur, "You have a private automobile. It's an Olds and the license number is ODT062."

Eagan looked at Mason with surprise. "That's my license number," he said, "but it isn't an Olds, it's a Cadillac."

"You were driving your automobile day before yesterday?" Mason asked.

Eagan looked at him with a puzzled expression on his face, then slowly shook his head. "I was chauffeuring Mrs. Trent. We drove up to Fresno."

Burger said, "That's all, George. You don't need to answer any more questions."

The chauffeur walked out.

Hamilton Burger turned to Mason and gave an expressive shrug of the shoulders, "There you are," he said. "If any attempt has been made to frame anyone, it's an attempt to frame this chauffeur. You'd better check the story of your client a little bit yourself.

"We'll arraign her at eleven o'clock this morning if that meets with your convenience, and we'll have her preliminary hearing at any time you suggest. We want to give you ample opportunity to prepare."

"That's very nice of you," Mason said, "under the circumstances. We'll have a preliminary just as soon as the judge can get it on the calendar—tomorrow morning, if possible."

Burger's smile was frosty. "You may catch us unprepared on *some* points, Perry, but you won't catch us with our wearing apparel disarranged. This is one case where you're on the wrong end. Your client is a shrewd, scheming opportunist.

"I don't know yet who she's teamed up with. I don't know who administered the poison to Lauretta Trent, but I do know that it was your client's car that crowded her off the road, and your client has told enough lies to make her exceedingly vulnerable.

"At least we'll get her bound over while we're looking for the other conspirator.

"And now, we'll leave you alone with your client."

Burger nodded to Lieutenant Tragg, and the pair walked out, closing the door behind them.

Mason turned to Virginia Baxter.

She said, "There's been a horrible mistake somewhere, Mr. Mason. That man has the general physical characteristics of the chauffeur—I mean, the man I talked with, the one who gave me the name of Menard. . . . Of course, *you* were the one who told me he was Lauretta Trent's chauffeur."

"That," Mason said, "was on the strength of the physical description plus the license number of the automobile he was driving. You're sure it was an Oldsmobile?"

"Yes. It wasn't a new Olds but I certainly thought that's what it was. . . . Of course, I could have made a mistake in the license number; that is, I could have been wrong on the last or something like that, but the first figure was a zero."

Mason shook his head, "No, Virginia, that would be *too* much of a coincidence. But you could have been victimized by someone who inveigled you into doing his dirty work for him. Suppose you try telling me the truth for a change."

"But I have told you the truth."

"*I'll* tell *you* something," Mason said. "If you insist on telling that story, you're going to be bound over for trial on a charge of murder; and if someone is using you as a cat's-paw and you don't give me an opportunity to get you into the clear by telling me exactly what happened, you're in very, very serious trouble."

She shook her head.

"Well?" Mason asked.

She hesitated a moment.

"I've told you the truth," she said at length.

Mason said, "If it's the truth, someone with a diabolically clever mind has carefully inveigled you into a trap."

"It's . . . it's the truth," she said.

Mason said, "I'm your attorney. If you insist that a story is the truth, no matter how weird or bizarre it sounds, I have to believe you and not show the slightest doubt when we get to court."

"But you don't really believe me?" she asked.

Mason regarded her thoughtfully. "If you were on a jury and a defendant told a story like that, would you believe her?"

Virginia Baxter started to cry.

"Would you?" Mason asked.

"No," she sobbed, "it sounds too . . . too—just too much of a series of improbable things."

"Exactly," Mason said. "Now then, you have one defense

and only one defense. Either tell me the absolute truth and let me take it from there, or stay with this improbable story. If you do that, I'm going to have to adopt the position that some shrewd, diabolically clever individual is deliberately framing you for murder. And the way events have been taking place, he's very apt indeed to have you convicted."

She looked at him with tearstained eyes.

"Of course, you realize my predicament," Mason said. "Once I adopt the position that you're being framed, if even the slightest part of your story turns out to be false, you'll be swept along into the penitentiary on a tide of adverse public opinion. The slightest falsehood will completely ruin your chances."

She nodded. "I can see that."

"Now then," Mason said, "in view of that situation and in view of that statement, do you want to change your story?"

"I can't change it," she said.

"You mean because you're stuck with it?" Mason asked.

"I just can't change it, Mr. Mason, because it's the truth. That's all."

"All right," Mason told her, "I'll take it from there and do the best I can with it. Sit tight."

The lawyer walked out.

CHAPTER EIGHTEEN

JERRY CASWELL, the deputy district attorney who had prosecuted Virginia on the charge of possessing narcotics and apparently firmly believed that there had been a miscarriage of justice in that case, had requested the district attorney's office to be permitted to present the People's case against Virginia Baxter at the preliminary hearing.

Now he entered upon his duties with a personalized zest and a grim determination that Perry Mason was not going to get any advantage because of ingenuity or quick thinking.

As his first witness, he called George Eagan.

The chauffeur took the stand, testified as to his name, address and occupation.

"Could you tell us what you were doing on Wednesday night?" Caswell asked.

"I was driving Lauretta Trent in her automobile. We had been to Ventura and were returning along the coast highway."

"Did you have any fixed destination in mind?"

"Mrs. Trent told me that she intended to turn off to go up to a motel that was up in the hills near a lake. She said she would tell me what road to take."

"She didn't tell you what road she intended to take?"

"No, just that she would tell me when to make the turn."

"Now then, are you familiar with the motel known as the Saint's Rest and the road leading to it?"

"Yes, sir. The turnoff is approximately three hundred yards to the north of the Sea Crest Café."

"When you approached that turnoff on Wednesday night, what happened?"

"Mrs. Trent asked me to slow down slightly."

"And then what?"

"Well, I realized, of course, that she was going to—"

"Never mind what you thought," Caswell interrupted. "Just confine yourself to answering questions as to facts. What happened?"

"Well, there were headlights coming behind and, since I — Well, I don't know how to express it without saying what I was thinking, but I was preparing for a left turn so I turned—"

"Never mind what you were preparing for; state what you *did*."

"Well, I swung far over to the right-hand side of the road, just as far as I could get, and waited for this car to pass."

"And did the car pass you?"

"Not in the normal manner."

"What did happen?"

"The car suddenly swerved, its front end hit the front end of my car, then the driver jerked the steering wheel so that the hind end swung over and crashed hard against the front end of my car. It knocked my front end way over, and the car went out of control."

"And what happened?"

"I fought the steering wheel, trying to keep the car from going over the bank, but I felt the car going. I shouted to Lauretta Trent to open the door and jump, and I opened my door and jumped."

"Then what happened?"

"I don't know what happened immediately after that."

"You were unconscious?"

"Yes."

"Do you know when you regained consciousness?"

"No. I had no way of knowing the exact time. I know *about* the time of the accident but I didn't look at my watch to determine the time until sometime later. I was upset and excited and I was feeling bad. I had a terrific headache and I was . . . well, I was groggy."

"How long do you think you were unconscious?"

"Objected to as incompetent, irrelevant and immaterial and no proper foundation laid, calling for a conclusion of the witness," Mason said.

"The objection is sustained," Judge Grayson ruled.

"Oh, if the Court please," Caswell said, "there are certain ways by which a person can tell how long he has been out—certain bits of circumstantial evidence."

"Let him give the circumstantial evidence then and not the conclusions he has drawn from that evidence."

"Very well," Caswell said. "Now, when you regained consciousness, what was your position?"

"I was sprawled out on the ground, face down."

"How near the road were you?"

"I don't know the exact distance, probably about ten feet, I would estimate."

"Who was there?"

"An officer of the highway patrol was bending over me."

"Did he assist you to your feet?"

"Not right away. He turned me over. They gave me some sort of a stimulant, then they asked me if I could move any toes. I could. Then they asked me if I could move my fingers. I could. Then they had me move my legs slowly, then my arms. Then they helped me to a sitting position, then to my feet."

"Do you know where they had started from?"

"Only from what they told me."

"How long was it after you regained consciousness before you were helped to your feet?"

"A couple of minutes."

"And then you looked for the Trent car?"

"Yes."

"Did you see it?"

"No. It was gone."

"And you told the officers what had happened?"

"It took me a little while to collect my senses. I was rambling a little at first."

"Then what happened?"

"Then there was the sound of sirens, and a wrecking car came up, and shortly after that another car came, divers went down into the water and located the Trent car in about twenty-five feet of water. The car was lying on its right side with the front end down; the left-hand doors were open. There was no one in the car."

"How do you know there was no one in the car?"

"I was there when the car was brought to the surface. I ran to it and looked inside. There was no sign of Lauretta Trent."

"Now, if the Court please," Caswell said, "I would like to withdraw this witness temporarily in order to ask ques-

tions of another witness. However, I am aware of the fact
that when I start to prove admissions made by the
defendant, the objection will probably be made that no
corpus delicti has been established. I wish to state to the
court that we are prepared to meet this objection here and
now; that the *corpus delicti* means the body of the crime
and not the body of the victim.

"There are several instances on record where murderers
have been successfully prosecuted, convicted and executed
where the body of the victim was never found. It is proper
to prove the *corpus delicti* by circumstantial evidence just
as any other factor in the case and—"

"You don't need to try to educate the court on the ele-
mentals of criminal law," Judge Grayson said. "I think
under the circumstances a *prima facie* showing has been
made. If Mr. Mason wishes to adopt the position that no
corpus delicti has been proven, I think he has the laboring
oar."

Mason got to his feet and smiled. "On the contrary, Your
Honor, the defense feels certain that the evidence now
introduced is sufficient to prove the death of Lauretta
Trent. We intend to make no issue in this case of *corpus
delicti* as far as the missing body is concerned. However,
the Court will bear in mind that the *corpus delicti* consists
not only of proof of death but proof of death by unlawful
means.

"So far, it appears that Lauretta Trent's death could well
have been an accident."

"That is why I wish to withdraw the witness at this time
and put on another witness," Caswell said. "By this witness
I can prove that this was a crime."

"Very well," Judge Grayson said. "However, the defendant is entitled to cross-examine the witness on the testimony he has given at this time, if he so desires."

"We will wait with our cross-examination," Mason sad.

"Very well. Call your next witness," Judge Grayson said.

"I'll call Lieutenant Tragg to the stand," Caswell said.

Tragg came forward and was sworn.

"Were you at the jail when the defendant was brought in and held for investigation?"

"Yes, sir."

"Did you have any talk with the defendant?"

"I did. Yes, sir."

"And did you advise the defendant of her constitutional rights?"

"Yes."

"And what did she say by way of explanation?"

Tragg said, "She told me that Lauretta Trent had telephoned her and arranged a meeting at the Saint's Rest. That she went up there and claimed she had been there for considerably more than an hour. That she became nervous and telephoned Perry Mason. That Perry Mason went up there to join her at the motel. That after he arrived he suggested that they go out and look at her car."

"And then what?" Caswell asked.

"Then they found that her car had been damaged. That a headlight had been knocked out and a fender bent."

"And did Mr. Mason make any suggestions?" Caswell asked gloatingly.

"She said that Mr. Mason told her to get in her car and drive out of the exit, to then turn around and come right back into the entrance. That when she did this, Mr. Mason jumped in his car and ran into her car, thereby compounding the damage so that it would be impossible—

"Just a minute," Mason said, "I object to the witness giving conclusions. Let him state the facts."

"I'm asking him what the defendant said," Caswell said. "Did the defendant say why this was done?"

"Yes, she said it was done so that it would be impossible to tell when her car was first damaged."

"What else did she tell you?"

"She said that George Eagan, Lauretta Trent's chauffeur, had approached her about forging a copy of a will."

"What sort of a will?"

"A will purported to have been made by Mrs. Trent."

"And did she say what she did in connection with that?"

"She said that she accepted five hundred dollars; that she forged two wills on the stationery of Delano Bannock, an attorney at law, now deceased, who had done work for Mrs. Trent and by whom she had been employed."

"Did she offer any proof of that statement?"

"She said that she had mailed herself a letter by registered mail containing the sheets of carbon which were used in making the forgeries. She said that following the advice of Perry Mason she had used fresh carbon paper so that it would be possible to read the terms of the forged will by holding the carbon papers to the light."

Judge Grayson said, "Now, just a minute. This is asking for confidential advice given a client by an attorney?"

"It is, Your Honor," Caswell said. "It would be manifestly improper for me to show this conversation except by calling for what the *defendant* had said. In other words, if the defendant should be on the stand and I asked her what her attorney told her, that would be calling for a privileged communication, but with Lieutenant Tragg on the stand, I may ask him what the defendant *said* in regard to her actions and in regard to explanation. If at the time of that conversation the defendant chose to waive the privilege of the confidential communication and state what her attorney has told her, then the witness can repeat that conversation.

"That is a chance an attorney has to take when he advises a client to do things which are for the purpose of confusing the law enforcement officers and, in this instance, for the purpose of compounding a felony.

"We will proceed against Mr. Mason in the proper tribunal and at the proper time, but in the meantime, we have a right to show what the defendant said her attorney told her."

Judge Grayson looked down at Mason. "You have an objection, Mr. Mason?"

"Certainly not," Mason said. "I have no objection to bringing out the facts in this case. At the proper time I will show that persons have deliberately framed a crime on this defendant and—"

"Just a moment, just a moment," Caswell interrupted. "This is not the time for Perry Mason to put on a defense, either for this defendant or for himself. He will have an opportunity to put on a defense for the defendant when I have finished my case and he will have an opportunity to defend himself before the proper tribunal."

"I think that's right," Judge Grayson ruled. "However, Mr. Mason has an opportunity to argue this point in regard to the objection."

"There hasn't been any objection," Mason said. "I want the witness to state what the defendant told him, to state everything the defendant told him."

"Very well, go ahead," Judge Grayson said. "I thought

there might be an objection interposed on the ground that
this was calling for a privileged communication. However,
I can appreciate that once the client has waived the
privilege of the communication and made a voluntary
statement— Well, there seems to be no objection, go
ahead."

"She stated that the witness, George Eagan, had been the
one who called on her?"

"Yes."

"And positively identified him?"

"Yes."

"Cross-examine," Caswell snapped.

Mason said, "You were talking with this young woman
late at night, Lieutenant?"

"Yes, she was not arrested until rather late in the evening."

"You knew that she was my client?"

"No."

"You didn't?"

"I only knew what she told me."

"And you didn't accept that as true?"

"We never accept what an accused defendant tells us to
be the truth. We investigate every phase of the story."

"I see," Mason said. "Then you aren't prepared to state
that what she told you about what I had advised her was
the truth?"

"Well," Tragg said, hesitating, "there were certain
corroborating circumstances."

"Such as what?"

"She gave us permission to pick up the registered letter
which was sent to her and to open it."

"And you did that?"

"Yes."

"And found the carbon copies of the purported will just as she had told you?"

"Yes."

"And for that reason you became inclined to believe *everything* she told you?"

"It was a corroborating circumstance."

"Then why didn't you believe her when she said that I was representing her?"

"Well, if it's material," Tragg said, "I did."

"Then why didn't you notify me that she was in jail?"

"I told her she could call you."

"And what did she say?"

"She said there was no use. That she couldn't understand what had happened but that this chauffeur, George Eagan, was the culprit and that she was freely and voluntarily telling us all of these facts so that we could go and pick up Eagan."

"And did you?"

"Not that night. We did the next morning."

"And what happened then?"

"In the presence of Hamilton Burger, the district attorney of the County, and in your presence there at the consulting room of the county jail we confronted the defendant with George Eagan. He said in her presence that he had never seen her before, and she stated that he wasn't the man who had called on her."

"Did she make any further statements?"

"She admitted that the man who called on her had never told her he was George Eagan, the chauffeur, but said that an identification had been made from a physical description and the license number on an automobile. She said that the man who called on her had given the name of George Menard."

"And you got the defendant to tell you all this by telling her that you were investigating the murder; that you wanted to apprehend the guilty person; that you didn't think she could be guilty; that she was too nice a young woman to be guilty of any crime of this sort; that you thought someone was trying to frame her and that if she would give you the facts immediately and without waiting to get in touch with me in the morning, that you would start an investigation which would perhaps have everything all cleared up so that she could go home and spend the night in her own bed. Isn't that right?"

Lieutenant Tragg smiled. "Well, I didn't say that personally, but one of the officers who was present made statements to that effect."

"This was in your presence and with your approval?"

The lieutenant hesitated for a moment, then said with a dry smile, "It is routine in dealing with a certain type of suspect."

"Thank you," Mason said, "that's all."

Caswell said, "Will Carson Herman please take the stand."

Herman proved to be a tall, slender man with a mosquito-beak nose, watery blue eyes, a firm mouth, high cheekbones and an emphatic way of speaking.

He testified that he had been driving south on the coast highway. That is, he was headed between Oxnard and Santa Monica. There were two cars ahead of him. One of them was a light-colored Chevrolet; the car ahead of the Chevrolet was a big, black sedan. He hadn't had an opportunity to make sure of the make of the car. "Did you notice anything unusual?" Caswell asked.

"Yes, sir, as we approached a turnoff road the black car swung far over to the right, apparently wanting—"

"Never mind what you think the driver wanted," Caswell interrupted, "just state what happened."

"Yes, sir. The black car pulled clean over to the shoulder of the road."

"And then what happened?"

"The Chevrolet got almost even with the car; then suddenly swerved over. The front of the Chevy hit the front of the other car a glancing blow and then the driver swung the wheel sharply so that the rear end of the Chevy came crashing against the front of the black sedan."

"Did you see what happened to the black sedan?"

"No, sir. I was following rather close behind the Chevrolet and it all happened so fast that we were past the black car before I had a chance to get a real good look at it. I saw it swerving and tottering and then I was past it."

"Go on. Then what happened?"

"The Chevrolet made a screaming turn up to a side road which takes off up a hill "

"What did you do?"

"I felt that it was a hit-and-run, and as a citizen—"

"Never mind what you felt," Caswell again interrupted, "what did you do?"

"I swung in behind the Chevrolet and tried to follow it so I could get the license number."

"Did you?"

"The road was full of curves, and I tried. I got the last two numerals of the license number, 65. I suddenly realized the road was lonely and realized my predicament. I decided to stop, turn around at the first available opportunity and notify the police.

"Because the road was so lonely and winding, it was certain that the driver of the car ahead would know that I was—"

"Never mind your conclusions," Judge Grayson interrupted. "You have been warned twice, Mr. Herman, we are only interested in facts. What did you do?"

"I slowed to a stop and watched the lights of the car ahead disappear. I may say that as the car swung around so that the headlights shone on the cut bank to the side of the road, I could see that the car had lost one headlight."

"What do you mean it had lost a headlight?" Caswell asked.

"Well, one headlight wasn't working."

"Then what?"

"Then I proceeded very slowly and cautiously until I found a place where I could turn around. I then went back down the road. There was a seafood restaurant about three hundred yards from the turnoff, and I stopped at this restaurant and telephoned the California highway patrol. I reported the accident. They said some motorist had already reported it and they had a radio car on the way."

"You didn't go back to see if the other car had been seriously damaged or any person was injured?"

"No, sir, I'm sorry to say that I didn't. I felt that the first thing to do was to notify the highway patrol. I felt that if any persons were injured, other motorists who had been coming along the highway would see the damaged car, stop and give aid."

"Cross-examine," Caswell said.

"Could you see the car ahead well enough to tell who was driving, whether it was a man or a woman, or how many people were in it?"

"There was only one person in it. I couldn't tell whether it was a man or a woman."

"Thank you," Mason said. "That's all."

Caswell said, "I will now call Gordon Kelvin to the stand."

Kelvin came forward with unhurried dignity, took the oath and testified that he was a brother-in-law of the decedent, Lauretta Trent.

"You have been in the courtroom and heard the testimony of the defendant's statement that she was asked to participate in the forgery of a carbon copy of a will?"

"Yes, sir."

"What can you tell us about the estate of Lauretta Trent?"

"That is objected to as incompetent, irrelevant and immaterial," Mason said.

Caswell retorted quickly, "If the Court please, this is a very material matter. I propose to show that the story told by the defendant was a complete fabrication; that it *had* to be a complete fabrication because the forgery of the carbon copy of a will would have done no good at all. I expect to show by this witness that the decedent, Lauretta Trent, had made a will years before; had given it to this witness in a sealed envelope to be opened at the time of her death; that this envelope was produced and opened and that it contained the last will of Lauretta Trent; that there could be no doubt or ambiguity concerning it and that any so-called carbon copies of other wills would have been completely ineffective."

"I'll overrule the objection," Judge Grayson said.

Kelvin said, "I have always been close to my sister-in-law. I am the elder of the two brothers-in-law.

"My sister-in-law, Lauretta Trent, kept her will in a sealed envelope in a drawer in her desk. She told me where it was some four years ago and asked that it be opened in the event of her death.

"After the tragic occurrence of last Wednesday, and knowing that there might be some question about proper procedure in the matter, I communicated with the district attorney's office and, in the presence of an attorney, a banker, and the district attorney, this envelope was opened."

"What did it contain?"

"It contained a document purporting to be the last will of Lauretta Trent."

"Do you have that document here?"

"I do."

"Produce it, please."

The witness reached in his pocket and produced a folded document.

"You have marked this document in some way so that you can identify it?"

"That document," Kelvin said, "is marked by my initials on each page, by the initials of Hamilton Burger, the district attorney, by the initials of the banker who was present and the lawyer who was also present."

"That should identify it," Judge Grayson said, with a smile. "These, I take it, are your initials written by you, yourself?"

"That's right."

Judge Grayson inspected the document thoughtfully, then handed it to Perry Mason.

Mason studied the document; passed it back to Caswell.

"I want this introduced in evidence," Caswell said. "I suggest that since this is the original will, it may be received in evidence and then the clerk may be instructed to make a certified copy which will be substituted in place of the original will."

"No objection," Mason said.

Caswell said, "I will now read the will into the record, and then it will be filed until a certified copy can be obtained."

Caswell read in a tone of ponderous solemnity: " 'I, Lauretta Trent, being of sound and disposing mind and memory, state that I am a widow; that I have no children; that the only relatives I have in the world are two sisters, Dianne Briggs and Maxine Kelvin; that my sister, Dianne, is married to Boring Briggs and Maxine is married to Gordon Kelvin.

" 'I further state that these four people are living in my house with me and have been for some years; that I am very much attached to my two brothers-in-law, as much so as though they were brothers of mine, and, of course, I have love and affection for my sisters.

" 'I further realize, however, that women—and, in particular, my two sisters—do not have the shrewd, innate business ability which would enable them to handle the numerous problems of my estate.

" 'I, therefore, appoint and nominate Gordon Kelvin the executor of this my last will.

" 'After the specific bequests herein mentioned, I leave

all of the rest, residue and remainder of my estate to be divided equally among Dianne and Boring Briggs and Maxine and Gordon Kelvin.' "

Caswell paused impressively as he looked around the quiet courtroom, then turned a page of the will and went on, " 'I give, devise and bequeath to my sister, Dianne Briggs, the sum of fifty thousand dollars; to my sister, Maxine Kelvin, a like sum of fifty thousand dollars.

" 'There have, however,' " Caswell read, and paused to glance around the courtroom significantly, " 'been a few people whose loyalty and devotion have been outstanding.

" 'First and foremost, there has been Dr. Ferris Alton.

" 'Because he has specialized in internal medicine and does not do surgery, he has locked himself in a branch of the profession which is somewhat underpaid as compared with the relatively remunerative practice of medicine in the field of surgery.' "

Virginia Baxter gripped Mason's leg just above the knee with hard fingertips. "Oh, it's so," she whispered. "I remember now. I remember typing that. I remember the tribute she made to—"

"Hush," Mason warned.

Jerry Caswell went on reading. " 'Dr. Alton has given me loyal care and is working himself to death, yet has no adequate reserves for retirement.

" 'I, therefore, give, devise and bequeath to Dr. Ferris Alton the sum of one hundred thousand dollars.

" 'There are two other persons whose loyalty and devotion have made a great impression on me. Those are George Eagan, my chauffeur, and Anna Fritch, who has nursed me whenever I have been sick.

" 'I don't care to have my death an event which will transform these people from rags to riches nor, on the other hand, do I want their loyalty to pass unrewarded.

" 'I, therefore, give, devise and bequeath to my chauffeur, George Eagan, the sum of fifty thousand dollars, in the hope that he will open up a business of his own with a part of this money as capital and save the balance as a reserve. I also give, devise and bequeath a similar sum of fifty thousand dollars to Anna Fritch.' "

Here Caswell turned the page rather hurriedly as one does when nearing the end of an important document.

" 'Should any person, corporation, or otherwise, contest this will or should any person appear claiming that I have a relationship with that person, that he or she is an heir, that I have through inadvertence or otherwise neglected to mention him, I give to such person the sum of one hundred dollars.'

"Now then," Jerry Caswell said, "that will contains the usual closing paragraph with the date. It is signed by the testatrix, and it is witnessed by none other than the late Delano Bannock, the attorney, and . . ." And here Caswell turned impressively to the defendant . . . "the defendant in this case, Virginia Baxter."

Virginia sat gazing at him openmouthed.

Mason squeezed her arm and brought her back to reality.

"Does that conclude the testimony of this witness?" Judge Grayson asked.

"It does, Your Honor."

"Any cross-examination?"

Mason got to his feet. "This will was the one you found in the sealed envelope?"

"Yes. The sealed envelope was in the drawer where Lauretta Trent said it would be. The will was in the sealed envelope."

"What did you do with it?"

"I put it in a safe and called the district attorney."

"Where was the safe?"

"In my bedroom."

"And your bedroom is in the house owned and occupied by Lauretta Trent during her lifetime?"

"Yes."

"The safe was already in your bedroom when you moved in?"

"No, I installed it."

"Why did you install it?"

"Because I had certain valuables and I knew that the house was big; and the reputation of Lauretta Trent for extreme wealth was well known; so I wanted to have a safe place where I could keep my wife's jewelry and such cash as I had in my possession."

"What has been your occupation?" Mason asked.

"I have done several things," Kelvin said with dignity.

"Such as what?"

"I don't think I need to enumerate them."

"Objected to as incompetent, irrelevant, immaterial, not proper cross-examination," Caswell said.

"Oh, certainly," Judge Grayson said, "I think this is background material and cross-examining counsel should be entitled to it, although I can't see that it will affect the outcome of the case or materially affect the evaluation the Court is placing on the testimony of the witness."

"There's no need of going into his entire life," Caswell snapped irritably.

Judge Grayson looked at Mason inquiringly. "Do you have some particular reason for this question?"

"I'll put it this way," Mason said, "so I can summarize the situation. All these various business activities, which you yourself state have been numerous, were unprofitable, were they not?"

"That is not true, no sir."

"But the net result was that you went to live with Lauretta Trent?"

"At her invitation, sir!"

"Exactly," Mason said, "at a time when you were unable to support yourself."

"No, sir. I could have supported myself but I *had* had certain temporary financial losses, certain business set-backs."

"In other words, you were virtually broke?"

"I had had financial troubles."

"And your sister-in-law invited you to come and live with her."

"Yes."

"At your instigation?"

"The other brother-in-law, Mr. Boring Briggs, was living in the house. It was a large house and— Well, my wife and I went there on a visit and we never moved out."

"And the same was true of Boring Briggs, to your knowledge, was it not?" Mason asked.

"What was true?"

"That he had met with financial reverses and had come to live with his wife's sister."

"In his case," Kelvin said, "there were circumstances which made such a course of action . . . well a—necessity."

"Financial circumstances?"

"In a way. Boring Briggs had met with several reverses and was unable to give his wife the monetary advantages which she subsequently obtained through the generosity of her sister, Lauretta Trent."

"Thank you," Mason said. "That's all."

Kelvin left the stand.

"All right," Mason whispered, turning to Virginia Baxter. "Tell me about it."

"That's the will," she answered. "I remember now typing that wonderful tribute to her doctor."

Mason said, "I'm going up to get that will and take a good look at it. I don't want you to seem to be paying any great attention to what I'm doing, but look over my shoulder, particularly at the attestation clause and the witness clause and see if that really is your signature."

Mason walked up to the clerk's desk. "May I see the will, please?" he said. "I'd like to examine it in some detail."

The clerk handed Mason the will while Caswell said, "My next witness will be a member of the California highway patrol, Harry Auburn."

Auburn, in uniform, advanced to the witness stand. He proved to be the officer who had inspected the scene of the collision at the Saint's Rest Motel.

Mason, turning the pages of the will, casually paused to examine the signatures.

Virginia Baxter said in some dismay, "That's my signature and that's Mr. Bannock's signature. Oh, Mr. Mason, I remember it all now. This is the will all right. I remember several things about it. There's a little ink smudge at the bottom of the page. I remember it happened when we were signing it. I wanted to type the last page over but Mr. Bannock said to let it go."

"There seems to be a fingerprint there," Mason said, "a fingerprint in the ink."

"I don't see it."

"Over here," Mason said. "Just a few ridges, but enough, I would say, to make an identifiable fingerprint."

"Heavens," she said, "that will be mine—unless it should be Lauretta Trent's."

"Leave it to Caswell," Mason said, "he'll have found it out."

The lawyer flipped over the remaining pages of the will, folded it, replaced it in the envelope, went up and tossed it casually on the clerk's desk, as though not greatly interested in it, and turned his attention to the witness on the stand.

As Mason walked back and sat down beside Virginia Baxter, she whispered to him, "But why in the world would anyone want all this fuss about forging two wills when there already was this will? It must have been that they didn't know of its existence."

"Perhaps someone wanted to find out," Mason said. "We'll talk it over later, Virginia."

Harry Auburn gave his testimony in a voice without expression, simply relating what had happened, and apparently with every attempt to be impartial but, at the same time, to be one hundred percent accurate.

He testified that he had been directed by radio to go to the Saint's Rest Motel to investigate an automobile accident; that this had been a routine call; that he had gone up the road to the Saint's Rest and found that an automobile belonging to the defendant and one belonging to Perry Mason had been in a collision; that while he was investigating the facts of the collision he asked for a check on the cars, and he was called back on the radio of his car.

"Now, you can't tell us what anyone told you on the radio," Caswell said. "That would be hearsay, but you *can* tell us what you did with reference to that call."

"Well, after receiving that call, I interrogated the defendant as to whether she had been using the car, whether she had been in another collision, and where she had been in the last hour."

"What did she say?"

"She denied using the car except to make that one loop in the motel grounds. She said that she had been in her room in the motel for some two hours. She emphatically denied having been in any other collision."

"Then what happened?"

"I checked the license number of her car; I found two significant figures; I checked the make of the car; I found enough evidence to take her into custody.

"Later on, I returned to the scene of the accident. I picked up pieces of broken headlight which had come from her car; that is, they matched the broken lens on the right-hand headlight.

"I then went to the scene of the accident on the coast road and picked up a bit of glass there which had come from a broken headlight; then I removed the headlight from her car and patched all of the pieces of the glass together."

"Do you have that headlight with you?"

"Yes."

"Will you produce it, please?"

Auburn left the stand, picked up a cardboard carton,

opened it and took out an automobile headlight. The lens had been patched together.

"Will you explain these different patchings, please?"

"Yes, sir. This small piece around the rim was the part that was in the headlight of the defendant's automobile at the time I found it. I have marked those two pieces number one and number two with pieces of adhesive tape which have been placed on them.

"The pieces of glass I found at the scene of the accident at the Saint's Rest Motel, I numbered number three and number four; and these three pieces, numbers five, six and seven, were picked up at the scene of the hit-and-run on the coast road."

"You may inquire," Caswell said.

"No questions," Mason said cheerfully.

Judge Grayson looked at him. "No questions, Mr. Mason?"

"No questions, Your Honor."

"Now then," Caswell said, "I would like to recall George Eagan to question him on another phase of the case."

"Very well," Judge Grayson said.

Eagan approached the stand. "You're already under oath," Caswell said.

Eagan nodded and seated himself.

"Did you ever at any time approach the defendant and ask her to tell you about a will?"

"I never saw the defendant in my life until I was taken to see her in the jail."

"You never gave her five hundred dollars or any other sum to make spurious copies of any wills?"

"No, sir."

"In short, you had no dealings with her whatever?"

"That is right."

"Never saw her in your life?"

"No, sir."

"You may cross-examine," Caswell said.

Mason regarded the witness thoughtfully. "Did you," he asked, "know that you were a beneficiary under Lauretta Trent's will?"

The witness hesitated.

"Answer the question," Mason said. "Did you or did you not know?"

"I knew that she had remembered me in her will. I didn't know for how much."

"You knew, then, that when she died you would be comparatively wealthy."

"No, sir. I tell you I didn't know how much."

"How did you know that she had remembered you in her will?"

"She told me."

"When?"

"About three months ago, four months ago—well, maybe five months ago."

"You did a great deal of cooking, preparing foods that Lauretta Trent ate?"

"Yes, sir."

"Outdoor cooking?"

"Yes, sir."

"You used quite a bit of garlic?"

"She liked garlic. Yes."

"Did you know that garlic was a good method of disguising the taste of powdered arsenic?"

"No, sir."

THE CASE OF THE HORRIFIED HEIRS

"Did you, at any time, put arsenic in the food you prepared?"

"Oh, Your Honor, if the Court please," Caswell interposed. "This is completely incompetent, irrelevant and immaterial. It's insulting the witness and it's calling for matters which have not been mentioned on direct examination. It is improper cross-examination."

"I think it is," Judge Grayson ruled, "unless counsel can connect it up. It is quite all right for him to show that the witness knew he was a beneficiary under the will, but this is an entirely different matter."

Mason said, "I expect to show that a deliberate attempt was made to poison Lauretta Trent by the use of arsenic on three distinct occasions. And on at least one of these occasions, the symptoms followed the ingestion of food prepared by this witness."

Judge Grayson's eyes widened. He sat forward on the bench. "You can prove that?" he asked.

"I can prove it," Mason said, "by pertinent evidence."

Judge Grayson settled back. "The objection is overruled," he snapped. "Answer the question."

Eagan said indignantly, "I never put any poison in Mrs. Trent's food. I don't know anything about any poison; I didn't know she had been poisoned. I knew she had had a couple of spells of severe stomach trouble and I had been told that they would be aggravated by eating highly seasoned foods. I had, therefore, talked her out of having another outdoor feed which she wanted. And for your information, Mr. Mason, I don't know one single, solitary thing about arsenic."

"You knew that you were going to profit from Lauretta Trent's death?" Mason asked.

"Oh, now, just a minute," Caswell said. "This is not a proper interpretation of what the witness said."

"I'm asking him," Mason said, "if he didn't know in his own mind he was going to profit from Lauretta Trent's death."

"No."

"You didn't know that you would be better off than your monthly salary?"

"Well . . . well, yes. She as good as told me that."

"Then you knew you would profit from her death."

"Not necessarily. I would lose the job."

"But she had assured you that she was going to make it up to you so that there wouldn't be any loss?"

"Yes."

"Then you knew you were going to profit from her death."

"Well, if you want to put it that way, I knew I wouldn't lose anything. Yes."

"Now then," Mason said, "how was Lauretta Trent dressed on this last ride?"

"How was she dressed?"

"Yes."

"Why, she had a hat, coat and shoes."

"What else was she wearing?"

"Well, let's see. She had a topcoat with some kind of a fur, neckpiece rather, that fastened on to the coat in some way."

"And she was wearing that?"

"Yes, I remember she asked me to cut down the car heater because she wanted to keep her coat on."

"She had been where?"

"To Ventura."

"Do you know what she had been doing in Ventura?"

"No."

"Don't you know that she had been looking at some property up there?"

"Well, yes. I know that we drove to a piece of property she had contemplated purchasing and we looked it over."

"And she had a handbag?"

"Yes, of course, she had a handbag."

"Do you know what was in it?"

"No, sir. The ordinary things, I suppose."

"I'm not asking what you suppose. I'm asking what you know."

"How would I know what was in her handbag?"

"I am asking you if you know."

"No."

"You don't know a single thing that was in her handbag?"

"Well, I knew there was a purse in there. . . . No, I don't know what was in there."

"As a matter of fact," Mason said, "don't you know of your own knowledge that there was the sum of fifty thousand dollars in cash in that handbag?"

The witness sat bolt upright in surprise. "What?"

"Fifty thousand dollars," Mason repeated.

"Heavens, no! She wasn't carrying any such sum in cash."

"You are positive?"

"Positive."

"Then you know what *wasn't* in her purse."

"I know that she would never have carried any such sum of money with her without telling me."

"How do you know?"

"Just by knowing her."

"Then the only way you know she didn't have that money with her is by reaching a conclusion based upon an assumption. Is that right?"

"Well, when you come right down to it, I don't *know* she didn't have that money with her," the witness admitted.

"I thought so," Mason observed.

"But I'm almost certain she didn't," Eagan blurted.

"Didn't she tell you that she was going to wave a sum of cash under the nose of the owner of this property? Or words to that effect?" Mason asked.

Eagan hesitated.

"Didn't she?" Mason insisted.

"Well," Eagan said, "she told me she was figuring on buying a piece of property up there. And she had told me she felt the owner was up against it for cash and that if she waved the down payment under his nose, he might accept it."

"Exactly," Mason said triumphantly. "And when this automobile was fished out of the water, you were there?"

"Yes."

"And there was no handbag in the bottom of the car?"

"No. I believe the officers failed to find any handbag. The back of the car was completely empty."

"No fur neckpiece? No coat? No handbag?"

"That's right. The officers made an heroic effort to find the body but the divers weren't risking their lives trying to find little objects. As I understand it, the floor of the ocean is rocky there."

"You don't know the driver of the car that hit you?"

"I am told it was the defendant."

Mason smiled. "You yourself don't *know* who the driver of the car was?"

"No."

"You didn't recognize the defendant."

"No."

"It could have been anyone else?"

"Yes."

Mason turned abruptly, walked back to the counsel table and sat down. "No further questions," he said.

Judge Grayson said, "Gentlemen, we got a late start today because of another case which was a carry-over. I am afraid we're going to have to adjourn for the evening."

"My case is just about finished," Caswell said. "I think the Court can receive all of the evidence and make an order disposing of the matter before adjournment. This evidence certainly indicates that a crime has been committed and that there is probable cause to connect the defendant with that crime. That is all that is necessary for us to show in a preliminary examination. I would like to have it completed tonight. I have other matters on my calendar tomorrow morning."

Mason said, "The assistant prosecutor is making a usual mistake in assuming that the case is entirely one-sided. The defendant has the right to put on evidence on her behalf."

"Do you intend to put on a defense?" Judge Grayson asked.

Mason smiled, "Very frankly, Your Honor, I don't know. I want to hear *all* the evidence of the prosecution, and then I want to ask for a recess so I may have an opportunity to confer with my client before making up my mind what to do."

"Under those circumstances," Judge Grayson said,

"there is only one course of conduct open to the Court and that is to continue the matter until tomorrow morning at ten o'clock.

"Court's adjourned. The defendant is remanded to custody, but the officers are directed to give Mr. Mason a reasonable opportunity to confer with his client before she is taken from the courtroom."

Judge Grayson left the bench.

Mason, Della Street, Paul Drake and Virginia Baxter gathered for a moment in a close huddle at the corner of the courtroom.

"Good heavens," Virginia said, "who was the person who came to me and wanted that forged will made?"

"That," Mason said, "is something we're going to have to find out."

"And how did you know that she had fifty thousand dollars in cash in her purse?"

"I didn't," Mason said, grinning. "I didn't say she had fifty thousand dollars in her purse. I asked Eagan if he didn't know she had fifty thousand dollars in her purse."

"Do you think she did?"

"I haven't the slightest idea," Mason said. "But I wanted to make Eagan say she *didn't* have it.

"Now then, Virginia, I want you to promise me faithfully that you won't talk with anyone about this case before you get into court tomorrow morning. I don't think they'll try to get anything more out of you, but if they do I want you to tell them that you have been instructed not to answer any questions, not to say one single word.

"Do you think you can do that, Virginia, no matter how great the temptation may be to talk?"

"If you tell me to keep quiet," she said, "I will."

"I want you to keep very, very quiet," Mason told her.

"All right. I promise."

Mason patted her shoulder. "Good girl."

He stepped to the door and signaled the policewoman who took Virginia Baxter away.

Mason returned to indicate chairs for the others. He started pacing the floor.

"All right," Paul Drake said, "give. What about the fifty thousand?"

Mason said, "I want a search made for that handbag. I want the officers to make the search. I think they'll do it now.

"Now then, Paul, here's where you go to work. I should have thought of this before."

Drake pulled out his notebook.

Mason said, "Lauretta Trent was intending to have Eagan turn the car to the left and drive up to the Saint's Rest Motel. She had a reason for going there.

"When Virginia told me that Lauretta Trent had telephoned her and told her to go to the Saint's Rest Motel and wait there for her, I felt that perhaps Virginia had been victimized by the old trick of having some third party identify himself or herself over the telephone and, since the telephone doesn't transmit the personal appearance of the person talking, it's a very easy matter to deceive someone in a case of that sort.

"However, the fact that Lauretta Trent did intend to turn to the left and go up that road is strongly indicative of the fact that she *had* telephoned Virginia Baxter.

"Now, *why* had she telephoned her?"

Drake shrugged his shoulders, and Mason went on.

"It was either because she wanted to give Virginia some information, on the one hand, or get some information from Virginia, on the other. The strong probabilities are she wanted to get some information from Virginia.

"Now, someone must have overheard that telephone conversation. There's not much chance that the telephone line could have been tapped. Therefore, someone must have heard the conversation at one end of the line or the other. Either someone was listening in Virginia Baxter's apartment, which isn't likely, or someone was listening at the place where Lauretta Trent telephoned."

Drake nodded.

"That person, knowing that Virginia Baxter was going to drive her car to the Saint's Rest, went up to the Saint's Rest, waited until Virginia had parked her car and was inside the motel room. Then that person took Virginia's car, drove it down to the coast highway and waited for Lauretta Trent to come along to keep her appointment.

"That person was a very skillful driver. He hit the Trent car just hard enough to throw it to one side of the road and then speeded up, threw the rear of the Baxter car into a skid which knocked the Trent car completely out of control.

"Then that person drove the crippled Baxter car up to the Saint's Rest Motel and parked it.

"Because other tenants had moved in in the meantime, the parking space where Virginia had parked her car was filled up, so he had to select another parking space."

"Well?" Drake asked.

"Then," Mason said, "he presumably picked up his own

car, drove it back down to the highway and into oblivion."

Drake nodded, "That, of course, is obvious."

"But is it?" Mason said. "He couldn't tell about the timing element. He couldn't tell whether someone riding along behind got the complete license number of Virginia Baxter's car instead of just the last two numbers. He had to have a second string to his bow."

"I don't get it," Drake said.

Mason said, "He had to have it so he could conceal himself in the event he didn't have time to get back down to the highway. Now, how would he do that?"

"That's simple," Drake said. "He'd rent a unit at the Saint's Rest Motel."

"That," Mason said, "is where you come in. I want you to go to the Saint's Rest Motel, check the registrations, get the license numbers of each automobile and run down the owners. See if you can get a line on anyone who checked in and then left without sleeping in the bed. If so, get a description."

Drake snapped his notebook shut. "All right," he said, "that's a job, but we'll get on it. I'll put a bunch of men on it and—"

"Wait a minute," Mason said. "You're not finished yet."

"No?" Drake asked.

Mason said, "Let's look at what happened after the car was crowded off the road, Paul."

"There were big rocks there," Drake said. "The chauffeur fought for control and lost out. The car toppled over into the ocean—you couldn't have picked a more perfect spot for it. I've checked it carefully. The road makes a left-hand curve there. As soon as you get off the shoulder, there are rocks—some of them eighteen inches in diameter—just regular rough boulders. There's ónly about ten feet between the road and the sheer drop straight down to the ocean.

"At that point there's an almost perpendicular cliff. The highway construction crews had to blast a road out of that cliff. It rises two hundred feet above the road on the left and it drops straight into the ocean on the right."

"Presumably," Mason said, "that's why this particular spot was chosen. It would be a perfect place to crowd a car off the road."

"That, of course," Drake said, grinning, "is elemental, my dear Holmes."

"Exactly, my dear Watson," Mason said. "But what happened to Lauretta Trent? The chauffeur told her to jump. Presumably she tried to get out of the car. The door on the left rear was unlatched. There was no body in the car; therefore, she must have been thrown clear."

"Well," Drake asked, "what does that buy us?"

"Her missing handbag," Mason said. "When a woman jumps from an automobile, she hardly bothers to take her handbag with her unless it contains a very, very large amount of money or something that is very, very valuable.

"That was why I had to find out from Eagan whether or not she was carrying something of great value. If she had a large sum of money or something of great value in her handbag, it's quite natural that she'd have told the chauffeur to be alert.

"Yet Eagan's surprise was too natural to be feigned. We're forced to the conclusion that, if there was anything of value in her purse or handbag, he knew nothing about it.

"Yet, when Lauretta Trent was faced with that moment of supreme emergency, that moment of great danger, she either grabbed up her handbag from the seat before trying to jump, or it was washed out of the car—otherwise it would be in the car.

"Now, my questioning about fifty thousand dollars being in the handbag will spur the police to go back and make a desperate search for that handbag with divers and submarine illumination. If the handbag is lying there among the rocks on the floor of the ocean, they'll find it. A body would be carried away by the ocean currents, a handbag would be trapped in the rocks."

Drake gave a low whistle.

"Then, of course," Mason said, "we come to the peculiar conduct of the heirs. Someone was trying to get Virginia to furnish a forged will which could be planted in the office copies of Bannock's wills."

"That is the thing that gets me," Drake said. "With a perfectly good will in their possession, why should anyone want to plant a forged will?"

"That," Mason said, "is what we are going to have to find out—and find out before ten o'clock tomorrow morning."

"And why the *second* spurious will?" Drake asked.

"That," Mason said, "is good practice in will forgeries, Paul. If in some way forged will number two is knocked out, then forged will number one has to be faced.

"Heirs are much more willing to compromise when they have two difficult hurdles to jump."

"Well," Drake said, "it's too much for me. I not only

don't think we have the right answer, but I don't think
we're even on the right track."

Mason smiled, "What track do you think we're on,
Paul?"

"The one that makes Virginia blameless," Drake said.

Mason nodded thoughtfully. "As her attorney, Paul,
that's the only track I can see."

CHAPTER NINETEEN

BACK in his office, Mason said, "How about working late tonight, Della, and then having dinner?"

Della Street smiled. "You know I never go home until you do when we're working on a case."

Mason patted her shoulder. "Good girl," he said. "I can always depend on you. Put some paper in the typewriter, Della. I'm going to give you a list of questions."

"Questions?" she asked.

Mason nodded. "Somehow I have a feeling that I'm letting my client down in this case simply because I'm not using my head and breaking the case down to basic fundamentals.

"Someone in the background is carrying out a preconceived plan or, rather, has carried out a preconceived plan.

"That plan makes sense to him, but the outward manifestations of it, which we see in the light of events which have taken place, simply don't make sense.

"When that happens, it means we're looking at only a part of the picture. Let's start taking things up one at a time and trying to see if we can get answers.

"We'll start with question number one," Mason said.

"Why did someone plant a shipment of contraband in Virginia Baxter's suitcase?"

Della Street duly typed the question.

Mason started pacing the floor. "First answer," he said, "and the most obvious answer is that this person wanted Virginia Baxter convicted of a felony.

"Question number two: Why did this person want Virginia Baxter convicted of a felony?

"First and most obvious answer is that he knew she was a subscribing witness to Lauretta Trent's will. He intended to do something which would indicate that will was a forgery and, therefore, wanted to be able to weaken her credibility as a witness.

"Question number three: Why did anyone go to Virginia Baxter and ask her to type two fraudulent wills?

"The obvious answer to that, of course, is that he intended to plant those carbon copies somewhere where they could be used to his advantage.

"Next question: Why could those spurious carbon copies be used to his advantage? What did he expect to gain by them?"

Mason, pacing the floor, paused, shook his head and said, "And the answer to that question is not obvious.

"Then we have the question: Why did Lauretta Trent want to talk with Virginia Baxter?

"The obvious answer to that is that she knew, in some way, conspirators were trying to use Virginia Baxter. Probably, she knew about the spurious wills. Or perhaps she just wanted to interrogate Virginia about the location of the carbon copies of the wills Bannock had drawn.

"There again, however," Mason went on, "we run up against a blank wall, because why would Lauretta Trent

THE CASE OF THE HORRIFIED HEIRS

bother about any will which she was supposed to have executed years ago? If she had wanted to make certain her will was the way she wanted it, she would have gone to an attorney and inside of an hour have had a new will properly executed."

Mason paced the floor for a few minutes, then said, "Those are the questions, Della."

"Well, it seems to me you've got most of the answers," she said.

"The obvious answers," Mason said, "but are they the right answers?"

"They certainly seem logical," Della Street said encouragingly.

"We'll put one more question," Mason said. "Why in that moment of supreme danger did Lauretta Trent grab her handbag? Or, putting it another way, why wasn't Lauretta Trent's handbag found in the automobile when the car was fished out of the ocean?"

"Perhaps she had the strap of her handbag over her arm," Della Street said.

"She wouldn't have been riding with the strap over her arm," Mason said. "Even if she'd picked it up at the time of the collision, when she was catapulted into cold ocean water she would at least have tried to swim. When you try to swim, you're using your arms; and when you're using your arms under water, a handbag strap isn't going to stay over your arm."

"Well," Della Street said, "we have a rather imposing list of questions."

Mason paced the floor for a few minutes, said, "You know, Della, when you're trying to recall a name and can't do it, you sometimes think about something else and then the name pops into your mind. I think I'll try thinking about something else for a while and see what happens with these questions."

"All right," she said, "what else would you like to think about?"

"You," he told her, grinning. "Let's drive out someplace where we can have a cocktail and a nice, quiet dinner.

"How about going to one of the mountain resorts where we can sit in a dining room looking out over the lights of the city and feel far removed from everyone and anything?"

"And I take it," Della Street said, pushing back her secretarial chair and putting a plastic cover on the typewriter, "we take this list of questions and answers with us?"

"We take those with us," Mason said, "but we try not to think about them until after dinner."

CHAPTER TWENTY

DELLA STREET, seated across the table from Perry Mason, regarded him solicitously.

The lawyer had eaten his broiled steak mechanically, as though hardly knowing what he was putting in his mouth. Now, he was sipping after-dinner black coffee, his eyes fixed on the dancing couples who glided over the floor. His gaze was not following any particular couple but his eyes were focused on the sea of lights visible in the valley below through one of the big windows.

Della Street's hand crept across the table, rested reassuringly on the lawyer's hand. Her fingers tightened.

"You're worried, aren't you?"

His eyes swiftly flashed to hers, blinked as he got her in focus, and his sudden smile was warm. "Just thinking, that's all, Della."

"Worried?" she asked.

"All right, worried."

"About your client, or about yourself?"

"Both."

"You can't let it get you down," she said, her hand still resting on his.

Mason said, "A lawyer isn't like a doctor. A doctor has

scores of patients, some of them young and curable, some of them old and suffering from diseases that are incurable. It's the nature of life that individuals move in a stream from birth to death. A doctor can't get so wrapped up in his patients that he suffers for them.

"A lawyer is different. He has relatively fewer clients. Most of their troubles are curable, if a lawyer only knew exactly what to do. But whether they're curable or not, a lawyer can always better his client somewhere along the line if he can get the right combination."

"How about yourself?" she asked.

Mason grinned and said, "I led with my chin. I knew, of course, that someone had taken Virginia's car and that it had become involved in an accident. I felt that it was a trap and someone had made an attempt to frame her.

"If that had been the case, I was perfectly justified in doing what I did.

"As a matter of fact, I was justified anyway. I didn't know any crime had been committed. I did know that an attempt had been made to frame a crime on Virginia a short time earlier and I was trying to protect— Of course, if I'd known a murder had been committed and the car had been involved, then my actions would have been criminal. After all, it's a question of intent."

The lawyer glanced back to the dance floor, his eyes followed a couple for a moment, then again became focused on the distance.

Abruptly he turned to Della Street and put his hand over hers. "Thanks for your loyalty, Della," he said. "I'm not much on putting those things into words. I guess perhaps I take you too much for granted, like the air I

breathe and the water I drink, but that doesn't mean I
don't appreciate all you do."

He stroked her fingers.

"Your hands," he said, "are wonderfully reassuring. You
have competent hands, feminine hands but, nevertheless,
strong hands."

She laughed self-consciously. "Years of typing have
strengthened the fingers."

"Years of loyalty have strengthened the meaning."

She gave his hand a quick squeeze; then, aware that they
were attracting attention, abruptly withdrew her hand.

Mason started to look at the distant sea of light again
then, suddenly, his eyes widened.

"An idea?" she asked.

"Good heavens," Mason said. He was silent for several
moments, then said, "Thanks for the inspiration, Della."

She raised inquiring eyebrows.

"Did I suggest something?" she asked.

"Yes, what you said about typing."

"It's like piano playing," she said. "It strengthens the
hand and fingers."

Mason said, "Our second question: *Why* did they want
to frame a crime on Virginia Baxter. The answer I gave you
is wrong."

"I don't get it," she said. "It's the most logical answer in
the world. It seems that would be the only reason they
could possibly have for framing a crime on her; then her
subsequent testimony could be impeached if she had been
convicted of—"

Mason interrupted with a shake of his head. "They
didn't want to convict her," he said. "They wanted to be
sure that she would be out of the way."

"What do you mean?"

"They wanted to get into her apartment, get her stationery and her typewriter."

"But they knew she was on a plane and—"

"They probably didn't know it in time," Mason interrupted. "She'd only been to San Francisco and had been away overnight. They had to be absolutely certain that they would have access to the typewriter and Bannock's stationery and be absolutely certain that Virginia wouldn't be home until they had done what they intended to do."

"And what did they intend to do?" Della asked.

Mason, his face flushed with animation as his mind speeded over the situation, said, "Good Lord, Della, I should have seen it all a long time ago. Did you notice anything peculiar about that will?"

"You mean the way in which she left the property?"

"No. The way in which the will was drawn," Mason said. "Notice that the residuary clause was on the first page. . . . How many wills have you typed, Della?"

"Heaven knows," she said, laughing. "With all my experience in a law office, I've typed plenty."

"Exactly," Mason said. "And in every one of them, the will has been drafted so that the specific bequests are mentioned and then, at the close of the will, the testator says 'all of the rest, residue and remainder of my estate, of whatsoever nature and wheresoever situated, I give, devise and bequeath to . . .'"

"That's right," she said.

Mason said, "They had a will. The last page of it is authentic. Probably the second page is authentic; the first page is a forgery, typed on Bannock's typewriter and on his stationery, but typed within the last few days.

"There's a substitute page in that will—and it had to be done on the same typewriter that was used at Bannock's office and whoever forged it had to have an opportunity to use that typewriter."

"But who forged it?" Della Street asked.

"On a document of that sort," Mason said, "the person or persons who made the forgery are most apt to be the persons who benefited by the forgery."

"All four of the surviving relatives are beneficiaries," she said.

"And the doctor, the nurse and the chauffeur," Mason supplemented.

The lawyer was thoughtfully silent for a moment, then said, "There was one thing about the first case we had for Virginia Baxter that puzzled me."

"What was that?"

"The officer stating that he couldn't divulge the name of the person who had tipped them off, but that person had been thoroughly dependable in his prior tip-offs."

"I still don't get it," Della Street said.

"Whoever wanted to forge that will must have known a police informer, bribed him to give false information and arranged to plant the dope in Virginia's suitcase."

Mason pushed back his chair, jumped to his feet, looked around for their waiter.

"Come on, Della," he said, "we have work to do."

The waiter not being immediately available, Mason dropped a twenty-dollar bill and a ten-dollar bill on the table and said, "That will cover the check and the tip."

"But that's way too much," Della Street protested, "and I have to keep a record of expenses."

"Don't keep a record of these expenses," Mason said. "Time is worth more than keeping accurate records. Come on, let's go."

CHAPTER TWENTY-ONE

PAUL DRAKE was seated in his cubbyhole of an office, at the end of a long, narrow rabbit-warren runway. Four-telephones were on his desk. A paper plate with part of a hamburger sandwich and a soiled, greasy paper napkin had been pushed to one side.

Drake had a paper container filled with coffee in front of him. He was holding a telephone to his ear and, intermittently, sipping coffee as Mason and Della Street entered.

"All right," Drake said into the telephone, "stay with it as best you can. Keep in touch with me."

Drake hung up the telephone, regarded the lawyer and his secretary in dour appraisal, said, "Okay, here you come fairly reeking of filet mignon, baked potatoes, French fried onions, garlic bread and vintage wine. I've gagged down another greasy hamburger sandwich, and already my stomach is beginning to—"

"Forget it," Mason interrupted. "What did you find out about the motel, Paul?"

"Nothing that'll help," Drake said. "A man checked in all right, and his bed wasn't slept in. He's probably our man, but the name and address he gave were phony; the license of the car he wrote down was incorrect—"

"But it *was* an Oldsmobile, wasn't it?" Mason asked.

Drake cocked an eyebrow. "That's right," he said. "The car was listed as an Olds. . . . They don't usually dare put a wrong make on the register when they're putting down the make of the car; but they do juggle the license numbers around, sometimes transposing the figures and—"

"The description?" Mason asked.

"Nothing worthwhile," Drake said. "A rather heavyset man with—"

"Dark eyes and a mustache," Mason said.

Drake raised his eyebrows. "How did *you* get all of this?"

"It checks," Mason said.

"Go on," Drake told him.

Mason said, "Paul, how many contacts do you have? That is, intimate contacts in police circles?"

"Quite a few," Drake said. "I give them tips; they give me tips. Of course, they wouldn't let me get away with anything. They'd bust me and take my license in a minute if I did anything unethical. If that's what you're leading up to, I—"

"No, no," Mason said. "What I want is the name of an informer police rely on in dope cases who answers the description of the man who checked in at the Saint's Rest Motel."

"That might be hard to get," Drake said.

"And again, it might not," Mason said. "Whenever they issue a search warrant on the strength of an informer's testimony, or even on the strength of a tip, they have to disclose the source of their information if they want to use the evidence they've picked up. For that reason, there's quite a turnover in informers.

"After an informer becomes too well known, he can't do

any more work because the underworld has him spotted as a stool pigeon.

"Now, my best guess is that the man we want has been an informer, has had his identity disclosed to some defense lawyer who, in turn, has tipped off the dope peddlers, and the stool pigeon finds himself temporarily out of a meal ticket."

"If that's the case," Drake said, "I can probably find out who he is with the description we have."

Mason gestured toward the telephones. "Get busy, Paul. We're going down to my office."

"How strong can I go?" Drake asked.

"Go just as strong as you have to to get results," Mason told him. "This is a matter of life and death. I want the information and I want it just as fast as I can get it. Put out a dozen men if you have to; get calls through to everybody you know; tell them it's a matter of law enforcement and offer a reward if you have to."

"Okay," Drake said, wearily, pushing the paper coffee container to one side, picking up the telephone with his left hand, opening a drawer in the desk with his right, and taking out a bottle of digestive tablets.

"I'll call you as soon as I get anything or, better yet, come down to the office and report."

Mason nodded. "Come on, Della," he said, "we'll wait it out."

CHAPTER TWENTY-TWO

Mason and Della Street were in the lawyer's private office.

Della had the big electric percolator filled with coffee, waiting for Paul Drake.

Mason paced the floor restlessly, back and forth, his thumbs hooked in his belt, his head thrust slightly forward.

At length he stopped from sheer weariness, dropped into a chair and gestured toward the coffee.

Della filled his cup.

"Why did you make all this to-do about the handbag?" she asked. "Do you have any information I don't?"

Mason shook his head. "You know I don't."

"But I haven't heard anything about fifty thousand dollars in cash."

Mason said, "There's something mighty peculiar about this case, Della. Why wasn't the handbag found in the car?"

"Well," Della Street said, "with a wild surf, a stormy night, a car toppled into the ocean—"

"The handbag," Mason said, "would be on the floor of the car. Or, if it fell out, it wouldn't drift far. I didn't say the handbag had fifty thousand dollars in cash; I asked Eagan if he didn't know it had fifty thousand dollars in cash. I wanted to inspire a host of amateur divers to search for that bag. I—"

Drake's code knock sounded on the door of Mason's office.

Della Street jumped to her feet, but Mason beat her to the door and jerked it open.

Drake, his face showing lines of fatigue, said, "I think I've got your man, Perry."

"Who is it?"

"A character by the name of Hallinan Fisk. He has been a long-time stoolie for the police in one of the suburbs but there was one case where the police had to disclose his name and one case where Fisk had to testify. Now he's a known informer. He thinks his very life is in danger. He's trying to get sufficient money from the police undercover fund to leave the country."

"Any hope of success?" Mason asked.

"Probably some," Drake said, "but the police don't have that kind of money. This is a dog-eat-dog world. It's not generally known, but the police in this outlying town sometimes pay off their informers by letting them cut corners.

"Fisk has been giving the police information on big-time stuff and also on dope. He's been making *his* money out of being a runner for a bookmaker. The police closed their eyes to this in return for tips on dope. Now that his occupation as a stoolie is out in the open, the bookmaker is afraid to have him around even though Fisk told the bookmaker he can virtually guarantee him freedom from arrest.

"The bookmaker is afraid that hijackers are going to lift his cash and that he may get himself bumped off. He's had a couple of anonymous telephone calls telling him to get rid of Fisk, or else; and in that business, that's all that is needed to make Fisk as desirable as a guy with smallpox."

"You get his address?" Mason asked.

"I think I know where he can be found," Drake said.

"Let's go," Mason said.

Della got up from her chair, but Drake motioned her down with his hand, "Nix," he said. "This is no place for ladies."

"Phooey," she said. "I know about the birds, the bees, the flowers and the underworld."

"This is going to be tough," Drake said.

Della Street looked appealingly to Perry Mason.

Mason deliberated a moment, then said, "Okay, come on, Della, but you're on your own. . . . How are you fixed for protection, Paul?"

Drake pulled back his coat to show a gun in a shoulder holster.

"If the going gets tough," he said, "we can flash my credentials and, if it comes to a real showdown, we can use this."

"We're dealing with murder," Mason said.

They carefully switched out the lights in the lawyer's private office, locked the door, and went down to Drake's car.

Drake drove down to skid row, which at this hour was a blaze of nighttime activity.

From time to time he looked dubiously at Della Street.

Drake finally found a parking place near the rooming house which was their destination.

Della, tucked in between the broad shoulders of Perry Mason and Paul Drake, was guided across the street along some thirty feet of sidewalk, then up a flight of stairs to a dimly lit little alcove where a counter held a plaque with the word OFFICE on it, and a bell.

Back of the counter were hooks containing various keys.

"Number five," Drake said. "The key isn't on the hook, so we'll take a look."

"He's not apt to be in, is he?" Della asked. "This is the period of high activity for skid row."

"I think he is," Drake said. "I think he's afraid to leave his room."

They walked down a corridor, dark, smelly and sinister.

Drake located No. 5, pointed toward the underside of the door.

"There's a light," he said.

Mason's knuckles tapped a peremptory message on the panels of the door.

For a moment there was no answer, then the voice of a man standing close to the door said, "Who is it?"

"Detective Drake," Drake said.

"I don't know any dicks by the name of Drake."

"I have something for you," Drake said.

"That's what I'm afraid of."

"You want me to stand here in the hall and tell it so everybody can hear it?"

"No, no."

"Well then, let us in."

"Who's the 'us'?"

"I have a girl with me," Drake said, "and a friend."

"Who's the girl?"

Della Street said, "My name is Street."

"Well, go find yourself another alley, sister."

Mason said, "All right, if that's the way you want it, that's the way it'll be. You'll pay the price. You wanted to get lost and the deal I have gives you a chance."

"*You* can do the getting lost," the man's voice said. "I'm

not opening the door for any crummy gag like this. If you want me to open up, get someone I know."

Mason motioned to Paul Drake, said, "You and Della wait here in the corridor, Paul. If he comes out, nab him."

"What do I do with him?"

"Hold him, one way or another. Push him back in the room. Put him under citizen's arrest if you have to."

"For what?" Drake asked.

"Hit-and-run," Mason said. "But I don't think he'll be out."

Mason walked down the long, smelly corridor to a telephone booth which smelled of stale cigar smoke.

Mason dialed police headquarters. "Give me Homicide," he said, when he had an answer.

A moment later when a voice said, "Hello, this is Homicide," Mason said, "I have to get Lieutenant Tragg on a matter of the greatest importance. How long would it take to get a message through to him? This is Perry Mason talking."

The voice at the other end of the line said, "Just a minute."

A second and a half later Lieutenant Tragg's dry voice came over the wire. "What's the matter, Perry, you found another body?"

"Thank heavens you're there," Mason said. "I'm really in luck."

"You are, for a fact," Tragg told him. "I just dropped in to see if there were any new developments on a case I am working on. What's the trouble?"

Mason said, "I want you to join me. I've got something big."

"A corpse?"

"No corpse, not yet. There may be one later on."

"Where are you?" Tragg asked.

Mason told him.

"Shucks," Tragg said, "that's only a short distance from headquarters."

"Will you join me?" Mason asked.

Tragg said, "Okay."

"Bring a man with you," Mason told him.

"Okay," Tragg said, "I'll grab a police car and be there within a matter of minutes."

"I'm waiting for you at the office at the head of the stairs," Mason told him. "This is a walk-up rooming house, second floor only—over a bunch of hock shops and honky-tonks."

"I thought I knew the dump," Tragg said. "We'll be there."

Mason stood waiting by the phone booth.

Two men came up the stairs, paused at the office, looked furtively around them, saw Mason standing there, started toward him.

The lawyer moved a step or two forward.

The men looked at his height, at his shoulders, looked at each other, then wordlessly turned, walked back to the head of the stairs and went down to the street.

A few moments later, Tragg, accompanied by a uniformed officer, came to the head of the stairs, paused and looked up and down the corridor.

Mason came striding forward.

Tragg paused by the counter, waiting for him, looking at the lawyer with kindly, quizzical eyes.

"All right, Perry," he said, "what is it this time? Here's your cat's-paw. Where's the chestnut you want pulled out of the fire?"

Mason said, "Room five."

"How hot is the chestnut?"

"I don't know," Mason said, "but once we get in and shake him down, I think we'll find the solution of the Lauretta Trent murder case."

"You don't think we have it already?"

"I know you don't have it already," Mason said.

Tragg sighed. "I could have saved myself a trip if I'd only been properly skeptical," he said. "What's more, the office takes a dim view of our running around on the hunches of defense attorneys trying to undermine cases the district attorney is prosecuting in court.

"Played up in newspapers, it wouldn't make a very nice story, now, would it?"

"Have I ever left you in the middle of a story in the newspapers that didn't look good?" Mason asked.

"Not yet," Tragg said. "I don't want you to start."

"All right," Mason told him, "you've come this far, come on down to room five."

Tragg sighed, said to the officer, "Okay, we'll take a look. That's all we're doing, taking a look."

Mason led the way down to where Paul Drake and Della Street were waiting.

"Well, well," Tragg said, "we seem to have a quorum."

Mason banged on the door again.

"Go away," the voice inside said.

Mason said, "Lieutenant Tragg of Homicide and an officer."

"You got a warrant?"

"We don't need a warrant," Mason said. "We—"

"Now, just a minute," Tragg interrupted, "I'll do my own talking. What's this all about?"

Mason said, "This man registered under the name of Carlton Jasper at the Saint's Rest Motel. He's also the stoolie who gave the police the bum steer on the dope in Virginia Baxter's suitcase. He's waiting for police funds to get out of town.

"He's been a professional informer for the dope squad and— You want me to stay here and yell the whole business out in the corridors, Fisk?"

There was a sound of a bolt on the door; then a chair being moved. The door opened to the limit of a safety chain. Obsidian black eyes peered out anxiously, came to rest on the police officer's uniform, then looked at Tragg.

"Let me see your credentials," he demanded.

Tragg slipped a leather container from his pocket, held it where the man could see it.

The man said, "Look up and down the corridor. Anybody there?"

"Not now," Mason said, "but a couple of torpedoes came up a few minutes ago. They started down to your room and then turned back when they saw I was a witness."

Shaking hands fumbled with the chain on the catch on the door.

The door opened.

"Come in, come in," Fisk said.

The little group walked into the room—a bedraggled place with a cheap, sagging bed, a paper-thin carpet in which holes had been worn in front of the cheap, pine dresser, its wavy mirror distorting reflections.

There was one cushioned chair, one cane-bottomed, straight-backed chair.

Fisk said, "What is it? You fellows have got to give me protection."

Mason said, "What was the idea of framing Virginia Baxter on that dope, and why did you go to the Saint's Rest and take her car?"

"Who are you?" Fisk asked.

"I'm her lawyer."

"Well, I don't need your type of mouthpiece."

"I'm not a mouthpiece," Mason told him. "I'm a lawyer. And here, my friend, is a subpoena for you to appear in court tomorrow and testify as a witness in the case of People versus Baxter."

"Say, what kind of a dodge are you pulling on me?" Tragg asked. "Getting me down here just so you could serve a subpoena."

"That's all," Mason told him cheerfully, "unless you want to use your head. If you do, you can cover yourself with glory."

"You can't serve me with any subpoena," Fisk said. "I only opened the door for the law."

"How come your fingerprints are all over Virginia Baxter's car?" Mason asked.

"Phooey, you won't find a fingerprint on the thing."

"And," Mason said, "when the officers went to Virginia Baxter's apartment to search it on the strength of your representation that there was dope hidden there, you managed to fix the door so you could get back in with the person who did the typewriting on Virginia's typewriter."

"Words, words, words," Fisk said. "I get so tired of having people try to frame things on me. Listen, lawyer, I've been worked over by experts. You amateurs don't stand a chance."

"You wore gloves in handling Virginia Baxter's car," Mason said, "but you didn't have gloves on in the Saint's Rest Motel. Your fingerprints are all over the room."

"So what? Sure, I admit I was at the Saint's Rest Motel."

"And registered under an assumed name."

"Lots of people do that."

"And gave a phony license number."

"I wrote it down according to the best way I could remember it."

Mason, looking at the man, said suddenly, "Good heavens, no wonder! There's a family resemblance. What's your relationship to George Eagan?"

For a moment the black eyes looked at Mason with cold defiance.

"That," Mason said, "is something we *can* check."

Fisk seemed to grow smaller inside of his coat, "All right," he said. "I'm his half-brother. I'm the black sheep of the family."

"And," Mason said, "you switched license numbers with Eagan's automobile and of course Eagan didn't notice— that was just in case anyone tried to identify you through the license number."

"Got any proof?" Fisk asked.

"I don't need it," Mason said. "By the time I put you on the witness stand tomorrow and the newspapers publish your picture and the history of your activities as a stool pigeon and double-crosser, the underworld will take care of you a lot better than I can. Come on, folks, let's go."

Mason turned and started to the door.

For a long moment Fisk stood there, then he grabbed

Mason's coat sleeve. "No, no! Now, look, look, we can square this thing."

He turned from Mason to Lieutenant Tragg. "I've given you folks the breaks," he said. "You folks can help me out. Get this mouthpiece off my neck. Get me out of town."

Tragg, studying the man intently, said, "You tell us the whole story and we'll see what we can do. But we're not buying anything blindfolded."

Fisk said, "Look, I've been in trouble, lots of trouble, lots of times in trouble. George had to get me out of it once when I was in bad trouble."

"Who's George?" Tragg asked.

"George Eagan, Lauretta Trent's chauffeur."

Mason and Tragg exchanged glances, then Tragg turned to Fisk and said, "All right, come on, what happened?"

"Well, I lost out with the police and lost all my connections and I was up against it. That was when this woman came to me who had helped out before."

"What woman?"

"The nurse, Anna Fritch. I'd dated her once or twice and I'd furnished her with dope over a period of years."

"Go on," Tragg said.

"She was teamed up with Kelvin. Kelvin thought he was going to get the bulk of the Trent estate—he and his brother-in-law, and their wives, of course. So he got this nurse to hurry the old gal over the divide.

"They made three passes with arsenic. They didn't dare to kill her with arsenic, but she had a bad pump and the idea was that all the upchucking from a small dose would make the pump give out.

"Then while the old dame was being sick the last time,

Kelvin found the will. He damn near dropped dead from the shock.

"So he had to change the will. They tracked down the lawyer's typewriter. The nurse was a good typist. If she had plenty of time she swore she could make a forgery they'd never detect, but she needed the lawyer's typewriter and stationery.

"That meant they wanted not only to get Virginia Baxter discredited so she couldn't spill their apples if she remembered the terms of the real will, but they wanted her in the cooler.

"They also wanted to either get Bannock's carbon copy of the real will or else scramble things so no one could ever get to first base by going to the old files—but they didn't think up this angle until later when I raised the question.

"Anyhow, first thing was to get this Baxter woman in the clink and get her convicted of a dope charge.

"Well, I did what I was supposed to. I bribed a guy to let me out to the plane to get my baggage on the ground; that it was an important shipment. I spotted the broad's bag as soon as it came off the plane; then said I'd lost my tags. They told me I had to identify the contents, so I got the suitcases opened and then said I'd made a mistake and, in the confusion, managed to plant the stuff I was to put in the suitcase.

"I thought that was all I was going to have to do.

"But that's the way it is with a broad. You get tangled up with them and they're always on your neck. So I had to take this girl's automobile and wait until George came along and then ram the car. I hated to do it, but George had been high-hatting me of late and—Well, a guy has to live."

"All right," Tragg said, "what did you do?"

"I did what I was told to," Fisk said, trembling. "I was to give it a good sideswipe. I didn't know it was going out of control and—I thought I was just framing a hit-and-run. . . . Well, that's the truth and now I've got it off my chest."

"That was Virginia Baxter's car you were using?" Mason asked.

"That's right. I was told she'd be up at the Saint's Rest and given the license number of her automobile. She hadn't much more than got into her room and got settled down than I left my car and took hers. Then, as soon as I'd done the job, I came back up and parked her car and took mine.

"The parking stall her car had been in had been taken by somebody else, so I had to park the Baxter car in a new stall. I was told to be awfully careful with that car, to give the Lauretta Trent car a shove with the front end of the car, but to hit it hard with the back end so the Baxter car would run all right."

"And how much did you get for that?" Mason asked.

"Promises. I was hot. I've got enemies and I've got to get where they can't take me for a one-way ride. This broad promised me twenty-five hundred, and she gave me two hundred in cash. I don't know how you found out about me, but . . . by God, if you put me on a witness stand and the newspapers publish this stuff, my life won't be worth a snap of my fingers. . . . Hell, they're gunning for me right now. . . . You said there were two torpedoes that came up the stairs?"

Mason nodded.

Fisk held out his wrists. "Take me into custody,

Lieutenant," he said. "Give me all the protection you can. I stand a chance of beating a rap, but you can't beat the big boy's torpedoes."

"Who's the big boy?" Tragg asked.

Fisk, shivering with apprehension, said, "I've never ratted on him. Always the little guys and always the outsiders; but if it comes to a showdown and I have to, I have to— Get me in a cell where I'm by myself; give me protection and a chance to take it on the lam and I'll tell."

Tragg looked at Mason, said, "Well, it seems there's butter on both sides of your bread."

CHAPTER TWENTY-THREE

MASON, Della Street and Paul Drake returned to the lawyer's office shortly before midnight.

The assistant janitor who operated the elevator after hours said, "There's been a woman trying to see you, Mr. Mason; says it's a matter of great importance. I told her that you said you'd be back, no matter how late it was, and she said she'd wait."

"Where is she?"

"I don't know. Walking around somewhere. She's been back four or five times and asked if you'd returned yet. I told her 'no,' and she said she'd be back."

"What does she look like?" Mason asked.

"Rather aristocratic-looking. Sixty-odd. Gray hair. Nice clothes. Quiet voice—not a crook, but something is sure worrying her."

"All right," Mason said. "I'll be up in the office. I'm going to be there long enough for Virginia Baxter to join me; then we're calling it a day."

"And what a day!" Paul Drake said.

"Virginia Baxter!" the elevator operator said. "You mean the girl they're trying for murder?"

"She's being released," Mason said. "Lieutenant Tragg's delivering her here in a police car."

"Well, what do you know?" the operator said, appraising Mason wonderingly. "You got her out, eh?"

"*We* got her out," Mason said, grinning. "Let's go."

The elevator shot up to Mason's floor.

Drake said, "Okay, I'll duck into my office and button things up, Perry. What are you going to do about that nurse?"

Mason grinned. "Our friend Lieutenant Tragg is taking the initiative there. You'll be reading in the papers about Tragg's brilliant deductive reasoning; probably that Tragg gave Perry Mason an opportunity to accompany him when he uncovered the key witness in the Trent murder case."

"Yes, I suppose he'll grab all the credit," Drake said.

"Tragg won't, but the department will. That's the way the game has to be played. See you in the morning, Paul."

Mason took Della Street's arm and led her down to the office.

He fitted his key to the door of his private office, switched on the lights, yawned prodigiously and walked over to the electric coffee percolator.

"How long will it be?" Della Street asked.

"Shouldn't be over ten or fifteen minutes," Mason said. "Tragg will have her out of there and leave it to me to keep her out of circulation. Tragg doesn't want anything interfering with his big story that'll hit the papers. He—"

A timid knock sounded on the corridor door.

Mason went to the door and opened it.

A tall white-haired woman said, "This is Mr. Mason?"

"Yes," Mason said.

"I couldn't wait any longer," she said. "I *had* to come to you."

She turned toward Della Street inquiringly.

"My secretary, Della Street," Mason explained, and then added, with only a moment's perceptible hesitancy, "and unless I'm very much mistaken, Della, this is Lauretta Trent."

"Exactly," she said. "I couldn't let things go to a point where that poor girl was convicted. I had to come to you.

"I'm hoping there's some way you can protect me until we can find out who is trying to murder me."

"Sit down," Mason said.

She said, "I am very naïve, Mr. Mason; I wasn't at all suspicious until Dr. Alton asked the nurse to get samples of my hair and fingernails.

"At one time I had done some research work in poisoning symptoms. I decided to get out of there and get out fast.

"Then when that car deliberately rammed us off the road and George Eagan yelled, 'Jump'—well, I jumped. I got skinned up a bit but, fortunately, I had seen that car was going to hit us and I was all ready with my hand on the door latch.

"I didn't have fifty thousand dollars in my handbag, the way you said in court, but I had enough cash so I could take care of myself.

"I saw that George was hurt. I went to the highway and, almost immediately, a motorist stopped. He took me down the road to the café. I called the highway patrol and reported the accident. They promised to have a car there right away.

"I just decided it was a good time to lie low and let things start to unscramble. I wanted to find out who was back of all this."

"And you found out?" Mason asked.

"When that will was read in court—I was never so shocked in my life."

"That will, I take it, was spurious."

"Absolutely!" she snapped. "One, or perhaps two, pages of it were genuine, the rest had been substituted. What I said in my will was that, since I had come to the conclusion that all of my relatives were barnacles simply waiting for me to die and without gumption enough to get out and do anything for themselves, I was going to give my two sisters a bequest that would be small enough so the men would have to go to work.

"I had that will in what I thought was a safe place. They must have found it, got the staples out of the pages, substituted those forged pages and decided to get rid of me."

"Apparently," Mason said, "you're due for a shock. Your relatives weren't the ones who were trying to hurry up your death, but the nurse, who was a good typist, evidently arranged with Kelvin to plant a spurious will—probably on a percentage basis with possibilities for unlimited blackmail after that.

"And in case Virginia Baxter remembered the terms of the real will, they planned to have her in such a position her testimony would be worthless.

"I'm glad you're all right. When they failed to find your handbag in the car, I had an idea you were alive.

"You've given Virginia Baxter a bad time, but it's nothing that can't be cured.

"We're waiting for Virginia Baxter to join us now."

Lauretta Trent opened her handbag. "Fortunately," she said, "I have my checkbook with me. If I made a check for twenty-five thousand dollars to you, Mr. Mason, would that take care of your fee? And, of course, a check for fifty thousand to your client to compensate her for all she's been through."

Mason grinned at Della Street. "I think if you make out the checks, Mrs. Trent, Virginia Baxter will be here by the time you've got them signed, and she can give you her answer personally."